The Order of Elysium

Book I
The Aetheric Wars Trilogy

Dean P. R. Buswell

For Lisa

In the time I took to create this, you've gone
from my friend to my partner and now my amazing wife.
Your support and encouragement, and my
unwavering desire to impress you, if no one else,
not only motivated me to finish but to do better.
You put the fire into my words when
I thought it had gone out,
so you are every part within these pages as I am.
Every line. Every word.

List of Characters

Wardens

Name	Role	Description
Aiden	Lance	Salem chapter's newest member.
Amber	Warden	Veteran transfer from a distant chapter.
Asard	Arch Paladin	The arch paladin and human leader of the Order of Elysium, and head of Sanctuary Prime.
Asha	Warden	Recently, and reluctantly, made loch warden of her own team.
Clarel	Arch Warden	Trainer and member of the council in Sanctuary Prime.
Delarin	Loch Warden	Previously Asha's loch warden and mentor.
Garret	Paladin	Loch warden and paladin of Salem.
Grim	Warden	Dark and sarcastic member of Asha's team.
Jason	Loch Warden	Reckless loch warden of Salem.
Jessica	Warden	Shotgun-wielding member of Sorterra's team.
Kallista	Warden	Sister to Sorterra and a member of his team.
Mason	High Warden	High warden of Salem, second-in-command of the chapter.

Wardens (Continued)

Name	Role	Description
Sorterra	Loch Warden	Loch warden and brother to Kallista. Friends call him Terra.
Tarek	High Paladin	High paladin and leader of the Salem chapter.
Tiago	Warden	Transferred back to Salem from Sanctuary Prime. Always making jokes.
William	Warden	A silent giant and member of Sorterra's team.

Humans

Name	Role	Description
Adley Black	Civilian	Expert on demonology and the occult.
Catherine Umbrator	Civilian	Adley's assistant.
The Ghost of Salem (Lynus)	Urban Legend	A mysterious man believed to be a myth among the wardens.
Narki Navia	Civilian	Mysterious trader of information used by Grim for the Order.

Angels

Name	Role	Description
Azrael	Seraph	Leader of The Ankor Legion. The Angel of Death.
Gabriel	Seraph	Leader of The Valkyr Guard and the creator of the Order of Elysium.
Kára	Erelim	Second-sphere erelim to Gabriel and second-in-command of the Order of Elysium.
Michael	Seraph	Dogmatic and ruthless leader of The Divine March.
Raziel	Archangel	Erelim to Michael.

Demons

Name	Role	Description
Eligos	Cambion	Working for an unknown master, Eligos fights to undermine the Order.
Hekate	Mephisto	Powerful, beautiful and sly. She is seen by many as the queen of her kind.
Lilith	Succubus	Queen of the second circle and her kind. She produces the white cambion.
Myn	Mephisto	A demon whose sole ambition is spreading demonic narcotics to humans.
Nephitus	White Cambion	The strongest of his kind, distinguished by unique markings.

Terminology Guide

Word	Description	Side note
Aethe-real/Aetheric	Any being/object that is from either heaven or hell. Not from Earth.	
Anchor	The process a demon uses to summon other lesser demons to Earth.	
Anchorage	An event wherein a temporary portal is opened up to allow masses of demons to be anchored to Earth, usually via an object rather than another demon.	
Arbiter	A second-sphere angel with the unique ability to extract the sins and misdeeds of mortals, dead or alive. They serve various purposes within most of the angelic legions.	
Arch Paladin	Human leader of the Order of Elysium, answering only to Gabriel himself, and Gabriel's erelim, Kára.	
Arch Warden	Elite wardens who call Sanctuary Prime home. They train new wardens and carry out important missions.	
Archangel	An angel of the highest order, created out of light by God himself.	
Blacks	The colloquial term used for the dark clothes wardens wear. Usually made up of plain black pants and shirt, along with mottle-black trench coats.	
Cambion	A half-human demon.	Usually created using specific methods employed by succubi and incubi, but can very rarely be the result of more traditional 'natural' methods.

Word	Description	Side note
Casteless	The lowest class of demon. Able to manifest on Earth only by taking possession of a living human host.	Some powerful demons can anchor the casteless into dead bodies.
Chapter	The collective of wardens within a city or region. In modern times, most chapters are made up of only a single sanctuary.	
Circle	Circles of hell, or simply 'circles', are the designation given to the various depths of hell. Generally, the lower the circle a demon comes from, the more powerful they are.	
Collector	A low-class demon that uses casteless demons to hunt down wardens to steal runes or other valuables.	
Aetheric Dust	Commonly referred to simply as 'dust', this substance is used to quickly dispose of aetheric organic matter.	
Erelim	An angel that serves as the second-in-command of a legion in service to a seraph.	
Etching	The process of wiping a person's memory.	
Fallen	Fallen are first- and second-sphere angels that have fallen from grace after expressing, and exposing themselves to, too much human emotion for too long a period of time. They retain their memories after they fall and most semblance of self; however, their personalities are drastically changed, always for the worse.	Not to be confused with husks.

Word	Description	Side note
Glyph	Angelic and demonic symbols that when applied to weapons or surfaces offer a variety of different effects. Most commonly they are used to enhance a weapon's effectiveness against the opposite aethereal force. E.g.: demonic glyphs on a weapon will hurt angels.	
Grace	The essence of angels. Grace is the force that makes an angel what they are, and it powers runes and angelic weapons. Grace may exist in other beings such as wardens, but in these instances, it's simply referred to as angelic essence.	
Harpy	A demon that resembles a cross between a young human woman and a large red bird. They are vicious and relatively easy to kill; however, they attack in large flocks.	
Hellgate	A permanent link to hell, all of which were sealed by Archangel Michael after the Second Aetheric War.	
High Paladin	The highest-ranking warden and the leaders of their chapters outside of Sanctuary Prime. They also brief the paladin teams.	
High Warden	The second-in-command of a sanctuary; they deal with training and briefings.	Additional high wardens are also assigned to any extra sanctuaries a chapter may have.
Husk	What is left of a third-sphere angel after they 'fall'. They feel no pain or emotion whatsoever, but are vicious and tenacious. Some legions of angels use them as a sort of attack dog and/or cannon fodder.	Not to be confused with fallen angels.
Ifrit	Large, powerful flying-flame demons that have a considerable anchoring power relative to their overall strength.	

Word	Description	Side note
Imp	A diminutive demon that varies in size and shape, but is generally winged and stands at about waist height. They are aggressive and tenacious, and while not much of a threat on their own, they often horde and/or keep near other more powerful demons.	
Incubus	A demon that enthrals and/or seduces human women to various ends.	The male equivalent to a succubus.
Inmai	Low-class demons. They are humanoid and grey-skinned with bone-like thorns all over their body. They generally hunt in small groups led by greater inmai, which are larger, have darker skin and fight with much more competence.	
Katharis	A warden who has infiltrated official government agencies, such as the police force, or general politics. Their job is to cover up large-scale aethereal activity, gather intel and cover up any risks of discovery by the general public. They also assist by diverting or delaying attention to Order business.	Kathari have complete operational freedom save from general instruction from Sanctuary Prime. However, they are also beholden to the authority of high paladins, within reason.
Lance	Initiate wardens who have yet to prove their worth as a warden.	
Loch Warden	One rank above a regular warden or paladin; they lead a team of 5–7 members.	A loch warden who is also a paladin simply goes by the title of loch warden, not loch paladin.
Lost Soul	Near-lifeless souls of hell that have lingered too long in the first circle and will soon rot away and become casteless demons, or will be consumed by stronger demons.	

Word	Description	Side note
Mephisto	Coming in a variety of forms and ranges of power, a mephisto is usually a humanoid, mid-class demon. They specialise in making deals with mortals, usually in exchange for their souls, which mephistos use as currency with other demons to buy power within hell.	
Mimic	A demon that can copy the form of a human whose blood it has ingested. Even a single drop is enough. Mimics look mostly passable from afar, but up close they look more like wax statues. They have powerful regenerative capabilities and retractable talons.	
Paladin	The elite teams of wardens. They are more heavily armoured and armed with two or sometimes even more runes. They are sent in to situations when subtlety isn't an option.	
Principality	A third-sphere angel who leads small groups of regular angels that perform day-to-day duties within their legion. Much like a loch warden.	
Rune	Angelic artefacts the size of large marbles. Given to lances once they are promoted to warden. Each rune variant provides the wielder with a powerful ability.	
Salem	Fictional city on the west coast of Australia. Salem is the city where most of the action on Earth currently takes place.	
Sanctuary	A base of operations for wardens hidden among the cities they protect. Multiple sanctuaries can make up a chapter; however, most only have one during modern times.	
Seraphim	The original seven arch-angels created by God.	All seraphim are archangels, but not all archangels are seraphim.
Sin	A Sin, not to be confused with the verb, or a sin demon, is the primordial being that personifies (or sources) each of the seven deadly sins.	

Word	Description	Side note
Sphere	Spheres denote an angel's rank and power. First-sphere angels are seraphim and other archangels, while third-sphere angels are regular rank-and-file angels. The second-sphere is for everything in between, such as some erelim and specialised angels like arbiters and virtues.	
Stygian Wall	A giant wall within hell that borders the second and third circles. It keeps lesser demons out of the inner circles and functions as a stronghold against angelic invaders.	
Succubus	A demon that enthrals and/or seduces human men to various ends.	The female equivalent to an incubus.
The Ankor Legion	The legion of angels led by Archangel Azrael. They are responsible for the collection and transport of human souls after death. Known more colloquially within most cultures as Angels of Death.	
The Divine March	The legion of angels led by Archangel Michael. They are the main fighting force against the demonic hordes and are not concerned about harming humans or wardens who get in their way.	
The Valkyr Guard	The legion of angels led by Archangel Gabriel. They are responsible for the protection of humans from demonic forces, and as a whole, they lead the Order of Elysium.	
The Virtuous Guard	The legion of angels led by Raphael. They serve heaven by guiding (usually covertly) wayward humans. Most of their numbers are made up of virtue angels.	
Valkyr	An angel who typically serves The Valkyr Guard, and who has the ability to see the deeds of a mortal upon their death and judge them worthy to join the Order of Elysium.	Valkyr range between second- and first-sphere angels, depending on their level of authority.
Vellum	A blank rune.	

Word	Description	Side note
Virtue	A virtue angel is the embodiment of one of the seven heavenly virtues. They serve The Virtuous Guard and act as guardian angels to humans who require their guidance.	Not the equivalent of a Sin. However, they are considered to be the angelic equivalent of a 'sin demon'.
Warden	Any human member of the Order of Elysium. It is also the rank held by the rank-and-file sanctuary members.	
White Cambion	A special breed of cambion created by Lilith using warden 'participants'. They have porcelain white skin and are seemingly impervious to most damage.	

In the beginning God created the heavens and the earth. Now the earth was formless and empty, darkness covered the surface of the deep, and the Spirit of God hovered over the waters. God said, 'Let there be light,' and there was light. God saw that the light was good, and he separated the light from the dark, and the darkness rotted and swelled and took physical forms of its own to infect the light and reclaim the earth in darkness.

The beings created by the darkness rebelled against God and the light. God reached into the light itself and created beings of his own, who would call him Father and fight to repel the growing darkness, and so the seven seraphim were born.

The first children of God, so-called angels and beings of pure light, descended upon the primordial evil that the darkness had created on the earth. As the angels fought to protect the earth, God continued with his plans and created mortals; these were creatures of seemingly infinite variety, and he loved this creation most of all.

God's love for humans was eclipsed only by the darkness' hatred for the light, and so the primordial evil spread to infect the mortal souls of man, creating demonic soldiers for itself, which soon grew to overwhelm the seraphim. In answer to this threat, God created seven-hundred new angels for each of his seraphim to serve as their legions of light. These angels were the archangels of the first sphere. Still, for every victory another threat emerged, and the battles started again as the darkness was unconfined and without restraint.

So God created another dimension, the seven circles of hell, where the evils of the dark could fester and rot until they could do so no more. For those human souls who resisted the infection of darkness, God rewarded with paradise after death, and from these souls his seraphim created new angels. These angels were of the second and third sphere, lesser than the archangels created by God, but they were angelic in their own right and lived to serve in their legions.

However, hell did so swell until its ferocity could no longer be totally contained within the circles of hell alone. Sin continued to seep from its depths and into the hearts of mortals until it was too much to bear.

God's gaze seemed to disappear from the world, while the manifestations of the primordial evil, **the demons,** *continued in their perpetual instinct to snuff out the light.*

Prologue

Somewhere in the second circle of hell

Ten years ago

A flickering red light danced across the smooth, pitch black rock that made up the long corridors of the sprawling demonic den. A steady clack of metal on stone echoed harshly down the hallway and into the chamber beyond, preceding the arrival of a tall, brightly clad figure who strode into the heart of the hellish structure. The figure was accoutered in heavenly ornate armour, and pearlescent white wings were folded on its back.

The chamber was filled with the pleasurable moans and quiet giggles of its occupants as they lounged around on darkly coloured silk pillows, fondling and playing with each other's naked forms in pits teeming with writhing flesh. On the opposite side of the den there were those that had been blindfolded, gagged and chained to the wall by shackles that dug into their wrists, rusting the metal with their blood; they were toys and tools both, ready for the lustful succubi and incubi. In the centre of the chamber was a lavishly decorated throne made from the same black rock as the walls of the den. Lounging in the chair was a dark-haired figure, draped in strips of thin charcoal silk that did much more than simply tease the curves of her all too human-like body.

'Long way from home aren't we, little angel?' she teased as she shifted forward in her chair.

'Were it that I could be anywhere else, it would be so,' said the angel. 'The fact is—I require your skills.'

'There are many who need my skills, angel,' retorted the beautiful she-demon with a fanged grin. 'But go on...'

'I need an army.'

'Then you have come to the wrong place,' she spat as she sat suddenly upright. 'I don't do armies. My succubi are not war factories for you or anyone else.'

'I heard differently,' stated the angel. 'Your power in this circle grows rapidly. Even the most savage demon lords are bending at the knee for a chance to be heirs of the armies you create.'

'I give them the weapons they require to raise their own armies, not the armies themselves,' she corrected firmly.

'And in turn they offer you loyalty and obedience,' the angel surmised.

'Yes.' The beguiling she-demon sat back with a contented smile. 'For without me they'd be simply fighting in the dirt themselves or wandering forever, lost in the first circle.'

'Such things are true for every successful soldier. No matter their skill, they owe their victories, at least in part, to the blacksmith that supplied their weapon.' The angel looked around the room with a pointed gaze. 'You are no different.'

The she-demon let out a quiet, sarcastic laugh. 'I owe no one. I am older than most of those even deeper in the realm and stronger than any of the whelps that managed to drag their way out of the first circle.'

'*Your* blacksmith is calling in a favour,' the angel stated, shifting his wandering gaze directly back to hers.

'You mean she—' the demon stammered, to which the angel simply nodded. 'I-I am in the middle of a war here. This stronghold was hard won, but the rest of the circle is—'

The angel threw a bag, which clinked as the demon snatched it from the air, and a glow of gold poured out as she inspected its contents. 'There are benefits of dealing with me and mine,' said the angel. 'A steady supply of this, coupled with your own talents, and this entire circle will be yours within a decade.'

The she-demon beamed with delight. 'Perhaps something could be arranged. How many do you want?'

'Two-hundred should suffice,' the angel replied.

The succubus stood up from her throne, her eyes wide with incredulity. 'Two-hundred? Do you even realise how long that would take? Even for someone of my calibre, I only have so many succubi and incubi at my disposal.'

The angel said nothing. He simply continued to look at her, waiting. She sighed. 'I can do it, but—'

'Good. But there is one other thing,' the angel cut in. 'You need to use wardens.'

'Cambion created from warden hosts?' she mused, staring off into the air, deep in thought. 'Interesting. I've never tried it, but I imagine the angelic essence within the wardens would create something more than simple cambion. Angels may not be able to breed, but this may be the next best thing.' She paused for a moment lost in thought. 'I'm sure I could do it, but securing the hosts may prove dangerous.'

'She would not have sent me here if you were not thought capable of dealing with such hazards,' the angel rebutted. 'Use the first batch to make the rest easier to acquire if you have to. It'll prove a good opportunity to see how they fare.'

'The process will be tedious, especially with your special request; it will take time,' she informed.

'Of that, I have plenty. Your cambion are simply the last means to an end that has been in the making for longer than even you have been alive, Lilith,' said the angel as he turned to leave, the flicker of red firelight marring the white of his wings as he stepped back into shadow.

Chapter One
Eligos

Salem, Australia - Western Harbour Dockyards

2025 - Present day

The shipping dock was far enough away from any of the populated areas that it was almost silent save for the lapping swell of the sea. The wind blowing gently in from the office window was enough to chill the air with a fierce tenacity that would have cut to the bone of any normal person, but Asha barely noticed, even as her subordinate shivered like a small dog.

Asha surveyed the body at her feet as the Aetheric Dust started its job of dissolving the remains. The face had contorted into unnatural expressions of pain and anger even now as it lay dead. This human had been the victim of a casteless demon—a demon too weak to take a form of its own, but instead took control of weak-willed individuals. The Order of Elysium encouraged their wardens to avoid killing possessed humans if possible, though it rarely was. This human host looked as though it had already been dead when the casteless demon took over, so it mattered little in any case.

Asha wiped her blade on a dark piece of cloth that hung from her belt then replaced her sword in its sheath, which was strapped around her, resting comfortably on her back. As the sword clicked into place, the quiet sizzling of the Aetheric Dust stopped, and where a corpse had been a few moments earlier, there was nothing but a bloodstain on the carpet. Upon entering the small office, which functioned as the dock's main administration building, the wardens had been attacked by three casteless demons, each of them occupying already-dead hosts that now lay in slowly growing pools of blood before Asha.

There was a quiet beep as Asha placed her hand to the left side of her face and pressed on the communicator inside her ear. 'Office building secure,' she reported. Her eyes swept the large office bullpen as she spoke, keeping an eye out for danger. The room was still; it was waiting for the morning workers to drag themselves in for the next day of drudgery. For now, as it had only struck midnight, the only ones with work to do were Asha and the rest of the warden team. The full moon that flooded the room with a cold light created many sinister shadows. These shadows could play tricks on a lesser mind, but she knew she had seen movement. 'For now, at least.'

'Copy that,' came the voice of Delarin, her loch warden, the team leader. 'Still no sign of the collector on our side of the dock. Wait there in the admin building for further instruction.'

Asha glanced over at the man they had partnered her up with. Anthony was the Salem chapter's newest recruit, or lance, as was his official title. He had been so quiet she almost forgot he was there, but that took nothing from the fact that he was a pain in her arse. She was beginning to think Delarin paired him up with her on missions as some kind of punishment. Unfortunately, experienced wardens like herself were becoming harder to bring together due to a global increase in warden casualties. This meant the Order was forced to shorten training times to replace them, resulting in a lot of on-the-job training. Something Asha always hated.

'What are we hunting, exactly?' asked Anthony.

'A collector,' she replied stiffly. By the look on the lance's face she knew she'd have to elaborate. 'Collectors are hive-minded demons that control large groups of casteless demons.'

A few feet away from them was another of the possessed humans they had killed. This one had also been dead long before Asha had run it through. Like the body before, this corpse had white markings smeared on its face. 'You see the white?' she asked the lance.

'What is it?' he inquired. 'Paint?'

Asha's jaw clenched in frustration. He should know this. 'It's the blood of the collector we are hunting,' she explained. 'They smear it on the casteless' face to share their vision and so they can give instruction—which is usually to find wardens like us and take our runes.'

Asha's rune sat in a small metal cage that hung around her neck on a silver chain, which is where most wardens kept it. She brought her hand up to it as she spoke and ran her finger around the orb. The rune let off a faint glow as it responded to her touch. Runes were the wardens' most powerful assets. Gifted to them once they were deemed competent, runes granted a variety of abilities that helped them fulfil their duties.

'I haven't received mine yet,' her companion said.

'I would not take comfort in that, Anthony,' replied Asha, visually sweeping the room for movement again. 'Demons are just as happy to kill you for fun, not just for your rune.'

That seemed to shut him up, and a ten-minute silence followed where Asha kept track of every shadow, lest one of them move. A voice broke over her comm unit.

'I've spotted the target inside the main warehouse.' The voice belonged to Grim, another warden on her team.

'Alright,' came Delarin's response. 'We'll make our way to that yellow track crane by the water. Regroup there.'

Grim was the first to respond to the order, then Asha acknowledged and led Anthony out of the office building.

Asha and her lance were the first to arrive, or at least Asha thought so until a patch of air above one of the crane's large wheels shimmered in the moonlight and Grim suddenly materialised, a large rifle in his lap. Anthony almost jumped clear off the ground.

'Dammit, Grim,' Asha muttered.

'What?' Grim teased.

'How many times do I have to tell you?' she growled.

Grim had always been adept at remaining unseen, even before he became a warden, and his rune simply accentuated his ability. Asha could tell Grim was going to say something in retort, but he didn't get the chance to as Delarin and Amber approached them. Amber was another newcomer to the team, though she was a transfer from another chapter and already a full-fledged warden. She was a whole different kind of pain to Anthony though. Where he was like looking after a friend's toddler, Amber was like a forced dinner party with an in-law who always knew best about everything.

'Anything to report before we go in?' asked Delarin. There was silence. 'Good. Amber?'

Amber straightened her back and lifted her nose slightly before she said, 'These casteless are corpses.'

Asha couldn't stand the way Amber spoke; it was as if she felt she was above the rest of them just because she came from a larger sanctuary. In fact, there wasn't much that Asha liked about her at all. That wasn't exactly out of the ordinary, considering her usual relations with people, but she didn't like the way Amber spoke to Delarin—like she was his equal. Whenever Asha said anything to the other wardens, however, Grim would just accuse her of being jealous.

'Of course they are.' Grim said in response to Amber's statement. 'So what?'

Delarin shot Grim an impatient look. '*So what* is that a collector isn't powerful enough to anchor casteless demons to dead bodies.'

'They shouldn't be able to anchor so many alone either,' Asha chimed in.

'Which means?' Anthony said, apparently having recovered from his near-heart attack.

'There's something else here,' murmured Amber. 'Something considerably more powerful than a collector.'

'Should we abort?' asked Grim dryly. 'It's probably a trap.'

'No.' Delarin was firm. 'Whatever this thing is, it has been a nuisance for too long. We have a duty to perform regardless. We just need to reassess the risks.'

'Grim, perhaps you should get up into the upper level and cover us. Out of sight,' Amber said, once again asserting herself as though she were in charge.

'Perhaps you should just let our loch warden give out the orders?' Asha snapped. 'The collector's pets have already seen us, so whatever else is in that main storage warehouse already knows we're here.'

'Enough, Asha,' Delarin ordered firmly. 'Grim, they both have good points. Make your way up to the upper level of the building, but don't give away your position unless I command it.'

Grim shifted himself off of the crane, fading to all but a shimmer as he set off towards the warehouse.

'Let's go,' commanded Delarin. 'Keep your eyes open.'

They spread out slightly and entered the warehouse via a small personnel door that was a part of the still-closed main door. The smell of fish and seaweed struck them hard as they entered; now it was all Asha could smell. The warehouse comprised a large single room with a vaulted ceiling, and it was littered with steel containers and wooden boxes. A metal catwalk ran a circuit above them—no doubt Grim was already in position up there. In the middle of the room was a raised four-by-four metre platform. A quick inspection

9

of the room showed no sign of any demon whatsoever, least of all their target.

'Amber and Asha, go that way,' Delarin instructed, pointing towards the far-left side. 'It's in here somewhere.'

Asha followed her orders and made her way over to the other side of the warehouse without checking to see if Amber was following her. She carefully moved around a blue sea container as she drew her sword from its sheath on her back.

All of a sudden the deafening rattle of rifle fire broke the silence. It wasn't the single clap of Grim's rifle, so it must have been Delarin's. She was about to call out to Delarin when the steel doors of the sea container behind Asha and Amber burst open with a bang. The doors swung all the way open with such force that they rebounded off the side of the container. Casteless demons!

Asha's rune lit up as she gathered its power, and its familiar cool tingle surged through her body. She slashed at one of the casteless at it ran towards her, cutting across its stomach. The demon took two more steps before ice crystals emerged from the wound. Asha swept forward with her sword, shattering the casteless' torso. Suddenly, the warehouse was crawling with the damned things.

Amber shouted something, and as Asha turned, she saw three more charging them. Behind the three closing in, on the raised platform in the centre of the room, Asha could see the collector. It was a disgusting bloated mass of floating flesh and tentacles. It locked eyes with her and let out a snarl.

Asha's focus snapped back to the casteless demons rushing towards her. She slashed the air horizontally with her sword, and a cold blast of air rushed towards her attackers, freezing their legs solid and causing the demons to fall and shatter on the ground in a clatter of white ice.

The collector's demons were uncoordinated and weak, clawing and biting recklessly. However, their tenacity drove them to keep attacking no matter their injuries until they were dead on the floor. The collector floated down towards Asha and Amber, who were already occupied fighting yet another group of possessed corpses.

'Shoot the eye!' Asha yelled at Grim. The collector had a single eye in the centre of its spherical lump of grey flesh.

'Sir?' Grim asked over the comm.

'Do it!' Delarin shouted.

A single shot rang through the air, and the eye of the disgusting demon exploded into a wet white cloud. The demon hissed violently, sounding like a large balloon filled with water that had been pierced. The collector sank down, struggling to keep afloat as it died, and then it collapsed on the ground, bubbly white liquid rapidly pooling around it.

The casteless didn't drop as expected, which meant the collector was not the one anchoring the demons inside their human hosts. Weaker demons needed to be anchored to stronger demons to manifest on Earth. With the demons being strong enough to possess dead bodies, together with the fact that the casteless remained standing, meant the wardens' speculation was right: There was something far worse here.

All at once, the casteless stopped. They were still alive but unmoving. Asha cut a few more down, but the rest simply stood rooted to the spot. Something caught her attention near the roof, but before Asha could warn the others, it descended.

Leather wings of dark purple unfolded from the figure as it came into view. They looked far too cut and torn to support flight, yet the dark figure glided down onto the platform in the middle of the room with surprising grace. The creature looked human for a second, but upon closer look, it had purple skin that rippled over the top of its muscular body and fangs that would rival any natural predator. It stood at least seven feet tall and was dressed in dark tattered cloth from the waist down, which covered its legs, but left its chest bare, save for black leather pieces of armour over its shoulders.

'Well done, little wardens,' it rasped. Its voice sounded human, but with a deeper tone echoing it underneath.

Asha froze. 'Cambion,' was all she could say.

'Clever, aren't you?' it replied sarcastically. 'My name is Eligos, and I've been tracking you wardens for a while now.'

Delarin and a pale-faced Anthony moved to Asha's side. Grim was still sitting up on his perch on the second floor, armed with his sniper rifle.

'Asha, get everyone out of here; I'll keep him occupied.' Delarin looked calm, but she knew the cambion demon would destroy him without their help.

Cambions were the result of a human woman giving birth to a baby who'd been seeded by a demon. Sometimes they came about from a willing coupling. Most times, however, a succubus would seduce or force herself upon a human man, his DNA then passing from the she-demon to an incubus, and then that demon would lay with a human woman. The process rarely succeeded, and the woman often died, but when it did, it resulted in a child who grew at three times the speed of a normal child, eventually becoming a dangerous half-human creature with more resistance to angelic and blessed weapons.

'Sir, you need us,' Asha stated firmly, getting her blade ready again. 'We can take him if we do so together.'

'If we all attack him, we could, yes. But how many of us would be left?' Delarin was being stubborn as usual. He was right though.

'I'll hold him off, Delarin,' Amber said, sounding just as stalwart as him. Asha had seen her fight many times, and the claims of her ability were true, but a cambion was a powerful demon and well above any of their abilities alone.

'Fine,' Delarin relented. 'Everyone else, get going.'

Amber stepped forward, a bearded, double-sided battle-axe raised in front of her. Eligos laughed at Amber, who thought herself good enough to stand against him. He looked her over. Asha couldn't tell if he was looking at her with lust, or like she was food. 'It is rare I see a mortal as delicious as you.' He sniffed the air. 'You smell very interesting indeed.' The demon smiled to himself, and his wings twitched in excitement.

The cambion then swiped a clawed hand towards Amber, and a green wave of energy cut through the air at her. She dodged the attack only barely, losing her footing and falling to the ground.

Asha stopped as she saw Amber getting to her feet, and she turned around to help. Asha could hear Delarin protest, but she didn't care. Amber wasn't her favourite person, but she wasn't about to run away while she died.

Asha took a position next to Amber as the cambion stood there taunting them. 'How sweet,' it mocked.

The cambion lifted a hand, which glowed sickly green before bursting into fire of the same colour. Eligos stepped forward and launched the fire from his hand. Asha ducked down instinctively, ready to dodge. However, the fire ripped through the air as it passed her, boiling the air around it as it sailed towards the others while they fled. The green fireball exploded as it struck Anthony. The lance went down instantly, a plume of smoke rising from his body.

Rage filled Asha, and she charged the cambion, leaping onto the platform and landing just in time to duck and weave under Eligos' fist as it sailed towards her head. She shot back up and swung her sword in a downward strike, but Eligos turned his body, and the sword met with only air. Eligos, still grinning, countered instantly with a hard punch to Asha's stomach, which knocked the wind from her lungs and sent her stumbling from the platform. Before Asha had even slammed back down to the floor, Amber was upon the demon. Amber swung her axe, but there was a flash of red electricity from the demon's hand. Instantly, the demon was wielding his own wicked blades, one in each hand, and used them to block Amber's attack. The surprise appearance of the blades must have thrown her off because Amber's reaction was half a moment too slow, and before she could bring her axe back down on the demon, he push-kicked her in the stomach, sending her to the ground mere feet away from Asha.

Asha was barely getting to her feet when Eligos leaped off of the platform. He moved so quickly, yet everything else seemed to slow down; something then knocked her back down to the ground as the demon came at her. Her vision blurred, threatening to black out completely as her head hit the floor.

She heard someone scream. 'Delarin!'

Asha looked up after the blur had cleared from her eyes, and she saw what had caused the distress in Amber's voice. Delarin had been the one to knock Asha to the ground, not Eligos. The cambion's face twisted into a satisfied grin as he pulled his blade from Delarin's body. Wardens were tougher than normal humans, but being impaled by the cambion's blades had no doubt killed him instantly. One through the stomach, and the other through the heart.

'Asha, we need to get out of here. Now!' Amber shouted. It was the first time Asha had been in complete agreement with Amber, but the cambion was already bearing down on them, preparing to strike again.

Before Asha could even think of what to do, a sound echoed through the warehouse. It was a horn call that brought everything, even the demon, to a sudden halt.

Asha looked up at the warehouse ceiling. It erupted inward with light as if the sun had suddenly risen in the dead of night, showering the floor below with debris. Three winged figures floated down from the roof, each gleaming in shining silver-plated armour.

Asha heard Amber curse. The angels' arrival gave them a second of distraction, but it made their situation even more dangerous.

'It's The Divine March,' Amber shouted.

The Divine March—angels, but not of the guardian variety. The angels of The Divine March were ruthless against demons and uncaring towards humans. They wouldn't think twice about the potential collateral damage to humans in the process of hunting their marks.

Asha moved to get over to Delarin's body, but Amber grabbed her by the arm and pulled her back, shouting to leave him. Asha looked over at the still-smouldering remains of the new recruit and the unmoving bloodied body of her mentor and friend. Her surroundings froze for a moment, and everything inside screamed at her to push Amber aside and run to Delarin, but the echoes of the violent battle now unfolding between the demons and the angels penetrated the haze and brought back her senses. Amber repeated her insistence, and after one final look towards Delarin, Asha made for the exit.

The shouts and clanging of metal on metal followed them as they cleared the warehouse into the cold air outside. Grim was sprinting towards them. 'What happened? I thought you guys were right behind me until I spotted the angels fly over.' He sounded out of breath. 'Where's Delarin?'

'He's dead,' Asha breathed, barely audible. 'So is the lance.'

Grim's face flashed with rage as he tried to push past Asha to make a run back in to the warehouse, but Asha stepped in front of him and pushed him back.

'We can't defeat him, especially now,' Asha cautioned.

'We need to leave while he's busy,' Amber said. 'Whoever wins that battle will come after us next.'

Chapter Two
Chosen

The last thing he remembered was also the only thing he remembered. Darkness. As he floated, disembodied in the dark void, coherent thought slowly began to flow back into his consciousness. Words started forming in his mind, and he was suddenly, once again, self-aware. One word in particular kept crossing his mind like a persistent itch, but before he could identify it, the darkness started to change around him. The pure black of the void began to dance around in grey swirls and eventually it faded into white. Brighter and brighter it became until it was a searing white light that forced him to close his eyes.

Everything snapped to black again, but this time it was different—it wasn't cold and empty. His eyelids fluttered once and then opened. He winced as his eyes adjusted to the relative brightness of the dimly lit space around him. The room was stone-walled and bare except for a pair of fluorescent lights on the ceiling. He was inside, yet there was a prominent draught that chilled his skin.

'You're awake.' The voice startled him, and he sat up to meet it. 'Do you remember your name?'

His name? It suddenly snapped together. That insistent word that kept invading his mind was his name. 'Aiden.'

'Oh, good!' the voice exclaimed. The voice belonged to a lanky middle-aged man whose dark blond hair was tied up in a small pony tail. 'You remembered that at least. What else do you remember?'

Aiden thought for a moment. 'Nothing.' His face wrinkled in confusion. 'Why don't I remember anything?'

'Being dead has that effect on the mind,' the man said as he shrugged.

'I'm dead?'

'Don't be stupid,' the man said, maintaining a smile. 'Of course not. You were dead. Now you're alive. Understand?'

'Not really, no,' Aiden said with confused indignation. This man was crazy. If he was dead, how can he be not dead? He remembered being in the dark, his consciousness filled with images and thoughts. Even now he continued to remember all sorts of things, though anything about a life before now seemed blurred or misplaced. Trying to remember anything before he had been floating in the void was difficult. 'Who are you and where am I?' Aiden demanded.

'Warden Tiago, at your service,' the lanky man replied as he did a sarcastic half bow. 'I'm the unlucky sod who's been tasked to get you up to speed. As for where you are… Sanctuary Prime is what we call this place.'

Tiago looked Aiden up and down with his pale green eyes, studying him.

'I don't understand why I can't remember anything before waking up here,' Aiden complained, keeping as calm and as patient as he could.

Tiago rolled his right shoulder, as though it were asleep. As he did, Aiden glimpsed a burn scar. 'Like I said,' Tiago stated. 'You were dead. But don't worry, your memories should come back to you soon enough.'

'Should?'

Tiago nodded. 'Yep. Some folks remember this or that of their past life. Some don't even end up remembering their names.' The man helped Aiden to his feet and gave him some clothes to put on, which was when Aiden realised he was naked. 'For example, I remember most of a happy six-year-long marriage. The things we did, where the reception was and the dress she wore. What I don't remember is the woman herself.'

'That's awful,' exclaimed Aiden as he pulled a plain white shirt over his head.

'Not really. I only remember how I felt about a person, not the person themselves.' Tiago shrugged. He then moved towards the door, looking back at him.

Aiden pulled on a pair of black cargo pants and followed Tiago out of the room and into a hallway—or rather what was more like a grey brick tunnel.

'Do you know what a zombie is?' asked Tiago as they passed a few more rooms like the one he was first in.

The question seemed a little random, but Aiden nodded anyway.

'Okay, good. You remember cultural references. That's a good start.'

'I'm a zombie?' Aiden asked, incredulous.

Tiago laughed. 'No, you're not a zombie.' He barked another laugh, and it was then Aiden noticed he had a two-centimetre scar on the left side of his mouth. 'You are not undead, a zombie, a vampire or in any special dimension you've probably read about. You simply were dead, and now you aren't.'

'I somehow doubt it's that simple.' Aiden was getting frustrated. Tiago made the whole dead-slash-undead thing sound so normal. 'You are not answering my question.'

'Because that ain't my job,' retorted Tiago. 'Nor my place.'

'Can you at least tell me where we're going?'

Tiago smiled, keeping his energetic demeanour as he led Aiden out of the tunnels into more of a homely area. The top half of the walls were a deep red colour that matched the carpet, while the bottom half had dark oak wooden panelling. The carpet felt comforting on Aiden's bare feet as they walked.

'Well,' said Tiago. 'You are only one of a few dozen that've been chosen in the last few days.'

Chosen?

Tiago continued talking as they navigated the halls, which seemed deserted except for them. 'In short, I am taking you to the answers you want.' Aiden gave up and decided to just follow instructions, all the while hoping his other memories would come back to him. The thought of never remembering anything nonetheless haunted the back of his mind as he followed Tiago through the sanctuary. Soon they arrived at a set of double doors. Tiago stopped and turned to him.

'Everything you need to know is through these doors, so listen well and don't worry,' Tiago advised. Yet somehow Aiden wasn't comforted.

Aiden did as he was told and pushed through the doors as Tiago disappeared farther into the hallway. It was like Aiden was walking through a dream. Nothing felt like it was supposed to, except for the headache creeping into his temples. That was real for sure.

The room he entered was populated by at least thirty men and women of all different ages and races, yet they all seemed to be talking to one another regardless. They looked just as confused as he felt.

The room was large, more of a concert hall than anything else, with a two-foot-high stage at the far end.

Aiden looked around at all the other people with a feeling of anxiety as he inched further into the room. No one paid him any attention as they continued to whisper to each other in concerned tones. Suddenly, the speaking stopped, and the collective focus shifted towards the stage where five strangely dressed figures were taking up positions.

The one addressing the crowd was a large muscular man. He had burn scars along the side of his face that were visible from even halfway across the room.

'Good afternoon, initiates,' said the man. His voice seemed amplified, though he held no microphone. 'My name is Asard, and I am the arch paladin of the Order of Elysium.'

Much like Asard, three of the other figures on the stage wore long black coats, which seemed to bleed shades of grey. The cloaks closed around them and were adorned with pieces of ornate metal armour on the shoulders.

The last person Aiden spotted was a woman with platinum blonde hair. There were two reasons she stood out from the others. First, she wore a full set of silver plate armour that had a golden filigree pattern, which circled and weaved all over the armour's surface, culminating in a solid symbol in the centre of the breastplate. The symbol was a golden-winged kite shield, which seemed to reflect light from a source that Aiden could not see. Second, folded up behind her, yet still arching several feet above her shoulders, was a pair of brilliant snow-white feathered wings.

'You have all been called upon to serve the Order, plucked from death itself to help us turn the tide in a war you don't even know exists,' Asard continued. 'The Elysium Order stands between human civilians and what is known as an Aetheric War. It is our duty to keep the citizens of the earth safe and unaware of what takes place in the shadows, and you have all been chosen to join us.' Asard then stepped back and exchanged a glance with the winged woman, who stepped forward.

'My name is Kára,' she announced. Her face looked as beautiful and perfect as an alabaster statue. 'I am Archangel Gabriel's erelim, his second-in-command and overseer of the Order of Elysium. I lead The Valkyr Guard, angels who have been assigned to scour the souls of the recently deceased, and choose among them the best warriors to help keep the rest of the mortal world safe from the war between my kind and the demonic hordes.' There was a pause, and the room fell silent as each person processed what she was saying. It sounded bizarre to Aiden, and everything seemed confusing.

'Even angels make mistakes,' she continued with a hypnotic monotone. 'So if you do not wish to be here, then you can be put back where we found you.' Her voice was calm and cold, yet soothing all at once.

Another silence fell upon the room, giving those in the room a chance to back out. But if they were as confused as Aiden was, none of them knew what they would even be backing away from, and the alternative of being put back into a shapeless void was terrifying. After a few moments passed, and no one spoke up, Asard stepped forward again.

'From tomorrow, you will all stay here for four days, learning what you can,' he said. 'Then you will be assigned a chapter sanctuary—a place you will call home from then on until its destruction…Or yours.'

Chapter Three
Sanctuary

On the first day, just like each day that would follow for the next few days, Aiden woke up in a small room just big enough to fit a small single bed and a metal military-style foot locker. He sat up in his bed and placed his feet on the worn grey carpet of the floor. He sat there on the hard mattress and looked around the room as his vision cleared from sleep and his surroundings came into focus. There were no window or clock that could give him any sense of time, nor did he know if he had slept for two hours or a whole day. It felt as though he slept well enough, however, because he didn't remember trying to fall asleep. It was as if the act of waking up from being dead had been as exhausting physically as it had been mentally.

He stood up and flipped the lid on the foot locker, pulling out the clothes they had told him to wear. Cargo pants, simple but tough-looking boots like those a tradesperson would wear, a simple V-neck shirt and a pair of briefs. All black. As he pulled the shirt over his head, he noticed himself in the reflection of a mirror on the wall opposite him. A surreal feeling came over him as he looked at his reflection for the first time since he had woken up. Deeply familiar but at the same time, a stranger.

To him, the eyes that studied themselves were gentle, like a calm sea in the midday sun, and blue with flecks of green. His hair was like a dark wood with lighter lines scattered through. It was short at the sides but his fringe touched the top of his eyebrows, almost covering the beginnings of what would no doubt someday become deep worry lines.

Once dressed, Aiden pressed a small button on the side of the metal door. It slid open from the middle, revealing the hallway beyond.

Aiden was still in Sanctuary Prime, but the hallway he now stood in was very different to any of the ones Tiago had led him through after he first woke up. Gone were the wood panels and the warm carpet; they were replaced by white polished concrete and metal walls like some sort of sterile hospital. Along the hallway were a dozen doors just like his from which more people emerged, looking just as anxious as he felt.

The hallway ended with two identical hallways coming in at a forty-five degree angle from either side, all three of which were separated by a large semicircle room. At the flat of this semicircle was a large metal door with no handle, only a panel next to it, with an illuminated red light and a darkened green light underneath.

Aiden stood with the crowd that had gathered from each of the three hallways. Assuming each room was occupied along each hallway, Aiden guessed there were thirty-six other people standing in the room, all waiting in a silent air of uneasy anticipation.

Several minutes crawled by before there was a loud click as the red light darkened and the green light lit up. Immediately thereafter the door slid open to the right, and a woman walked out. Aiden remembered the five figures that had taken to the stage when they were addressed after waking. There was the winged woman, and then four others dressed in all black. This woman reminded him of one of the four as she wore a long black coat and pieces of metal armour that sat snugly over her shoulders. Although her pieces of armour were metal, they were coloured matte black and didn't reflect the hard lights of the room.

'My name is Arch Warden Clarel.' She stood with hands clasped together behind her back and spoke in a clean and authoritative manner. 'I am one of the seven arch wardens that serve directly under Arch Paladin Asard as head of training. Under normal circumstances I would have my trainers handle this class, but the Order finds itself presently outside of normal circumstances. However, that is not important right now. Follow me.'

The woman led them through the facility's cold metal interior. At several junctions they passed there were more doors like the one they had waited behind, each one manned by armoured men and women in black coats. Aiden shuddered at the ideas that were going through his head as to why such a high level of security was necessary. Luckily, the so-called classroom was not too far away, and he did not have more time to consider the possibilities.

'This is where most of your training will be taking place for the next four days,' the woman said as they followed her into the classroom. It was nothing like Aiden would have expected of a classroom. The floor was a grey rubber material that felt firm but spongy under his feet. The walls, however, were the same featureless surgical steel metal of the hallways.

'Today's lessons will educate you about the world you are now a part of and will continue to be a part of until you die your second and final death, at which point your soul will be treated as it would have originally, had the valkyr not intervened.'

A tangible feeling of unease seemed to sweep through the crowd around Aiden, but the inaudible command of silence that Clarel's green eyes seemed to growl kept them quiet.

'First things first,' she said. 'As of right now, you each hold the rank of lance within in the Order of Elysium, and will do so until your loch wardens deem you competent enough to hold the rank of a full-fledged warden.

'Second, the head of the Order is the Archangel Gabriel. However, Arch Paladin Asard is our human leader and the highest authority you will probably ever need to be concerned with,' she continued, unmoving in her stance or tone. 'While you are here at Sanctuary Prime, you may see angels within the halls. Do not approach them or try to communicate with them in any way. Whatever they are here for is more important than you, and if they choose to obliterate you, you'll be swept up and forgotten within the hour.' There was a dead quiet before a subtle smirk crept across Carel's face. 'I'm kidding, but still, don't get in their way or else there will be consequences.'

As they stood there silent and afraid to ask questions, Clarel lectured them on the nature of the Order and the war that was being forever waged in the background of humanity. She called it The Aetheric War and said it was the third and longest war since creation. Over the next four days, Aiden waited for Clarel to tell them about the first two Aetheric Wars, but she never did. The only time she mentioned them again was to explain that it was the aftermath of the second war that had led to Gabriel's decision to create the Order of Elysium.

At the end of the second war, Lucifer's attempted invasion of the earth from the circles of hell led to his complete destruction at the hands of Archangel Michael. Soon after these events, God disappeared from the throne of heaven. Even the angels couldn't form a consensus as to how or why their creator had vanished. Some believed God saw his creations as failures and simply abandoned them, while others, like Michael, believed it was a test and that wiping out sin altogether would win God's love back and he would return. Most, however, simply continued to have faith that God's disappearance was simply part of some grand plan, and that the best thing to do was follow the same divine law they always had.

This way of thinking did not convince Michael, however, who instructed his legion of angels, The Divine March, to destroy any demons they could uncover. Normally, Gabriel would have been there with him, but Gabriel was charged with humanity's protection, and Michael had grown to blame humanity and their sin for God's disappearance. Although Michael did not go out of his way to harm humans, Gabriel protested the collateral damage that was being inflicted upon humanity as The Divine March sought to eradicate the demons intent on taking over the earth.

This led to Gabriel forming the Order of Elysium, vowing to protect humanity against all aethereals, even the March, if necessary. Clarel said the wardens existed to serve Gabriel in his attempts to keep humanity safe from not only demon-kind, but the war itself. The angelic crusade against demons, and the demons' thirst for humanity's collective soul, was the Third Aetheric War.

Clarel had lectured for two hours before she allowed them to sit on the floor, and then for another three hours more before she finished up the session.

'Currently, as far as any of us know, the demons are without direction and disorganised without the central leadership that Lucifer had provided in the second war. However, our numbers within the Order are dropping. As such, we are going to condense a month's worth of training into the next four days to get you out into the world faster.

'As wardens, our bodies hold a small amount of angelic essence from the process that brought us back,' Clarel explained. Despite speaking for hours now, her stern, hard tone had remained unchanged. 'This allows us to sleep less, eat less and heal faster, which means don't expect much of those things for the next four days. Except maybe the last one.' For the first time in the whole lecture, her tone changed ever so slightly to match the smallest of smirks twitching at the corner of her mouth. 'Now, follow me.'

First, Clarel led them to a shooting range where they practised with various firearms. In the first two hours they trained, Aiden hit the target plenty of times—that wasn't hard. But his grouping and overall precision wasn't going to impress anyone.

After that, Clarel led them to another room much like the first one they were in, where they trained for six hours with swords. These were blunt, but still full metal, and Clarel scolded anyone who held back. Aiden did much better with the swords than he did with the firearms, but when he returned to his small room to sleep, he was covered in yellow and purple bruises. The hard mattress didn't help the pain either, making it difficult to get comfortable. Despite this, his exhaustion led him quickly to sleep.

The instructors allowed the lances a three-hour sleep before an alarm sounded, waking them all up. Despite the short rest, Aiden felt refreshed. The fact that his bruises were completely gone helped considerably. So once again he got dressed, and they all gathered in the semicircle room in front of the metal door. This time the silence was filled with idle chatter. No one spoke to him though, so instead, he listened to their conversations. Some were talking about the previous day of training, while some shared what memories of theirs had returned to them already.

This time Clarel led them to a canteen where they ate what Aiden could only describe as wet sand with a hint of banana served with a large glass of water. They had thirty minutes to force down the 'food' and meet Clarel in the hall. Almost everyone was there in ten.

The next two days were more or less the same thing. Three hours sleep, followed by thirty minutes of food, and then twenty hours of training with swords, firearms and lectures. The lectures covered many subjects from demon types to how demons enter the earth realm and Order hierarchy and rules, but at no point did she go very deeply into a topic. When someone braved a question, she answered with different variations of the same thing each time. 'You'll learn more once you're assigned to a chapter.'

The fourth and last day of training started the same way, but instead of standard lectures, Clarel led them through a new hallway. This hallway had them go through another large metal door like the one in the semicircle room, only this one was controlled by a security team within a reinforced booth in the wall. The room they arrived at was like the others, simple and square, only instead of the clean, cold metal, it was all concrete. The patchy colour of the concrete led Aiden to believe it had been repaired frequently. If that wasn't enough to set a bout of anxiety through the group, there was all manner of symbols and lines drawn on the walls and floor. Some symbols seemed to be cut off where grey concrete met with a slightly different shade of grey. The last thing that was different about this lecture was that a cloaked figure stood in the corner. The hood on his warden's uniform was up, obscuring his face, and at no point did Clarel address his presence.

'Before I continue, are there any questions?' she asked. Aiden's curiosity got the better of him, and before he knew it his hand was in the air. She nodded to him.

'What are angels?' he asked carefully. 'They're not like us, right? So what are they, exactly?'

'Hm,' Clarel mused. 'That is a good question. Easy to answer, but hard to properly understand. To put it simply, angels are beings of light. To say they exist as forces of energy within heaven is the best way I can describe them. However, the forms we see are physical manifestations of that energy, made from their own grace, which is, in essence, what makes an angel, an angel.

'Seraphim, and other archangels, are far more powerful than their counterparts as they were created by God himself nearer to the beginning of the world as we know it. As such, their bodies are almost pure light. Second- and third-sphere angels on the other hand are mortal souls that have ascended and been forged anew by other archangels. As such, they bleed just like you and me, except for the fact that their blood is golden.'

'They bleed?' Aiden pressed. 'So they can be killed?'

'Unfortunately, this war does require us to sometimes fight and kill angels,' Clarel explained. 'The angels serving Michael in The Divine March often get a bit overzealous. So yes, second- and third-sphere angels can be killed, although they are more resistant to attacks, even more so than us. Which brings me to my next point...

'Besides our physical enhancements, wardens have other aetheric assets at their disposal.' Clarel held up a sword, one of the flat sides facing the group. She ran a finger down the flat of the blade over several cerulean blue etchings. 'These are called aethereal glyphs.'

Someone raised their hand, at which Clarel made the barest of nods to. 'What does aethereal mean?'

Clarel gave the lance the meanest-looking glare Aiden had ever seen. 'I'm glad you've been paying attention to my lectures,' she snapped. 'Aethereal is the term we use to mean non-human, specifically it means anything angelic, demonic or otherwise. Which brings me to my point. Unless anyone else has a stupid question about something they should already have heard me say?'

She waited, daring someone to ask a question, then turned her focus back to the blade in her hand. 'Specifically, these glyphs are angelic.' Clarel turned the blade over so the opposite side was facing them. This side had glyphs as well, but instead of the smooth organic-looking angelic glyphs, these were deep red with jagged edges and harsh angles. 'These are demonic. When applied to a weapon, these glyphs will enhance said weapon's effectiveness against the opposite force,' she explained. 'Having both glyphs, such as these, will make a weapon more effective against both demons and angels; however, not as effective as just focusing on one.'

'How does that work?' someone asked, without even bothering to raise a hand.

'I do not teach the intricacies of glyphs, but if you want to learn more about them, you will have to ask your loch warden once you're assigned to a chapter. But I doubt you'll have time to ask.

'The other application of glyphs is on objects or surfaces.' She gestured around the concrete room to all the glyphs that were scribbled on the wall. 'Demonic glyphs in this case are used to summon demons, while angelic glyphs are often used to contain demons or protect the summoners in some way. You won't be learning that here either, but I will do you the courtesy of a single warning: Using glyphs in an attempt to summon demons is punishable by death to anyone without express permission by the leader of a sanctuary and the supervision of an angel.'

Her gaze upon the group felt like a tonne of stone. 'The only reason I am telling you about it is because humans are stupid, and glyphs are the most common method occultists use to summon demons.'

She then walked over to a patch of concrete bare of any markings and drew on it with a piece of black chalk.

'That being said...' she uttered something under her breath and the glyphs she had drawn on the floor erupted into a frenzy of crackling red arcs of electricity and smoke. The surprise of it made most of the group, including Aiden, flinch away and take several steps back. When Aiden looked back, there was a creature standing over the glyphs. It looked like a human, only its skin was grey and it had several white thorns sticking from its body. It snarled and lunged forward, only to be stopped by an invisible force just above where Clarel had drawn several angelic glyphs. This angered the creature, and it hissed and growled, punching the invisible barrier but making no sound as it connected with air.

'This is a lesser inmai demon,' Clarel said. 'Demons can be summoned like this by those on Earth, but stronger demons can anchor other demons to themselves, summoning them to their sides at will. Kill the main demon and the others are sent back to hell,' she explained as the demon hissed at her. 'Most demons powerful enough to anchor can only summon a handful at a time, however, so it won't always be like taking the king in chess, but it is always a wise move to prioritise any demon who could be anchoring others.'

As soon as Clarel had finished speaking, Aiden saw a pulse of red light emanate from her coat sleeve, and at once the hissing from the demon ceased. Aiden looked back at the demon. Four crimson slivers of what he could only describe as shards of glass had pierced the demon through in a criss-cross pattern from above, pinning it in a standing position. Seconds later the glass dissolved, and the inmai dropped to the ground. Its dark red blood pooled around it, creating a perfect circle to frame its lifeless body.

'One of the top priorities within our duties as wardens is preventing evidence of aethereal existence,' she said, gesturing to the dead demon on the ground. 'So if this were in public, we'd have a problem.'

Clarel reached into her coat and pulled out a small silver flask not unlike something one would use to carry around liquor.

'This is Aetheric Dust,' she said, holding up the flask and unscrewing the lid. 'Or simply dust, as we usually call it. This will dissolve any deceased organic matter.' She sprinkled a small amount of a fine grey powder over the demon's body from within the flask, and it was as if each speck of dust was a tiny carnivorous creature eating away at the demon. In thirty seconds the body was gone, leaving only a dark brown stain on the ground where the blood had pooled.

'It will not always be possible to clean up as you go,' Clarel admitted. 'Every sanctuary has at least one team that will handle the big jobs of cleaning up, but in small encounters you are expected to clean up after yourself. We have agents within governing bodies in every city in the world to help cover up any mistakes, but the less chance we leave of something being found, the better.

She looked over the group as if she were assessing each one of them in her mind. At least a dozen seconds ticked by before she spoke again. 'This is the end of your training, or at least the end of your time here.' To Aiden's surprise, her voice had lost most of its authoritative intensity, though it was still by no means warm. 'Do you have questions before you're assigned to a sanctuary?' A full minute passed in silence. 'Good. Return to your bunks and await instructions.'

Aiden sat on his bed thinking back over the last few days. It all seemed to blur into a single confusing day. Despite everything they had crammed into just four days, Aiden didn't feel much different to when he first woke up. Everything was strange and overwhelming. He felt like he had just been floating through and absorbing as much as he could to make sense of his situation.

'Ready?' The familiar voice broke through Aiden's thoughts. It was Tiago. 'We leave in about five minutes.'

Aiden had nothing to pack, save for the clothes Tiago had given him, so he had been ready an hour ago, as ready as he could be at least. 'Where am I going?'

'They have assigned you to the Salem Sanctuary,' he said.

'Salem? In America?' He had never been to America before. As Aiden came to think of it, he didn't remember where he had come from. So he could have for all he knew.

'No, not America,' was all Tiago said.

Aiden was about to ask him to elaborate but was distracted at the sight of his bag. It was a blue sports bag and looked full to bursting.

'You're coming to Salem with me?' Aiden asked him, gesturing at the bag.

'Yeah,' Tiago answered. 'Rookie handlin' was starting to bore me. Though more to the point, I used to be assigned to Salem, and now for some reason they need me back, which makes two've us.'

'What about the others I trained with?' Aiden hadn't made friends with anyone, but he felt a strange kinship with them through their shared helplessness.

'Too many sanctuaries, not enough wardens.' Tiago gestured to Aiden's bag, urging him to pick it up. Aiden then followed him out into the metal hallway. 'That's why The Valkyr Guard are expanding their search criteria for more and more souls to bring back.'

Aiden trailed Tiago as they navigated the halls that had been his home for the last four days. Despite there having been thirty-odd new lances, the hallways they walked down were just as quiet and uneventful as every other day. It was as if their graduating was no big deal. No show. No congratulations. Just another step towards what was now his duty.

'Isn't there some sort of ceremony?' Aiden asked as they walked.

'Celebration is for the living,' Tiago chuckled.

'I thought you said we aren't dead.'

'We aren't,' Tiago said. 'But having died even once kind of excludes you from the pleasures of the living.'

'Pleasures?' Aiden asked, dubious.

'Y'know, like junk food, sex and the luxury of caring about ceremonies for the smallest of achievements.'

'We can't have sex?' Aiden didn't even know if he had done that before. Not that it was something he had thought about.

Tiago's roar of laughter caught the attention of everyone in earshot. Even an angel turned to look at him. 'Are you asking if the Order frowns upon it or if we are still capable of such humanly things?'

'Both?'

'Yes,' Tiago chuckled again. 'These are just things that tend to be omitted from our lives as wardens.'

As the pair walked through the sanctuary, they eventually climbed a flight of wide stairs that led them to the more homely part of the sanctuary. As they continued on their way out, Aiden could see a small group of confused-looking people following another warden. The warden nodded and smiled at Tiago, who returned the gesture as they passed. These people, all of different age and race, looked just as bewildered as Aiden had felt four days ago. The next batch.

Aiden and Tiago arrived at the Salem International Airport and travelled in a taxi for about an hour before Tiago asked for them to be dropped off in front of a bar just as the sun was beginning to set. Tiago then led them on foot through the city while he told him about Salem and his experiences while previously assigned there. He used to be a loch warden, which was the name given to wardens who were in charge of their own team, but then something happened to him. He lost command of his team and was sent to Sanctuary Prime just over three years ago. He didn't say what happened exactly, and Aiden was smart enough to know not to ask.

The city itself seemed to go on forever in every direction. The centre was dominated by kilometres worth of skyscrapers and high rises, while the density of the city streets thinned out towards the north and south and even more so as its boundaries populated the hills to the east. Immediately to the west of the highest concentration of tall buildings was the ocean, which looked as if it were on fire as the sun dipped below the horizon. In a city so large, the nights were almost as busy as the days, which, according to Tiago, meant the wardens were always busy here. Even now, early in the night, Aiden could see the nightlife starting to move. The good and the bad.

'So where is this sanctuary, and how come we got out of the taxi?' asked Aiden.

'We ditched the taxi 'cause a taxi pulling up outside of a secret entrance to a secret hideout makes it a little less secret.'

'Fair enough.'

'The Salem Sanctuary is on the beach, or at least that's where the main entrance is. The sanctuary itself is underground,' Tiago said, which made Aiden's first thought that of having to sleep in a cave, and he scowled involuntarily. Tiago chuckled. 'Twenty-something years ago, Salem experienced an earthquake, and while not all that damaging in most places, it weakened the supports of a cavern under a residential suburb that the city council knew nothing about. An entire street collapsed into it a few days later.

'Unable, or unwilling, to afford the extra cost to remove all the rubble from the hole in the ground, the council simply built over it. Now, most of the buildings were pretty much wrecked, and the cavern floor was flooded, but there was an old mansion on that street that had survived, almost intact too. The wardens who were workin' out of an abandoned rail yard at the time decided to scout out the cavern. They did repairs, made it safe to live out of and moved in over the next few months. The old rail yard was once again abandoned, and the mansion became the new Salem Sanctuary.'

'Don't they worry it'll collapse again?' Aiden asked. They were now walking down a set of limestone steps that led to the beach.

''Course not.' Tiago feigned offence. 'The city put in their own new supports when they built over the cavern, but *we* strengthened them ourselves when we moved in.'

'Wait, you were here when they moved out of the rail yard?' Aiden looked at Tiago in disbelief; he didn't look much over thirty, let alone having already been in the Order twenty years ago.

'Was twenty-six when I became a full-fledged warden, and a few days later we moved into the mansion,' he explained. 'I much prefer the mansion. The rail yard had a strange smell to it.'

Aiden thought for a bit. 'But that would make you...' He struggled to do the math in his head.

'Figuring out age gets screwy with us because of the whole ageing more slowly thing on account of the angel blood in us,' Tiago said with a smile. 'But I died when I was twenty-five and I've been a warden for thirty-one years, which makes me...' He pretended to count on his fingers as he added the numbers.

'Fifty-six,' Aiden whispered in disbelief to the man who looked not much past half that.

They had been walking along the beach, keeping the water to their left, and a large limestone wall to the right. The limestone wall soon gave way to rock and stone that jutted towards the sea. Aiden surmised that this was where the rock they had bothered to move was dumped. Tiago explained that they had cleaned it up a bit and now it looked more like a natural feature. Tiago walked up to a spot where the limestone met the rock. There was an archway and a metal gate there. As Tiago grabbed the gate and swung it open, it seemed to let off a dull glow.

'Seems obvious,' Aiden said.

'Well, that's because you know it's here,' Tiago said as he stepped into the tunnel, which turned to the right and then again to the left. 'Besides, its key feature isn't subtlety; it's the fact that only wardens can open it.'

After turning the first left, the tunnel descended via a set of stone stairs then opened to the cavern Tiago had told him about. It was a long cavern with a mansion at the other end. The whole space was lit up by half-a-dozen floodlights attached to the house facing outward, illuminating the rock in an even light. As they walked towards the building, Aiden noticed a lot of the piles of rocks were in fact mounds of bitumen dotting the cavern floor, still left over from the earthquake collapse.

The mansion was a large Victorian-style house with two main floors and what appeared to be an attic that had been crushed by falling debris. Tiago pushed open the double doors, and awaiting them on the other side was a woman, whose face, upon seeing them, seemed to fall.

'You?' The woman seemed annoyed. 'Come crawling back, have you?'

'Not so much crawling,' replied Tiago. 'More like begged, really.'

'I suppose even I would get bored watching over lances for as long as you have.' Her voice was cold. It was obvious there was no love between these two, despite Tiago's sarcastically playful demeanour towards her. 'I'd be begging too.'

Tiago laughed. 'You misunderstand; *they* begged *me*,' he revealed with a satisfied grin. 'Seems you guys are a bit overwhelmed here.'

Her eyes narrowed. 'If that were true, I doubt they'd send a man who hasn't even been in the field for over three years, and such a scrawny lance.'

Aiden realised this woman was talking about him. He was scrawny, but he maintained that he was stronger than he looked, especially now.

'Oh, I almost forgot,' Tiago exclaimed, nearly sounding excited. 'Asha, this is Aiden, your newest team member. Aiden, this is Asha, your loch warden.'

Her? She was to be his leader? Aiden didn't expect he'd find this woman pleasant to work with.

'I know who he is, you idiot. I've been briefed,' she snarled. 'Or do you think I stand here all day, every day, for the fun of it?'

Tiago dismissed her attitude with a shrug and said, 'In any case, I'll show him to his quarters and send him to you ASAP.' He then snapped a sarcastic salute, and she walked away with a roll of her eyes, muttering something under her breath.

'Don't mind her too much,' Tiago advised, suddenly sounding more serious. 'You're here because her team's loch was killed about a week ago during a demon ambush. Along with a lance,' he added sheepishly. 'Her loch sacrificed himself to save her. She got promoted. She's not exactly happy about the whole thing as you'd imagine.'

'Is that why she's…' Aiden tried to find the appropriate adjective without it sounding offensive, but he struggled.

'A bitch?' Tiago blurted out, then chuckled. 'No, she's always been like that.' He then waved him on, signalling Aiden to follow. 'I'll show you to your room so you can get some sleep.'

Chapter Four
A little stick

The red glint in the eye of a passer-by was all Lynus needed to begin his hunt. He didn't have to follow the three men far before they slipped into a bar two streets away. As he entered after them, he lowered the hood on his blue jumper. Even in a backstreet bar like this where there was no dress code, a man shrouded in a hood was bound to draw more attention than he'd like.

The inside of the bar was in stark contrast to its rundown front. The tidy rectangular room of red brick featured two dozen circular tables spread out in front and to the sides of the squat U-shaped bar, which started on the right-hand side of the entry. Lynus stepped around the length of the bar, careful not to be bumped into by any of the patrons that littered its stools in various states of intoxication.

He scanned the room as casually as he could for the men. He looked over each group that stood around the tables or sat at one of the cushioned booths that ran along the bar's back wall. Hanging on the wall was a large collection of photos—local celebrities that had come to the bar mixed in with group photos of regular patrons and monochrome photographs of men standing next to barrels of whisky and complicated-looking brewing equipment. A picture in the middle of the wall stood out, if not because it was four times larger than any of the other photos, then because it had a lamp above it making sure shadow would never obscure it. It was a portrait of a rather rotund, balding man in a black and white suit, wearing a homburg hat typical of those worn by men back in the sixties. With one hand grasping the other and resting on his stomach, the man in the portrait seemed to survey the room with a still and silent gaze that tugged on a familiar part of Lynus' memory.

He pulled his focus away from the photos once more, and his eyes soon fell upon the men he had followed into the bar. They were standing around a table together, several metres away from the short side of the bar opposite the door they had entered.

Lynus found a spot where he was close enough to keep an ear on their conversation, while still being able to see them. To avoid looking out of place, he ordered a glass of water with ice. He knew he was over-thinking his efforts to remain inconspicuous but demons often spooked easily, and when they felt threatened, people got hurt. Lynus wanted them at the end of his blade but needed them in a less-crowded place to do so.

He sipped on his water as he strained to overhear the conversation between the three male demons that stood mere metres away from him. It was hard to hear over the din of the bar, but he heard the words 'blood', 'deal', and 'rundus'. Two of which were words that were never good coming out of the mouth of a demon. As for the third, he did not understand what a rundus was—perhaps he had misheard the word 'rune'. The thought of which made him now consciously aware of the weight of the rune that hung from a silver chain around his neck in a small metal cage. It was a rune that he had taken from a demon almost a year ago, who no doubt had taken it from a warden or an angel. It was in fact the second of what was now a small collection of the angelic marble-shaped devices at his disposal, though this was by far his favourite.

As he stood leaning against the bar, looking as uninteresting as possible, his focus shifted towards another man who had walked into the bar and joined the other three. The first three were well-built and muscular, but they seemed to shrink to half their size as the newcomer joined them at the table. He was not only a head taller than the others but larger in every sense of the word. He had thin, dirty blond dreadlocks, and his face was heavily scarred from what Lynus assumed was likely due to long-term possession.

Lynus hated these kinds of demon most of all: demons who took human form. Worse still were those who did so by possessing humans—casteless demons—as they were known by those who knew such things at all. At first, killing these casteless while a human soul still lived within the body was difficult. He had failed to do so on more than one occasion, and these failings taught Lynus that it was kinder to kill the human than let the demon continue possessing them. Certain others he knew of would disagree on this point, however.

After a short greeting, the newcomer walked over to the bar as Lynus looked away again. The smell of stingingly sweet cologne filled Lynus' nostrils as the man stood next to him and waved the bartender over. Lynus wondered if there were any demons that possessed an extrasensory ability for mortal danger, since if Lynus had wanted to, the disgusting creature that inhabited this poor man's body could be dead in a matter of seconds. He concluded that they didn't because most of them believed themselves above a proper mortal death, or too far below it as was more appropriate. As if the demon had read his mind, he sneered at Lynus while he shoved a wad of cash into the bartender's hand. A small jolt of adrenaline shot through Lynus, but as the man turned back around to join the other three, Lynus figured he had earned the dirty look not because of suspicion but simply because Lynus dared to look at him. Demons—easily spooked.

Once the dreadlocked demon had returned to the other three, he led them all through a door next to the bar's toilets to Lynus' left. As soon as they had closed the door behind them, Lynus stood up slowly and took another sip of his drink. He headed towards the back of the bar and slipped through the door to follow them.

The door led to a short hallway with two doors to the right spaced about five metres apart, and then another door at the end of the hallway, which had just closed as Lynus entered. Lynus got to the door and waited a few seconds to allow the demons time to check that they had not been followed. But when Lynus opened the door, it led into an empty alleyway bordered off by the walls of the bar; the neighbouring building and two high chain-link fences to his left and right were capped off with rusted and broken spools of razor wire.

The only logical explanation, even in a scenario involving demons, was they had entered into the vacant building that had once played host to yet another bar. So far, between the chance of finding the demons that had provoked his hunt, to being able to follow them so easily, he had been lucky, but as he turned the handle of the door into the vacant building, his luck ran out. It was locked.

Lynus had in his possession at least two runes that could blast the door in with little problem, but his curiosity demanded that he remain undetected. He wanted to know what these demons were up to. So with no other choice, he drew upon the power of the deep purple rune that hung around his neck.

The de-materialisation of his body started at his eyes as they began to smoke purple, as if an exotic fire had started inside his head. The smoke spread in an instant and suddenly he was nothing more than a cloudy shadow that took the shape of a man. He wasted no time, and as if a man becoming smoke was not strange enough, the smoke passed through the door and reformed on the other side. The instant the smoke reformed, he materialised, becoming solid flesh once more.

The purple rune was not the strongest by way of brute strength within his small arsenal, but it was by far the most useful. Lynus had not mastered the rune, however, and although he theorised it was possible to sustain the ghostly image, he could only use it in short bursts when he needed it in combat, as even that drained the power within the rune rapidly. The more practice he got with it the more efficient he had become. As it was though, making *himself* incorporeal, even for such a short time, had likely drained almost half its power.

Admittedly, he had somewhat come to rely on his ghost rune, and having it already half drained would leave him starting the fight further from the point of strength he'd have preferred. Lynus reasoned this by reminding himself that there were only four to kill, and those that possessed humans and did nothing more than skulk about the city streets were usually small-time demons. This reasoning fell apart when he surveyed the room, and his luck continued its shift downhill.

Immediately after the door stood, to his relief, a stack of shelves cluttered with boxes and various other storage containers that offered cover. More shelves similar to it were lined up to make an S-shaped pathway through the first half of the large room, leading out to the mostly empty second half. Lynus crouched down, making his way around the first bottom curve of the S-path so he could see who it was the demons had come to meet—or rather *what*.

A foot taller than even the dreadlocked demon stood a purple-skinned figure with large torn wings furled up that rested on its muscular back. Its black eyes surveyed the four that stood before him, but he did not speak. The demon was a cambion, the result of the demonic coupling of human and demonic genetics. It was a rare but powerful offspring that had all the strengths of a demon, and only a few of the weaknesses. Not even a blessed blade would faze it much more than a regular one. Lynus silently cursed himself. He would have been able to kill the cambion with his purple rune at full strength, albeit with a little difficulty. He'd have to utilise his rune a lot more than he usually would to dispatch the other four demons quickly enough to put himself on an equal footing with the cambion, but in doing so he would then no longer *be* on an equal footing, especially now.

Lynus considered striking immediately while he still had the element of surprise but it occurred to him that this was an odd meeting, which piqued his already stimulated curiosity. Demons skulking about empty buildings wasn't remarkable. A demon using much weaker demons to do its bidding wasn't either. But a cambion? This meant Lynus had stumbled on something much bigger than he first thought.

The cambion spoke. It was a dual-tone rumble that Lynus couldn't understand. '*Amikko quod sangvilu et amikko voosrus kerebus.*' The cambion placed identical brown backpacks in front of each of the demons as they listened to what he was saying. He spoke to each in turn, giving different instructions, and after he had spoken to all, they picked up the bags and placed them on their backs.

Lynus decided not to attack but simply to follow. For now. He turned on the spot to wait for them back in the bar. The cambion wouldn't follow them back inside, and from there he'd be able to single one out to follow. He took one step and then he heard a heart-plunging clatter of metal as an empty tin can fell from the shelf he had been leaning against. So much for that plan.

He stood up straight as the demons called out, then he stepped out to where they could see him. The four demons stood in place, looking at him with confident and hungry smiles, feeling safe in the presence of the cambion who stepped in front of them. The cambion's eyes tightened as it caught Lynus' gaze with a sinister grin. He extended his purple bat-like wings and shot straight into the air with a single thrust, not towards Lynus like he expected, but towards the ceiling and through the large, broken roof window and into the open sky.

'Eligos?' one of the abandoned demons muttered, his face looking more confused than confident as it watched the cambion leave. The others, however, looked at Lynus with maintained confidence.

'You're that looky-loo at the bar, eh?' said the dreadlocked demon. 'Wrong place to come snoopin'. Kill 'im!'

Shots rang out that made Lynus duck back behind cover. Guns? Most demons enjoyed getting their hands dirty with a blade. These guys were lazy. Or desperate. Whatever was in those bags was worth forgoing the pleasure of killing up close and personal. Guns were a minor deterrence. He had never tested out his ghost rune's ability to stop bullets, and he wasn't about to test it now, so he'd have to try something else, at least until he could get close.

He drew upon the power of his red rune instead. It was the first rune he ever collected, and the one he was most practised with. He felt the warmth of it ripple through his body and coalesce in his right hand as he willed the flames to erupt from his palm, covering his hand. The fire didn't burn, or at least it didn't burn him. He flung his hand with a sidearm throw as if passing a ball through the gaps in the shelving. There was a brief lull in the gunfire as the demons scampered to move out of the way of the ball of fire, but the shooting resumed faster than he could move to take advantage. The bullets tore through boxes and stacks of paper, sending sheets fluttering around Lynus' head.

The flames engulfing his hand went out as he redirected the rune's power through his body. He risked being shot for a brief moment as he stood up straight, his legs shoulder-width apart. If the demons had been quicker, they would have been able to get an easy shot off through one of the empty shelves now level with his head. Lynus raised his hands to his side and pushed them forward into the shelf. The whole shelf erupted into flame and lurched forward, it's now-flaming contents flying towards the demons.

Lynus released the rune's power and dashed out into the open while the demons were distracted by the flaming pieces of rubbish that had bombarded them. One demon was frantically patting out the flames that had caught on his shirt, while another raised his gun again. It was too late for the demon, however, as Lynus had grabbed the demon's wrist. Lynus called on his ghost rune, and there was a flash of purple as the arm holding the handgun fell to the ground. Lynus turned the gun in his own hand, fired a round into the one-armed demon's shocked expression, then two rounds into the chest of the demon coming at him on his right, and another in its head when it wasn't slowed by the first two.

The demon to his left that had caught fire had been overwhelmed by the hungry flames and was now rolling on the ground screaming. As he rolled, he set fire to two of the backpacks, which caught alight quickly. Lynus could hear the smashing of glass as the heat broke whatever was inside. He turned to face the dreadlocked demon, the ghost rune ready to finish the job. Instead of the demon's cocky grin, he saw the back of his head, his blonde dreadlocks swinging over the top of the two brown backpacks he carried as he ran towards the door Lynus had come through. Lynus dropped the gun and unleashed a ball of fire, but the demon had left the room before the flames even struck the brick. So he gave chase.

Lynus burst back into the bar just as the demon had pushed through the front entrance. He was able to rush through the demon's wake of thrown- and pushed-around patrons to help catch up, which turned into a sprint through the streets. It was the middle of the day, so when the demon became desperate and fired wildly as Lynus sprinted after him, it caused a panic. Luckily, no one got hit, and unfortunately for the demon, it made him easier to chase. But it would attract unwanted attention. Lynus had to kill him quickly.

Lynus had just run through a stitch in his side when the demon made a sudden turn into a back street, and then into an alleyway that opened into a space where large square bins were kept. The demon stopped in the centre of the alley, the confident grin returning to his face.

'Thought you might be a run-of-the-mill demon hunter, but with those runes I figure you as one of those wardens.' He spat on the ground. 'Well, I guess I'll just have to kill you and call it a bonus.'

This demon's returned confidence puzzled Lynus only briefly as seven dark shapes stalked around the corner of the far side of the alley. Inmai. Grotesque grey-skinned humanoid creatures that had white bony thorns all over their bodies. To Lynus it looked like they had rolled around in a rose bush.

Lynus reached behind him, pulling out a small metal shaft from a holster strapped to his back, and held it in his hand. The object itself was only slightly longer than his palm, which it sat comfortably within. It was clean silver and had filigree engraving all around it that gave off a dull white glow.

The dreadlocked demon roared with laughter. 'You're going to need more than a little stick, boy!'

Lynus agreed, and just as the inmai demons twitched in his direction, there was a brief flash of white light centred on Lynus' *stick*. The light coalesced and solidified into the form of a shining sword. The filigree, along with the glow, extended from the hilt and ran through the otherwise simple blade. Its cross guard was thin and golden, forming a clipped S-shape that looked to Lynus like a rolling wave of ember.

Lynus wasted no time. He plunged the sword into the first inmai's chest. It glided out just as easily as it did in. Two of the grey-skinned demons threw themselves at Lynus simultaneously. He stepped in as he side-swung the sword into the ribs of one inmai, which sank half way into the demon's body, its blood and innards sizzling as the sword rushed out of it. There was another flash of purple as Lynus used his ghost rune again; this time an incorporeal copy of himself appeared and blocked the other demon's attack, quickly countering with a thrust of its own ghostly sword before disappearing as quickly as it had appeared. He turned to the rest. These were lesser inmai, uncoordinated without their larger, meaner leaders, so their attacks were slow and clumsy. He killed the rest without even needing to call upon his ghost again.

Before the dreadlocked demon could process Lynus' victory and make another run for it, Lynus was upon him. Lynus pushed him against the wall and held his sword less than an inch away from the man's throat. The sword gave off its natural glisten, unmarred by any of the blood or dirt from the fight. Lynus had never seen it become dirty with even a single mark, almost as if it refused to become fouled by such things.

'You're not a warden,' the demon croaked.

'Catch on to that, did you?' Lynus taunted.

'Wardens aren't dumb enough to walk around packing angelic weapons,' he growled.

Like the runes, the sword was another thing he had collected from his time in Salem. It was, of course, not a regular sword. Aside from its obvious power in a fight, the fact that it worked a lot like a rune made it easy to conceal. He had to will it into being, just like the powers and abilities from the runes; otherwise, it was just another pretty bauble.

'Wardens use runes,' Lynus replied.

'Given to them by angels,' said the demon. 'You've got to be mad with a death wish to steal one.'

'Who said I stole it?' Lynus remarked. 'Could have killed one. Just like I'm going to kill you if you don't tell me what and where you're so desperate to deliver to.'

'Wouldn't work if ya killed—,' the demon's sentence was cut short as Lynus pressed the blade of the sword against its throat. The demon's blood sizzled slightly as Lynus broke skin.

'Answer the question,' Lynus growled as his eyes smoked purple again.

The dreadlocked demon's face warred between emotions of rage and fear. 'I know who you are...' he stuttered and then spoke very quickly. 'It's a drug. New. They ordered me to deliver samples to the Golden Rundus Casino.' That was disappointing. All this mystery for a simple drug run. The drug might be new, but demons spreading narcotics among the human population was not. As much as Lynus would love to, even with his runes and his sword, he'd be pushing his luck trying to take down an entire drug ring alone, especially if it involved a cambion like that purple-skinned thing he'd seen earlier.

The demon continued despite Lynus' now-fleeting interest. 'A mephisto called Yuenlyn Myn is waiting for the delivery.'

Upon hearing the word 'mephisto', Lynus' interest came rushing back.

'A mephisto?' he asked with a look of suspicion.

The demon nodded as much as the sword hovering over his neck would allow.

Before Lynus could press for more information, there was a sudden rush of wind behind him and the unmistakable *whoosh* of large feathered wings. Lynus turned, cutting the demon's throat as he did. It slid down into a sitting position against the wall, dead. Standing before him, there it was: the unwanted attention. Four angels now took up occupancy within the alleyway. Two guarded the only exits with their white wings still extended, while their leader and a fourth stood in front of him, keeping their distance as they eyed the sword. Each of the angels had silver engraved metal along the top of their wings, ending in sharp blade-like points. On their silver chest pieces, they displayed a golden engraving of their insignia—a simple-looking sword not unlike his, but this sword insignia had wings whose tips stretched up almost meeting above the blade. The sword itself was pictured as being wreathed with flame. The Divine March had found him again.

'Hand over the sword,' the leader said plainly. 'It does not belong to you. Place it upon the ground and walk away.'

Lynus stopped, deep in thought. Not about handing the sword over as that would never happen, but he assessed his situation. Judging by the golden trim on this angel's armour, he was a principality, a leader of a small group such as the one before him now. They were the bottom of the angelic hierarchy—rank-and-file soldiers—but Lynus knew better than to underestimate any angel. With a fresh start, Lynus would have plunged straight into battle, but he had just been in two fights in the last thirty minutes, and his resources were becoming spent.

'If you're all the March could send, I don't believe they want it badly enough.' Lynus pulled all the power that remained in his fire rune and erupted a wall of flame from within that moved across the alleyway in all directions like a wave. He quickly recovered and darted towards the principality. It kicked off the ground and took flight to dodge Lynus' sword. Lynus followed through and instead impaled the unprepared angel that had been behind its leader. The angel shouted in pain as it tried to push Lynus away. Lynus saw one of its wings wind back up for a strike. Lynus pulled the sword free just as the angel's wing snapped forward to attack, but he was too quick, lopping the angel's wing off and following up the attack with a slice at the angel's neck. The sword embedded deeply, and there was a brief flash of white light from the angel's eyes as it died.

Lynus swung around to face the other angels who had now not only recovered from the blast of fire, but had swords drawn and were rushing towards him. The first one to reach him had taken flight, soaring close to the ground with its sword wound up ready to strike like some sort of angelic wasp. Lynus jumped to his right, rolling and popping back up, now facing all three as the two lesser angels approached. They attacked as one. Lynus engaged them both, sending out his ghostly avatar each time they attacked to block one while he attempted to counter another.

If nothing else, angels were at least more coordinated than most demons, which made them more challenging opponents. Not only that, there was the fact that when two angelic weapons met, they did so with equal force, so Lynus' edge of having an angelic weapon was almost mitigated. Luckily, for reasons Lynus assumed were from fear after what happened to their comrade, the angels were at least keeping their blade-tipped wings well away from Lynus' sword.

Lynus couldn't keep this going. He would run out of rune power soon. When the next attack came, Lynus didn't block either angel. Instead, he stepped back and let his ghost take both blows. This opened the angels up to a proper attack. He swung the sword down, slicing a diagonal cut down one of the angel's necks, through its plate armour and right down to its waist. He flicked the tip of his sword up and pushed upward, impaling the other angel from under the rib cage; its eyes flashed white as he withdrew the sword, quickly slashing a second time at the first angel whose eyes also flashed white.

Lynus looked around for the last angel, panting. The principality angel had not joined the fight. Instead, it circled around them and was now leaning over the angel Lynus had killed first. The angel stood up and faced Lynus again; he now wore a necklace with a white rune attached to it, taken from the body of his comrade. He also wielded the dead angel's sword in the other hand. He walked towards Lynus with no expression upon his face, both swords angled down as he walked.

Lynus sucked in two deep breaths and erupted into a sprint towards the angel. He drew on the last of his ghost rune's power as he ran. Dark purple smoke enveloped him, giving his whole

51

body an eerie shimmer and turning his eyes into purple fire. The angel struck with both swords. Lynus didn't move to dodge. The angel's attack hit nothing but air as Lynus darted through the angel, spun and struck out with two quick slashes across the angel's back, gliding through the plate, skin and bone like it was all just made from paper. Paper didn't scream in pain though. The angel swung around for another attack, but Lynus had already ducked under its reach and slashed again. The angel fell to a knee and Lynus wasted no time finishing the angel off with a stab through the neck, carving through the angel's rune. There was a bright flash of light from the rune and the eyes of the angel as it fell.

He didn't need to pull the sword out. It deactivated on its own, and Lynus staggered away from the body. The purple smoke that had surrounded him evaporated, and he fell to one knee. He allowed himself to fall to the ground and roll onto his back, staring into the sky. Clouds blanketed the sky now, and a soft spray of rain fell. Lynus groaned in pain from exhaustion.

He heard footsteps and someone called out. *Shit*, he thought, *a civilian*. Lynus mustered up as much energy as he could and got to his feet, running for the street before someone spotted him. He would find a place to lie low, rest and let his runes recharge. Then it was time to go to the casino.

Chapter Five
The new lance

As Asha walked down the central hallway on the second floor of the sanctuary, the door at the end of it opened and Amber walked out, shutting the door behind her. She passed Asha without a word or a glance. Asha ignored it and made her way to the door Amber had just exited. She knocked on it, and a voice on the other side beckoned her in.

Asha entered the room and shut the door softly behind her. The office featured a large mahogany desk on the far side with a window behind it that would have shown a sprawling garden once upon a time. Now it was nothing but an empty cavern, so the owner of the office had the red velvet curtains drawn shut. On the desk was a small lamp that lit up the workspace and the hard-lined features of the man who sat there, watching Asha as she approached.

'You called for me, sir?' Asha stood up straight, hands by her sides and faced the man sitting at the desk.

'Sit,' instructed the man. He wore the black clothes of the Order, though his coat was hung up and his pauldrons, which were mostly ceremonious, were set down on the other side of the room on a small table by the door. Asha did as the man instructed and sat down on the chair opposite.

'High Paladin Tarek, I—'

Tarek held up a hand, and she stopped. The man was pushing sixty, as far as his physical age was concerned, but his exceptionally well-trimmed silver hair gave him an air of distinction and authority. He was the Salem chapter leader, the high paladin, and Asha would follow any command he gave. Though even if the man before her wasn't her superior, she'd follow him regardless due to the deep respect she had for the man himself for having survived as a warden for over a hundred years. One-hundred and sixteen to be exact, Asha had once found out, putting his actual age at around one-hundred and thirty due to the slower ageing process. Wardens of his calibre were usually promoted to Sanctuary Prime by this point to serve on the Order's council, or at the very least as an arch warden. She had once gathered the courage to ask him why he preferred his position as chapter head. She knew that Tarek, if he had the ambition to, could have been standing in place of the arch paladin, instead of Asard, who was at least a decade younger. He had simply replied that a demon's blade was kinder than bureaucracy's rope.

'I have heard quite enough of your protests,' he said. 'I know you don't think you are ready to be a loch warden, but we are running out of options. Besides, you are familiar with the team, and I am nowhere senile enough yet to place Grim in charge.'

'It's not that, sir,' she said, dejected, having missed Tarek's attempt at humour. 'I—'

'Like I said,' Tarek interrupted. 'I've listened to your concerns, Asha. It wasn't your fault and as much as I'd like to say otherwise, we don't have the luxury of solace.' It sounded harsh but Asha knew it was the truth; however, all she could think about was screwing up as a loch and making their situation that much worse.

'This time last year I had fifteen warden teams, three of which were paladin teams. Now we are down to nine, and only two of those are paladins.' Tarek sighed deeply, looking lost in thought for a moment. 'But never mind that,' he said. 'That's not why I called you here. I have an assignment for your team.' He handed over a piece of paper. It was a printout of a news article from a freelance news site.

Asha took it, her eyes scanning the headline, *'Supernatural Murder Scene!'* It described how the writer of the article found dead otherworldly creatures in a back alley. There were pictures in the article showing the scene. With a dozen bodies littering the alley, it looked like the scene of a mass murder merely with one difference. Only one body looked human; the others were aethereals.

'The bodies weren't dusted,' she said, immediately cursing herself for stating the obvious. 'I take it that these bodies were left by something else, and this civilian has found them.'

Tarek nodded. 'This was published online about two hours ago. I want you to take *your* team to the site, dust the bodies, gather all the info you can and find that reporter.'

'Is this the same reporter that's been a pain in our arse for months now?' Asha was referring to a persistent camera-wielding civilian who seemed to have a particular interest for the supernatural. This by chance led him into their path more than once, making himself a problem when it came to keeping certain things out of the public eye, whether he knew it or not.

Tarek nodded. 'Yes, it is. It's time he was dealt with,' he advised. 'I have already put in a request for a special etching.'

'I'll assemble—' she paused, looking at her feet for a few long moments before meeting Tarek's gaze. 'My team.'

She got up to leave, but as she reached the door, he called out to her again. 'There is something else you should know,' he added. Asha could see his jaw clench, and his lips became a thin line. 'I have it on good authority that the demon that killed Delarin escaped the March. Be careful. He's still out there and he's still out for warden blood.'

Asha nodded and turned away quickly so that Tarek didn't see her face twist into a mix of anger and heartache. As she closed the door behind her, the thoughts racing through her mind were not of caution. She wanted nothing more than to run into that demon again.

***

Aiden stood on an abandoned street. It was void of all life or detail. The wind did not blow, and the sun did not feel warm on his face. The signs on the walls and on the shop windows seemed familiar, but he could not read them. At the corner of his eye, he thought he saw something. He spun around, but nothing was there. Back to his left he thought he saw a group of people walking down the path, but as he looked and tried to focus on them, they were gone.

He was suddenly aware that the world around him was like normal, full of life and bustling activity, but only at his peripherals. Whenever he turned to look, the space was empty, as though another world existed just outside of his view.

He walked down a narrowing street. The buildings themselves did not move, yet with each step he took they seemed to inch closer until he could see them meeting some distance in front of him. He turned to walk back, but it was the same behind him. He started to panic and ran into an alleyway, and soon everything was black. He felt around him, and his heart sank to find something enclosed him.

He felt as though he was moving; the enclosure he was in swayed back and forth, and he could hear shouting outside of the box. Again familiar, but he did not understand the words. He could hear fighting and more shouting—it sounded like a battle. Suddenly, he jolted up against the top of whatever he was trapped inside. He felt weightless as he fell.

He could hear his name…

'Aiden!' Asha pulled the pillow from behind his head and dropped it onto his face. 'I need you ready in five minutes.' She threw down a duffel bag by his feet as he moved to a sitting position on the bed. 'These are your blacks for now, put them on.'

Asha had made a very aggressive first impression, and even now as she stood by the door, her icy blue eyes watching him with impatience, it surprised him to notice how fair her face was despite her demeanour. She had all the beauty of a nice sword. She was just under six foot and lean, attractive, but with fierce, sharp features. Her hair was short and wavy, hanging a half-inch below her ears, jet black in blunt contrast to her pale skin.

'Before you meet up with us, Tarek wants to see you in his office,' she announced.

He nodded sleepily, and she left the room shutting the door behind her. Only then did he realise he had no idea where Tarek's office was, or who Tarek was for that matter.

He rubbed his eyes one more time as he picked up the bag. He could still feel the residual sensation of falling from his dream. Never before had he had a dream like that, not that he could remember at least. He took out the contents of the bag Asha had given him. Black cargo pants, a belt and a black t-shirt. Almost exactly what he had worn during his four days of training. It looked more minimalistic than what Asha was wearing when she had come in, but even more so than some of the wardens he had seen at Sanctuary Prime.

He quickly dressed himself and left his room only to wander aimlessly around the hallway outside for far too long. Eventually, he found someone who gave him directions to a door that had a label on it: High Paladin Tarek.

Sounded important. Surely he had not been here long enough to get himself in trouble. He knocked, and a voice ordered him inside. The man at the desk inside stood to greet him and said, 'Nice to finally meet you, Aiden.' He walked around his desk to shake Aiden's hand. 'I am High Paladin Tarek, and I am in command here in Salem.'

'It's nice to meet you too, sir.' Aiden was nervous. This man, although clearly aged past his prime, had a gaze that froze him solid yet commanded him to move all at once. He hated himself for being anxious; he was better than that. Or was he? He felt he shouldn't be, but something scared him. He was scared of never remembering. Scared of what he was getting into. Scared of everything. And he despised it.

'Sit, son.' Tarek walked to the other side of his desk again and took his seat. Aiden sat opposite.

'You look worried,' Tarek stated.

'Sir,' he struggled to speak his mind, but pushed through it. It was either being scolded at for asking too many questions or go about this new, confusing life not knowing. Despite being intimidated by this man, the thought of never regaining his memory commanded most of his trepidation. 'It's been almost a week now, and I have not remembered a single thing of my past.'

'As I am sure someone has made you aware, some people remember nothing.' Tarek sat back in his chair unfazed, or perhaps even bored with the question. Aiden realised that he probably wasn't the first person to ask this question, and yet here he was asking like so many confused pups before him. What made him think he was special?

'Your past does not matter anymore, Aiden. All that matters is now, and what you need to do. Out there.'

'I've been having some strange dreams though,' Aiden continued. 'When I was in training, they were all pretty vague. Now though—'

'They are just dreams, son,' said Tarek. 'I wouldn't think much of them, but don't go around talking about them to the others, either. Asha is still getting used to her new role, and the last thing she needs is to think you are not ready to be out there.'

Aiden felt defeated and suddenly out of the courage to keep asking. He didn't feel ready for the field, but he figured admitting that out loud would bring more trouble than not, so instead he just nodded. 'Yes, sir.'

'Now, I called you in to get you acquainted with how things work around here,' Tarek said. 'Demonic activity has been increasing in Salem over the past six months, and we have only a handful of teams. I'm still not happy that they only gave me two new wardens, especially after I lost two last week.' He seemed to be staring off past Aiden, no longer actually talking to him but rather thinking out loud. His eyes snapped back into focus. 'But that's not your problem. I believe you have met Asha?'

'Yes, sir,' replied Aiden. 'Tiago introduced me to her when I arrived. She's my—' He tried to remember the word for team leader, but it didn't come to him.

'Loch warden. That's right,' he said. 'She's a bit high strung at times, but just do what she asks and you'll do well with her. She cares about her team, even if she doesn't partake in expressing that.' Tarek opened a draw on his desk, pulled out a piece of paper and handed it to Aiden.

'The sanctuary is bigger than it looks from the outside, and can be confusing.'

Aiden looked at the piece of paper. It was a vaguely detailed map of the mansion. He could have used this ten minutes ago.

'You may eat and sleep whenever you want,' Tarek advised. 'But make sure you are always prepared to be summoned for an assignment. Aside from a demon invasion, of which there has never been at this sanctuary, there is no excuse for tardiness to assignment briefings.' He smiled with effort, Aiden thought, to comfort him.

Training had been very structured, and very strict, which made this seem odd. Being able to do what you wanted so long as you showed for assignments was, at least in contrast, very relaxed for a place that housed demon hunters. Or angel hunters. Whatever they—he —was now.

'Now,' Tarek said as he stood from his chair. 'I believe your team is waiting for you.' He placed his finger on a section of the map. 'This is the briefing room they'll be in.'

Aiden stood too and headed for the door before he turned to face the high paladin as Tarek spoke. 'And Aiden, as far as your memory is concerned, learn from Tiago's mistakes and know that if you keep searching, you may not like what you find.'

Tiago? When Aiden first woke up with only Tiago to explain what was going on, he had explained his lack of memories with an example of his own. He mentioned nothing that seemed troubling to Aiden, but Aiden decided not to press the issue. He was running late as it was.

Aiden walked into the briefing room within just a few minutes of leaving Tarek's office. The room was outfitted with four dozen lockers set up as three rows of four on either side of a large metal table in the centre. Running along the back of the room were weapon racks, which were lit with a cold blue light. The racks were stocked with assault rifles and handguns, but according to the map Tarek had given him, this wasn't where they kept the bulk of the weapons. If this is what they held in just a briefing room, Aiden couldn't help but wonder what toys they held in a fully stocked armoury.

Standing around the table in the middle of the room, the rest of the team waited for him. There were four in total. Asha stood with her back to the weapon racks; she was facing the door as he walked in. To her left was Tiago. Those two he knew. The man and woman who stood to her right-hand side were unfamiliar.

'Grim. Amber,' Asha introduced, 'This is Aiden, the new lance.'

The first one to her right was Grim. He stood about five foot ten with a large rifle in hand and nodded a greeting. Grim's black hair was a standard short-back-and-sides cut that had been grown out with a few tufts of hair hanging loosely over his forehead. He reminded Aiden of a hawk, with the green-gold eyes of a bird of prey and a thin but heavily toned body. His bare arms looked like twisted ropes bundled together by skin.

Amber on the other hand had soft features and eyes of dark blue that looked as welcoming as a pool on a hot day. Standing next to Grim, Aiden could see she was a couple of inches shorter than him. 'Welcome to the team,' she said, giving him a genuine and friendly smile. He couldn't help but stare at her a little, not just because she was strikingly beautiful, but because everything about her spoke of comfort and a slight sense of repose. Like Asha, she seemed built for battle, but unlike Asha's tall and toned physique, Amber was more feminine and had curves visible even through her warden coat. She had light olive skin unmarred by any noticeable scars. Her hair was copper red, and despite it reaching to between her shoulder blades, she was wearing it loose save for a few clips that kept it from her face.

All of them were wore their warden blacks, a term they used for the general dark clothing the members of the Order each wore, defined mostly by the long mottle-black trench coats. Aiden had not been given a coat yet and he dared not ask for one now, and Grim seemed to be perfectly comfortable without one.

'Our orders,' Asha said before Aiden could return Amber's greeting. 'Are to investigate a battle site.'

'Battle site?' Aiden asked out loud as he thought it. He immediately regretted asking when Asha shot him a cold glare.

'Well,' Tiago started. 'Demons and angels usually try 'n keep to the shadows, but when they meet, they are more concerned with killing each other, so we need to clean up the mess before the general public catch wind.'

'Which is a problem because this battle site has already been photographed,' explained Asha. 'Luckily by a freelance journalist who isn't taken seriously. Most of what he puts out is considered a hoax by the public, but it can still cause a problem for us if it's not dealt with.'

'I looked over the article,' said Amber. 'It appears he intends on further investigation of the site, so we should expect him to be there.'

'Good,' Asha said coolly. 'We have orders to bring him in for etching.'

Aiden wondered what etching was, but he thought better of asking.

Aiden had managed to get three hours of sleep since he arrived in Salem, which as a warden was almost the same as sleeping through the night, so when he stepped outside it was somewhat of a shock to find it to still be night. By the time they arrived at the alley after a brisk twenty-minute walk, it had only just struck midnight.

The entrance to the alleyway was a driveway that allowed residential entry to the two apartment buildings on either side of the alley. The only thing dissuading the general public from wandering down the alley was the fact that it was barred off by a boom gate operated by a swipe machine. One after the other, they ducked under it and made their way down the small road, which turned down and into a ramp to an underground parking area that was empty as far as Aiden could see. Instead of following it down, the team stood by the corner where the alley opened up to the back of the surrounding buildings.

Aiden stood by Tiago and looked into the alley where, just like the article had described, about a dozen bodies lay strewn about the concrete.

There was what looked like a human slumped up against a far wall, but the rest were a mix of the grotesque grey-skinned inmai demons and angels, which wore decorated silver plate mail.

'March angels by the looks of those insignias,' Amber stated. On the front of each of the angel's chest pieces was a gold engraving. It was hard to see from where they were and with the lack of proper lighting, but to Aiden it looked like a winged, flaming sword.

Asha took out a mobile and after a few quick thumb presses held it to her ear. 'We've got about a dozen to dust here,' she said. Aiden could hear faint voices speaking on the other end of the phone but couldn't hear the words they were saying.

'Sir, we need at least thirty minutes to dust and secure the area.' Asha replied. 'Okay. No. No sign of anyone. Yes, sir.'

She took the phone away from her ear and hung up, placing the phone back into her coat.

'The katharis is giving us thirty minutes before he has to bring in the authorities,' she said, addressing the team.

'Bloody Kathys,' Tiago cursed. 'Do they even know how dusting works?'

'Considering clean-up is their primary job, I'd say they do,' Amber replied.

'How're we going to dust a dozen aethereals in thirty minutes?' Grim asked.

'By shutting up and getting to work,' Asha snapped. 'Tiago, show the lance what to do. You two, pick a corpse and start dusting.'

As the rest of the team moved into the open area of the alley, Tiago turned to Aiden and gave him a metal flask.

'This is what we call dust,' he said. 'I'll show you.'

'What's a katharis?' Aiden asked as they walked over to the corpse of an angel.

'A major part of our job is keeping the aethereals a secret from the world,' he said as he unscrewed the top of his flask containing the dust. 'Regular humans would lose their minds if they ever found actual proof of aethereals.'

Aiden watched as a small amount of a grey sand-like substance poured out of the flask and on to the body of the angel. The dust seemed to glow slightly red as it went to work dissolving the body. 'But, dusting on-the-job only ever really happens in ideal circumstances,' Tiago explained. 'More often than not, we have to come out to clean up after an angel–demon throw down, or have to come back after an assignment if we cannot do it during, for whatever reason.'

Tiago led Aiden over to another body as the first continued to dissolve, a demon this time. 'The kathari are special wardens who work undercover, usually in government, and pull strings to help us do our job.' He gestured to the body on the ground. 'Your turn. Careful to pour at the right angle so the dust comes out at the correct velocity. It's real complicated stuff.' He broke into a wide grin as he passed Aiden the flask.

Aiden poured some of the dust, and it went to work just as it had on the angel beforehand. Tiago then walked him back over to the first one to show him that after only a few minutes the body had dissolved, leaving nothing behind except for a vague shadow of what had been laying there, which would be washed away by the next rain.

'In this case the katharis that Asha spoke to works with the local police and is delaying them from showing up,' Tiago explained. 'Then once they're here, he'll do his best to discredit anything that they do find, if anything. They also cover up anything we miss and handle mass etchings.'

'Which is?' Aiden asked.

'What? Etching?'

'Yeah,' Aiden said. 'Asha said it before as well. What is it?'

'If we find that reporter, you'll find out,' Tiago advised.

As the team continued to dust the bodies, Asha had noticed Amber stop and stand over one of the demons.

'What is it, Amber?' Asha asked.

'These demons. They're just inmai demons,' she said.

Seeing these creatures was a far cry from seeing them in the pictures, or even that one living demon that Aiden had seen in Prime, and he couldn't help the feeling of fascination that seemed to be growing inside. He walked over to Amber and looked at the body of the demon she had been scrutinising. It was the same ugly species that Clarel had used to demonstrate summoning glyphs.

'I don't see four angels falling to such weak opponents, even third-sphere angels such as these,' Amber stated.

'Sphere?' Aiden questioned.

Amber explained to him that they organised angel ranks into three spheres. Angels of the first sphere were the most powerful of all other angels, whereas angels of the third sphere were rank-and-file angels tasked with day-to-day duties. The second sphere was for everything in between.

'What about this one?' Aiden had moved to another angel that, unlike the other two, had gold trim on its silver armour.

'He's a principality,' Amber explained. 'Still third sphere, but this one acts much like the angel equivalent of a loch warden.'

Aiden looked at the principality angel. Something caught the light of the street lamps and directed his attention to what he almost mistook as a two white chunks of rock. He picked them up, holding them up to what little light there was, and found they fit together to create a small pure white sphere.

'Grim!' Asha broke Aiden's concentration and drew his attention to where she was now pointing. 'It's that fucking journalist!'

'I'm on it.' Grim dashed towards the direction Asha had pointed and gracefully scaled a downpipe before climbing onto the second-storey balcony of the building.

The journalist must have ducked behind the balcony wall before Aiden looked because Aiden couldn't see anyone. That was until a man was thrown from the balcony, landing somewhat safely in a large bin.

'God dammit, Grim, now get him out of the bin!' Asha shouted as his head appeared over the side of the balcony.

'There was a bin there?' he shot back, but even from here Aiden could see the hint of a smirk.

The journalist scrambled out of the bin, falling to the ground as he did.

'Aiden, grab him,' Asha ordered.

Aiden half-ran towards the journalist before he could get to his feet. He grabbed the man by the sleeve, but the journalist easily shook out of his grasp. Aiden reacted quickly, grabbing the man again with his other hand. He held him tighter this time and pulled him back. The man stumbled, almost falling again, though by now Asha had come over, shoving him hard, which helped him to the ground anyway.

'Who are yer people?' the man asked with wide eyes. He spoke with an accent, but Aiden couldn't pick it. 'If yer 'ere for th' same reason as me, I don min' sharin'. S'lang as folk know aboot it.'

'And why *are* you here?' Amber asked. Aiden looked at Asha; she looked annoyed at Amber for jumping in.

'T'take photos, o' course,' said the journalist. 'Name's Sullivan. I hava website you've likely—'

'Shut up!' Asha raised her voice to get over his ramblings. She grabbed his camera from him, much to his pathetic protests. She ignored him as she smashed it against the ground into a hundred tiny pieces.

'Ya doolally boot!' Sullivan yelled.

Asha grabbed the man's face, and her hands and rune glowed blue. When she took her hand away, his mouth was covered with ice, 'I said shut up. Aiden, restrain him.'

Aiden did as he was told as the rest continued their observations.

'So if inmai could not kill this many angels,' Tiago said. 'And that guy over there is dead…'

'There must have been a third party,' Amber concluded.

'Get whatever info you can from the remaining bodies and finish dusting them. We're running out of time,' Asha ordered.

The team did as they were told, except for Aiden who was still watching over Sullivan. The journalist was wide-eyed as he watched the bodies dissolve as the dust began its work on the other bodies.

'Ah knew it!' he shouted, the ice having thawed enough for him to speak again, 'T'all makes sense now! How come ah cud neva fin' solid proof? Who are yer people?'

'It doesn't matter what you see tonight or what I tell you, so save your breath,' growled Asha.

'Wha'are you talkin' aboot?'

'In about an hour you won't remember a thing,' Asha said. Sullivan's eyes widened even further, darting back and forth, looking for an escape.

'You're gettin' etched.' Tiago almost seemed excited. 'Have not seen an etching in a while,' he mused to himself.

'Well, since you are so enthusiastic about it, you can take him,' Asha said flatly. 'We'll finish up here.'

Tiago walked over to Sullivan and pulled him to his feet by his jacket. 'C'mon, Civ.'

As Tiago walked away with the reporter, Aiden walked over to Asha and pulled out the objects he had found, handing them to her, 'One of the angels had it.'

'Hm,' she mused, looking at it closely. 'Looks like a rune, but not like I've ever seen before.'

Grim joined them, carrying what looked like vial of yellow liquid. 'That human over there is, or was, a casteless. He had this on him.' Grim held it up for them to see.

'That looks like angel blood.' Amber took the vial from Grim and studied it. 'Except not.'

'Make sense,' snapped Asha.

'Angel blood doesn't coagulate; there's no need since their skin heals so quickly. Notice how fluid this is?' she asked, tipping the vial. 'Archangels bleed literal light, but other angels' blood glows gold. This is more of a basic yellow, like it's lost its essence or something.'

'You an expert on angel blood now?' Asha asked sarcastically.

'Trust me,' Amber stated. 'I had a lot of down time in my old sanctuary, which had a large library of books on angels.'

'Why would a demon have an angel's blood?' asked Aiden.

'They drink it.' Amber's eyebrows moved together as if she had just tasted something foul. 'It's a drug to them. It's fatal to humans though.'

'I could ask Narki Navia,' Grim offered. 'He knows everything happening on the street, and if that's really a drug of some sort, he'll know where it came from, or if not, at least what it is.'

'Okay,' said Asha. 'Grim and Amber, go see Narki and find out what you can. If this is dangerous, we need to keep it away from the public. Aiden and I will visit an old friend of my own regarding this rune.'

Chapter Six
Common knowledge

S o, how did you get a nickname like that?' Amber asked
Grim as they were travelling down a busy street. It was almost one in the morning, and the nearby nightclubs were
in full swing. Everywhere they went boomed with music and
drunken yells of fun and violence. They continuously dodged the
civilians stumbling into the street as they headed towards Grim's
contact. If the vial of blood they had found was in fact being used
by humans as a drug, Narki would know and happily tell them. For
money.

'Must be my sunny disposition,' he replied dryly with a hint of
a smirk.

'Do you remember much of your old life?' Amber questioned.

This woman was too curious for Grim's taste. 'Do you always
ask such personal questions?'

'I like to know the person I am likely to die fighting alongside.'

Grim wasn't sure if she was being wry or pessimistic. Either
way, he couldn't disagree with her logic.

'Well, what about you?' he asked indignantly. 'Do you remember anything?'

'No.'

She was insufferable.

'To answer both questions,' he said, giving in, '*Grim* was my handle in my previous life.' She had a point; it would be nice to know more about each other. Amber had been in the team for three weeks now and in Salem for two months, and he knew nothing about her. 'Your handle?'

'Yeah,' he said. 'I did work for the Vlacinov crime family here in Salem in the nineties before I died.'

That seemed to take her aback for a moment.

'Killed bad guys for other bad guys,' he added quickly. 'They never hired me for anything other than killing rivals. Knew I'd reject anything else.'

'Odd that you be assigned to the same city in which you lived,' she said.

'Yeah, well, even before I died I didn't have much of a life left.' Grim said sullenly. 'Let alone a life that would impede my work now.'

'I'm sorry,' Amber whispered.

'Me too.'

'So this guy we are going to see,' Amber blurted. 'How did the sanctuary come to be using him?'

'They don't,' he said. 'He's an acquaintance of *mine*.'

'So you don't allow others to associate with him?'

'More to the point, he won't talk to anyone else from the Order. In fact, he doesn't officially know about us.'

'Officially?' Amber queried.

'He knows almost everything going on in the city. If something leaves someone's lips, the smart money would go onto him finding out about it one way or another,' Grim explained as they turned a corner. This street was narrower than the one they had been walking down, and turning down it was like shutting the door on a party; only the loudest of the drunkards and the distant thrum of music could be heard. 'I believe he knows enough about us to know what we do, and that it's in his best interest to limit his association with us.'

'Why go to him at all then?' she asked. He felt a little like he were being interrogated. He wasn't used to this much conversation.

'We know quite a bit about demons and angels in the bigger picture, but the devil is in the detail, so to speak. Narki has more connections to the human underground than we could ever manage. As I'm sure you know, that's where demons like to do their work, which also means he's aware of aethereals. He's proven useful plenty of times.'

They walked in silence for the next few minutes before they arrived at a store front with a blacked-out front window. They pushed open the front door with a blue neon sign above it that read, 'Narki's'.

The inside of the store was untidy with scraps of paper on the floor and half-built contraptions piled up on various shelves. There was no cash register as one would expect, instead just a counter that was in front of a door at the back of the room. Behind the counter sat a wiry caramel-skinned middle-aged man who was leaning back in his chair. He had a baby-blue feather tattooed on the underside of his left forearm that cradled the back of his head. Unnaturally white dreadlocks streaked with light blue dangled over his face, and his eyes were closed, but Grim could see the hint of a grin form as they approached.

'Narki,' Grim said in an attempt to get his attention.

'Grim,' replied the man without opening his eyes.

Grim pulled out the vial of blood they had found in the alley earlier and placed it in onto the counter in front of Narki with a dull clank. 'We need info.'

'Of course you do,' Narki replied through a yawn as he opened his baby-blue eyes and sat forward. He looked at Grim and then at Amber. 'The only other reason you'd be here is to introduce me to this lovely woman.' He smirked and gave Amber a wink.

When Grim was alive, Narki was only twenty years old. Now Narki would be well into his forties, but looked as though he had not aged past thirty. Grim had no doubt that Narki's charm would have worked on many women, but not Amber, who returned his lazy flirt with a scoff and an impatient eye roll.

'Oh, I'll introduce you to something…' Amber growled.

Narki chuckled and looked down at the vial on his table. 'On this I'm guessing.' Narki picked the vial up between his index finger and thumb, inspecting it for a just a few seconds before placing it back down. 'Fifty,' he said, tapping the table three times in quick succession.

'Really?' Grim asked indignantly.

'Really really,' Narki replied. 'Trust me.'

'If only.' Grim placed down a fifty-dollar note in front of Narki who snatched it away.

'Aether.'

'Ether?' queried Grim. 'Like the anaesthetic?'

'No. Aether,' Narki repeated before spelling it for him. 'It's an up-and-coming drug. Named as such because of how high it gets you. Heard rumours of it in other cities. It's dangerous stuff.'

'Why does it look like angel blood?' Amber asked.

'Because it is,' he asserted. 'Or at least it's synthetic angel blood.'

'Synthetic?' Amber asked, seemingly unwilling to trust what she had just heard. 'How could someone make angel blood?'

Narki moved his head side to side, popping the joints in his neck. 'They don't,' he finally admitted. 'It's just human blood mostly.' The two wardens stared at him, and when he finally realised that they were expecting him to elaborate, he continued. 'Real angel blood is mixed in with human blood at a one in one-hundred ratio.'

'So it's just diluted angel blood?' probed Grim.

'Not just; I'm sure they add other stuff to it to make it more palatable and very addictive, but essentially, yeah. Unlike real angel blood, it's useless to demons as a recreational drug, but the rest of us would get the same effects that the demons would with real angel blood, although without the pesky side effects of having your blood literally boil out of your eye sockets.'

'What kind of effect will users have if they take it?' Amber queried.

'Think of all the best qualities of most street drugs, with none of the downsides. Makes you alert, strong and horny,' Narki revealed.

'And no danger at all to the user?' Grim asked.

'Well, besides memory loss from overindulgence and becoming super-agreeable,' he replied.

'So why would a demon be carrying it?' asked Grim.

'They're the ones who distribute it,' Narki said matter-of-factly.

'You make it seem like this is common knowledge.' Amber seemed offended. 'If it were, how come this is the first we've heard about it?'

'Everything is common knowledge to me, gorgeous.' Narki was blunt, but Grim could hear the pride resonating within his voice. 'It has not hit the streets here in Salem, not en masse anyway. Not yet.'

'Why are the demons distributing drugs to humans and where are they getting this synthetic stuff?' Grim demanded.

'For fifty I told you what this is,' Narki grinned.

Grim placed another fifty-dollar note on the table.

'You know me, Grim. I like to stay away from aethereal business. That's your job.' Narki placed a hand over the note and dragged it towards him, pocketing the cash. 'I don't know who's creating or supplying, or where and when they will be releasing it onto the streets,' he continued. 'But, I've heard some interesting things coming out of the Golden Rundus Casino lately.'

***

Adley Black, the name 'black' being ironic given the new grey hairs he'd found on his head this week, approached the stall. It was a shady sort of stall that would sell things in an alley at this hour, just the type he wanted to see, and his intuition was rewarded instantly. He spotted what he had spent earlier that night tracking down. He picked up the small orb and held it between his ringed index finger and thumb. This was the rune he had been looking for, so the rumours were true, though the rune was definitely dormant.

'Good evening, sir,' Adley said to the man behind the stall as he brushed off a piece of errant fluff from his white shirt. 'I wish to buy this. I'll give you two-hundred for it.'

'No, not two-hundred. Three-hundred and ten,' the stall owner demanded.

Adley laughed. 'I'm doing you a favour here, trust me. You won't find someone else to offer even what I am for it.'

The seller behind the stall grunted. 'Three-hundred and ten.'

'Come now, this is a game, is it not?' Adley smiled a charming smile. 'Yet despite having opposing goals, this is a game we both can win. Tell me, do you know what this even is?'

'It's just a pretty trinket,' the merchant replied with a smile. 'Yer think yer smooth, but I'm not selling this for less than what I told ya.'

Adley shrugged and put the rune back down. 'Well, I guess we both lose then, huh?' he said flatly before turning to walk away. Five steps later, he was urged to turn around at the behest of the stall owner. He smiled to himself, straightened his sport jacket and turned back to the stall.

'Fine, you can take it for two-hundred,' the man huffed.

'That was my offer last time I was here,' Adley grinned. 'Since I had to come back, I'm only offering one-fifty. My time is precious, my friend.'

The other man slammed his hands down on his stall, making all his little trinkets jump. 'Fine!' he yelled, tossing the little sphere at him. 'Take it and leave.'

Adley snatched the trinket out of the air and graciously handed over a trio of fifty-dollar notes.

'Since you gave me such a generous discount, I'll give you some free advice. If you are going to sell this stuff, I would suggest you do your homework, my friend,' advised Adley, holding up the rune to the street light. 'I would have gladly paid thousands for this. I guess you still lose.' He smiled and walked away. Angry yelling followed him down the street.

It wasn't a long walk from the alley to his study. He walked along the footpath as the occasional night-clubber stumbled by on their way home, but from what he could tell, a lot of the people were not going to their own homes. Judging by the noises coming from the alleyway he had just passed, some were not even waiting to get home at all.

Adley held up the object he had just purchased. It was pure white, but did not glow like it should. He had hoped that it had already been charged, but it seemed as though his luck had run out. Though on second thought he considered himself lucky, for if it had been charged, it may have attracted a less desirable possessor, making it harder to get a hold of.

He turned left down another alleyway and pushed open a worn-down faded blue door.

'Hello, Mr Black,' came a woman's voice. 'I heard there was quite the commotion down at the club. Are you alright?'

'Of course, my dear,' he reassured as he walked over to the desk she was sitting at. The room was no bigger than a two-car garage but looked much smaller than that since it held several desks littered with books, folders and various papers with messy scrawlings on them. But this room was only a prelude to his main study.

The woman who had spoken was perched delicately at the largest desk near the centre of the room. She wore her pitch black hair up in a bun on top of her head, and a dark blue pencil dress. Her honey-coloured eyes followed him as he took a seat opposite her. 'I got the information I needed and left that shambles of a place. Demons everywhere.'

'You got it then? Are you sure you'll be able to use it if you're not a warden?' she asked.

'Of course, Katherine.' He then took out the sphere he had purchased off of the ignorant man on the street. 'Technically anyone can use them. Wardens just have better access to them and proper training. Unfortunately, the rune is not active, and so it will remain unless I can find someone to…' He trailed off for a second, looking towards a door at the back of the room where there was the sudden sound of growling and high-pitched voices. '…charge it. What is that sound?' he asked, noting that Katherine did not seem particularly fazed by it.

'I planned ahead, sir,' she said as she used a single finger to push up her thick black-framed glasses so that they were resting comfortably upon her small pointed nose. 'In the event the rune was inactive. I summoned a…tracker. To help find someone who could activate it.'

'Katherine, there is only one kind of person who can activate this.'

'Precisely,' she declared, seemingly quite pleased with herself. 'And since it has been months since you've even spoken to a warden, and they neglected to share the location of their sanctuary, this demon will help find one and in turn, an angel.'

'Species?'

'Imp, sir.'

Adley walked into the room where the imp demon was being held. The room was small and empty besides himself and the demon, and now his assistant, who scurried in behind him as he shut the door. Katherine had once suggested an airlock door, but Adley was confident that the glyphs of containment painted over the otherwise pure white room would hold almost anything Katherine could summon. And her little book had a few fairly powerful summoning spells in it, which was the very reason he had recruited her to help him. She had proven herself invaluable over the past several years.

'What do you want, you worthless sack of piss!' the imp hissed. It was no taller than Adley's waist and dark brown in colour with light brown wings that Adley was always surprised were big enough to enable flight. Of course, in his studies he had learned long ago that the normal rules of physics did not quite apply to aethereals. The ability to summon objects and balls of fire, as well as traversing between realms when called by certain practitioners, were all things that defied the common understanding of science.

'It's not about what I want any more, little one,' Adley taunted.

'You filthy human. Did you summon me here just to have a laugh!' the imp shouted.

'No, but that's the thing, isn't it? You *are* here, and you can't get back on your own, so if that is what you want, you will help me.'

'Spit it out then,' said the imp with an impatient flutter of his wings.

'I need you to track a warden for me,'

'Well, there's a surprise. That's all anyone ever seems to want of me these days.'

'Can you help me or not?'

'For a few drops of angel blood, anything is possible.' The imp smiled, showing its needle-sharp teeth.

Adley had certain avenues to keep a small supply of angel blood, which had been handy when questioning various demons. Even some of the most stubborn casteless played right into his hands when he flashed a vial of the stuff. Adley never stopped being amazed at how something so simple could make such a big difference. He gave the beast what it wanted, and it beamed with delight then started laughing.

'What's funny?' demanded Adley.

'No need to go looking; there's a warden headed down your alley right now!' The demon started cackling again.

'*Ki Maluukes!*' Katherine huffed. The demon disappeared in a display of red lightning and smoke, snickering all the while.

Adley could hear his front door creak open and voices in the front room. 'Be a dear, Katherine, and clean up that summoning circle while I tend to our visitors.'

As Adley entered the room, he saw two people standing next to Katherine's desk. He recognised one of them, but not the other. 'Asha!' he exclaimed. 'Long time. What brings you here, my dear?'

'This.' She handed him something he recognised instantly. A broken rune.

'Hmm. Follow me,' Adley instructed as he walked through a door into a room with walls lined with bookshelves. His inner study as Katherine mockingly called it. He walked over to a desk on the far side of the room and sat down, placing a pair of glasses on.

'How'd you manage to break it?' he asked.

'We didn't. We found it on an angel. A dead one,' she replied.

He held the rune up to his eye, twisting a second lens on his glasses that magnified and focused his view on the rune.

'It's definitely a rune that has been cut in half somehow, which as a fact on its own is extraordinary, but this…this is what is interesting.' He ran a finger over the flat side of the rune. 'The cut is exceptionally smooth. Any idea what kind of weapon could do this?'

'Are you actually asking me?' Asha asked, clearly irritated. 'Or do you already know the answer?'

Adley couldn't help but smile. Same Asha as every other time he'd had dealings with her. 'I do.'

'Well?'

'Well, there is something I need in return.'

'You're asking for payment?' Asha's voice was raised, and he could hear her temper rising. 'Have you forgotten our arrangement?'

'Of course not,' he said with a smile. He was spotted one night and almost killed while tracking a group of demons. A warden named Delarin and his team, Asha included, saved his life. Adley had explained to them that he was somewhat of an expert on demonology, and in return for not being etched, he offered them his knowledge whenever they needed it. Delarin had warmed to him easily enough, but Asha never quite got there and had always considered him to be no better than the other occultists in the city. 'I'll give you the information you want, of course, whether you help me or not. I'm asking as a favour, my dear.'

'Tell me what I need to know, and I'll think about it.'

'You there,' Adley directed himself at the stranger who had walked in with Asha. He seemed quite young, not much older than twenty. If that. 'What do you know about Michael?'

The stranger looked uneasy. He looked at Asha before speaking. That hesitation meant one of two things: She was in charge of a team now or he was new.

'He leads The Divine March,' said the young warden. Or more to the point, stuttered it.

'Correct,' said Adley. 'He leads the bulk of heaven's angelic warriors.'

'Get to the point, Black,' Asha snapped.

'Michael's. Sword.' Adley put emphasis on each word separately. 'It is the only thing I know of that could possibly do this to an object of angelic origin. But there is a problem, you see. Michael doesn't have the sword anymore, so that means he isn't involved in this.'

'Gotta tell you, Adley,' said Asha. 'This isn't exactly information worth granting you a favour for.'

'What exactly is going on here? Where did you find this?'

'You don't need to know that,' Asha stated flatly.

'You came to me for help, remember? The more information you give me the more I can provide.'

'The rune was found on a dead angel. Principality class,' she revealed begrudgingly.

'Hmm,' Adley mused. 'What do you know of the Ghost?'

'The Ghost of Salem, as in the urban legend that's been going around for the last year or so?' Asha's brow scrunched up in incredulous curiosity. 'The man who has allegedly put down countless demons, yet is hunted by heaven?'

Adley nodded, 'It's not an urban legend, my dear. A bit hyperbolised, I'm sure, but he is real, and I think he's involved in whatever you have going on here.'

'What makes you think that? What about the sword?' Asha asked.

'Well, during my time with various demons—' he stopped, realising she may take that the wrong way. Humans consorting with demons made the Order nervous. 'Nothing nefarious, I'll have you know. Just some relatively friendly demons willing to share information with me.'

'You're rambling again.' Asha's voice was cold.

'Sorry. Yes, ah…' He had to think back on what he was talking about. 'Right, well rumour has it that the Ghost, whoever he is, actually stole the sword from Michael.'

'How could a mortal human simply steal anything from an archangel, let alone his weapon?' asked Asha.

'Well,' Adley said. 'That's the other thing. Some say he isn't a normal human. That he is part angel, or part demon, or…various other things.'

'Stories tend to get exaggerated, Black. What is he really?'

'Hybrids don't exist, of course.' Adley shrugged. 'Not sure, but he's definitely something.'

Asha rolled her head back and stared at the ceiling for a few seconds. 'Thank you, Adley.' Asha walked out of the library room followed by her lance.

'Wait!' He reached her as she was leaving the front door. 'What about my favour? My information was adequate wasn't it?'

'It was,' she said. 'Consider me ignoring you being overly friendly with demons as your favour.' She and the recruit then walked out.

'Bitch.'

Chapter Seven
Sad stories

B ack at the Salem Sanctuary, Aiden followed Asha through the sanctuary into the etching room. Grim and Tiago had arrived beforehand, but Amber was nowhere to be seen. The room itself was a simple square room with white walls. The only other thing inside was a padded table with four sets of straps on it that were currently tightened over the unconscious reporter they had captured from the alleyway. Standing by Sullivan's head was another figure dressed in robes of white that matched the wings curled up on its back. The angel looked as if it were in a trance, totally disconnected from any interaction with anyone, save for a quick glance towards Aiden and Asha as they entered, before returning its focus to the man on the table.

Aiden stood next to Asha at the man's feet and watched Tiago as he placed what looked like a blank business card on the reporter's forehead. The angel then placed two fingers on the card and pressed down firmly. The card began to glow an aureate gold, and the civilian's eyes fluttered for a few seconds before eventually closing again.

'What's happening?' Aiden whispered to no one in particular, somewhat mesmerised by the glowing.

'This is an etching,' replied Tiago. 'We have the tools to take a civilian's memories in the event that they see things they shouldn't.'

'What then?'

'Then the civilians get put somewhere safe and wake up like nothing happened,' Grim explained.

'But surely he will remember everything else?' Aiden was, as always, confused. 'He was investigating the Order before tonight, so won't he just go back to doing that eventually?'

Grim nodded. 'Normally. When we etch people, they lose the last twenty-four hours. Give or take,' he said. 'That's why the angel is doing it. They can pick and choose which memories to take from as far back as they wish. It's not a perfect process, and mistakes can be made, or he might just end up following the same path to us again eventually, but besides killing him, there's not much else we can do.'

Aiden continued watching. The card now had hard black-cornered markings on it that continued to appear as the process continued. Once the markings filled up the card, Tiago began unstrapping the man from the table.

'What happens to the card?' Aiden asked.

Grim shrugged. 'Never cared to ask.'

'Grim,' said Asha. 'Take the journalist and dump him behind a bar or something. You know the drill.'

'You're just gonna leave him?' Aiden was surprised that they would treat someone so carelessly. 'That's horrible.'

'We have to do a lot of horrible things to keep people safe, lance,' Asha growled. 'Get used to it. Grim?'

'I'm on it.' Grim walked over to the man's unconscious body and began moving him out. The angel was the first to leave.

'Aiden, get some food and sleep if you need it,' Asha advised as she followed the angel out. Grim, with the reporter over his shoulder, followed close behind. Tiago gave Aiden a smile and turned to leave, but Aiden called him back.

'Yeah?' Tiago turned to face Aiden as the rest of the team continued on.

'I spoke to the high paladin about my fear of not getting my memories back.' Aiden tried his best to keep his nervousness out of his voice. He wasn't nervous about asking Tiago the questions he had, like he was with Asha, he was afraid of what the answer might be. 'He said that if I continue to look for answers, I may not like what I find, and he said that I should learn from your mistake.'

Tiago's face, for the first time in Aiden's experience, went abruptly dour. 'High Paladin Tarek is a wise man,' was all he said.

'What did he mean?' Aiden was insistent.

'I was actually a lot like you,' Tiago recalled. 'I didn't remember anything for months, and when I did, important parts were missing. Remember how I said I had a wife, and that I remember everything except anything specifically about her?'

Aiden nodded. 'You said that you remembered everything about her except who she actually was, and so you had all the happy memories but none of the sadness that would come from losing her.'

'I lied,' he said. 'At first that was true, and it's a useful way to explain things to new wardens, but I insisted on finding out. I kept thinking about it and asking questions.' He shook his head as if disappointed in himself. 'I started havin' dreams about her until all of a sudden it all came rushing back to me. All the memories I wanted came back; the memories of the person I loved.' His expression became disconnected then, as if he were remembering it all over again. 'Those memories didn't come back alone, either. I also remembered our last moments together. I regretted it immediately and even asked to be etched. Just my luck, I was told that warden's can't be etched.' Tiago forced a laugh and a smile, but to Aiden it just seemed bitter.

'Why did you regret it?' Aiden knew he was pushing on a boundary but he decided that he needed to take the opportunity while it was present. He convinced himself that he'd be different. That he wouldn't regret it.

'I found out how she died.' Tiago's face seemed to go a few shades lighter.

'What happened to her, Tiago?'

'I killed her.'

Aiden found himself making a conscious effort not to move away from Tiago in surprise.

'It was an accident,' he said blankly. 'I was a cop and used to work crappy, long hours. One night I had come home early. Didn't feel too good. Found her in bed with another man. I flew into a rage. Literally threw the guy out of the house, and me and her started screamin' at each other. All I remember of the fight was how angry I was because she was making excuses instead of feeling ashamed and sorry like she should have. All I could think of was tryin' to make her share the pain I felt. I couldn't, so I took my gun out and pointed it at her. If she wouldn't feel wretched for what she did, I wanted to make her feel fear instead. I had no intention of shooting her, but as I went to lower the gun…I dunno what happened. Maybe my finger twitched, or it was a freak misfire. It didn't matter; the result was the same: it hit her in the chest. I called an ambulance and tried to do first aid. But she died in my arms, looking up at me with a face of horror, pain and sadness that's seared into my mind even today. I put the next bullet in me, and the next thing I knew I was in Sanctuary Prime, just like you were.'

Aiden was mortified. He wasn't sure what to feel, but the story made him feel a little sick to the stomach. Every impression Aiden had of Tiago was that of joy and playfulness. It was a nice balance with everything else around him. He would never have guessed his circumstances of death to have been so dark. Tiago started to walk out of the room after Aiden failed to say anything.

'I'm sorry,' was all Aiden could think of.

'Don't be,' Tiago got to the door and turned back to him. 'We all have sad stories, Rook. Otherwise, we wouldn't be here.'

The room Aiden stood in was dark, yet he could make out the obscure shadows of furniture. A dresser. A bed. A small, soft lamp that flickered on as Aiden looked at it. Now the shapes became solid, as did the man lying in the bed. Aiden stood there as the whole room seemed to move under his feet, bringing him closer to the man. He stood over him. The sleeping man was noticeably pale, even in the low light. Beads of sweat clung to his forehead and streaks ran down the side of his face along his greying hairline.

Aiden could suddenly feel eyes burning into the back of him. He spun around, peering through the dark room at a woman in a green dress, who had a fleeting familiarity about her face. Before Aiden could catch it, she changed. She stepped forward from the shadow, and her face twisted and contorted into rage as she lunged for him.

Aiden's eyes shot open, and he was back in his own room. He had barely been in Salem for twenty-four hours and already he had experienced two dreams. Tarek had said it didn't matter what they had done in their past lives, only what they did now. He couldn't help but think of how many other wardens in the sanctuary had met similarly horrid ends, just like Tiago. It briefly made Aiden consider that he might be better off not knowing. Briefly. He shook the thought from his mind and got dressed, pulling out the map Tarek had given him, and left the room.

Even with the map he was lost, but managed to stumble his way into the mansion's lobby. It was a lot more active than when he first arrived with Tiago. Wardens in blacks and casual clothes alike cut across the white-tiled floor of the lobby and into the various hallways that connected it. The walls were a light brown with circular patterns in a slightly darker hue that were barely noticeable unless you looked closely enough. About a metre away from the front double doors there were the beginnings of a four-metre wide dark red carpet that ran down the centre of the room and up the main staircase. On the second floor landing there was another centre hallway and hallways on either side. It looked strange to see some wardens walking around in such civilian-like clothing, but even the warden blacks looked like cheap knockoff costumes compared to what he saw next.

Six figures marched down the central staircase with such purpose that all other wardens moved well out of the way the moment they saw them. They wore warden blacks, but had thick black leather armour covering them underneath and across their neck and shoulders. They wore black hoods and matching fabric masks over their mouths, leaving only their eyes visible.

'Paladins,' said an unfamiliar voice that startled him.

Aiden turned to his left where the voice that had shattered his bubble of awe had come from. There stood a young woman. She looked like she was in her mid to late twenties, so a little older than he was at twenty-one. She stood there looking at him with a casual confidence that told Aiden she wasn't new like he was, despite her apparent youth. Like a lot of the others, she wasn't wearing the black clothing of wardens. Instead she wore cargo pants and a loose-fitted top with some obscure logo on it. No doubt a pop-culture reference he didn't understand. She looked at him expectantly with light brown eyes. He realised he had not replied, but rather just stared at her for far too long.

Duh. Good job, Aiden.

She smiled, seemingly amused by the fact he was still struck dumb by the paladins, or was it her that had caught him off guard to the point where he couldn't find his words? She was pretty but plain looking, though something about her demanded admiration. Her chestnut brown hair was tied up into a bun on her head, which made her appear slightly taller than him. He then realised he was staring again. 'Paladins?' he finally stammered.

'Yup,' she said. 'You're the new lance, huh?'

Aiden nodded, 'What gave that away?'

'The fact you've been standing there staring at the lobby for about a full minute now.' She smiled at him again, showing the barest of dimples at the corners of her mouth.

'You've been watching me?'

'Yup, so we're even,' she said matter-of-factly, a smile playing across her face as one eyebrow hitched up. 'Don't think I didn't see your eyes giving me a once-over just now.'

He didn't even realise he had been doing it, but she was right. Aiden could feel the blood force its way into his cheeks. The thought of him blushing in front of this girl only made it worse. He tried to change the subject. 'My name's Aiden.'

'My name is Kallista,' she said. 'But my team calls me Kalli.'

'So, what's the deal with the paladins?' Aiden asked. It was nice to ask a question and not have to worry about a death glare from Asha.

'Paladins are what we should all aspire to be,' Kalli recited as she puffed out her chest, and her face was masked with a serious expression. 'Too serious for my taste. They are our elite. When teams of wardens fail, the paladins are sent in. Though they mostly deal with the more serious demons. Y'know the big ones from the lower circles of hell.'

Aiden recalled one of Clarel's lectures back in Sanctuary Prime. She had explained that hell was, first and foremost, a very real place. It consisted of seven regions, or circles, that were home to demon-kind. Demons were forces of domination by their very nature and their collective desire, the reason for their original existence, was to destroy the creations of God and his light. However, for the most part, they were trapped within hell, and so dominated each other instead, fighting for supremacy over one another. This fighting drew the victors closer into the centre circle of hell, where they were closer to the source of darkness that lay even further locked away at hell's heart. Not only were the demons that ended up deeper in hell stronger for their victories, but their proximity to the primordial darkness bolstered them further. Luckily the deeper inside they were, the harder it was for them to be summoned to Earth, and the less likely occultists were brave enough to summon them. It seemed even they had some sense.

'They don't exactly look very subtle,' he said.

'Neither are the demons they fight. There comes a certain point where subtlety isn't practical.' She grabbed the map from his hands. 'Lost?'

'Yeah. Tiago told me to come to the blue mess hall for breakfast,' he said, looking around.

'Well, there are two mess halls in the mansion.' Kalli tapped her finger on a section of the map in the south wing's ground floor. 'This is the yellow, and the blue one is here.' She was now tapping on an adjacent area in the north wing.

'Thanks.' A few seconds of awkward silence passed as he tried to figure out whether he should leave or...what?

'Well,' she said to Aiden's utter relief. 'I've got some more strangers to spy on. See ya 'round.'

***

The room Grim was in slowly came into focus as he opened his eyes. He experienced a few moments of absolute confusion as he tried to figure out where he was, or how he got there. The last thing he remembered was placing the reporter behind a bar. Then the alley went dark. Now he was here with no memory of anything in between.

He focused his vision and got his bearings. His wrists were tightly bound behind him with something cold and hard. His feet were bound as well by what looked like steel wire. The only light in the room was the late morning sun filtering in through a dirty cloth that hung over a small window. The rest of the room's walls were bare, and the floor consisted of cracked and chipped concrete. Grim's mind went wild with the possibilities of who had abducted him and why. Police? No, too trashy a place to keep him. The mob? They think he's dead. Demons were the most likely, but why abduct him?

Grim looked down at his feet again. The wire was more like a cable and was wrapped around his legs just above his knees, and another was around his ankles. He tried forcing it, but it didn't give whatsoever. He looked closer and noticed that the wire was seamless; there was no physical way to tell where the cable came together. He rolled to his side, trying to get to his feet, but rolled back to a sitting position as the door opened.

'Grim,' the figure said as it walked into the room, ducking slightly under the door frame as it did. Not human. That revelation gave Grim a bit of solace as the Order was naturally a bit contentious about killing humans. The being before him wore a similar coat to that which wardens wore, only this was a mix of white and gold. The coat was sleeveless, and at the waist it opened up to reveal legs clad in silver plate armour. Its face was hidden behind a hood, but even past the shadow he could see the light reflect off the man's white irises—the mark of a high-ranking angel.

'What do you want with me?' Grim demanded.

'You?' It seemed amused despite its monotone. 'You're already doing it.'

'I should have known better than to have expected a straight answer,' Grim snarled.

'Yes,' replied the angel. 'You should have. Then again you've done many things you should have known the better of, haven't you, Markus?'

Grim glared at the angel. No one in this life knew his real name, except for Tarek, Asha and likely the higher-ups in Prime. 'Who are you?'

It ignored his question, but Grim already knew what it was. An arbiter. What it didn't explain is what this arbiter wanted with him. Arbiters were dominion-class angels of the second sphere. Meaning they were not your average angel, so it meant Grim was in more trouble than he was prepared to deal with. Arbiters had the innate ability to look into a mortal's soul and see all the sinful deeds of that person, which in their position in heaven they used to judge entry through the 'pearly gates', or so the story went. Though in the wardens' collective experience, arbiters used the ability for manipulation—and the evil deeds of man as a source of power. That was a fact, and it was all that mattered to Grim right now.

'Whatever you are going to do with me, I suggest you do it quickly,' Grim said flatly. 'They'll know I'm missing by now.'

'That's the point.' The angel looked at Grim without expression. 'How many more people will die, I wonder, before you learn patience?'

Grim said nothing. It had already begun; the arbiter was searching his soul already and seemed quite pleased with what it had found. 'You don't know what you're talking about.'

The arbiter studied Grim. Grim knew what it was doing, and he knew there was no way, at least known to the Order, to fight against it. It was reading him. Looking for scars to rip open and feed off.

'I'm the only one who knows what they're talking about,' it said. 'You're ex-military. A marksman. Your wife Eleanor died. So you left the army to look after your daughter, only to find your job prospects few and far between.' It looked around the room, its eye twitching as it did, as if it were sensing something. 'So you joined one of Salem's local mobs. You quickly became a valued weapon for them. Destroyed the enemies they threw you at as you slipped deeper and deeper into sin, earning your apt nickname.'

'As if you're any better,' Grim snarled. 'You angels, killing the innocent, all the while claiming that we are just unavoidable collateral. That it's for the *greater good*. That it's for us. At least the people I killed weren't innocents.'

The angel began casually pacing back and forth in front of him in the way that one would if they were simply bored waiting for something.

'I see no difference in your failed justifications,' it said as it passed in front of him again, 'You told yourself that you were killing horrible people. That you were doing it for her.'

Grim cursed and thrashed about as much as he could with his arms and legs bound so tightly. The arbiter did not even break its stride.

'Your emotions and your attachments already caused your downfall once. Are you so eager for it to do so again?' the angel probed.

Grim swore. 'I didn't have a choice,' he said. 'I had to make a decision.'

'You made the wrong one,' stated the angel.

'You think I don't know that?' he yelled. 'My target was going to release sensitive information about the mob I was working for. Including information about me and my daughter.'

'Except the man you shot and killed wasn't your target, was he?' The angel was baiting him. He enjoyed seeing Grim distraught by his failure, although you couldn't tell by looking at his expressionless face. 'Who was the man you killed, Grim?'

'Don't ask me questions you already know the answer to,' Grim chided.

'Information is not my goal here,' the arbiter countered.

'So you captured me just to torture me?'

'No,' it said. 'I'm just passing the time.'

'I'm not going to be your entertainment,' Grim maintained, looking away from the arbiter.

'I have no doubt you know what I am and what it is we do: extracting the sins of mortals. Judgement is our job, but the feeling we get from the emotions and memories attached to those sins is our pleasure.' The angel put his arm behind his back and produced a stave. It looked like oak, but lines of gold ran through it. Other than that, it was an unremarkable polearm. 'You think that every soul I deal with is willing to illuminate their darkness to me? I have ways to get to it myself, but I guarantee that you'd wish you had just told me and made it easier for the both of us. And sweeter for me.'

Grim had heard stories of the staffs that the arbiters used. Their complexities were far beyond anything a human could fathom, but the end result was that it was a torture device that worked on the human soul, not just the body. The effects it apparently had on the soul of a dead human were horrific, so Grim dared not think what it'd do to him while alive.

'The people I worked for were in the middle of finalising a truce with another crime family,' Grim relented. 'The man I shot was the son of that family's boss.'

'You see?' Although no expression showed upon its face, it sounded smug. 'You killed the wrong man because you were impatient.'

'I killed the wrong man because I thought it would save my daughter.'

'And how did that work out?'

Grim glared at the angel. 'For the truce to go ahead despite the mistake, my employers pinned the blame solely on me, saying I was acting independently. I agreed to go along with it because I knew that if I didn't, they'd kill my daughter.'

'Except they lied to you, didn't they?' His tone was mocking.

'They didn't tell me they had already handed over my daughter to the rival family, and when I found out I carved my way into where they were keeping her,' affirmed Grim, his face tightening. 'But—'

'But they stopped you in the end,' the angel interrupted. 'Kneeled you down in front of your daughter and made you watch as they dragged a blade across her pretty little face for each of the men of theirs you killed. The last thing you saw were her tears mixing with the blood of her rosy cheeks as she screamed at you to help her. But you didn't help her did you, Markus?'

Grim fought back the tears that threatened to overtake him. He wasn't going to give the arbiter the satisfaction. He had long ago convinced himself of the truth. There was nothing he could have done. He never wanted the life he had found himself in. The only thing that still haunted him was that he didn't know if she was dead or alive.

'Why are you doing this?' Grim asked through a clenched jaw.

'This? Because I enjoy it,' the arbiter acknowledged.

'That's not what I meant and you know it, you piece of shit!'

'You are bait,' it admitted.

'Why?'

'Why would I tell you that?' it asked. 'You will die here. Make no mistake about that. But I am not foolish enough to tell you anything.'

'My team will come for me,' corrected Grim.

'I'm counting on it.'

'I think you're underestimating them,' Grim avowed.

'And I think you put too much confidence in a team that can't work together to literally save their lives, led by a woman who has no confidence in herself or her team,' the arbiter derided. 'Who in turn is led by a man who wouldn't be able to spot a traitor if they declared it to all the world in front of him.'

'The March is spying on us?' Grim was incredulous, though it would explain how accurate the arbiter's description of his team was. The team had lost a leader and a lance in as many months. Asha was still trying to cope without Delarin, who had been her mentor since she arrived in Salem as a lance herself. Yet she was now in charge of a team in a very dangerous time for the Order. Things were relatively quiet in Salem, yet the Order was losing wardens faster than it ever had before. Morale was low, but the Order kept up the pressure nonetheless, and as a result more and more assignments had been labelled failures. The possibility of a spy would also help to explain a lot of that too. Their intel was almost always off just enough to cause them problems.

'Is The Divine March using spies?'

The arbiter stood up straight and lifted his chin ever so slightly. 'Treachery is the dagger of demons and renegades. The March has no need to stoop so low.'

With that, the arbiter left the room, and Grim could hear the scratching of clawed footsteps move around on the other side of the door and above him. He wanted to rip the arbiter apart, but he couldn't escape without help, and even if he could, an arbiter was well out of his league.

Help would come soon.

***

Asha stood in front of the high warden. Mason was a stout man with short silver hair and a miserable attitude. Asha respected his position, if not the man himself. Still, she would much prefer dealing with High Paladin Tarek. Though she understood that Tarek was far too busy for warden briefings, so the duty of handling the warden teams was delegated to the high warden, who was considered the high paladin's second. In Salem, that position was unfortunately occupied by Mason. If Mason were honest, he'd admit

that the position was far easier now since the teams had been re-
duced, but Mason was not honest and liked to pretend he was
more important than he was. Asha got the feeling he didn't like
her. In fact she knew he didn't, and he was still not happy about
her promotion, which made her a little more okay with it.

'Sit,' he ordered. His office was far less impressive than Tarek's,
but the red carpet and jarrah bookcases that lined one of the side
walls gave it the same warm feel, despite the man who occupied it.
Asha sat down on a chair that matched the desk and the bookcases.

'I take it you and your team brought in more than just a troublesome civilian.'

Asha was not sure if that was a question or not, and if it was,
she wasn't sure his condescending tone made it worth a response,
'We did.'

'Well then?' he prompted.

'We found evidence of a new drug on the street,' she said in
the calmest voice she could muster. What she wanted to do was
freeze that smug face and break it against his desk.

'Why should we care about some drug? Civilians are always doing such things.' His smugness was the thing that made Asha hate
him the most. Not just that it was irritating, but his idea that he
floated above everything often stopped him from thinking about
things. He had been a warden for just over seventy years, yet never
seemed to have learnt to think about the *why* of a problem. As with
this, he should have been considering why she thought it worth
mentioning, rather than trying to dismiss it. He was either lazy or
didn't hold much confidence in her. She couldn't decide which was
more offensive.

'You should care because it's sourced demonically. Or maybe
even angelically.'

'What kind of drug?'

'Apparently, it's a human-safe version of angel blood,' she divulged. 'It's human blood, but with diluted properties of angel

blood. Its street name is aether. People inject or ingest it, and it causes increased alertness, arousal, strength and suggestibility. Higher doses can cause amnesia, but otherwise it has very few negative effects, and no long-term ones at all, besides addiction of course. I fear because of this, it'll spread quickly, and who knows what the ones supplying it are planning to do.'

'So your concern is a drug that makes people feel good and a little forgetful,' Mason drawled, once again missing the bigger picture. He was about to make further sarcastic comment, but Asha spoke before he could.

'My concern is that higher suggestibility makes long-term users more susceptible to demonic activity, like possessions and the occult. It makes it even easier for them to be manipulated,' she said, once more pushing down the urge to break his teeth. 'Or the supplier could suddenly swap the diluted angel blood for the real thing, killing hundreds, if not thousands of people. Which is neither a quick nor painless death.'

He didn't say anything for a few moments, seemingly putting some actual thought into his words. 'You have a point, but our job is to kill aethereals. Why should we worry about the poor choices of civilians?'

'Our job is to keep other humans safe from aethereals and their machinations,' contended Asha, gritting her teeth. 'Not just their blades.'

'Speaking of civilians,' he segued, knowing he was wrong, so shifting the conversation. 'What is this about a demon hunter?'

Asha let out a deep breath, trying her best not to sound as exasperated as she felt. If he didn't outrank her, she may well have given into her fantasies of smashing him by now. 'We found a rune that had been perfectly cut in half,' she confided. 'My contact is adamant that the Sword of Michael would have been the only thing able to make such a clean cut on a rune. Or a cut at all for that matter.' Asha could see Mason's eyes narrow and brow crease as she mentioned her contact. 'But I'm not sure his reasons for thinking that are reliable.'

High Warden Mason never liked the fact that Delarin was allowed to have his own sources outside of the Order and clearly didn't like the idea that they were now hers. He argued that lochs should not be allowed to have contacts that were not officially handled. Tarek had overruled him, saying that that as long as Delarin kept them in line and did not divulge unnecessary information, he could keep using them.

Adley Black, the self-proclaimed demonology expert, was easy enough to deal with. His curiosity for anything they brought his way, and fear of being etched, was more than enough to keep him in line.

Narki was another story, though strictly speaking he was Grim's contact. Narki was overly confident in himself, or underestimating of the Order, but he always knew more about the darker crevices of Salem than the Order, which kept him useful enough to keep in their pocket.

'And what makes you suddenly doubt your contact?' His eyes narrowed, and he failed to contain a smirk, which sent a flare of anger through her.

'I don't doubt him,' Asha said defensively, although that wasn't completely accurate. 'What he says makes sense, but I'm not sure I believe some urban legend is running around with the Sword of Michael.'

'Ah, the supposed Ghost of Salem. I've heard the stories. What does your expert think exactly?'

'Somehow,' she said, 'this civilian has taken the sword and is now using it as he sees fit.'

'So, we've already got a cambion on the loose in the city,' Mason mused as he sat forward, his fingers intertwined and resting against his mouth for a moment as if thinking. 'And now we have a new drug on the street, a civilian running rampant with the most powerful weapon known to us, and...' He picked up a computer tablet and furrowed his brow at it. Mason used the device to monitor the comings and goings of the front gate. 'Grim still has not returned. Have you heard from him at all?'

Grim? Asha had completely forgotten about Grim. Come to think of it, he had been gone for far too long. 'I sent him to drop off that reporter we etched early this morning.'

'You sent him alone, in this climate?' he exclaimed. 'Well, I guess I don't need to tell you your next assignment. Our numbers are low as it is. Find him.'

Numbers are low? She wanted nothing more than to drop the *numbers* by another one, but she decided to focus on getting Grim and then scream at him for going off-grid on her. After the loss of the lance and Delarin, she couldn't take losing Grim too. Even if he was an arse.

'Oh,' Mason said before she could turn around to leave. He placed a black sheathed blade on the table. 'I had a team dust the site where Delarin and Anthony died and—'

'Killed,' she corrected with a voice of fire and ice.

Even Mason's voice seemed to subtly soften from his usual arrogant tone. 'Tarek has asked me to give this to your team. Do with it what you will.'

Chapter Eight
Husks

I n its prime, the Salem chapter would have assigned up to four teams to each of the sanctuary's four briefing rooms. Now though, Asha's team got one all to themselves while the other three teams had to share with one another. Tarek always gave the paladins their assignments in the main briefing room closest to his office.

Asha stood in front of the square metal table that was centred in the room. In front of her, and laid out across her open palms, was the sheathed blade that High Warden Mason had given her. She looked at it with unfocused eyes, looking *through* it more than *at* it. It was Delarin's. He would always argue the strategy of a gun over a blade in battle. He and Asha had many debates on the topic over the years she had spent as a warden under his command, which was in fact *all* the years she had been a warden. Contrary to this, Delarin held a fascination for ornate and ceremonial swords and had always kept this one on him when on an assignment. His idea of practicality and love for beautiful blades coalesced into a blade of simplistic beauty, which she held in her hands now.

She reverently removed it from its hard black nylon sheath. The sword in its entirety was made up of a single midnight-coloured piece of steel. It was pitch black except for the dark silver where the cutting edge began, and the grey cord that wrapped around its ergonomic handle. Three small blunt but curved protrusions separated the edge of the blade and the grip of the sword. Cut into the sword's spine, close to the handle, were six large fang-like serrations that curved up and back towards the grip. The blade itself was about eighteen inches from grip to its slightly curved tip.

Asha replaced the blade into its sheath and, as it clicked into place, the door to the briefing room opened and Aiden walked in. Upon seeing his usual nervous face, a feeling of regret crept into her chest. Delarin had been a practical man through and through, which was what made him not only an efficient and effective leader, but a well-respected one. He could do what Asha believed she could never, which was find a balance between emotion and duty. He always seemed to know when it was necessary to sacrifice personal feelings and attachments and do what was best for his team and the Order, and when it wasn't. She didn't always agree but always supported his decisions. All except one.

It was with these thoughts of Delarin that Asha was able quell the feelings of regret and nervousness she had about what she was to do next. She knew it was the right thing to do for her team. Perhaps the sword would be a good luck charm in his hands.

'You wanted to see me?' Aiden said as he approached the table. 'Where are the others?'

'The others will be here soon.' Asha gestured to Delarin's sword, which she had placed on the metal table. 'I wanted to give you this before the assignment briefing.' Asha watched Aiden pick up the weapon and examine it. He did so with about as much care as anyone else would have thought appropriate, but to Asha it was like watching a child paw at the Holy Grail with corn chip dust all over their fingers. She wanted to lecture him on just how important the sword was, but she knew that would have been inane and pointless. It was, after everything, just a sword. Trying to instil her attachments into him wouldn't help him fight with it.

'Take good care of it because I won't be ordering you another,' she warned. 'And be ready to use it.'

Soon the others arrived as she had instructed, and she gave them a quick briefing on their next assignment. Grim had not returned from dumping the reporter after they had etched him, which although it wasn't entirely unlike him to wander off, he usually stayed in contact when he did whatever it was he did when he disappeared into the city streets. So now they had to go investigate. A missing member of the team was the last thing she needed, as was the flood of the worst-case scenarios that broke into her thoughts. She locked the flood away behind a mental barrier and led her team out.

It was a Sunday morning as they ventured into the hazy streets of Salem. The shops were closed, and the carpark was mostly empty, so Asha was not worried about exposure. Besides, a group of people walking around in strange clothes on the morning after a Saturday night was not too far from the ordinary in Salem.

'Guys?' Aiden called out the team. Asha looked over to Aiden who was standing beside a large green bin behind a bar. Beside him was a man struggling to get to his feet. It was the reporter from last night.

Tiago walked over with a grin on his face. He helped the confused man to his feet.

'Wha urr ye fowk?' the man mumbled. His accent seemed thicker and harder to understand than it was last night. 'Whaur am ah?'

'Bit of a rough night, eh?' Tiago reached into his pocket and pulled out a pair of pills and handed them to the man. 'You'll need these for your headache.'

'Wha headache?' the man said. A few moments later the man's face scrunched up in pain. 'Och…'

'So, you just carry around painkillers?' Asha asked mockingly.

'When I heard I'd be on your team, I figured I'd need them,' Tiago retorted with a strained straight face. 'So I bought a carton.'

Asha ignored him and pointed at the reporter. 'Aiden, see him off.'

Aiden walked the man off the street and watched as he stumbled down the footpath. When Aiden returned to the group, Tiago was crouching down beside a bin bag. 'Looks like blood,' he surmised.

Asha took place behind Tiago and looked over his shoulder. There was a small splatter of blood on a bin bag, barely noticeable against the black of the bag.

'Could be Grim's,' observed Amber.

'Could be anyone's,' Asha retorted.

'Yes, but if it is Grim's, I can use it to locate him.'

'How?'

'I have a locater crystal.' She put a hand into a small satchel bag she had hanging over her shoulders and pulled out a small crystal about the size of her thumb. 'The blood looks dry, and there isn't much of it, so I'm not sure how accurate this will be.'

'It's worth a shot,' said Tiago holding out his hand.

Amber gently pushed passed him, ignoring his open palm, and scraped the tip of the crystal against the bag. The bag tore but Amber seemed satisfied.

'It's about as good as we'll get. How many more of these do you have?' asked Tiago.

'Just the one left,' Amber said. Asha looked at the crystal dubiously. She'd never seen or even heard of a locater crystal before, but then Salem was never well outfitted when compared to some other chapters.

Amber inspected the crystal. There was a tiny speck of red near the tip of the crystal, which expanded and spread until the crystal went from white to a deep red. Amber held the crystal up and then let it go. The device floated there for a second before shooting up into the air, shattering with a loud crack, and projecting a beam of light that arched across the rooftops.

'Tiago, get up on the roof and see if—' Asha gave the order but Tiago was just cresting the wall and standing on the roof watching the crystal's light fall down above an area a few kilometres to the east.

'Looks like it went towards the Asseti Industrial Strip,' Tiago shouted from the rooftop. 'It dissipated before it touched down on his position.'

'Last time I was there they had an area fenced off in preparation for demolition,' said Asha. 'It's pretty much abandoned. If that thing is accurate, then I'd say he is in there somewhere.'

Tiago descended the building, and they made their way through the city streets populated only by the occasional partygoer still staggering home. The partly cloudy sky let in plenty of sun, but the chill of winter filtered most of its warmth, and a slight breeze carried the cold between the buildings. Eventually, they crossed over a road and were now at a short chain-link fence, easy enough to vault over and into a small stretch of brush.

'Tiago, run ahead and make sure the place is still abandoned,' Asha instructed. 'We don't want to arrive at the main fence-line and be spotted if they've resumed the demolition.' Tiago nodded and ran off into the scrub towards the buildings ahead.

Asha drew her sword from a sheath hidden on her back under her warden coat. It looked fierce but elegant. The grip was wrapped in white leather leading up to a diamond-shaped chappe, which was decorated with a circular ice-blue pattern. The cross guard featured a similar pattern that travelled its length and followed it as it gently curved up into a forty-five degree angle. The blade was tinged blue and had half-a-dozen glyphs etched into the length of the fuller on either side. Angelic on one side, demonic on the other.

'Do most wardens use swords instead of guns?' Aiden asked, gesturing at Asha's sword.

'No,' she said flatly. She scolded herself for being blunt, but loch or not, lances still annoyed her. Still, it wasn't his fault he wasn't trained properly. 'Plenty of wardens prefer guns,' she said, trying to soften her tone. 'But swords are easier to enhance with glyphs, so are more effective.'

'Each bullet would need to be enhanced, right?' he asked. At least he seemed to catch on faster than most.

'Exactly,' she affirmed. 'We get supplied special magazines with bullets stamped with glyphs, but they're usually in short supply, and Salem often gets forgotten when it comes to the good ordnance.' It was a fact that always bothered Asha, not because she had to do without, since she preferred swords anyway, but because she had had to put up with Delarin complaining about it. He had always managed fine without the enhancements when he needed to though.

A minute later, Tiago returned. 'The condemned area looks like it's on the main fence-line,' he informed. 'And there's no one about so we won't need to be sneaky.'

'You sure this is where the light touched down?' asked Asha.

'Well, it didn't touch down.' Tiago pointed over towards a pair of multi-storied office buildings. Neither had a single window that had not been smashed. 'But it dispersed just above those buildings.'

The team walked over to the fence-line. Asha ran the tip of her sword down the fence along a pole. The aluminium links frosted over and a quick kick was all that was needed to break them loose, allowing them to push the fence and gain entry.

'All right. Aiden you're with Tiago in that building,' Asha said, pointing to the building to their left. 'Amber and I will go to the other building.'

Tiago nodded, looked to Aiden, and jogged towards the smaller of the two buildings. As Aiden followed, Asha could see his knuckles go white over the grip of Delarin's sword.

Asha walked ahead of Amber down the darkened hallway. The wall's paint was chipped, bubbled and covered in graffiti, most of which displayed crude messages. The hallway opened to a large room that had smaller glass-walled rooms on either side of it with the entrance to another hallway on the opposite end. Only a few beams of light pierced the darkness through the boarded-up windows. Most of the room was filled with cubicles made of plasterboard, many of which had large holes smashed into them.

Suddenly there was a noise to Asha's left. A scratching. Like a rodent scurrying around in a roof, only bigger. She looked towards the noise but saw nothing. She turned to look at Amber, who nodded slightly—she heard it too. Amber branched off to the right, down the centre of the room, as Asha walked towards the scratching noise. The small glass rooms were private offices, meeting rooms and a photocopying room. Some rooms still had the furniture while others were nothing but dirty, torn carpet.

Asha walked into one of the meeting rooms where she noticed the window wasn't boarded-up. She peered out and could see the building the others were searching. In fact, she could see a figure pass one of the windows on the second storey, followed soon by another. *They had better be searching thoroughly and carefully*, she thought. Whatever managed to take Grim by surprise was not something Asha wanted to take lightly. For something to not only sneak up on him but also to take him with what seemed to be little effort was almost unthinkable.

Asha turned back to the meeting room entrance but stopped mid-step. Blocking the doorway and the only way out was a figure dressed in nothing but dirty white rags. It stood slightly hunched, its wiry arms hanging limp with small blades in each hand. The pearly white hair that covered the creature's face flicked away as its head twitched to the side. Its eyes were jet black, and its skin looked porcelain white, almost as if its expressionless face would break if it moved.

The creature's arms suddenly burst to life, and it charged at Asha. She parried a blow to the left, followed by another one quickly to the right. She jumped back to dodge a second left side swipe. The creature darted forward and swung with the right again; she blocked again and countered with a kick to the side of the creature's leg. It fell to one knee, but before Asha could follow it up with another attack, the creature rolled to its feet and swung its blades wildly.

She fell backwards, dodging the blades, but now she was on her back. The creature was relentless and without even hesitating it was at her again, standing over her as it slashed its blades like a crazed animal, all in an eerie, expressionless silence. Asha locked her blade with one of the daggers, and before the creature could bring the weapon away, Asha sent a pulse of rune energy up into her blade. The air around the creature's dagger crackled and froze the blades together. Asha yanked the sword to the right, and her attacker stumbled to the side, one of its daggers still attached to her sword. Asha leaped to her feet and pulled the sword again, causing the creature to lose its footing and fall forward. The ice that fused the swords together snapped, and the dagger fell to the ground. The creature reached for the weapon as it tried to get back to its feet, but Asha lunged forward and plunged her sword into the thing's back as it crawled for its weapon. Its empty black eyes fluttered and closed.

'Asha!' Amber was yelling from the main room. Asha ran from the room to see another dozen of the same vacant creatures she had just killed. 'Husks.'

'Yeah,' she agreed, with barely enough breath left to sound facetious. 'I noticed.'

'Tiago, be on alert for husks,' Asha said over the comm unit. Husks were angels, but of course not the usual type of angel. They were feral angels that had spent too long on Earth and had been driven mad by human emotion; they had thus fallen from grace and lost their wings. An angel without wings could not recharge their grace—their source of strength. Grace was to an angel what a soul was to a human, and without it, the weaker angels devolved into feral beasts. The combination of madness and soullessness made them excellent cannon fodder for the angels who used them like wild dogs. Asha readied her sword and sprinted at the nearest husk.

***

Aiden and Tiago had entered the building, which ended up being a small motor pool. The vehicles that had been abandoned here were vandalised, although they were more rust than metal anyway. Having found no sign of Grim, they made their way up to the second floor. This floor was much more illuminated because the main corridor was on the far side of the building, allowing the sun to flood in through the broken windows. 'Do you hear that?'

Aiden listened carefully. He could hear it. It was a sharp hissing noise that stopped and started with varying lengths of time. 'What is it?'

Tiago said nothing but shrugged and held a finger to his lips as he moved forward. Aiden followed a few steps behind. They got to the end of the corridor where it cornered around to the building's east side. Tiago pressed his back against the edge of the wall as he peered around.

'Civilian kids,' Tiago whispered. A wave of relief swept over Aiden.

'What do we do?' he asked.

'I know they have taught you that we need to keep out of the public eye at all costs, and we need to make sure our work is never witnessed and blah, blah, blah,' Tiago said. 'But try not to over-think these things.' With that he raised his pistol.

Aiden's eyes almost fell out of his head, and Tiago grinned. 'You're not going to hurt them are you?'

'Of course not. You know the Order's law regarding the harming of civilians.' Tiago still wore a mischievous grin. The Order's law regarding harming normal humans was simple: don't. Of course, there were some foreseeable exceptions, although even criminals and civilians trying to harm others were not allowed to be killed. This meant dealing with civilians was more of an art than a science. 'But they don't know that.'

Tiago turned the corner, and Aiden followed. The two boys were spray painting the wall and didn't see Tiago or himself until they were a few metres away. They turned and jumped back in fright.

'Are you cops?' one of them stuttered.

Tiago pulled back the slide on his gun. 'Not exactly.' The kids froze in place, unsure what to do. 'I wanna help paint the walls,' Tiago said with a wild grin. The kids ran towards the stairs and headed down, swearing to each other, with Tiago's laughter following them down.

'Are you not worried they might tell the police?' Aiden asked.

'And say what?' Tiago asked. 'That while they were trespassing and defacing private property…'

'Well, no, but—'

'You know how I said not to over-think it?'

'Yeah?'

'You're over-thinking it.' Tiago lowered his gun. 'Even if they did, the kathari would deal with it.'

'So that whole thing about being discreet?' Aiden asked. Tiago had begun walking down the corridor and turned down into the stairwell that the two boys had just fled down, but rather than go down they went up to the third floor.

'Being all sneaky is still important since all kinds of things can go wrong if we are not always doing our best to stay in the shadows. It's what we do, after all,' he said. 'The kathari in this respect are only for small things like not ending up in jail for trespassing. Like we're doing now.'

'And scaring the crap out of teenagers,' Aiden added.

They climbed the stairs and were now passing through another corridor like the previous one, only this one was on the south side of the building, and he could see the building that the other two were searching. Tiago was in front while Aiden followed a few steps behind. They looked in the rooms that they passed but there was no sign of Grim or much of anything for that matter, except the thick layers of dust along many of the window sills.

'It doesn't seem like anything has passed through this level recently,' Aiden observed as he dragged his finger across a window sill. As he did, the comm unit Asha had given him came to life. 'Tiago, be on alert for husks.'

'Nothing human anyway…' Tiago murmured to Aiden as he stuck his head in a doorway and looked around. He confirmed acknowledgement of Asha's message and then they continued their searching.

'What's a husk?' Aiden asked.

'Third-sphere fallen angels,' Tiago answered as they walked.

'Fallen angels have ranks too?' he asked.

'No, no,' Tiago said. 'What I mean is, when a third-sphere angel falls, they turn into a husk.'

'And stronger angels?' Aiden asked. 'What do they turn into?'

'Not husks, I can tell you that,' Tiago said, peering into another room as they passed. 'Much worse. Less creepy though if you're into silver linings.'

After a few minutes more of searching, Aiden spun around suddenly to the sound of a dense CRACK. It was the sound of snapping wood and falling debris. Both of them rushed over to the window to see dust and dirt flood out of the windows of the building opposite.

'Asha!' Tiago yelled over the comm. 'Are you two okay?'

There was no reply for a few long seconds. 'Amber, the floor gave way beneath me,' came Asha's voice. 'Don't take him on alone. I'm going to make my way back up.'

'Asha, what's going on?' Tiago asked again.

'Tiago, get over here,' Asha yelled, out of breath. 'We've got—' the transmission cut out.

'Got what?' Tiago asked frantically, but before he could reattempt contact, five creatures, all with small blades in each hand and pitch black eyes peering out from a curtain of pure white hair, came sprinting down the corridor.

Before Aiden could even register what was going on, Tiago was firing down the hallway into the mass of flesh that ran at them. The creatures each took a few shots before they finally crashed into the ground, dead.

'Husks,' Tiago shouted. He continued to fire as more came charging around the corner. The corridor was wide enough for three people to stand abreast but it wasn't wide enough to swing a sword effectively, so while Tiago was able to shoot at them like fish in a barrel, Aiden wouldn't be much use in the fight. Regardless, Aiden readied his sword with a slight tremble to his hand.

'We need to get back down to the ground floor where we can fight these things properly.' Tiago ran back down the corridor towards to the stairwell, and Aiden moved to follow, but in his panic, he tripped over his own feet.

His fall was unbroken, and his face hit the ground hard. For a moment he could see nothing but blackness and hear nothing but the sound of his blood roaring through his head. Tiago was pursued by the bulk of the husk group and had already turned the corner and was out of sight, apparently not having witnessed Aiden's incompetence. He would have been relieved if it were not for the pair of creepy angel things bearing down on him. He had barely enough time to roll onto his back and bring his sword up before the husks attacked him with tenacious savagery. Each strike against Aiden's sword sent a sharp pain up his right arm as he tried to keep his guard. They didn't stop. They didn't slow. They just kept smashing into his blade as if it were a stubborn nail in a piece of wood. His first real assignment and his first real chance to prove himself and he was about to be killed. Not even by a powerful demon, but by some angelic reject.

But what did it matter anyway? He never asked to be brought back. He never asked to be thrust into fighting against two sides of some secret war in a world he had already departed from. Aiden had decided to go along with it because it was better than what seemed to be a void of nothingness. He figured he should at least see where the path went, and this is where it appeared to end. Humans could only be brought back once. Wardens were resilient but once they were dead, that was it. Well, at least he had tried.

What was he thinking! He hadn't just wasted the last week just so he could die on his back during his first real encounter. He became suddenly angry at himself for being willing to give up so easily. How pathetic. He would not give up yet. Aiden kicked out and connected with the husk on the right, giving him a slight enough reprieve to deflect the other husk's next attack.

Once the next attack made contact with his blade, Aiden turned the blade to the right, causing the husk's dagger to slide harmlessly off his own blade. Harmlessly that was until it landed in his right hamstring. The pain was incredible, but he tried his best to block it out as he noticed the husk was stuck, but the other one had recovered and was about to start its attacks again.

With the husk bent over Aiden trying to retrieve its blade, he took the opportunity he had created to counterattack. He switched his weapon from his right hand to his left and stabbed it directly into the creature's ribs. He could feel the flesh and muscles rip and tear as the blade entered the fallen angel's ribcage. Still, no expression of pain or fury passed over the husk as it went limp. Now Aiden had another problem. His blade was halfway into a fallen angel who was now dead on top of him, he had a dagger in his leg and another husk about to finish him off. He wanted to feel sorry for himself. Assure himself that at least this time he had tried, and it was a good effort. But all he could think of was the pain. The pain in his leg and the pain to come.

Just as he was expecting to be cut to ribbons, three shots rang out that left a slight ringing in his ears. The other husk staggered and then dropped dead to the ground, daggers still in hand.

'Well, got your first kill, eh?' Tiago holstered his pistol and was sauntering down the corridor towards him. He saw Aiden's leg and made a feigned look of disgust. 'Your first wound too! Busy day for you then.'

Aiden's ears had stopped ringing and could now hear the intense pumping of his blood rushing through him. His whole body shook, and Tiago was making jokes. Aiden opened his mouth to tell him to shut it, but no sound came out.

Tiago pushed the husk off Aiden and pulled the dagger from his thigh with as much tenderness as a shovel to the face. 'Doesn't look too bad,' Tiago said as blood escaped the wound at an alarming rate. 'Relax. If you were a civilian, I'd be worried, but the blade hit nothing important, so the bleeding will stop eventually.' Tiago bent over and ripped off a piece of cloth from the nearest husk's body. He fastened it around Aiden's wound and helped him to his feet. 'Better than nothing, and besides, the wound will close soon enough.' The pain that lanced through him when he put his weight on his right side almost made Aiden fall back down. Instead he readjusted his weight, and they limped him down the corridor.

'Are the others okay?' Aiden winced with every step.

'Haven't heard from them since the attack,' Tiago answered. 'They are both more than capable. They'll be fine, but we need to get you out. Fighting in such enclosed spaces, especially wounded, is not exactly ideal.'

'Don't we have something that can…I dunno. Heal?' Aiden and Tiago slowly made their way down the stairwell. 'Like, shouldn't Asha have a rune or something? I'm not so terrible that I'm the only person to get stabbed during a job, surely.'

Tiago laughed. 'What did you learn at Prime?'

'We were mostly taught how not to get killed.'

'Did you miss a few classes?' Tiago laughed again and patted Aiden's injured leg. 'I'm thinking you mean like a healing rune.'

'Yeah,' Aiden said, wincing through his pain.

'They don't hand runes out willy-nilly, Rook,' he said. 'Runes are rare as it is. Healing runes are especially highly requested by sanctuaries. Wardens only get one rune each. The only exception there are the paladins.'

'Where do runes come from?' Aiden asked as they reached the ground floor.

'That's a good question,' Tiago said. 'Angels craft them by infusing a symbol into something called a vellum. Different symbols grant different abilities to the wearer.' Tiago stopped walking and let Aiden walk on his own. It still hurt for him to limp, but he could do it on his own now that the bleeding had stopped. 'Where the vellum comes from, I have no idea. Could be God's own balls for all I know.' Tiago laughed.

'What does yours do?'

Tiago took out his handgun and released the magazine. He tipped it so Aiden could see it from the top down. Empty, except for a small sphere embedded where the bullets would have been placed. He then put the magazine back in and fired. The ringing in Aiden's ears returned briefly when the gun fired as though it were loaded. 'Infinite aetheric ammo for my handgun. Not powerful enough for anything too much larger.' Tiago smiled.

'Aetheric ammo? Like angelic bullets?' Aiden probed. He wondered if it worked as well as glyphs.

'Well, I mean angels don't really use guns exactly, but if they did, this is how they'd work,' Tiago said with a grin. 'The bullets are manifested by the power of my rune, and so are aethereal in nature, but as they're technical objects and not a living force, we call them aetheric ammo.'

'Ah, right. Ghost bullets,' Aiden said with sarcasm.

'Exactly.' Tiago laughed. "Lots of runes have abilities that summon aetheric objects. Some demons can do it too.'

Their conversation was brought to a sudden halt as Asha burst into the building followed by a large clutch of husks.

***

Grim's arms ached from being bound for so long, even though he had given up on trying free himself hours ago. He was alone now, and had been for most of the day, though every so often a husk would come in and stand by the door, stare at him with empty black eyes and then leave. It was only creepy the first five times.

Hope had faded. That is until Grim had heard a commotion within the building. It had sounded and felt like the building was coming down on itself, but Grim wasn't that lucky. Though it did mean that his team had found him, or demons were raiding the place.

The door opened, and the arbiter walked in, closing it behind him. Despite what must have been a large part of the building coming down, the angel did not seem perturbed.

'Your friends have come,' it said. 'I no longer have any use for you.' Without missing a step, the angel took out a dagger. Part of Grim was relieved. Part of him was angry. Mostly he was just too tired to care. He knew he couldn't get out—he had tried for hours.

There was another crashing noise, but this time it was the door being broken open. Several husks and a woman were tangled up in one another. The woman got to her feet, noticing Grim with a look of brief surprise.

'Grim!' Amber exclaimed before turning back to the husks. Two of them jumped towards her, and she swung her axe, cutting one down easily. The second grabbed hold of her, but she spun and threw it to the ground, finishing it before it could rise again. She pulled the axe free but didn't have enough time to wind up for another swing at the third one as it attacked. Instead, she flicked out the pommel of the axe against the husk's face, which staggered it back to buy herself enough time to attack properly. She stepped forward and swung. The creature went down, the axe near cleaving the creature's entire head off of its shoulders.

The arbiter turned to face Amber, his daggers disappearing in a flash of light. He pulled out what looked like just the handle and guard of a sword. Light suddenly flowed from it, solidifying into a massive greatsword. Despite its sinister intentions, the blade was beautiful. Its white steel glowed golden ever so slightly, and its cross guard was in the shape of white feathered wings. Amber stood defiant and unwavering, however, her relatively small, double-sided battleaxe at the ready.

The arbiter was the first to attack. He lunged forward with more agility than Grim would have thought possible for someone holding such a large weapon. Amber defended herself and countered with minimal effort. She moved with such grace that as she attacked, blocked and countered, it was almost possible to imagine that they were dancing. Perhaps it was his exhaustion, or perhaps he was giddy with hope, but Grim suddenly noticed just how beautiful Amber was as she fought to save his life.

The angel swung his sword down on a diagonal angle aimed at Amber's neck. She lifted her weapon in response and managed to hook the blade behind the beard of the axe. She twisted and pulled quickly with enough speed that the angel didn't have time enough to brace. The greatsword slipped from his hands, but Amber was not expecting the angel to counter so quickly without a weapon and learned a hard lesson in the form of the angel's fist to the side of the face, which sent her reeling.

From what Grim could see, she wasn't moving, and her breathing seemed laboured. The arbiter stood there for a full five seconds before he walked towards her, but he stopped again, picked up his greatsword and turned back around to face Grim.

'I believe you spoke of me underestimating your team,' the angel stated. 'After you, she dies. Then the next one and the next one. Until I have my prize.' The angel pulled his sword back ready to thrust it through Grim's chest. He lay on the ground doing the only thing he could do: wait. He'd soon find out if his daughter had died all those years ago.

The angel thrust the sword, but Grim heard the thunderclap of metal on metal as Amber blocked the attack, but only just. The arbiter's sword still found a mark; it just wasn't Grim. Grim could see the tip of the sword protruding from the right side of Amber's back.

Amber had not gone down yet though. The angel was defence-less for the moment, and Amber swung her axe one last time before falling to her side with the sword still lodged in her chest. The swing of her axe caught the arbiter in the side with enough force to break the skin and send him staggering back. Still, he did not fall, but as he regained himself, golden blood seeped through the angel's clothing and ran down to his legs. It had been a deep cut, but Amber's already regrettable sacrifice was wasted. The arbiter would kill Grim anyway, and now his incompetence had cost the life of yet another person he cared about.

As if waiting for the most dramatic time to do so, Asha, Tiago and the lance came through the door, husk blood splattered all over their clothes. The arbiter spun around to face them.

Grim didn't see what happened next as white feathers, which seemed to come from nowhere, blocked out his vision. The feathers cut through the air in a frenzied swarm around the angel, quickly moving closer and closer as they continued to orbit until the angel was no longer in view, just a spinning cocoon of feathers that exploded outwards with such a gale that it forced Grim's eyes shut. When he opened them, the angel, and the feathers, were gone.

'Bastard got away!' he heard Asha curse.

'Well, that was flashy.' That had to be Tiago. Though his tone changed once he spotted Amber.

Chapter Nine
Bonds of blood

A full thirty hours had passed since Lynus' latest brush with The Divine March. He had managed to get a few hours' sleep and a meal, and he could feel that his runes were all fully charged. He wasn't about to go headfirst into a mephisto's nest with anything less than full strength. This included acquiring a small combat knife that he hid clipped to his belt behind him.

Lynus had snatched up one of the drug runner's bags before he left the alleyway the previous day. It was empty now, but he had figured it would come in handy. With it slung over one shoulder, he walked down through the carpark towards the Golden Rundus—Baker Hill's finest gambling establishment. The sun's light had not yet drained from the sky but the carpark was already full. The Rundus was more a dive than anything, nothing like the larger casinos in the city, but somehow a bigger pit of sin than most. Suits and formal wear didn't fool Lynus into believing that the people wearing them were model citizens.

As Lynus approached, he saw the muscle-headed bouncer stir and stand up straight with his chest out in a sad attempt to look intimidating. Wearing his blue hoody and dark blue jeans, Lynus didn't exactly fit in, and it was clear the bouncer had already decided that he wasn't going to let him inside.

'I.D?' the bouncer grunted. Lynus had been watching the place for a few hours now and never saw a single person carded.

Lynus shrugged the shoulder with the bag on it. 'I don't know what this is, but they told me to bring it here,' he said casually. 'There'll be a pissed off mephisto coming down on your arse if you don't let me in.'

The door guard grunted again and reached for his two-way. 'One of the last ones has finally arrived with the blood,' he said into it.

'Where're the others?' The door guard now spoke to him. 'And what took you so long?'

'Wardens,' Lynus said, hoping it would answer both questions.

The doorman grunted again as the door opened and Lynus was waved inside. 'Yuenlyn is definitely gonna be pissed alright.'

Two more very large men escorted Lynus inside, through a small hallway heavily decorated by tacky plastic palm trees, and into the main area of the casino, leading him towards the far end of the building. The room was filled with overbearing lights, sounds and drunken fools. Most of the casinos in the cities would kick out the stupidly drunk, even the less respectable ones. Here, however, it was like someone had drugged all the animals in a zoo and then let them loose. People drank, smoked, gambled and displayed unseemly affection with one another, yet no one seemed to bat an eye.

Lynus' best guess was that this Yuenlyn person the bouncer mentioned was the demon in charge. The mephisto the dreadlocked demon had mentioned. Mephistos were usually a malleable mixture of cowardly and clever. They often made deals, cut people in or gave favours to continue their work unobstructed. Most humans who actively came looking for demons like Yuenlyn were either highly trained demon hunters or people way in over their heads. The former of which was only looking to clean up the filth and nothing more; the latter—well, they often lacked the conviction and intelligence to not get identified as a meal instead. The really unlucky and foolish ones got what they asked for. Lynus had a bigger goal in mind, though, and had been keeping an ear to the ground for any trace of a mephisto for months, and he was finally about to get his hands on one. Again.

They pushed Lynus through a set of double doors and told him to go to the end of the hallway. He walked down the ugly cream-coloured corridor, which had private rooms and small offices along its length. He did as he was told and knocked on the door at the end.

'In,' came a voice from the other side.

Lynus moved into the room but said nothing as they shut the door behind him. There were another three bodyguards in the room, not including the giant man who had opened the door. The room was dirty and looked far more run down than a building of its age should. It also smelled like sweat and overripe fruit.

'You're late.' The man who spoke was a middle-aged Asian fellow with short hair and an amused expression. 'But then, I would expect you had a hard time finding the place since you weren't invited. Eh, Ghost?'

Lynus tensed, expecting to be attacked right away. Ghost was the name he had apparently earned during his time in Salem. Demons and angels alike referred to him as such. He had to admit he did like the amount of fear that seemed to be attached to it. Though, seeing Yuenlyn's smirk, he figured there was no fear of him here.

'Welcome to my new casino. Recently acquired,' he said. 'My name is Yuenlyn Myn. Please, call me Myn. Easier on the tongue.'

There was a moment as Myn waited for a response from Lynus, who gave him only silence. Mephistos generally had a bad habit of talking too much. A tactic for confusing and charming their usual prey. Lynus was not usual prey, and he would let Myn talk himself out a bit.

'Mr Vargo, the previous owner of this establishment, and I couldn't seem to agree on the use of my gifts.' Myn grinned, but his eyes remained focused on Lynus. He looked at one of his bodyguards and pointed at the ground by his feet. As the guard moved over to where he had pointed, Myn stepped out from his desk, walked around to the opposite side and then leaned back onto it with his arms behind him. Lynus briefly considered gutting him right there. The bodyguard dragged out the bloodied corpse of Mr Vargo and left the room, but the smell of him lingered.

'It's very curious that a man who makes his earning from mortal vice would be so argumentative about his ethical stance on distributing my wares,' Myn contended. The grin had disappeared from his face altogether now. 'So, why all the trouble, Ghost? Why come here? Are you going to kill me? I would prefer you didn't.'

'I haven't decided yet,' Lynus taunted. 'Perhaps I will.'

Faster than Lynus would think possible for men of their size, two of the bodyguards lunged at him. Lynus pulled out the combat knife from his belt, spun to the right and planted the blade into the guard's neck while his smoky avatar did the same to the left. The purple figure quickly returned to Lynus as he ripped the knife out of the man. He turned to deal with the other two guards but stopped mid-step as an orange semitransparent blade floated in front of his face.

'So, you really are him.' Myn sounded gratified. 'The Ghost of Salem.'

'A demon using a rune,' Lynus countered. 'Really are without shame, aren't you?'

'Gotta protect yourself in this business.' Myn laughed as he walked back around his desk and sat behind it once more.

'Where did you get it?' Lynus asked.

Myn held up his arm. Attached to it was a black leather band within which contained the small orange-yellow ball. 'This? Is that why you came here, Ghost?' Myn asked impatiently. 'To ask about my rune?'

'Not exactly.' Lynus' steeled expression faltered for a moment as he remembered. 'I've lost something, and I want it back.'

Myn lowered the blades, and they dissolved. 'And you want to make a deal with me?'

'No. I'm done making deals,' he spat.

Myn let out an explosive sigh of impatience. 'So why come to me?'

'I want your boss,' Lynus said matter-of-factly. Strictly speaking demons didn't have bosses in the conventional sense, but some types of demons, the more intelligent ones like mephistos, generally had a strongest among them that held a lot of influence over the rest.

'My boss? No, I don't think you want him, but I think you mean Hekate?' Myn let out a derisive laugh. 'You're done with deals, but want to look for the queen of deals herself? How do you know she's even in Salem?'

There was a short moment of silence before Myn's face turned from impatience to realisation, then to amusement.

'Ah, I see. Not even the great Ghost of Salem is immune to his human stupidity, eh?' Myn mocked. Lynus glared at him. 'You lost something in a deal you thought you could find a loophole for, and now you're pissed off and want her to undo it. Gotta tell you, I expected more from the great Ghost of Salem.'

'You'll get more, and so will she when I remove her head from her deceitful body,' Lynus snarled.

Myn laughed again. 'Oh, well if anyone could, it would be you, I suppose.'

'Glad you think so,' Lynus proclaimed.

'And why is that?'

'Because it means you know I can and will kill you if you don't help me.'

Myn shrugged. 'I kind of just assumed you would do that anyway,' he conceded. 'But so long as we are talking about a d—' he cut his sentence short and amended his words. 'About an arrangement, I'm sure I can be of assistance. But first, if you please, sate my curiosity.'

'What?' Lynus looked at the demon warily.

'Most of the people I deal with are foolish idiots who are far too easy to please. Chuck a bit of money at these morons and they are willing to throw themselves into eternal damnation,' he said. 'But you're not a fool. What did you ask for? I heard rumours, but they can't be true.'

Lynus stepped forward, pulled out the handle of his angelic blade and activated it with a brilliant flash of light. The tip of the sword was mere inches away from Myn's throat.

'So it is true.' Myn smiled nervously. 'The Sword of Michael.'

'Where is she?' Lynus asked, sword still level with Myn's throat.

'The Central Salem Graveyard,' he answered.

Lynus deactivated the sword and turned away to leave. Before he pulled the door he said, 'And you're wrong. I am a fool.'

From the moment Lynus set foot in the cemetery, he could feel eyes upon him. By now he was sure Hekate knew he was here, and if she knew he was here, she likely knew why and wasn't going to be caught off guard.

The Central Salem Cemetery was indeed the largest cemetery Lynus had ever seen and sat almost exactly in the middle of the city. As he walked among the headstones and small gardens, which looked bright and colourful even at night, he took a moment to admire the cathedral that the cemetery was attached to the side of. Its darkened silhouette loomed in the distance as though it were a guardian of the dead. During a full moon, the cathedral's spire windows would light up like a beacon, making the stained-glass artwork visible as if it were day. Tonight, though, the dense cloud cover cast only darkness over the sombre city of tombstones.

Even in the dark, out of the corners of his eyes, Lynus could see shadows darting around. Eventually he stopped walking, looking from left-to-right, seeing if he could catch sight of whatever was following him. He saw nothing at first, but he heard chittering and the low growls of what he identified as imps.

His assessment proved to be correct as one of the vicious little demons lunged at him. He ducked and spun to face it, but more jumped at him, their sharp claws slashing at his face. They were small and easy to deal with alone, but from what Lynus could tell there were at least a dozen, maybe more. They were of various shapes and sizes, but the largest of them was about four-and-a-half feet tall, the smallest of them only around two feet. All had grey skin, but only some had wings, while others had small horns on their heads. Some had both. All of them had razor-like claws.

Lynus reached behind him, pulling out and activating the Sword of Michael. The blade glimmered as if in the midday sun. He swung the sword left and right, cutting through the imps, each one being sliced in half with ease as the sword half cut, half burned the demons. It felt like cutting sponge cake with a butcher's knife. The sword glided through them with no resistance at all as they lunged at him.

But it only worked for so long. A seemingly endless tide of teeth and claws spilled from the darkness, and he was soon having to put a surprising amount of effort in. As powerful as the sword was, it was still his own reflexes, skill and muscle he needed to rely on to land the hits so the sword could do its work. Lynus quickly found himself having to dodge more imps than he could counter. He thought about using one of his rune abilities, but the last time he met with Hekate he only had a single rune, and he didn't want to tip his hand in case Hekate was watching. If she proved to be uncooperative, he didn't want to underestimate her.

Among the swarm of imps and their tenacious chittering, Lynus heard the crack of thunder overhead, and then a blinding flash of light along with the screams of the imps as the light burned them away. Almost as soon as it had come, the light receded, and Lynus could make out a figure standing just a few metres away from him.

By the time the light had faded completely, there were no more imps, only the figure standing before him. He held a massive sword, one that would require a normal human to use both hands, but this stranger held it aloft in one hand with ease. As Lynus' eyes readjusted, he could see the stranger's face much clearer now and quickly fell back into a defensive stance, his sword held up ready to fight again. The figure's eyes were white. Not the pale-grey white of a blind man, but the vibrant, pure white of an angel of high calibre. The sword it held was much like his in design, simple yet elegant.

'Ghost,' it said.

'Whoever you are, I suggest you leave me to my business,' Lynus snarled.

'I'm the arbiter that has wasted months tracking you down,' it said. 'I went as far as trapping an entire team of wardens because I thought you were among them. I see why they call you what they do.' The angel stepped forward with an open palm. 'But you've had your fun, now give me the sword so that I may return it to Michael.'

'If he wants it so bad, why does he not come after it himself?' Lynus growled.

'One of few things that can destroy an archangel is the weapon of another archangel, or their own...' the arbiter said. 'Do you really think Michael would risk you landing a lucky shot with all your flailing? Of course not! He has far greater goals than to deal with you himself.'

'I'm not going to hand this over and then stand by while you wipe out humanity just to win a war,' Lynus shouted.

'Don't be so naïve,' the arbiter said in a calm voice. 'The human world is infected with the darkness of sin. It is sick and dying all on its own. Michael will purge all of these diseased cities to cauterise the wound. Whatever hides elsewhere will be easily sought out and destroyed. Millions of humans will die, but that is just unfortunate collateral. We will show the humans that survive how best to serve God and continue with better lives than they have now.'

'You angels are just as bad as the demons,' Lynus spat. 'You'd kill millions of innocent people to get what you want. I was taught that angels protected and guided us, but it turns out you are nothing but monsters and cowards.'

Ever since Lynus had taken the sword, its owner had sent out angels to hunt him down. Lynus had wondered why all this time Michael had not come himself, but now it was apparent that even he was afraid of the power of the sword. Lynus always suspected he himself was wielding but a fraction of its capabilities, but now he had a good idea of just how right he was. At first Lynus refused to give it up until he had made proper use of it for his own selfish reasons. But during the battles he had fought with the angels who tried to take it away from him, he had found out firsthand just how little care The Divine March had for humans. The destruction they often inflicted upon innocents just to kill a few demons was vast, so keeping the sword from Michael had become so much more important.

'Michael's hand has been forced by the sins of man. He turned to aggression to stem the tides of darkness in this world,' announced the arbiter. 'Gabriel and his kind still continue to wield compassion and love as a weapon, and it gets them nowhere because the time for that is long past.

'You humans were given free rein. Over time you have taken advantage of this, gorging yourselves and indulging your baser instincts to the point where there is more sin than not. That's what has caused the demons to be strengthened over the past thousands of years. That won't happen again. Michael does this for your own good. Someday soon, humans will know true happiness, away from sin. They will learn to be thankful for what Michael will have done for them when his actions win back God's love and God re-enters this darkened world.'

Lynus had heard enough and lunged forward, striking fiercely with his sword. The angel quick-stepped backwards, dodging Lynus' attack, and then lunged forward into a counterattack. Lynus brought up his sword to defend, and even though the attack was blocked, the sheer power behind the angel's attack knocked Lynus' sword to the side.

Lynus stepped back to readjust his stance, but the angel and his giant sword were already upon him with another attack. Acting on pure instinct, Lynus drew on the power of his purple rune to dodge the attack fast enough. Black-purple smoke enveloped him briefly as he moved just enough to the side to dodge the blade's downward strike. His eyes were still glowing purple as he countered with a lateral slice aimed at the angel's ribcage.

The attack connected, but against an angel it had none of the spectacular cutting power that the imps had been victim to earlier. Though unlike a normal sword, it still forced the angel to retreat a few steps, hissing in pain. The angel regained his composure, standing up straight and looking down his nose at Lynus.

'As skilled as you are in use of that blade,' the angel said, 'its potential is wasted on you. In its true master's hands it can perform feats a thousand times greater. You wield but a fraction of its worth.'

'Yeah, well, it's good enough to kill you, so I think I'll keep it,' Lynus shouted out as he attacked again. In response, the angel suddenly unfurled his magnificent white wings, the blast of wind from which stopped Lynus in his tracks. Now hovering in the air, the arbiter burst forward with tremendous speed.

The angel swung his sword as he barrelled towards him, and Lynus blocked, but as the swords connected, the angel planted his knee in Lynus' gut with all the force of his flight. The angel landed gracefully on his feet while Lynus was thrown backwards, the wind being forced from him as his body hit the ground, the power of his ghost rune dissipating.

As Lynus willed the air back into his lungs, the angel stared at him with intensity. Lynus knew what he was doing, and could feel him inside his mind like a severe headache pushing its way into different parts of his skull.

'Vengeance,' it said finally. 'Vengeance is all you type seem to want. Something killed your brother and now you blindly charge after it, killing anything that stands in your way just like you did when your father died. Even other humans aren't spared your wrath for the mistake of getting in your way. And you call us the monsters.'

It continued digging, to the point where even when Lynus had gotten his breath back, the pain from inside his head kept him down.

'Oh, I see. It didn't just kill your father. It killed you and your brother too. Oh my, then that makes you...' It paused for a moment. 'A warden. So you and your brother became wardens and then you let him get killed a second time for your lust for revenge.' The angel actually chuckled at that a little, much to Lynus' surprise.

'Nice to see you developing a sense of humour,' Lynus snapped with dry sarcasm.

'Yes, well it would seem I've been down in the human world for far too long chasing after you.'

Lynus recalled that while angels didn't treat emotions the same way humans did, the longer they stayed on Earth, the more susceptible they became to feeling human-like emotion, which eventually caused them to go mad. The stronger the angel, the longer they could stave succumbing to insanity. Except for the archangels as they were thought to be immune and freely expressed emotion.

Lynus felt the angel leave his head, and the enormous pressure that sat upon his mind was lifted. As the pain passed, Lynus got to his feet. He was done screwing around with this arbiter and once again called upon his ghost rune's power. Lynus' eyes flashed bright purple like an arcane forge fire, and dark purple smoke rose from his whole body as he darted forward, faster than any normal human could. The angel wrapped a wing around itself to block the incoming attack, but Lynus grabbed the wing with his bare hand.

In a swift motion, Lynus extended the arm that held the angel's wing, and his ghost form rushed out, taking the wing and snapping it backwards. His ghost form disappeared just as quickly as it had appeared, suddenly materialising on Lynus' right side, darting towards the angel. It grabbed the other wing and forced it out as Lynus brought down his sword, slicing through the wing, following up with a push-kick to the angel's stomach.

All this happened in just a few short moments, too quickly for even the arbiter to react, only howl in pain and anger. Lynus stepped forward, slicing at the angel again and again. Each time, his ghost form appeared and attacked as well. The angel was unable to defend itself fast enough without the use of its wings, and eventually Lynus buried his sword through the angel's chest. The angel's eyes went wide then twisted into anger as it fell to the ground.

Suddenly the ground shook and the angel's body glowed a pure white so bright it almost burned to look at it. The glow of the body took shape as a pillar into the sky that dissipated as quickly as it had formed, leaving a naked body on the ground. Even the leftovers of its wings were gone now. If Lynus didn't know any better, he'd have thought it to be a human.

A slow clapping broke Lynus' fury, and his eyes faded back to normal as he looked around the cemetery.

'Looking for me?' He instantly knew who it was. She looked the same as he remembered from their first meeting, wearing the same slim-fit black dress with a plunging neckline and a slit up one side to just above her hip. She had wavy black hair, framing a sharp yet delicate and altogether beautiful face. She was, in fact, so stunning that even Lynus couldn't help but stare lustfully into her poisonous green eyes for a moment, the purple smoke easing back into his body until he appeared normal again.

'Don't think I don't have enough energy to kill you too,' Lynus said with thunder in his voice.

'What is it you hope to accomplish by killing me? Do you think it'll get your brother back?' Her voice matched her appearance. She whispered, but there was a sultry coarseness to it.

'You tricked us, and for that you have to die,' Lynus asserted.

'Don't be such an impertinent child, Lynus,' she said smoothly. 'You're going to kill everyone who does wrong by you?'

'You didn't hold up your end of the deal! We were not finished, and you took him instead of me,' he countered.

'No, Lynus, *you* said your soul, but *I* never specified which of you, and that is what we shook on,' she said. 'It is not my fault that you do not listen.' She walked around him in a casual fashion, but was clearly keeping her distance. He had used too much of his rune's power, so there wouldn't be much left to call on for a few hours. In his state after the battle, she had the upper hand in a fight, but she still seemed rightly cautious of his weapon. 'You got your weapon to take your revenge, and I took a soul.'

'Out of all the weapons you could have chosen, you sent us after this?' Lynus lifted Michael's sword. 'Why? Did you plan to take it off me for yourself, or were you scared of what Michael plans to do with it?'

'You've been slaughtering angels and demons indiscriminately for over a year now,' she purred. 'Surely you've figured out by now that the sword you carry isn't something just anyone can wield, and demons are not on the list.

'As for Michael's plans, well, I'd be a fool not to be concerned, so, yes, I suppose that is a fortunate turn.'

She was lying, but Lynus knew he wouldn't get the truth from her.

'I don't know what you monsters do with souls once you've got them,' Lynus interjected, his eyes narrowing in contempt. 'But I want it returned, and me taken instead.'

'Well, since you've been doing your thing in the city, I must admit you've become quite a trophy to be won.' She smiled at him with the hungry eyes of a pining lover. 'But... I don't have your brother. Angels killed him as I am sure you remember. I never claimed him when he died.'

'What are you talking about?'

'Besides the fact that the angels barred my way?' she asked. 'Warden souls are not like human souls. Someone else claimed him before either I or The Valkyr Guard could,' she explained. 'You should thank me for my kind nature, you know. I may have failed to get the soul, so technically the deal is unfulfilled, but I'll let it go as a favour to you.'

'Who?' he asked, ignoring her twisted brand of humour. 'Who claimed it?'

'If I had to guess, I'd say one of the Ankor, those angels of death. Ferrying souls is their job after all. Though...I heard whispers it was The Divine March. That would make sense considering they're the ones who killed him. I'd say they have his soul imprisoned somewhere, likely to be used as bait for you, so I'd be careful how you go about this crusade of yours.' Her voice was tinged with concern, but Lynus couldn't tell if it was sincere or not, nor did he care.

There was a long silence as Lynus thought about all the implications, and what he had been doing. The truth was, with his brother by his side their mission had been simple enough. Find the thing that had murdered their father and kill every demon or angel that got in the way. Now though, Lynus had made literal deals with demons and had become twisted into something far greater than revenge. He thought for just a second that the arbiter had been right—that he was foolish for being motivated purely by revenge. Even now, he suddenly realised he didn't even know what he had hoped to get from Hekate's death. Even if she were lying and had his brother's soul, Lynus had no way of knowing if killing her would release it.

'I want to help you.' Her enthralling voice broke into his thoughts and brought him back to reality.

'Why would you do that?'

'I overheard that angel say a few nasty things,' she admitted with a beguiling smile. 'Things pertaining to my likely death. And I rather enjoy being alive, here on Earth especially. Not all demons want the same things, Ghost.'

'I've not met a demon yet who's wanted much more than death and destruction,' he retorted.

'You need to get out more then, love,' her smile turned downright seductive. 'Don't get me wrong, most of us do just want to wreak havoc, and even the special agendas of some still involve death in some way or another. But not all, my dear. You'd be wise to remember that.'

'Well, let's make a deal then,' Lynus proposed. 'I don't kill you, and you tell me where I should start in getting my brother's soul back.'

Hekate threw her head back and laughed. 'Even if I were inclined to give into such a juvenile threat, and I am not, you haven't been looking after yourself, Ghost. You're tired and worn and right now I'd wager I could hold my own, even with you wielding that unsightly thing.

'But perhaps there is something you can help me with off the record. No official deals or bonds of blood, just my word and yours. How's that sound?' Hekate looked at him expectantly.

Lynus stopped and thought for a moment, after almost reflexively denying her. He wasn't so stupid as to make another deal with her, was he? That's how things had become so twisted to begin with. But this was his only trail—his only lead. Without her help, he would hit a dead end and be no closer to finding out what happened to his brother as when he started. Demons had a knack of weaving things in their favour so they were always in control. They made sure they had the upper hand and were always in the position to gain more than they gave. Especially mephistos. He didn't really have the option of saying no though, and she knew it.

'What is it?' he asked finally.

'There is a man, and I need him to die,' Hekate explained ever so casually.

'And you can't kill him yourself?' Lynus asked. 'Is this collection for a deal he's made? What's wrong, can't find him?'

'When a soul is ready for collection, they shine like a beacon to me through hell itself and beyond. I can always find a soul that belongs to me.' She let that fact hang in the air for a few moments before flashing a smile and a short, delicate laugh. 'Yes, he made a deal,' she confirmed. 'And I could kill him, but I *want* you to for reasons I have no desire to divulge. Do you want to take me up on my generous offer or not?'

'Fine,' Lynus huffed. If this man had made a deal, he was likely only an occultist no better than the many he had killed before. 'What's the name?'

'Adley Black.'

Chapter Ten
To protect humanity

Aiden woke as if startled by a dream, but for once there
was no dream for him to ponder. He wasn't sure how
to feel about that. The dreams of lost memories that
taunted and teased him were the only thing he had to cling to of
who he was. Who he used to be. The person he was now felt to
him like nothing more than an unfamiliar, cheap copy. He stared
at the ceiling of his tiny room, willing his memories to come back,
but it was like scooping water with a net. He could feel the tugging
deep inside, but all it left him with were the droplets of basic func-
tion. Memories of how the world around him worked, but nothing
that told him how he fit into it.

A low, bubbly growl roused him from his stupor—it was his
stomach. He peered up at the clock above his door. Five-thirty
p.m. He had only been asleep for a few hours. Aiden pushed aside
his thoughts and got out of bed. After dressing in his black cargo
pants and a plain white shirt, he left his room.

His room was one of six others on the right-hand side at the
end of a short hallway, which did not seem wide enough to allow
even two average-sized wardens to pass each other. Judging by the
map High Paladin Tarek had given him when he had arrived,
Aiden surmised that these six rooms used to be one room that had

been sectioned off when the wardens took the place over to accommodate their numbers.

The short hallway led to another, much larger and more conventional hallway that looked far more like it belonged as part of a mansion with the wood panelling and deep red wallpaper. It was lined every so often with more doors that led to more small hallways with another six doors. It reminded Aiden of Sanctuary Prime.

Aiden made his way through the sanctuary and found what was known as the blue mess hall. Technically the yellow one was closer, but Aiden had only been to the blue one and didn't want to get lost. The mess hall was a large room with wooden floorboards filled with a dozen dining tables large enough to seat six people. The walls were plain white, with a dark blue stripe running along the centre. To the left as Aiden walked in was a smaller room that housed wall-to-wall cupboards filled with various types of food. The kitchen was also home to two large silver fridges, four microwaves and a deep freezer filled with frozen meals and meat. Aiden could hardly imagine someone spending, or even having the time, to cook a decent meal in here, yet it seemed at least to be possible. Instead, he poured himself a bowl of a cereal consisting of gold-coloured flakes.

He sat alone, sinking deep into thought again until a voice brought him back to reality. 'What'cha thinking about, Rook?' Tiago asked, taking a seat next to him.

After the last conversation he had with Tiago about memories of their past lives, Aiden did not want to bring up what was really bothering him. 'About Asha,' Aiden blurted instead. He was going to continue, but Tiago's quick tongue got in first.

'You're a brave man,' he remarked. 'There are plenty of other eligible ladies around here.'

'That's not what I meant.' Aiden played with his cereal with his spoon, the golden flakes now having more or less dissolved into a mush. 'She seems edgy since we got Grim back.'

'She's always edgy,' Tiago said. 'I was in Salem when she first arrived. Even as a lance she always seemed ready to stab things. One thing I learned after a long while is that behind the point of her sword, she cares. She just isn't good at showing that side of herself.'

'Why not?' Aiden asked, looking up from his bowl.

'In our world we are surrounded by death, and people we get close to tend to die,' he said, his voice rather solemn. 'Everyone deals with that in their own, often screwed-up way.'

'Like you and your jokes?' Aiden asked.

'No, that's because he genuinely thinks he's hilarious.' Kallista, the girl who had helped him find the blue mess the first time, walked in and into the kitchen area. She came back out with a piece of fruit-bread in her mouth. She tore off a bite as she sat opposite Aiden. 'I heard what happened to your friend. How is she?'

'Still in the infirmary,' Tiago said. Amber was still unconscious, and even as a warden, her wounds were near fatal. 'Grim has barely left her side. He feels responsible.'

'It's not everyday someone takes a sword to the chest for you,' Kallista granted. 'I'd feel responsible too.'

'Not every day, no, but at the moment it's more like a monthly occurrence,' Tiago muttered.

Kallista turned to look at Aiden. 'How are you settling in since I saw you last?'

The truth was he was settling in poorly. He still felt lost and was just moving with an invisible current, unsure about where he was or what he was doing at any given time. He was glad for Tiago since he had had little interaction with Grim, and truth be told, Grim intimidated the hell out of him. Asha was his leader, but he didn't yet feel like he could approach her—she didn't seem to like him very much. Then there was Amber, but even despite how kind she seemed, Aiden hadn't interacted with her a lot either. That just left Tiago to help him. 'I'm getting there. Slowly.'

'God will guide you,' Kallista encouraged with a smile. Tiago didn't bother to hide a rather loud scoff.

'What?' Kalli snapped at Tiago. 'You're always giving me a hard time for my beliefs. What about you?'

'What *about* me?' Tiago asked defensively.

'What do you believe?'

'There's nothin' to believe,' he said. 'They *told us* that God is gone. That's why Michael is so pissed at us.'

'You seriously believe everything they tell you?' Kalli took another bite from her bread, waiting for a response.

'Think about it, Kalli.' Tiago sat forward. 'Our Order was established what, like over three-thousand years ago?'

Kallista nodded, waiting for him to get to his point. Aiden got the feeling it didn't matter what it was though.

'And why? Because Gabriel needed an army to help defend humans against demons, right?'

Kallista nodded again. 'Yeah, what's your point?'

'Did he though? Angels had fought against demons for who knows how long before then, with no help from humans. Suddenly angels were fightin' angels, half of which wanted to wipe humans away as well. God abandoned us. If he even existed to begin with.'

'Have you ever seen an angel fight another angel?' Kallista asked.

'Not myself, but other wardens have heard the stories, just as you did when you were in Sunday school. Lucifer and his legion of angels betrayed the others, and that's what caused the Second Aetheric War,' Tiago said. 'What they probably didn't mention in your little church was that just after that, God left the building, leaving Gabriel to defend humanity against Michael's temper tantrum *and* demons.'

'So they say, but I don't believe it,' Kallista disagreed with a defiant smile.

Tiago shrugged.

'I thought Grim was the pessimist of your group,' she said. 'Besides, even before the Order, angels used wardens. All the heroes of the ancient world like Hercules, Agamemnon, Beowulf, Karna. They were all wardens before the Order was created.'

'Exactly.' Tiago slammed down his palm on the table in his excitement that Kallista seemed to have proven his point for him. 'Gabriel was fine using a warden here and there when he needed to. Then God left, and Gabriel needed a more permanent solution.'

'I don't believe God has left at all. I believe he simply left heaven and his spirit came to earth to enter us. To help us. He is still here within all who hold out against sin and continue to have faith,' she replied. 'And I am not alone in that belief. I've even heard some angels say such things.'

'Not Michael though, right?' Tiago sneered.

'Michael is angered by us because we, as a whole, have perpetuated sin to the extent that he believes caused God to abandon us. He believes the angels are being tested, and if he wipes away all demons on earth, all sin will disappear too and God will return.'

'Which makes killing humans justified?' Tiago snapped.

'Of course not,' she whispered. 'The point is *he* thinks it does. Besides, it's not like the March go out of their way to hunt us down.'

'They would if he knew the other angels wouldn't stop them,' Tiago retorted.

'Maybe,' she shrugged. 'But I believe he simply doesn't care if humans get in the way because he assumes we are all sinners, and he is misguided by the idea that killing us by accident or otherwise doesn't matter as long as eradicating demons on the earth brings back God.'

Kallista turned to Aiden. 'What about you?'

Aiden shook his head. 'Haven't really been here long enough to figure it all out yet.'

'I mean before,' she said as she shoved the last piece of bread into her mouth.

'Before being a warden?' Aiden shrugged, trying to play off his very real concerns as indifferently as others seemed to. 'I still don't remember much from before.'

Kallista stood up, moved over to the rubbish bin and dropped a piece of crust into it. 'Don't worry. Trust me; it pays to just focus on what's going on in front of you.' She ran her hand over Aiden's shoulder as she left the room in what Aiden guessed was a gesture of support. 'See ya's later.'

Tiago watched her as she left, likely staring inappropriately, which was, Aiden realised, what he was doing too. 'Speaking of eligible ladies,' Tiago said with a sly grin. 'I think she has a thing for you. I've annoyed her enough times now that she never comes in here anymore. Normally goes to the yellow on the other side of the sanctuary. Just be careful of her brother.' He laughed.

'Maybe they ran out of fruit-bread at the yellow mess. Or maybe she secretly enjoys debating theology with you.' The last thing Aiden cared about was women, although he had to admit to himself that he felt an attraction to her. Something about Kalli put Aiden at ease. In this new world surrounded by pessimists, her optimism was a refreshing comfort, albeit a fleeting one.

'So,' Aiden was keen to change the subject. 'Why is Asha extra pissy since we rescued Grim? Is it Amber?'

'Could be part of it. They don't get along, but she's still part of the team,' he said. 'But I think it has more to do with Grim's debrief.'

Aiden looked at him as Tiago's tone grew darker.

'According to Grim,' Tiago explained, 'the angel that captured him let slip that there was a mole within the Order, likely within the Salem chapter.'

'Like a spy?' Aiden asked. 'Working for whom?'

'Dunno,' he replied. 'Doesn't matter either. Any warden that's reporting to any enemy of Gabriel's for any reason, angel or demon, is a traitor, plain and simple.'

'Does that kind of thing happen often?' Aiden queried.

'Rarely, but there have been cases in the past,' Tiago said. 'At the end of the day, super or not, we're still only human.'

This idea that a warden could work against the Order defied everything Aiden had come to understand about the nature of being a warden. He thought of wardens as being morally infallible. Angels chose them after all. Though Aiden also remembered what they had said when he'd first woken up, that even angels made mistakes.

'Surely the others aren't taking the angel's words as fact,' Aiden said. 'It was a March angel after all, wasn't it?'

'I'm not exactly an expert in the way angels think, but generally speaking, angels don't often have much reason to lie,' he said. 'Besides, the idea of a mole would explain a lot of things.'

'Any suspects?' Aiden asked.

'None,' Tiago said. 'I guess that's why Asha is so pissed. This sanctuary has been like a home to those of us that've been here for so long, and the wardens in it are like our family. Just the idea it's likely someone within these very walls cuts deep.'

There were a few long moments of silence as Aiden thought it over, while the rest of his cereal turned into a gluggy mess. He pushed it aside.

'So do we have any missions or…' Aiden asked. Pretty much ever since he had arrived in Salem, they had been busy. This was as much downtime as he had experienced.

Tiago barked a short laugh. 'Assignments,' he corrected. 'We aren't secret agents.'

Aiden gave him a blank stare as he waited for Tiago to answer the question.

'And no, most warden teams are already on assignments—that's why it's so quiet around here. Our team isn't exactly in fighting condition right now so we've been handed a bit of a break,' he finally said. 'I'd suggest getting yourself familiar with the sanctuary while you can. Relax for a bit or you'll end up like Grim, always brooding about.'

Aiden took Tiago's advice and explored the mansion that was the Salem chapter's sanctuary. He asked Tiago to be his guide, but Tiago declined, opting instead for sleep, which he had not had a chance to do since Grim's rescue.

Aiden's first stop was back to his room where he retrieved his map, which made the sanctuary look far simpler than it felt in reality. Aiden wandered aimlessly for the most part, using the map to guide him in general directions to make sure he covered everything.

Looking at the mansion from the front, the width of the sunken building ran from north to south. The sanctuary's lobby was the main thoroughfare to the rest of the building and featured a large staircase at its centre, which led to the second floor via two hallways. These ran the width of the building and another hallway ran perpendicular to them, the end of which led to High Paladin Tarek's office. The other two hallways on the second floor both eventually turned to the east and ended at the back of the building. Once upon a time they would have given access to the third floor, which had mostly been just an attic, but now it had been crushed by the cave-in and never rebuilt. Occupying the second floor was the armoury, which took up most of the north wing, a couple of briefing rooms, High Warden Mason's office in the south wing and a small mess hall that Aiden could not see on the map.

The bottom floor was similar in design except the two main hallways made two large squared C-shapes. The hallways started at the north and south sides of the lobby and ran the width of the building before turning to the east and eventually back in on themselves, where they met in the middle of the eastern side of the mansion and then formed a centre hallway that led west and back into the lobby. The south wing was almost entirely made up of warden rooms, which were identical to his own. The yellow mess hall was located half way around on the inside of the south-most end. The north wing was made up of a couple more briefing rooms, the infirmary, bathrooms and the blue mess hall. The largest occupier of space in the north wing, however, was the training room.

Aiden walked in to take a better look. Spaced out within the room was everything you'd expect to find in a regular gym: various types of weights and lifting equipment, rowing machines, bikes and even a boxing ring. More akin to a martial arts studio, the training room also had a section of floor permanently covered with padded mats, which also had racks holding wooden swords at each corner.

Inside the boxing ring was Asha, who had set up a dummy and was training with it, although to Aiden it looked more like the dummy owed her money. A lot of money. He turned to leave, but he spun back around when she called his name.

'Come over here,' she said as he faced back towards her. She got out of the boxing ring and moved over to the padded area, gesturing him to follow her onto the mats. He stood on the padding in front of her. It was far firmer than he had thought it would be. Soft enough to break most of a fall, but not so soft that it'd cause your feet to sink into it and compromise your footing.

'Tiago tells me the new training regime at Prime is to handball everything to the lochs,' she said.

Aiden nodded. 'Clarel said—'

'Arch Warden Clarel,' Asha corrected.

'Uh, what?' Aiden stammered.

'I guess one of the things they neglected to teach was respect for superiors,' Asha surmised. 'She earned that title. Use it.'

'Sorry, Loch Warden,' he said looking at his feet.

'Just Asha is fine,' she replied coldly.

'But you just s—,' he started, but she silenced him with a raised index finger.

'I know what I said. Continue.'

'Arch Warden Clarel usually answered most questions with the fact that we'd learn everything else we needed to know from you,' Aiden explained.

'When I was a lance, training went for a month, did they tell you that?' Aiden shook his head. 'Ridiculous that they spit you lances out after only a few days. I guess I'll try to fill in the holes they left.'

'So I can ask you questions?' Aiden asked with strained caution. Asha gave him a curt nod. 'When will my memories return? Some others at Prime had started to remember bits of theirs, but so far I've remembered nothing. I know it's different for everyone but—'

'Questions relevant to our job, lance,' she snapped. Aiden looked away from her, trying to suppress his look of dejection. After a few moments she then asked, 'How did you go with your training? Was there anything you picked up easily?'

'Training with a sword came naturally, far easier than using a gun,' he said. 'Felt sort of familiar.'

'Well, then, you have that at least,' she offered. 'I know it isn't much, nothing like a real memory, but muscle memory is still very much a piece of the puzzle you are trying to put together.'

Her shift in tone took Aiden somewhat aback. It wasn't warm and cuddly, but it was better than being growled at.

'Sorry, but I don't follow,' Aiden said.

'I don't know what rules The Valkyr Guard follow when they pick people,' she relayed, 'but most of the time the people they choose are fighters of some sort, usually in the literal sense, which means during training at Prime, most new wardens will find themselves naturally excelling at one thing or another.

'The fact that you did better with a blade means two things: They picked you for your ability to fight, and that you had some previous training with swords or similar weapons. It's not much, but it's far from nothing.'

To Aiden's surprise, this revelation did make him feel a little better, although it lasted only for a moment as he remembered his first, and so far only, battle with the husks. Clearly he was one of the mistakes that angels sometimes make.

As if reading his mind, Asha gestured at his leg. 'Still have a lot to learn though.' She then turned to a nearby rack and grabbed two of the wooden swords displayed there, tossing one through the air to Aiden who caught it with a modicum of grace. 'I had hoped to get you in here before we had a real fight like that. That's what life is like here though, so I'd advise you get used to being ready for anything.'

He took the practice sword and held it loosely in his right hand, still eager to sate his curiosity. 'What about your past life?' he asked. 'Did your memories come back easily?'

Asha did not reply. Instead she darted forward and struck with a downward swing. Aiden was quick enough to raise his stick in response and block it, but Asha had stepped into the blow, and Aiden realised only as she shoved into him that her right foot was planted firmly behind his. He tipped over like a falling tree straight onto his back. He was sure if the ground wasn't padded it would have knocked the wind from him. He made a mental note—that wasn't a lesson in proper footing.

Aiden got back to his feet, and she was at him again. This time it was a sideways swing, which he was not quick enough to block, and was punished for his sluggishness with a blow to the ribs. She did not relent, however, and had twirled her wooden sword in an arc and swung again, aiming for the opposite side. This one he blocked, and the two wooden swords cracked together and bounced off each other. She tried for another downward swing, which was blocked with another loud crack, followed by another sideways swing. This time he stepped back, opting to dodge it instead of blocking. Her swing sailed through the air hitting nothing, her arm now overextended. He waited for another attack but for a single moment nothing happened. In the next moment, she was attacking with a flurry of blows, none of which he blocked, and then suddenly he was on his back again.

'What the hell was that?' she demanded.

'What?' he asked as he got back on his feet.

'I leave myself wide open and you do what, nothing?' Her eyes were furious, and the air seemed to get ever so slightly colder.

'I...' he stammered.

'Exactly,' she snarled. 'You hesitated! That will get you and more importantly, others, killed out there. What is it you think we do here? What is the Order's purpose?'

'To protect humanity,' he said, trying to will confidence into his voice and failing.

'To protect humanity,' she repeated louder, driving the point in. 'Not ourselves!'

Aiden considered apologising, but somehow he felt as if that would feed her anger.

'She's right,' came a raspy voice. The air next to Asha shimmered, and Grim appeared just off the mats. 'At least that's what the angels tell us.' He gave Asha a sour look that was returned with equal severity. 'I for one can't see how being dead benefits anyone. Apart from the obvious.' He said with a dark grin as he gave his black warden coat's collar a tug.

'I'm not talking about being reckless, Grim,' Asha snapped. 'I'm talking about accepting the risks our duty comes with.'

Grim shrugged. 'Go easy on him.' His eyes fixed onto hers. 'Sometimes a bit of hesitation can be a good thing.'

Asha's face softened, and she dropped her gaze from Grim's. 'Fine, you train him.' Her tone was cold once again. She replaced the wooden sword on the rack on her way past as she marched from the room.

'Uh,' Aiden sputtered. 'Thanks.'

'Don't mention it,' he said. 'Besides, I actually wanted to thank you for your part in my rescue.'

'Didn't do much, except get stabbed,' Aiden replied. 'It was mostly Amber. How is she?'

Grim didn't respond right away, and his gaze drifted past Aiden into empty air. It was then Aiden realised the rings around his darker-than-usual eyes. 'She's stable, but unresponsive,' he finally said, looking back to Aiden. 'But she's a warden, so she'll pull through soon enough.'

'What did you mean by what you said about the angels?' Aiden asked.

'You're still adjusting to being in the Order, Aiden,' Grim acknowledged. 'I won't confuse you by painting your views with my brush.'

'I think I'm as confused as I'll ever be; besides, I don't have a brush,' Aiden said. As he spoke, he realised this may have been the first time he had ever spoken to Grim. 'Doesn't seem like anyone can agree on much when it comes to aethereals.'

'Trust your team. Trust us, and yeah, I know she's a bit psychotic sometimes, but even trust Asha,' he said. 'We'll look after you well before any angels would. That's all I'll say. The rest I'm sure you'll make your own mind up on in time.'

Aiden was about to push for more, but there was a loud crackle as the sanctuary's announcement speaker system came to life. 'Garret, Asha and Sorterra, assemble your teams and report to the main briefing room. Priority Alpha.'

Chapter Eleven
Salem arena

G rim and Aiden arrived in the main briefing room to see High Paladin Tarek standing at the head of the room's long table. He nodded a greeting at them as they entered. Soon thereafter, Tiago entered the room and stood next to Aiden without a word. Aiden had followed Grim and was now standing at one of the table's long sides. The room looked like a larger version of the briefing room Aiden had been in before, only it had no lockers, more display screens, including a large one behind Tarek, and the table would have fit at least four full teams rather than just one.

They all looked left down the table as a door on the opposite end of the room opened and High Warden Mason entered, taking his place next to Tarek. He was a short man, only reaching Tarek's shoulders. Aiden was not sure if it was his stature, the permanent scowl or the small bulge that had formed in his midsection, but something about the high warden did not inspire confidence in Aiden, even though he was Tarek's second-in-command.

Aiden's head swung to the right as the main door opened and a whole other team of wardens joined the room. Three men and two women joined the table, and as they did, Aiden's heart skipped a beat as he recognised one of the women. It was Kallista. Even amidst the serious air of the room, she flashed him a quick smile as they took up a position opposite his team.

Not a moment later, Asha entered the room and stood next to Grim. She was followed closely by yet another full team of wardens, only these were different. Aiden wasn't sure if this was the same team he had seen the previous morning, but they definitely had the same daunting air about them. Paladins, who wore the typical warden blacks but under it they wore thick black leather armour. Aiden remembered what Kallista had said about them, how they were used when a situation was bad. Seeing them here with all the others caused a knot to form in Aiden's stomach.

'Good evening, wardens,' Tarek said as the paladins took up positions at the opposite head of the table to Tarek. 'Thank you for assembling so quickly. We need to act fast.'

'As you all heard, we have a priority alpha about to take place,' High Warden Mason said. 'Not only is this an alpha priority, but it is a high population event.'

Aiden recalled his few days of training in Sanctuary Prime. Among their theory lectures they had learned that, above all things, the first and foremost responsibility of the Order was to fulfil the purpose of the Order's founding. Not to kill demons, although that was their more common duty, but to protect civilians from becoming collateral damage when a fight between The Divine March and demons had boiled over to the point of putting humans at risk. Normally the March was effective and precise and put demons down without too much harm to civilians, but not always, and they never cared who got in their way when the fight got out of control. This was ultimately the reason Gabriel had founded the Order of Elysium. The high warden's mention of a 'high population event' was a term that meant that a lot of civilians were at risk, and the thought of a combination of the two made the knot in Aiden's stomach tighten.

'Kathari scouts have spotted and are currently tracking a large group of angels flying over the city,' Mason explained. 'They have counted at least fifteen, and although their flight path does not seem direct, they appear to be heading in the general direction of the Salem Arena.'

One of the large display screens behind Tarek and Mason lit up to show a map of the city. A yellow triangle denoted the ever-changing position of the angels, while a red circle encompassed the location of the Salem Arena. 'There is a concert playing at the arena tonight, and I don't need to remind most of you that a force of angels this large, more often than not, means they're hunting something big, and if that hunt leads them to the arena, we're in trouble.'

'You three teams are the only ones we have at our disposal at the moment. If our prediction is correct, we don't have time to recall others,' Tarek said. 'Garret, you will take the lead on this assignment.' Tarek gestured to the paladin team's loch. Even without the armour, Garret looked menacing enough to go toe-to-toe with most demons. He was a tall, largely-built man with a serious gaze; his face was dotted with small scars and a single large one that ran down the left side. 'We will initiate the operation under the assumption that this will come to a head at the arena. That is our biggest concern, but just be prepared to alter mission parameters if that ends up not being the case.

'I want the paladins to contain whatever it is the angels are hunting. Keep exposure to a minimum, but safety of civilians remains priority,' Tarek continued. His gaze now shifted from the loch warden to Asha and then to whom Aiden assumed was the other team's loch. 'Asha and Sorterra, your teams' job will be to support Garret's, primarily by protecting civilians as they evacuate. Kathari teams are en route to the area as we speak and will herd any civilians coming out to a safe area where they will be seen to.' Aiden knew that was the polite way of saying 'etched'.

'Are there any questions?' High Warden Mason asked, followed by silence. 'Good. Get your teams ready as soon as possible and get to it.'

The teams had received word half way through the twenty minute drive to the arena that the warden's prediction had come true. The angels had indeed ended up engaging in a battle with demons inside the Salem Arena, and by the time the three warden teams had arrived on the scene, the entire building was totally walled off by police cars. To Aiden's surprise, a police officer waved in all fourteen wardens, including the five armoured up, despite the looks of confusion from some other officers.

The teams rushed in through the front doors of the entertainment complex and into its lobby, where people had already started screaming and running for their lives as red feather-winged creatures swooped down and clawed at them. The paladins darted ahead and intercepted some demons in a shower of bullets and flashes of runic power.

'Asha,' Garret yelled. 'Take your team upstairs and cover the south side of the upper area. Sorterra, take yours to the north. Keep those harpies busy and away from the civilians.'

Asha and Sorterra acknowledged the order and then sprinted from the lobby and up a large flight of stairs that led to the complex's upper lobby. Sorterra's team ran off to the right once they ascended, while Asha, Tiago, Grim and Aiden took the path to the left. The upper foyer ran in a ring around the entire complex, encompassing and allowing various points of access to the actual performance stage further within. It was decorated with hanging banners advertising upcoming shows and events and had food service and bars in strategic locations as it went around.

Not even an hour ago, this whole ring would have held thousands of patrons eagerly waiting to take their seats so they could

scream and applaud with enthusiasm at whatever group of enter-
tainers they were here to see. Now it was flooded with those same
people screaming for all different reasons. Aiden could not imagine what the Order would need to do to cover something like this
up.

Aiden heard an ear-splitting screech as something slammed
into him, knocking him to the ground. He heard a shot ring out,
and dark red blood from the demon spattered him. It let out another angry, bird-like screech as another shot sounded, and it fell
dead. The next thing Aiden knew, Tiago was helping him up. He
drew his sword as soon as he got to his feet. Tiago left his side as
he shot into the air at more of the demons that Garret had called
harpies. Aiden quickly examined the demon that now lay dead at
his feet.

It looked like a young woman, only just over the cusp of adult-
hood, naked except for spiky red feathers that covered its spine,
wings, head and legs, from its waist all the way down to its feet—
or rather, its talons. The rest of its body was exposed and looked
uncomfortably like a human except for the fact that it had wings
rather than arms.

Another harpy lunged for him, but he was quicker this time
and sliced it out of the air. It landed close to the other, and he
finished it with a stab through the heart. Aiden looked around. The
others were all engaged with one or more of the demons as they
tried desperately to distract them from the civilians. Mostly the demons seemed far more interested in engaging the threat the wardens posed, but some harpies still attacked the arena's patrons. Already Aiden could see several dead.

Aiden spotted a harpy diving from the high ceiling. He hesitated for a split second before the memory of Asha's scolding
flashed in his mind. He sprinted forward, crash-tackling a woman
from the demon's path. The demon came down hard in front of
them and stumbled from the unexpected landing. Aiden lunged

with his sword and impaled the demon through the stomach. It screeched and swiped at him with a clawed foot, tearing a small slit in the arm of his coat, but it didn't break his skin. Aiden pulled the sword out and rammed it straight back in a little higher. This time the demon died without another sound.

As they fought, the stream of panicked people thinned, leaving only a few stragglers dragging behind, many of which were injured or helping others who were. What didn't slow was the amount of harpies; they did not relent. Suddenly there was an explosion of brick and mortar as the wall to Aiden's left exploded outwards, and from inside a toilet block, an angel burst through.

It was a March angel. It tossed aside the harpy it held by the neck, which flopped to the ground like a rag-doll. A dozen harpies scampered away at the sight of the angel and in that moment, the fighting stopped. The angel eyed the wardens. One by one, he gave them a quick examination. Then he glided off after more harpies.

A voice came in over the team's communication units. 'Asha, Sorterra. Give me an update,' Garret commanded.

'I think we're clear on this side,' Asha replied. 'The angels seem to be more interested in fighting the harpies than us.'

Sorterra's voice now came through the comm unit. 'Still got a few more civilians to get out.'

'Good,' Garret said. 'We're in the main arena, same goes for the angels here. We've found the angel's main target too: ifrits.'

Aiden had never heard of ifrits before, but if the angels had so many of their own hunting them, and they could anchor so many harpies, they were obviously bad news. 'Asha, head around and help Sorterra finish off the harpies on that side and then I want both of your teams to join us in here.'

Asha and Sorterra acknowledged. Without having to be told, the team made their way back around towards the stairs as fast as they could while swatting away errant harpies. As they approached, more angels ascended. Three of them came into view, which stopped the team in their tracks. Two of them looked almost identical to each other and the one that had burst through the wall earlier. The third one standing between them, however, was heavily armoured, including a silver and gold helmet, reminiscent of ancient Greek soldiers. It was styled with etchings of flame-shaped filigree that matched the rest of his armour. Much like the other angel, these angels gave the team nothing more than a cursory glance before heading deeper into the complex.

'Garret,' Asha said over the comm unit. 'Raziel is here. The angels are under his command.'

'Say again, Asha,' Garret came back. 'Please confirm. You said Raziel?'

'Yes, sir,' she replied.

'Are you sure?'

'Yes, I'm sure,' Asha responded.

There was a long pause before Garret responded again. Or at least it felt long. 'Copy that, Asha,' he said. 'I will notify the kathari. All teams emphasise your distance with the angels. Give them no reason to attack.'

'You heard him,' Asha said to them. 'The enemy of my enemy is my friend.'

'Our friends are dicks,' Tiago said with a grimace.

Asha gave Grim a pointed look, to which he replied with a grunt. 'No promises,' he said. Asha glared at him, but decided not to argue. Instead, she led them around the ring towards Sorterra's team.

Asha's team joined up with Sorterra's and soon made easy work of the remaining harpies. They did a quick status check and found almost everyone with nothing more than a few scratches. Aiden's eyes widened when he saw Kallista, who had a bleeding claw swipe from below her ear to the middle of her collar bone. Despite this injury, she smiled a greeting at him, and he remembered that within a few hours there would be no evidence of a wound at all. Nonetheless, her brother Sorterra seemed to fuss over her, trying to affix a bandage to the bleeding, to which she gently yet firmly pushed away.

'Ready?' Asha asked once Sorterra had given up.

'Ready,' Sorterra said after giving Kallista a huff.

The two teams ventured further into the complex and after passing through a short hallway, entered the main area. Salem Arena was the largest performance complex in the city. It had a capacity of twenty-thousand people during non-sporting events and could be reconfigured for almost anything. Tonight they had the ceiling closed, but during some events they would open it up to reveal the sky above. The teams had entered from the side. Below them, down almost two dozen rows, was the railing that led down to the stage, left abandoned with musical equipment and instruments. The railing encompassed the floor seating area in a wide half-circle, in which a large group of angels fought with seven large masses of fire that had taken humanoid form.

Scattered around the rows of seats were the paladins, keeping a watchful eye on the proceedings below. For a few long moments, the teams did the same. They observed as the angels fought with these demons called ifrits.

The ifrits loomed over the angels at almost twice their height as they fought with claws and fire. Their skin was black like charcoal, with raging fires for eyes. They all looked male, but with demons, who really knew. They were muscular from head to toe, although they didn't have toes—or legs. Instead, from the waist down, they seemed to evaporate into a swirling gust of fire that propelled them around the room, fighting the angels in the air and on the ground. The ifrits looked as though they had once been adorned in silken robes of purple and maroon and had suddenly burst into flames, becoming what they were now.

They wore large middle-eastern style belts that held together the singed remnant pieces of coloured cloth, which danced around in the whirlwind of flame below them. The only intact piece of clothing they had were their hoods, even then they were pierced by two small yet sharp-looking horns at the top of their heads. They had similar protrusions running along the side of their necks, shoulders and down their exposed arms.

Most of the angels fought the ifrits in small teams, but Aiden watched as the angel they had called Raziel shoved his guards aside and fought with one of the creatures by himself. Raziel held his angelic sword above his head, and in several quick flashes of light, a dozen blades materialised above him and cut through the air towards the demon. The ifrit roared in defiance at Raziel; the inside of its mouth glowed like the inside of a forge, and its long-fingered hand glowed orange like super-heated metal. It waved its hand in front of it with a single movement, and the swords that threatened it melted away, the slag hitting the demon, sinking into its fire-cracked skin, doing no harm.

The instant the swords had melted away, the demon brought its arms up in front of it, palms facing each other several inches apart. A fountain of lava erupted from the ifrit's chest, passing between its hands and jetting towards Raziel. Raziel brought down his sword, slicing the pillar of magma down the middle with a flash of light. The molten stream split into two. One-half arched upwards and penetrated the arena's ceiling, while a paladin narrowly avoided the other as it ploughed into the far row of seats.

'Asha,' Grim said. 'Look!' Grim pointed to a group of three angels fighting an ifrit. A fight that was getting dangerously close to the upper rows of seats.

'Sorterra, stay here. Guard this side. My team with me,' Asha ordered as she made her way along the railing towards the other side. 'Garret, you've got some friends getting a bit close.'

'We see them,' Garret replied over the comm. 'Get over here! We could use you.'

The team made their way around as quickly as they could, and by the time they arrived, most of the paladin team was there as well with the ifrit and four angels overhead. It was all they could do to avoid wayward spouts of fire.

Suddenly the ifrit took a hit that knocked it violently towards the arena wall. Aiden heard one of the paladins shout, and another sprang into action. When the ifrit crashed into the wall, instead of going through it, it was repelled by a wall of shimmering light.

'That hit hard,' Aiden heard one of the paladins say over the comm. 'Drained almost a quarter.'

'Asha,' Garret said. 'You have a cryomantic rune, yes?'

'Yes, sir.'

'Do you think you could bring that ifrit down a notch?' he asked.

Asha hesitated for a fraction of a second. 'Probably enough to give the angels an edge, yes.'

'Do it.'

Asha moved quickly, flicking her sword in an upwards motion, and Aiden noticed a subtle change in the air around her blade as she angled it towards the demon. As the shimmer got within a metre, it solidified and erupted into crystals of ice that struck the ifrit's whirlwind of flame. The flame melted instantly with a hiss and bellow of steam, but the ifrit roared with either frustration or pain as it dropped several feet out of the air, suddenly unable to keep afloat.

The demon caught itself with a flare of fire, like a jet engine reigniting. This didn't seem to hurt the demon but Asha's goal was clear as it gave the angels a free shot, which they did not waste. One angel let loose a spear of light that ripped through the demon then sailed downwards into the rows of seats and struck a paladin too slow to avoid it. The spear impaled the warden, and a silence rippled through the teams as their minds caught up with their eyes.

'Morgan!' someone shouted.

Garret rushed over to the speared paladin, but it had pierced crucial organs, and the warden was already dead. It was unclear to Aiden whether the angels now saw the wardens as a threat because of Asha's attack on the demon, or they decided to pre-empt the logical response to their mistake, but either way the result was the same. The angels now bared down on them.

Flashes of colour erupted from the group of paladins as they drew power from their runes and fired gouts of flame, lightning and bullets. The angels backed off, protecting themselves by folding their wings in front of them.

'Grim, fire at will,' Asha ordered over the comm.

'Way ahead of you,' he replied, deadpan. He had taken a position higher in the rows of seats. Aiden could not see him, but heard the loud crack from each of his shots. One of the angels that had been closest to them, thinking it was at a safer distance, unfolded its wings to stay airborne and received a round from Grim in its shoulder as a reward for its poor judgement.

'Nice shot,' Asha said over the comm.

'Not nice enough,' he commented.

A few more shots rang out as Grim fired, but he did not manage to land another clean hit now that the angels had retreated to the ground, their armoured wings protecting them.

'Grim, save your ammo. Wait for a good shot,' Asha instructed. 'Garret, we—'

'Everyone regroup on me,' he ordered, his voice was stern but strained with rage. 'We need to take down these angels.'

'Sir,' Sorterra said. 'Our orders are to contain the demons, which are almost defeated. The angels—'

'Just killed one of my own!' he shouted over the comm unit. 'They die too.'

'He's right, Terra,' Asha asserted. 'We can't let them get away with that; besides, they won't let us go now, and we won't get away with Raziel commanding them.'

'I'll contact the kathari and advise the change in situation,' Sorterra said flatly. 'My team will fight until backup arrives, but I won't sacrifice *my* team just to avenge one of yours. We're not demons.'

'Agreed,' Garret broke in. 'Ranged fighters, I want you up in the stands. Everyone else joins me on the floor.'

'Aiden,' Asha said. 'Stay close but don't get in my way.'

Aiden followed Asha and the others as they found a set of stairs that led them down to the arena floor, while Kallista, Tiago and a handful of others took positions up high with Grim. The arena floor was littered with charred and flaming seats that had been tossed aside in the fighting. Among them lay several dead civilians as well as all but one of the ifrits and five of the angels.

The paladins took the lead. Two of them had taken positions up high, leaving three on the ground with the other warden teams. Sorterra's team was the same. Kallista and another of Sorterra's team had joined Grim upstairs. Sorterra was holding two kukri knives, each about forty centremetres long, bending down in the middle at a twenty degree angle. They looked as if they had lightning surging through them.

Standing next to Sorterra was the largest warden Aiden had ever seen, holding the largest sword he had ever seen. The sword's gigantic blade curved and rippled like solid fire. Then there was a woman who still had a hood drawn over her head and a shotgun in her arms that had a blade attached under the barrel almost as long as the gun itself.

'He said all ranged fighters up there, Jessica,' Asha barked at the woman.

'Bayonets aren't ranged,' she replied with a grin.

'Trust me,' Sorterra said to Asha. 'The gun is secondary.'

Seeing the wardens form up, four of the angels advanced upon them. As one glided along the ground towards Asha, a shot rang out, and the angel dived face first into the dirt. Asha lunged forward to take advantage. The angel rose, but she swung her sword and the angel's wings were suddenly frozen to the ground. It broke free moments later, but it was enough time for Asha to get in and cut into the angel's wing. The angel screamed in pain, but got to its feet. Another loud crack echoed through the arena as the angel lunged at Asha. It faltered, and Asha impaled it through the stomach. Aiden saw the angel lift its blade to swing, but he did not see what happened next as he was knocked the ground.

Suddenly he was looking up at an angel, its spear pulled back and aimed at his chest. As the angel thrust its spear, Aiden heard a loud snap followed by a buzzing crackle as lightning dissipated off the angel's breastplate. It was unhurt but stumbled back with the force of the attack. Aiden did not understand where it had come from and allowed himself no time to wonder; instead, he got to his feet and readied himself to defend.

Instead of attacking, the angel looked over its shoulder and dived to the side. Aiden's instincts kicked in, and he did the same as the body of the last ifrit demon came crashing down. Raziel landed among the battle, his sword ablaze, and Garret was on him in an instant. He held his own, but Raziel was too strong for him. For every decent hit Garret got in, Raziel got three. Garret blocked an attack but faltered from the force of it. Aiden made the snap decision to try to help. But what could he do? *Anything was better than doing nothing.* Before Aiden could move, however, a booming voice rippled through the battle.

'Enough!'

Aiden looked to the source of the voice that had stopped the battle in its tracks. All he could see was a blinding golden light, which condensed and shrank until it took the form of two more angels. These were different from the ones attacking them though.

161

Instead of the flaming sword insignia of the March, these angels were adorned with a golden emblem of a winged kite shield. The angel that spoke was like no other Aiden had ever seen.

His eyes were not simply yellow like some angels he had seen, but an aureate so breathtaking it was as if they were a cradle to the sun itself. The only thing that offered distraction was the angel's wings, which held a rival brilliance. He had not only one, but two sets of massive wings that were spread out behind him.

'Gabriel,' said Raziel so plainly it was as if he was answering Aiden's internal question. 'Do not interfere. We are on Divine March business.'

'I see that,' Gabriel acknowledged. 'You are fulfilling the duties of The Divine March with the same level of grace and skill I know to expect from Michael's charge.'

'Seems to me, Gabriel, that dead humans are a failure of The Valkyr Guard,' Raziel hissed. 'It is your job to babysit the humans; it cannot be helped if they get in the way.'

'You may be Michael's erelim, but Gabriel is still your superior in every way!' growled a female angel next to Gabriel, looking ready to strike. 'You will show the proper respect or—'

'Or what, Kára?' Raziel asked. 'You may be allowed to unleash your Order savages to carry out your will, but you are bound to the laws of the Divine Authority.'

'As are you bound to those same laws, Raziel,' Gabriel warned. 'You have struck down one of my wardens, and I will not stand for it.'

'The laws may prevent us from attacking each other without sanction, Gabriel,' Raziel sneered. 'But I could order my angels to slaughter every one of your human pets and there would be nothing you could do about it,' Raziel laughed.

'Raziel,' Gabriel said as if about to teach wisdom to a child. 'You could try, but I wonder, which of my duties are you willing to wager I'd uphold foremost? My adherence to the Divine Authority's laws or the task of protecting humans that was given to me by our Father himself before his departure?'

Raziel looked taken aback, and his slightly smug expression melted into a slate of non-expression. 'We are done here,' he announced, and with that his remaining angels took flight, leaving via the various holes within the arena's ceiling.

As Raziel left, Aiden watched Gabriel and his companion walk across the arena's floor towards Garret. As he walked, his wings folded and rested on his back, and his eyes became a human-like blue.

'You have done well,' he said to Garret, placing a hand on his shoulder. 'Recover your dead. I will personally make sure this is cleaned up.' He turned to the others and smiled at them. It was a smile that made Aiden's residual fear and adrenaline from the battle disappear in an instant. 'You have all made the Order proud here and have earned rest. Go, and I will see you all back within the safety of sanctuary walls.'

Chapter Twelve
Gabriel

H igh Warden Mason had collected Asha, Garret and Sorterra the moment they stepped through the sanctuary's front double doors. They followed Mason down the second floor's centre hallway until they reached the end, where two angels stood guard on either side of Tarek's office door. The angels eyed them each as they passed the door's threshold.

In the office, all occupants stood looking at the lochs as they entered. Two of Gabriel's honour guard angels stood side by side by the far wall, while Tarek stood behind his desk next to Gabriel. A female angel stood to Asha's right between her and Gabriel— the same angel that had appeared with Gabriel at the arena. She had a pretty face, but a stern and severe look upon it that seemed as though it could peel a man's skin off. Gabriel's physical form was not much taller than a normal human, yet everything around him seemed to shrink in his presence. His eyes had remained a human-like dark blue, rather than the golden fire they had been when she first saw him. He had perfectly straight white hair that fell to his shoulder blades.

The next ten minutes passed as each of the lochs shared their version of events at the arena up to and including Gabriel's arrival. Gabriel and Tarek seemed pleased with their overall success. After they completed the debrief and Gabriel congratulated them all on a job well done, they were dismissed, except for Asha, whom Tarek gestured at to wait. The others looked at her with curiosity as she watched them leave.

'Thank you, High Warden Mason,' High Paladin Tarek said, raising a hand towards the door. 'You may return to your duties as well.'

Asha could see Mason about to protest, but he thought better of it, nodded deeply and left.

'Asha, isn't it?' Gabriel's voice was strong and sounded as if he could command a mountain to move, yet still soft enough to send a shiver down Asha's spine that felt like it turned her insides to mush. His voice nearly rendered her speechless.

'Y-Yes, sir,' she stammered.

Gabriel smiled, which is something she wasn't used to seeing on an angel's face, although she knew archangels were different when it came to their ability to show emotion. The smile felt genuine, which was comforting. 'Before Raziel interrupted our plans, we were on the way to see you,' Gabriel informed her. 'We understand that you have information on the demon hunter they call the Ghost of Salem?'

'That's correct, sir,' Asha nodded. 'We found evidence of the use of the Sword of Michael, which we believe to be in this civilian's possession.'

'The theft of Michael's sword is, needless to say, of great interest to us,' Gabriel said, his voice still cutting through to Asha's core.

'You need us to take the sword for you?' Asha asked as politely as she could.

'No,' Gabriel shook his head. 'Angels are not allowed to wield the weapons of other angels without their express permission, not even a seraph like me, and I am doubtful my brother will give me said permission.'

'So, there is red tape even in heaven.' Asha realised as she said it that it sounded far less impertinent in her head.

The female angel took a step towards Asha. 'You had best watch your tongue,' she commanded, but was instantly silenced as Gabriel raised a hand. She glared at Asha but stepped back as she was ordered.

'Please excuse, Kára. She tends to be a bit excitable,' Gabriel said. 'We do not want you to take the sword; we simply wish for you and your team to find this Ghost and employ him to our cause, or failing that...to kill him.'

'But isn't he just a human?' Asha asked.

'Yes, but a very skilful human with great potential,' Gabriel said. 'He managed to steal a seraph's weapon, after all.'

Asha considered this. Seraphim were archangels, and they were the strongest of them. Gabriel and Michael being the most well-known among the Order. Which did indeed beg the question, 'How did he manage to do that anyway, sir?'

'We believe he had help from a rather powerful demon,' Gabriel revealed, 'with unfortunate access to a tool of equal strength. How this demon came about it or what the demon benefited from this arrangement is unknown to us, but in any case it leaves us with an opportunity. An opportunity I wish you and your team to take advantage of.'

'Where do we even begin to look?' Asha asked. Her confidence was rising in Gabriel's presence, but she took care not to speak out of turn.

'Your report said you found a vial of modified angel blood.' Kára's voice had changed to a more familiar monotone, a tone Asha was more accustomed to when speaking with angels. 'That could be a coincidence. It might not be. Follow it.'

Asha's memory jolted. Grim had said his contact, Narki, had told them exactly where to look for the source of the angel blood. 'Sir, we think we know where the drug is coming from: The

Golden Rundus Casino,' she said. 'But we never had the time to follow up on the lead.'

'Tarek,' said Gabriel. 'I do not wish to meddle in your duties as the commander here, but might I suggest you send Asha and her team to this casino? Perhaps they will get lucky and catch this Ghost there.'

Tarek nodded deeply. 'Of course, sir.'

Gabriel smiled at Tarek and then swept his gaze towards Asha once more. She felt a subtle tingle all over and a weakening in the knees. 'Get your team rested and head there as night falls.'

'Yes, sir.' Asha said. She hesitated for a moment and then asked, 'If I may ask, why my team?'

'Your team are the ones who found this crucial evidence,' Gabriel explained. 'Besides, something tells me to have faith in you.' He smiled that kind smile again. It felt like all her doubts about this damned war were being stripped away and replaced with warm hope.

'Sir,' she said, addressing Gabriel. 'I have a wounded team member who has yet to regain consciousness. She was impaled by an arbiter's blade. I apologise if I am out of line in asking this, but is there anything you can do to help her? Her name is Amber. She's in the infirmary in the north wing.'

Gabriel looked at Kára, as if for approval, or at least that's what it seemed to Asha, which was odd. Kára was Gabriel's erelim, his second-in-command. She led the valkyr angels, which made up the bulk of Gabriel's legion, but Gabriel commanded The Valkyr Guard, including the Order of Elysium therein. In any case, Asha's confusion over the social interactions with angels simply deepened.

Kára nodded. 'I will help but I must be with her alone.'

Asha did not question it, she was just happy that the angel was going to help. Asha half bowed and said, 'Thank you.'

Eager to learn what Gabriel had to say, especially after seeing the other lochs leave, Aiden and Tiago were waiting in the lobby for Asha to return. As Asha emerged, she explained to them what the new situation was.

Tiago was laughing. 'So we are supposed to find a man so elusive that most wardens think he doesn't exist, by hopefully bumping into him.'

Asha's jaw clenched and her lips parted, but the female angel that had been with Gabriel walked up to them, quickly silencing them both.

'This way.' Asha gestured to the north hallway that led back to the blue mess. Aiden followed behind the pair with Tiago as they made their way through the north wing.

They came to the infirmary where Amber was laid up, and on Asha's orders, waited outside as they entered. Shortly after, Grim and Asha came back out. Grim still looked rather worn, and his usual clean-shaven face had grown coarse.

'What's that angel doing in there with Amber?' Grim demanded.

'She's healing her,' Asha snapped back.

'Be a bit happier about it,' Tiago added, clasping Grim's shoulder.

'Why should I?' Grim snarled, shoving Tiago's hand away. 'We're the ones out there dying for this damn war. Us wardens shouldn't be the ones taking blades to the chest. The angels should do that. So I won't be happy or grateful, since this is the *least* these fucking angels can do to help us.' By now his voice was raised and no doubt the angel inside the infirmary could hear him, but he didn't seem to care.

Asha moved to speak, but the door to the infirmary opened, and the angel walked out and proceeded down the hallway without so much as a glance at anyone as she moved past them. Asha and the others stepped into the room one by one as quietly as they could.

The infirmary was a long room lit with a soft, comforting light and lined either side with single pipe-framed beds. Of these, all but one were empty, which is where Amber had spent the last day and a half unconscious. Now she was sitting up in the bed, watching the team as they came in. Despite looking a little groggy, she looked as if nothing had ever happened.

Tiago was the first to get to her bedside. 'How ya feeling?' he asked her, his face brimming with a smile.

Amber ran her fingers through her auburn hair and gave them a small smile. 'What happened?'

'Well,' Tiago said, 'you jumped in front of a sword and got yourself skewered. It was all very meaty.'

Amber's eyes widened suddenly, 'Is Grim alright?'

Aiden thought Grim had walked in with them, but as they all turned to look at him, he was nowhere to be found.

Asha gave an impatient huff. 'He's fine.'

'He locked himself up in here with you for most of the time you were out,' Tiago answered.

Amber shifted back and tossed her blanket aside, twisting her body so that her feet rested upon the wood floor. She pressed down with her feet as she tested whether her legs were ready to support her. 'And how long was that?'

'Almost two days,' Asha said. 'Now that you're up I need you ready to fight again by tonight, so do whatever you need to be ready for that. Same goes for the rest of you. Briefing will be at seventeen-thirty.'

'What about Grim?' Tiago asked.

'Let me deal with him.'

It took Asha years to get used to just how large the sanctuary mansion was. Even with the amount of wardens living within it, there were still many parts of the building in disrepair due to disuse. What used to be the mansion's beautiful backyard was now a cavern, not unlike the one at the sanctuary's front. However, this cavern was also home to the mansion's greenhouse, which had been heavily damaged in the fall. Hundreds of colourful and vibrant plants would have been grown there at some point, now though it had been refurbished into a shooting range.

The shooting range was not somewhere Asha frequented, being useless with firearms herself, but it was one of Grim's favourite places to haunt. She knew she'd find him around there somewhere. If not at the range itself, then brooding somewhere within the cavern. She had made this trip more than once.

She found him perched on a mound of large rocks, fidgeting with his rifle. He knew she was there, but said nothing.

'What's your problem, Grim?' Asha demanded

'Have Gabriel and his flock of pigeons left yet?' Grim asked, not looking up.

'Yes, they have. Now answer my question.'

'Seems my problem just left, apparently.' Grim was being frustrating on purpose. He was an excellent warden and an even better marksman, but sometimes he acted like a child.

'Is that the same *problem* that just saved Amber's life?' Asha said. She didn't share his dislike of angels, but she understood it. But whether or not he showed them respect, at the end of the day, they were all fighting the same enemies.

'No, it's the same *problem* that put her in that position to begin with,' Grim hissed through gritted teeth.

'In case you forgot, we are soldiers in a war, Grim. Dying is part of the job,' Asha reminded, trying to keep calm. Grim had always had a dark demeanour about him, but for him to get truly angry over something was rare, so Asha did her best to keep from making it worse. She needed him level headed.

'You believe that, do you?' retorted Grim, knowing full well what the answer was.

'It doesn't matter what I believe. It is what it is,' she replied with a strong air of conviction. It was a phrase wardens used often, '*It is what it is*', but Grim knew she didn't believe it because he was one of the few who was feeling the recent deaths just as hard as she was. The difference was that Asha had accepted it as the way of things in this life. She hated it as much as anyone, but at least accepted it far better than Grim ever had. 'We were all given the same opportunity to go back to being dead when we were first raised. We knew being killed a second time was an occupational risk.'

'And that makes our deaths justified? How many wardens do you think have actually chosen to go back to death?' he asked. Asha had never heard of anyone ever having refused membership into the Order. 'We wake up scared and confused and most don't believe the things being said to them at that point.'

'We've been wardens together here in Salem for twenty-five years, Grim. Dozens have died in that time, so why are you taking this so hard all of a sudden?' Asha probed. Grim had been a warden for two years longer than Asha, which meant they had worked together for almost each of their entire second lives as wardens.

'The angel that held me captive was an arbiter. He had one of those fucking torture staves, so I had no choice but to tell him the circumstances of my death, just so he could get off on it while he waited for the rest of you to show up.'

'I'm sorry about that, Grim. But I don't understand,' Asha said.

'It opened old wounds. And old hope of finding my daughter.' Grim's anger seemed to have passed, but was now replaced with clear heartache.

'Even if you found her, what kind of effect do you think that would have on her?' Asha asked. 'How old was she when you died? Ten? You are physically younger than her now.'

'Only by a few years,' he said defensively, giving her a dismissive wave before she could reply. 'If I found her and I told her I was her father, I'm sure I'd be arrested and thrown into an asylum,' he said. 'But I want to know if she's alive and if everything I put us through was worth it.'

'You know it's forbidden to fraternise with people from your old life,' Asha warned. It was for this reason that wardens were generally placed in cities away from their old lives. There were a few though, that for one reason or another, were placed in sanctuaries in the same cities where they had died.

'Unless it benefits the Order, right?' Grim said, referring to the criminal contacts he had that the Order took advantage of.

'Hypocrisies aside, it's not worth discussing. You know they won't let you,' Asha said firmly.

'I know, but you asked what my problem was. Now you know,' Grim said. His tone still reeked with a bad attitude, but he seemed much calmer now at least.

'I'm sorry, Markus. Really,' she said softly. 'At least I know how my family faired after I died; I can't imagine not knowing.'

'You don't need to be sorry,' he offered, matching her quietened tone. 'We're just as good as family, and you've been dragged through the same crap I have over these years. I just wish I could trust the Order like you do.'

'How do you manage to go out there without trust for the Order?' she asked incredulously.

'Because I trust you,' Grim stated. 'Just like I trusted Delarin.' Grim's hand danced over his rifle one last time to the sound of mechanical clicks before he slid down the rock and landed in front of her. 'Now, we got an assignment or what?'

Asha half-smiled. 'Be ready by sunset, arsehole.'

Chapter Thirteen
This time he dies

A iden had slept for five solid hours once instructed to by Asha, almost half a day by warden standards, yet even so, he had several hours before the briefing to get in some training with Tiago. They weren't alone in the training room either. Amber had followed Asha's instructions to get into fighting form by that night, and Grim was sparring with her in the boxing ring.

Once five-thirty p.m. had ticked over, the entire team met in the briefing room. Asha had kept the briefing short, though there wasn't much to say. The vials of yellow liquid that the team had found that night in the alleyway had turned out to be a concoction of heavily diluted, yet still potent, angel blood. This angel blood, mixed with who knows what, was about to be released into the public as a drug called aether. Asha expressed her concern about one of the drug's side effects, heightened suggestibility, and how that effect alone could increase occultist activity, which was no doubt the drug's intended purpose. However, as important as that was, the reason for going after the source of the aether had now shifted from that to finding the Ghost of Salem, who was tracking the angel blood as well.

After the briefing, the team made their way up into the street where they followed Asha across the road from the beach and then down an alleyway. The sun had sunk under the horizon by now, and clouds that threatened rain choked out the remaining light. Above the sanctuary, where the mansion had once sat as king over an immense property, was a commercial-industrial sector. Nearby stink from the refinery kept most beach-goers several kilometres either side of it, while the streets they were walking through were occupied by various small businesses, storage units and other low-profile buildings that didn't attract a lot of attention. Most of the sector's traffic was people coming to and from work, cutting through the neighbourhood to avoid more congested areas. Aiden wondered if it was for this reason they had rebuilt the mansion below or if the re-zoning of the area wasn't simply a lucky coincidence.

After just a few minutes of walking, the team arrived at an alleyway garage and took off down the road in one of the Order's black vans.

'The current owner of the casino is a mephisto demon, taking the name Yuenlyn Myn,' said Asha from the driver's seat. 'He's not a particularly strong mephisto as far as they go, but even the weaker ones shouldn't be underestimated. He's bound to have plenty of demons anchored to him for protection.'

'What's a mephisto exactly?' Aiden asked.

'Remind me to loan you my copy of *A Pocket Guide to Demonology*,' joked Tiago.

Asha scoffed. 'That book is full of crap.'

Tiago shrugged. 'It's *mostly* right,' he said, before turning back to Aiden. 'T'put it simply, mephistos are deal-making demons. They have some control over mortal souls and like to collect them.'

'I heard they eat them,' Grim sneered.

'That's dumb. How d'you go about eating a soul?' Tiago slung back.

'Fuckin' demons, man. I dunno.' Grim shrugged.

174

'So an occultist summoned this guy?' Aiden asked.

'Occultists playing around with crap they shouldn't is one of the most common ways demons get to our world. Another, much rarer case, is that some stronger demons can sort of, uhh...' Tiago thought for a few seconds trying to figure out the right word to use. Aiden had the feeling he was trying to dumb it all down for him.

Amber cut in. 'Some demons are drawn to Earth by sin,' she said. 'They come here by themselves. The weaker demons have to possess a human to do this in order to stay, while stronger demons manifest on earth all by themselves, using the extra power they get by being closer to the centre of hell, where the primordial darkness is said to be locked away. They can take on a weaker human version of themselves. This mephisto is one of the latter.'

'If they can do that, then why would they not just all do it all at once and invade us?' Aiden asked.

'They have invaded us; humans are just too stupid to know it,' Grim huffed.

'They have not,' Asha snapped.

'With all the crap that goes on because of them, they may as well have,' he retorted. 'They want to destroy any light they can get their claws into, and I say they're doing a pretty good job at it.'

'Which is why it's our job to protect it by protecting humanity,' Asha growled back at him.

'Besides, demons are not foolish as a whole,' Amber added. 'Usually sheer force isn't their strategy because angels would have the advantage in a straight-up fight. They like to infiltrate and corrupt the population from the inside like the disease they are.'

'And when it is?' Aiden asked.

The air in the vehicle seemed to darken at that. 'Sometimes, when a particularly strong demon gets through, they can open what we call an anchorage, which is essentially a portal demons can come through. Even a small anchorage can support hundreds of demons at a time.'

'Only seen one while I've been a warden,' Grim said. 'It was just strong enough to reach the second circle of hell. A lot of imps, harpies and inmai to kill. They were easy enough, but the succubi were harder to hunt down, so even that was a nightmare to clean up.'

After that, there were a few minutes of silence before they parked the car in front of the Golden Rundus. They all wore the same plain black shirt, except for Tiago, who wore a black button t-shirt that had thin grey lines running down the front and back, and no coat. Aiden, however, had finally been given his own coat by Asha after the briefing. It was thick and had a dozen pockets inside, but was far lighter than he had imagined it would be.

Each of them carried their respective weapons hidden away within the folds of their blacks. Even Aiden had managed to hide away his sword on his back, with Asha's help.

'Demon at the door,' Amber pointed out as they walked with purpose towards the front of the casino. Standing by the door was a large man with a stern look. He looked like a normal human at first, but as they got closer, Aiden felt uneasy when he looked at the demon. It was like looking at a living wax statue that was perfectly passable as a human being in every way, but something about it was wrong.

'Amber,' Asha said as they came up to the entrance to the casino.

The bouncer moved to speak, but Amber had already lunged forward and slashed her dagger across the demon's throat. The bouncer's eyes shifted from brown to an ember orange, and it snarled. Amber struck out with the dagger again, but this time she drove it into the side of the bouncer's head. The demon continued to growl a moment longer before it died, its body withering in upon itself until it was almost skeletal.

'Mimics,' Asha said, 'Probably more inside. Don't let them latch.'

'Before we do this, should we come up with a safeword?' Tiago questioned, barely containing a smirk.

Asha rolled her eyes but then said, 'Mary.'

Tiago and Grim nodded.

'Safeword?' Amber asked.

Asha's eyes widened ever so slightly at Amber. 'A codeword. Didn't your old team ever encounter mimics?' Asha asked.

'It's so if they latch on to your brain and suck out your face to wear, we know who's who,' Tiago explained.

'We never thought about using a codeword,' Amber shrugged. 'I guess my loch figured it was obvious.'

'S'pose you can never be too careful,' Tiago said. Asha just glared at her.

'Amber and Aiden, go around the back way,' Asha ordered. 'See if you can find a way in back there and find where they're hiding the aether.'

***

Amber and Aiden did as ordered and made their way around the side of the building. Running the length of the casino's side was a large red brick wall, which looked as if it went all the way around the building; however, it wasn't long before a chain-link fence barred their way. Without a word, Amber struck it with her axe, which sheared a perfect cut through it. She sliced at it again and a section fell away, allowing them easy access through. Soon they found a way into the casino through a back door that led into an employee breakroom.

'Where do you suppose the aether would be?' Aiden asked.

'I'm not sure,' she replied. 'Considering it's human blood based, I'd assume the demons would prefer to store it somewhere cool.'

Aiden walked over to a fridge and opened both of its doors. Empty. Amber laughed. It wasn't a mocking laugh, but rather a delicate gentle laugh. 'Gotta check everything,' Aiden said as he shrugged.

***

Asha led Grim and Tiago into the casino. The various machines continued to make obnoxious sounds, but the casino was void of the usual drunken patrons that, on any other night, would later fill the seats.

'Well this is ominous,' Tiago exclaimed with frivolity in his tone.

The group eased forward, spreading out with caution, each scanning the inside of the building. The main area of the casino was just one giant room, mostly filled with slot machines and other games of chance with card game tables on either side of a large walkway that went down the centre of the room. Along the left were a variety of small outlets that would serve food—if there were anyone to serve food to. In three evenly spaced spots among the outlets were staircases giving access to the second storey, which ran the length of the left side as one long balcony, giving those that dined above a view of the entire casino floor.

As they approached the centre of the casino pit, Asha noticed movement in her peripheral vision to the left. She snapped her head around and saw two large men, identical to each other and the one they had killed on the way in. They each stood on either side of a well-dressed Asian man.

'Welcome, wardens. Hmm, I was told there'd be five of you.' Asha allowed herself a feeling of slight relief upon realising Amber and Aiden were as yet undetected. 'All the better,' he grinned. 'Kill them.'

The two mimic bodyguards leaped down the stairs in a single jump, landing in a sprint towards Asha. Asha heard Tiago and

Grim fire their weapons behind them and knew they were suddenly beset on all sides by demons.

Asha swung her sword into the air and an almost-solid shimmer cut through the space between her and the demons. As it neared the demons, the shimmer burst outwards in an explosion of ice that encased the demons' legs. Following the momentum of the attack, Asha swung the other way, this time aiming to make contact, blade to flesh.

As the demon's feet were rendered immobile by the ice, it held up hands to block the blow. Asha felt the blade bite, but the demon had transformed its fingers to twice their length, now gnarled and bony. The demon grinned as Asha's sword became trapped within its grasp. She twisted the blade and pulled, slicing the demon's fingers off. It howled in pain, but seconds later the fingers started to regrow. She darted forward for another attack, and the demon brought its still-regenerating hands up to block again, but Asha severed the demon's arm this time. When the demon roared and swiped at her with its remaining limb, she stepped back, dodged and countered, removing its head.

At that moment, the second mimic broke free of the ice surrounding its feet. It rushed forward, but she lowered her sword to her side and rammed her free hand into the demon's face. A flash of blue ran down the length of her arm like a light travelling under ice. In just a few quick movements, Asha froze and then shattered the mimic's head.

Asha looked behind her. Tiago was taking cover behind a slot machine, covering Grim who had swapped out his rifle for a large combat knife and was slashing at the demons. The mimics' regenerative abilities undid a lot of Grim's attacks, but between the two of them, they were dealing with the mimics easily enough.

Asha turned back around to face Yuenlyn, who had descended the staircase. His demons were losing, yet if it worried him he didn't show it. Rather, he moved closer to her, wearing a friendly smile as if approaching a friend spotted at a party. He was without a weapon that Asha could see, but suddenly there was a quick flash of light and half-a-dozen translucent orange blades appeared, hanging in an arc above him and glowing like hot embers. Yuenlyn's hands twitched, and the blades darted through the air straight towards Asha. The first couple she could shatter with quick sword strokes, but as he continued to summon and fire more and more at her, they forced her to dodge more than she could slice out of the air. As she dodged each of the flying blades, she stepped forward to try to close the distance, but he moved back just as quickly, skilfully able to keep her at an equal distance.

Asha drew upon the power of her rune again. An icy blue light ran down her arm, stopping at her left hand. The light seemed to solidify, turning her entire hand blue, and although a layer of frost formed around her hand, she felt no chill on her skin. As she swatted another blade, she flicked out her left hand, and from it something leaped out and arched through the air towards the mephisto. It looked like a ball of blue fire the size of a football, but rather than the tongues of flame for a tail, a snowy substance created a trail as it sailed through the air towards its target.

Yuenlyn summoned several blades, which rather than use as projectiles, he brought together to block the blast of the frozen fire. While the mephisto stopped his attack for a second, it gave Asha the break she needed to close the distance between her and the mephisto. Yuenlyn was quicker than Asha had predicted though, and as she swung, he recuperated just in time to block with one of his floating blades. As he did, he instinctively brought up his arm, as if to enforce the block. It was then Asha noticed the item around Yuenlyn's arm. A black leather band with an orange sphere not much bigger than a marble affixed to it.

'Filthy demon!' she growled through gritted teeth as she pushed against the floating blade. 'That does not belong to you!'

'So people keep saying,' he remarked, his overconfident grin withholding.

He summoned another blade and thrust it through the air towards her, which forced her to disengage and jump back to avoid it. It shattered against the ground. A bolt of pain lanced up Asha's arm as one of the shattered pieces embedded into her arm before dissolving, letting her blood flow freely. Willing herself to ignore the pain, she made ready for another onslaught of Yuenlyn's attacks. But as she looked up from her arm, she saw Tiago and Grim, having finished off their attackers, running over to her. As Tiago fired a few shots at the mephisto, he ducked for cover behind a poker table. Grim and Tiago reached Asha, and the demon took off, sprinting between several rows of slot machines for cover as Tiago fired after him.

Asha placed her left hand over the wound on her right forearm and gnashed her teeth in pain as she placed a layer of frost over it. It stung and sent a bitter chill through her arm, but it would keep it from distracting her long enough to stop bleeding on its own. The potential frostbite would be a problem for later.

'Grim, don't worry about me,' she shouted. 'Go after him!' She pointed towards Yuenlyn just as he disappeared behind a door at the back of the casino. 'Tiago, with me. We'll head him off from the front.'

Asha and Tiago made their way to the door but before they could make it outside, the door exploded inwards with a blast of green flame.

***

A chill made its way through Aiden as he looked at the hundreds of yellow vials along the shelves inside the walk-in fridge they had found inside the casino's kitchen area. Naturally it had been held shut with a padlock, but Amber could break the lock as easily as she had cut the fence outside. Aiden estimated over two-hundred vials, and who knew how many doses each vial contained.

They pulled down the aluminium shelving units, sending several dozen vials shattering to the ground at a time and coating the fridge's floor as if it were a slaughter room. The blood pooled together as it trickled towards the drains. Satisfied, they left the fridge, closing the large door behind them. As it thumped shut, the door to the kitchen burst open. An Asian man in a suit, followed by one of the large mimic demons, ran into the kitchen. They stopped in surprise as they saw the two wardens.

'Demon!' Amber shouted at the man. 'You take the mimic. I'll deal with the mephisto.'

Before anything else could happen, an explosion from the main casino floor surged through the kitchen. The mephisto flashed a wide grin like a child who had just won a game, then the two demons rushed them. Amber darted ahead, knocking the mephisto to the ground while the mimic charged at Aiden. He steeled himself and raised his sword. The demon slashed at the blade, knocking it to the side. Aiden almost lost his grasp, which would have ended the fight straight away. He recovered and responded by swinging his sword back, taking aim at the demon's stomach. His clumsy attack missed, and the demon swiped again in response; this time, however, with more luck than grace, Aiden sidestepped the attack and managed to stab his attacker.

The blade pierced the demon's stomach with surprising ease, and the moment Aiden realised that he had in fact made contact, he stepped in and forced the blade further in, causing it to erupt out from the creature's back. It swore and snarled, but it did not die. Instead, the demon struck out again, clawing at Aiden's face with hands that had grown in length and become almost like talons. The demon's attack landed, slicing his left cheek. He could feel the warmth of his blood as it ran down the side of his face.

Aiden's fear, more than his fortitude, ensured a tight grip on his sword as the demon thrashed about to free the blade from its stomach. Before he knew what he was doing, Aiden had pulled the sword out and swung. The blade sliced the demon's throat open. He hadn't actually meant to hit anything particular; he had just hoped to make contact. It snarled and hissed once more as its body shrunk like a tomato rapidly drying out in the sun, going a dark green colour as it did. He looked over to Amber.

'Stay back,' she called out to him. 'I've got this one.'

The mephisto sneered with derision, but Amber easily blocked or dodged each of his attacks. Her fighting style was a bold contrast to Asha's. She fought like Asha had told Aiden not to. Amber left many opportunities unclaimed as she continued to dodge and block with not just ease, but graceful fluidity. The more vicious and frustrated the mephisto got with his attacks, the easier it seemed to become for her. It was only when he grabbed one of his summoned blades in each hand and lashed out in an overly aggressive attack that she sidestepped and countered with a deep blow to Yuenlyn's chest, embedding the axe's blade almost to the shaft, killing the demon without another sound.

'That's that then.' Aiden's breath was heavy. He steadied himself on a nearby prep-table.

'I wouldn't bet on it,' Amber said, looking around concerned, as if she was expecting another attack. 'We just put an end to what must have been an enormous endeavour as if it were an evening patrol.'

'Remind me not to go on evening patrols,' Aiden said, catching his breath. He held a hand up to the scratch on his face. It stung, but the bleeding had stopped.

'I am using hyperbole, of course,' she said. She bent over the mephisto's body and took off its black band, which held an orange rune, pocketing it inside her coat. 'We had reason to believe they were getting ready for city-wide distribution. Yet there were not nearly enough vials of aether inside the fridge for that.'

'We haven't seen the Ghost either,' Aiden added. 'Maybe it was a trap for him.'

'If so, we just walked into it,' she remarked.

***

The blast must have knocked Asha unconscious because the next thing she knew her eyes snapped open and she was now looking up from the ground several metres away from what remained of the door. Tiago helped her to her feet, and they both retreated towards Grim, who had run back to help, abandoning his pursuit of the mephisto. Asha made a mental note to scold him later as the blur cleared from her eyes.

'When will you humans learn?' The voice that spoke was course and seemed to echo within itself. 'You fight that which you don't even understand and struggle against forces you couldn't possibly defeat.'

The fury that rose through Asha drowned out most of what the demon had said, instead all she saw was red as she shouted, 'Eligos!' and charged him.

The demon knocked her aside with a swipe of a clawed hand, sending her flying several metres away. 'Vermin,' it rumbled.

Tiago rushed to Asha's side. The demon watched with a vague disinterest as Tiago once again helped her up.

Eligos stepped further into the room, his dark purple wings unfurling as his pitch black eyes looked over the group. The deep purple-skinned demon stood nearing seven feet tall and had scars that marked its skin in the form of demonic glyphs. It wore clothing not too different from what the Order's paladins wore, only much more minimalistic with only a few pieces of leather armour over its shoulders and midsection, leaving most of its chest exposed.

There was an almighty *crack* as Grim fired his rifle at the demon now walking towards them. Three rounds cut through the air, striking the demon in its chest. It staggered back only slightly before continuing forward. Eligos snarled and swiped at the air in front of him in an upwards motion. A sudden wave of green spectral energy surged towards Grim, slamming into him and knocking him through the air. He landed hard on one of the sets of stairs nearby. Eligos turned to Asha and sniffed the air, looking thoughtful. 'I smell that you have new blood for me to spill,' he declared. 'The last ones were no fun; they died far too easily.'

'Asha, we need to leave.' Tiago's voice was as serious as it ever got.

'No,' she snapped. 'This time he dies.' With that she got to her feet for another charge. Eligos let loose another wave of green energy through the air. Asha ducked under it as she ran and slashed at Eligos with her blade. Dark red blood spilled from the cambion's wound. Eligos grunted in pain as he sidestepped another attack from Asha and grabbed her by the throat, lifting her off her feet. As he held her in the air with one hand, he grabbed her wrist with the other in an attempt to wrestle her weapon away from her. She struggled, and heard more shots ring out. Not the high calibre of Grim's rifle, but Tiago's handgun with its rune-powered rounds, which impacted with almost as much force. Force enough at least to cause Eligos to recoil and drop Asha.

Suddenly Grim was by her side. With his rifle discarded, he attacked with his combat knife. Eligos retaliated and swiped a claw at Grim, who jumped back. As he did, Asha stepped in to attack in his place. They kept it up only for a short time with Tiago firing anytime in between, but suddenly Eligos snapped back his wings and with a frustrated roar brought them forward with great force. The force of the gust from the wings sent Asha and Grim flailing backwards.

By the time they made it to their feet again, Eligos was hovering in the air. The wounds on Eligos' chest and arms had already stopped bleeding.

'Asha, we need to go,' Tiago urged again, with more insistence than before. 'We can't beat him.'

'It's too late for you,' Eligos smirked, now grinning down at them. 'Even if you killed me, all you love will be dust before you can get to safety. As I speak, my demons are fighting over the meat left on the bones of your fellow wardens inside of your so-called sanctuary.'

'He's lying,' Asha said. 'He's trying to get to us so we'll do something stupid. Don't listen.'

Eligos just laughed and then lunged at them, a spectral sword materialising in his hand as he closed the distance. Grim moved in front of Asha but was knocked aside as Eligos passed them through the air, while Tiago was kicked backwards as the demon landed. Asha looked over at Grim, who laid unmoving on the floor several metres away. Eligos then swung at Asha, but she managed to block with her own weapon.

Instead of a follow up attack with his weapon, his free hand shot out and closed around her throat again. She managed to swing her sword and embed it into his side, but he did not let go although he hissed in pain. This time it was clear he did not intend to let her escape. His clawed hand squeezed, and she felt the pressure of breathlessness build in her chest as her heart thumped away. She had let go of her sword, its blade still embedded in the demon's side, and helplessly tried to pry Eligos' hand away from her throat. Just enough to reopen her windpipe. Enough for one more breath. Instead she felt more pressure. She didn't feel the claws pierce her neck, but she felt the warmth of her blood as it ran down the curves of her shoulder and chest, wetting her clothes. Suddenly she fell to the ground when he tossed her aside with a howl of agony.

Asha tried to look up at what had happened, but as much as she tried, her eyes refused to focus. She also didn't believe what they were showing her. Eligos now had a new wound across his stomach, and Aiden had replaced her in the demon's grasp. Eligos face twisted in disgust as he leaned inward and inhaled deeply through his nose. The look of disgust twisted into that of irritation as he threw Aiden aside. Asha's vision blackened for what must have been longer than the second it had been for her. When she opened her eyes again, Eligos was engaged by another.

Amber had joined the fight. Asha struggled to her feet as Amber fought with the cambion. She stumbled over to Tiago and shook him. He didn't respond but Asha could see he was breathing.

'What do we do?' Aiden asked. His eyes screamed panic, but with a small flare of pride through her pain, she noticed he still held his sword ready.

'Stay with Tiago and keep him safe,' she turned to look around the casino floor and then back to Aiden. 'Have you seen Grim?'

Aiden shook his head, and Asha swore. 'Stay with him,' she ordered again.

Asha collected her sword from the ground and ran over to help Amber. As she did, Eligos stretched his wings and shot backwards through the air. Amber stood her ground as Asha took up a position next to her.

Amber gave Asha a subtle nod with a look in her eye that told Asha they were both thinking the same thing: he dies or they do.

Eligos hung a foot off the ground and eyed them with fury from afar. 'You won't be the first little team of wardens I've wiped out,' he snarled. Asha saw his wings twitch as if about to charge for another attack, but before he could, he was forced back to the ground. He roared in pain, but it took a few seconds before Asha could figure out why.

Grim had leapt from the balcony. As he dissolved his invisibility, Asha could see him hanging from Eligos' back from his combat knife as if it were a climbing pick.

Eligos thrashed around and managed to dislodge Grim, and Amber immediately took the advantage. She rushed forward and buried her axe into Eligos' abdomen, dodged a counter, then brought back her axe and swung it to hit a second time, which brought the demon to its knees.

'Perhaps I won't be your end, wardens,' Eligos chortled through gritted teeth. 'But the time of the angels is over, and I have already earned my place in the world that will rise after he burns this one to the ground. A *novos orvis*.'

Amber stepped forward and swung the axe at the cambion's chest. Eligos spat blood as he shouted out in pain. 'You are nothing more than fodder, light-slaves,' he hissed through bloodied teeth before crumpling down to the ground, finally dead. Amber stood over Eligos' body, staring at it as she caught her breath, waiting to extinguish any more signs of life.

'Well, that was rather sinister.' Tiago had come over rubbing the back of his head with a pained look on his face, Aiden in tow. 'What do you suppose that was about?'

'It doesn't matter. We need to get back to the sanctuary,' Asha said. 'Now.'

Chapter Fourteen
If it bleeds like a duck

iden slammed the car door shut and half-ran, half-jogged to keep up with the others who were rushing back to the sanctuary.

'There's no sign of an anchorage,' shouted Tiago as they ran. 'There's no way demons could have the bulk to carry out a full scale attack on us.'

'By all means, stay behind then,' Asha shouted back at him. 'Otherwise, shut the hell up.'

Asha reached the limestone retaining wall that ran alongside the sand of the beach. She stopped suddenly to look out across the beach towards the sanctuary entrance. Aiden, along with others, stopped beside her and looked out onto the beach, half expecting to see a battle taking place. It was calm.

'The demon lied,' Tiago chuckled. 'Who would'a thought it?'

Aiden saw Asha give him a stern look.

'Asha!' someone was shouting. It was a woman's voice familiar to Aiden. The woman ran up to them trying to speak through laboured breaths.

'Catch your breath,' Amber advised. 'Then speak.'

'No time,' the woman said, getting close enough that Aiden could recognise her. It was Kallista. 'Demons. In the sanctuary,' she said, still panting.

'But how?' Tiago asked, his eyes wide.

'What kind of demons?' Asha demanded at the same time as Tiago.

'My brother is still in there!' Kallista eyes were welling up with tears, and a fresh cut painted the side of her face with a dark red streak coming from the side of her head.

'Calm down, Kalli.' Amber spoke softly and placed a hand on Kallista's shoulder. 'We need to know what you do.'

Kallista took a few quick, deep breaths before answering. 'I was with my team in our briefing room. Getting ready to go on a patrol,' she said, wiping tears from her eyes. 'All of a sudden we could hear gunfire and fighting coming from the lobby. We rushed out to see what was going on, and demons were charging inside, led by some kind of winged demon I've never seen before.

'We cut down the demons that rushed us, but the one that led them healed faster than we could cut it, even with blessed blades.'

'Maybe it was an angel,' Grim offered.

'Why would an angel help demons?' Aiden asked.

'Dunno,' he said. 'Wouldn't surprise me though.'

'It wasn't an angel!' Kallista's voice filled with a sudden anger. 'Cursed weapons were not hurting it either. Gerard went down, and my brother called for us to retreat into the sanctuary. We were going to hold out in our briefing room, but before we could get there another of those winged demons came through the front door. It was then when I got separated from the rest of the team and fought my way out.'

'If they came through the front door, that means they figured out a way to break through the seal on the gate,' Grim said. 'It also means the cave will be crawling with demons.'

'I'm guessing the whole place is crawling with demons by now,' Tiago deduced. 'Not just the cave.'

'We should take the back entrance,' Grim recommended.

'There's a back entrance?' Aiden asked incredulously. 'How do we know they didn't get in that way?'

'It's where I escaped from,' Kallista said, much calmer now. 'It's a maintenance tunnel left over from the old sewer system. Leads out into the back cavern near the gun range.'

'Let's get moving,' Asha ordered. 'We need to get in there and help whoever is left.'

'No arguments here,' Grim agreed. 'Can't wait to put down those demon arseholes.'

'I'm so glad,' Asha said sarcastically. 'Let's get in there and search for survivors.'

'Survivors?' Grim blurted out. 'You talk like we've already lost. Let's get in there and kick these sons of bitches out!'

'We will kill as many as we can, Grim,' Asha said. 'But we need to focus on helping our friends.'

'Obviously,' Grim spat out. 'And the best way to do that is to kill everything that's not them.'

'Enough!' Asha growled. 'We're wasting time. Let's go.'

'I don't suppose you can pray to the angels for help?' he asked darkly, looking at Kallista before sprinting into the street.

The rest of them followed, and a few moments later they were in a small alleyway. Grim was at the end of the alley as a section of the far wall slid open with a rumble.

'Kalli and Aiden, you're with me,' Asha instructed. 'We will search the south wing for Tarek. The rest of you take the north wing and find Sorterra and his team.'

'We'll go in first and make sure it's safe in the tunnel,' Amber said.

'Okay. Go,' Asha prompted with a nod.

Aiden watched the three disappear one at a time into the maintenance hatch that was in a compartment inside the wall. Asha gestured for Kallista to follow, but as she ducked into the compartment, an ear-piercing screech cut through the air.

Aiden heard Asha curse. He turned but at first couldn't see anything except the walls of the alleyway and the street beyond. As another screech pierced the air, two red blurs sped past the alleyway.

'Above!' Asha launched half-a-dozen balls of frozen fire, striking one of the four red figures diving upon them. A blue ball of frost struck one of the red figure's wings, freezing half of it. The demon spiralled out of control, its wing shattering against the building wall, sending a hail of frozen red feathers over the alleyway. What was left of the creature was sent screaming into the ground in front of Aiden, who finished it with a stab through the heart.

Aiden heard another screech above him and suddenly a harpy was bearing down on him with talons extended. The demon's claws grasped Aiden's shoulders, puncturing the skin and forcing him to the ground. It let out a shriek and for a moment all sound seemed to leave the world, before rushing back in the form of a persistent ringing. The demon's mouth opened, showing teeth that looked even sharper than its talons. As it was about to strike, a flash of light slammed into the demon's chest, sending it flailing off of him in a scream of pain. There was another bolt of light that flew past Aiden and struck its chest, finishing it.

Aiden looked over to see where the bolt had come from. It was Kallista, holding a bow made of light. She fired another projectile that looked like it had materialised from nowhere. It cut through the air, lightning crackling around it.

Aiden took out his sword, just as another one of the flying creatures lunged for him. He instinctively brought his sword up and the creature impaled itself on his blade. The sudden dead weight of the creature pulled down on the sword, but Aiden was able to pull out the blade as it hit the ground.

More of these creatures came flooding into the alleyway. At least a dozen of them came screeching and clawing at the three wardens. Red feathers flew around the alley as the harpies were slain with blade, bow and frozen fire. But still more came.

'Get into the hatch!' Asha was barely audible over the sound of the demons.

Kallista and Aiden rushed to do as ordered. Aiden lifted the hatch, and Kallista hurried down the ladder to the tunnel below. Once she was down, Aiden followed, and once he was inside the tunnel, he looked up towards the hatch anxiously waiting to see Asha follow.

Above the horrid screeching of the demons, Aiden could hear Asha yell something and then shout out in pain. Then she was suddenly falling down into the tunnel, one of the flying demons tangled up around her.

Kallista jumped up onto the ladder to close the hatch as Aiden dived towards Asha, slamming himself into the demon, knocking it off of her. Asha got to her feet and sliced the demon's head clean off. 'Fucking harpies,' Asha snarled. She looked at Aiden. 'Thanks.'

Aiden suppressed a smile of pride. An easy task considering Asha's next words, 'Next time just use the damn sword though,' she said.

Asha led them down the pipe-shaped tunnel, which was blocked off in the other direction. The tunnel itself had long since dried up, but the pungent smell of sewerage yet lingered, though they did not have to put up with it for too long as the tunnel opened up via a hole in the side, leading to a large cave. From here Aiden could see the entire backside of the mansion, including the greenhouse, which had been converted into a shooting range. All around the cavern were the dead bodies of small demons Aiden had never seen before, killed by the others who went in ahead.

'Be ready, you two,' Asha warned. They slowed their pace as they entered the mansion. The door entered into a small room that was an intersection for the ground floor's three hallways. Directly ahead of them would lead them to the lobby, which they definitely wanted to avoid. To their right was the hallway the others would have gone down to find Kalli's team. Asha led them to the left.

***

So far, besides a few imps in the greenhouse cave, the journey into the sanctuary had been uneventful for the other half of the team. There were bodies everywhere inside, but Tiago figured it was good to see that most of the bodies were demons, but even one dead warden *inside* the sanctuary was too many. Judging by the amount of dead demons, there couldn't be too many demons left. Without an anchorage event, this many in one place was abnormal. Whatever *was* anchoring them here was powerful, and Tiago didn't feel as keen to meet whatever it was as Grim did.

Tiago led Amber and Grim through the northern halls of the sanctuary towards Sorterra's briefing room, a room he shared with a loch called Jason. Tiago wasn't a big fan of Jason, but he hoped he had the sense to hole up there too. The more wardens they could find the better, especially if they had to fight their way back out.

Tiago clasped the handle and pushed open the door to the briefing room. A blur of motion welcomed him to his right, sending him to the ground. Before he hit the ground, his pistol was out and aimed up at his attacker, but no follow-up attack came.

'Aw, hell,' said his attacker. 'As if the demons weren't bad enough, now I gotta deal with you too?' The man gestured towards the door as Amber and Grim came in, closing the door behind them and stepping over Tiago. 'Can't you just send in more demons instead?'

'Sooty!' Tiago said with a broad smile as he got to his feet, smoothing his clothes. He patted the man on the shoulder. 'Good to see you're keeping your reflexes sharp.'

'How many times, Tiago?' Sorterra groaned, knocking his hand away. 'It's Sorterra.' Sorterra was Kallista's brother, a fact that refused to be forgotten by the striking family resemblance they held. They were twins and shared the same emerald green eyes, the same dark hair and the same sharp nose. There were some obvious differences, such as Sorterra had a much wider frame and a groomed stubble, which he always seemed to have, and he kept his hair short and tidy.

Sorterra was not alone, which sparked hope. Standing around the briefing table were five other wardens all dressed in their blacks. One of them was wearing the usual dark coat of the wardens, but stood out from the rest as he was wearing black leather pauldrons that covered his shoulders. He was short and seemed to wear a permanent scowl on his face, which only intensified as he stood up and spoke.

'What's the situation out there?' he blurted.

'You mean to tell me you've just been hiding in here?' Grim demanded of the man, raising his voice. 'Forgotten how to swing a sword, Mason?' Grim's voice dripped with venom and spoke the man's name as though it carried the risk of disease just to speak it. Tiago had seen Grim be impetuous plenty of times before, especially towards Mason, but never so badly.

'How dare you!' The short man's face twisted in anger. 'I am still the high warden here,' he hissed through gritted teeth.

'Yeah, well, write me up after all this is done if you're still alive,' Grim retorted.

The two men glared at each other for a few long seconds before Terra interrupted the staring contest. 'You guys came from outside, right?' he asked. 'Is my sister okay? Is Kalli safe?'

'She's with Asha,' Amber reassured, which seemed to put him at ease a little.

'Good.' Terra nodded deeply as a thankful gesture. 'Now, what's going on out there?'

'We cut down a few demons in the caves, but it was eerily quiet otherwise,' said Tiago. 'What happened?'

'We were in here getting ready for a patrol in the northern suburbs,' Sorterra explained. 'We rushed out to the lobby when we heard fighting. Then this pale winged demon waltzed in and started cutting wardens down. Gerard was the first to fall, so I ordered a retreat to here. Kalli got separated.

'We ran into High Warden Mason, who was fighting just outside. We had hoped others would rally here but none have besides you guys. Now we just need an opportunity to get out, which seems like now if everything is as calm as you say it is. Though I really don't want to run into those white demons again.'

'Is it true that neither cursed nor blessed blades hurt them?' asked Amber.

Sorterra shook his head. 'Not exactly. Normal weapons did nothing at all, but cursed and blessed weapons broke the skin, but not to the same effect they should have. They still healed too quickly.'

'Wait.' Tiago paused in thought. 'Cursed *and* blessed blades had the same effect? But wouldn't that imply...'

'Hybrids?' Grim suggested, halfway between shocked and disgusted, his eyes wide with disbelief.

'Impossible,' Amber declared with such conviction it was as if nothing in the world could argue against her. 'I've never heard of an angel procreating, let alone with a demon.'

'I'm sure the angels do plenty of things we're not aware of,' Grim said, returning to his glib demeanour. This idea of angels consorting with demons would only further darken his opinion of them.

'Well, if it bleeds like a duck...' Tiago said.

'Enough of this.' The high warden got to his feet. 'I am still the high warden, and I say we need to get out of here.'

'We need to drive these demons out of our home!' Grim had taken a step towards the high warden and was now looking down at him.

'How do you propose we do that?' Mason snapped, looking up at Grim with equal ferocity. 'This white demon is unstoppable, and who knows how many there are. We can't take the sanctuary back by just charging at them.'

'If they bleed, we can kill them,' Grim argued. 'We can't just leave everyone else here to die; we have to try.'

There was silence as everyone considered the situation. Amber was the one to break the silence. 'I agree with Grim,' she said. This seemed to surprise Grim, who smiled. It was a smug smile, but a smile nonetheless.

'Well, when do I ever go against the current?' Tiago said with the grin of a child who was about to do something they shouldn't.

'Always?' Sorterra offered before letting out a long breath of exasperation. 'I'm sorry, sir, but so long as Kalli is in here, I'm not leaving.'

High Warden Mason huffed. He was a rude and arrogant man, but for all his talk he wasn't particularly brave, and without the high paladin to back him up he wouldn't dare try to assert his authority over them. 'Fine,' he relented. 'If death is your choice, I won't stop you, but I won't feel guilty about not deciding to throw myself onto a demon's sword.'

'You'd need a conscience to feel guilt,' Grim hissed as the high warden pushed his way past them towards the door with two other wardens in tow.

The two wardens that were left stepped forward, a woman and a man, the latter of whom gave a simple wordless nod. He looked to be in his fifties, his black hair was speckled with grey, which contrasted with his dark skin.

'Thank you, William,' Sorterra said.

The second warden was a woman who kept her hood up covering her hair but not the clearly visible scar running straight down from under her left eye, just missing the corner of her mouth, all the way down to her jaw line. 'Gerard wouldn't have wanted us to skitter away like that coward,' she said.

'You're right, Jessica, but we need to be careful,' Sorterra said, looking to Tiago. 'What's the plan?'

Tiago let out a short laugh. 'Plan? Our *plan* was to find survivors, and we found you. That was really the extent of our orders.'

'God forbid you think for yourself,' Sorterra said as he rolled his eyes.

'Asha went to the north wing, so we sh—' Amber stopped talking suddenly at the sound of movement outside of the room.

Silence fell, and each warden's gaze rested upon the door. Tiago un-holstered his handgun as slowly as he could. Sorterra and the others followed his example, each brandishing their own weapons. Grim's weapon had been destroyed in his last fight, but he had found a replacement on the weapon rack at the far end of the room. It wasn't quite as large the rifle as he usually had, but it was still somewhat improved by the blade that was attached to its barrel. He pointed it at the door, along with the intense concentration of six wardens.

Suddenly there was a loud crunch. The door splintered and broke inward as a demon burst through it. The demon stood the height of an average human, and its dark grey skin was riddled with bone-white spikes with two larger spikes, which looked more like horns, protruding from the top of its head and curving back and down to its neck. The creature's red eyes darted around the room to each of the wardens, clearly surprised by how many it had found. Each of them moved to attack the demon, but Grim had already placed a bullet into its skull before anyone else could respond.

As the demon hit the floor, Grim cursed. 'So much for stealth.'

'I have no doubt more demons heard that,' Amber cautioned. 'So now is probably the best time to get out of here before more inmai show up.'

The rest of the group murmured a shared agreement and one by one they entered the hallway where their fears became a reality. They were beset on either side by four inmai demons.

Amber and Terra faced the four on one side, while William and Jessica took up a position facing the other four. Grim and Tiago took their places behind them with their firearms levelled. The demons, however, held no such mind for any sort of strategy, pushing each other to claw viciously at the wardens, who did their best to cut the creatures down while avoiding their blood-stained claws.

The warden's blades cut to bone, but the demons refused to go down. Even as their dark red blood covered the floor and soaked into the carpet, they swiped and roared in defiance. Eventually the demons fell, leaving the wardens with laboured breaths and bloodied blades. But before anyone could speak, there was movement at the end of the hallway that halted any thought of recuperation.

At the end of the hallway stood another inmai. Just like the ones they had killed, it was covered with white thorns and had horns protruding from the top of its head. This inmai was larger in every aspect, however, and its grey skin was so dark it was almost black. It was a greater inmai, a leader of the lesser variant. It stood an entire foot taller than the other demons and held level a spear that was a few inches taller than even that. It walked towards them with casual confidence.

'Quick,' Terra shouted. 'We can't fight that here. This way!' Sorterra led them down the hallway just as the demon ran at them. They sprinted through the hallway until it opened up into the sanctuary lobby. The demon was right behind them, but now at least they were spread out and wouldn't be turned into a shish kebab with a single thrust of the demon's spear. It didn't stop the beast from trying anyway, and it attacked the nearest warden, which was

Grim. With no weapon on hand that could deflect it, Amber jumped forward to save him, swatting the spear to the side with her axe.

The failed attack didn't deter the demon, and it was already attacking again, this time at Amber who jumped backwards to avoid the attack altogether. Tiago fired his handgun as quickly as it allowed, and as the inmai turned to face him, Amber lunged forward and swept low, burying one of the axe's blades in the creature's leg. She pulled it free to attack again. The demon swung the butt of the spear. She ducked, swung her axe and caught the pole of the spear in under the beard of her axe. She tugged hard, and the spear snapped. The demon hissed in frustration and slashed the side of Amber's face with the spear head. Tiago went to fire but took more time to aim with Amber so close. Before he got the shot off, Grim's rifle exploded, and a large calibre round penetrated the demon's neck. Amber was quick to turn back to face the demon and finish the job with a strike to the heart.

There was a brief moment of calm where the only sound was the wardens' heavy breathing, interrupted by the sounds of footsteps as a surge of the smaller inmai demons flooded the top balcony. The main horde forced their way down the stairs, and William, Jessica and Sorterra moved quickly and fought the flood of demons at the foot of the stairs. The others did their best to stem the overflow that leaped from the banisters.

They held them back for what seemed like forever. Tiago shot as many demons as he could, focusing on any that even looked like they thought jumping down was a good idea. Despite this, a few continued to get through, leaving Amber to deal with them, which she did with sharp efficiency, but they couldn't keep it up forever. To make it worse, another of the larger inmai demons had appeared on the top floor and was attacking Terra's team with its spear over the heads of the lesser demons.

Tiago shifted his focus to the horde on the stairs. They'd be soon overrun otherwise. Tiago watched Sorterra as he fired into the crowd of demons. He struck out with a flat palm and sent a bolt of electricity through a demon. As it died, its skin burned and crackled as the electricity surged through it, which arched out and electrocuted other nearby demons. The electricity that arched out was not enough to have the same effect, but it left the demons vulnerable so that William could get in and finish them. It seemed like it was enough to push them back, but Tiago noticed Terra clutching his side, his movements becoming sluggish.

Sorterra wasn't the only one who had taken a blow. Jessica had several claw-shaped lacerations on her arms and a tear in the clothes on her stomach. William had claw marks on his arm, and blood from a head wound covered most of his face. Things were quickly turning against them. Just when Tiago was sure there could be no more, two more groups, each led by another of the greater inmai, emerged from both the north and south hallways.

Tiago heard someone yell something. An order to move or to run, Tiago couldn't be sure which. The voice was drowned out by the sudden roar of flame that burst from the southern hallway, scattering the demons therein. As the flames dissipated, three armoured figures sliced their way through the demons with flashes of flame and steel. In the time it took for anyone to realise they were paladins, the demons in the southern hallway were destroyed. The sight of the paladins gave the others a breath of renewed vigour as they charged in, instantly pushing the horde of demons back up the stairs. Two more paladins entered the lobby and joined Amber as she engaged the demons coming from the north hallway, while Tiago and Grim took up positions next to each other and took shots where they felt they were needed most.

The paladins were amazing to watch. The protection of the armour they wore under their warden blacks allowed them to fight with more ferocity. Even as the demon's claws snatched at their throats, they barely flinched.

In under a minute of fire, blood and the clanging of steel harmonising with the demonic screams of the dying, it was all over. Asha and the others, along with the high paladin, emerged from the southern hallway as the paladins wiped the blood from their weapons and took up a position next to Tarek, all without saying a word.

'Terra!' Kallista was suddenly flying across the room and into her brother's arms. 'Thank God you're okay.'

'Yes, let's thank God…' Tiago muttered as he ran a finger over a gash on his arm.

'Kalli, what happened to you?' Sorterra was checking her for wounds like a worried father.

'I got outside and found Asha and the others,' she said.

'And you came back?' he asked incredulously, with a touch of worried anger in his voice.

'Of course I did!' she shouted. 'I wasn't leaving you here! Besides, there are harpies guarding the entrance.' Kallista turned to Tarek. 'I think they may be picking off wardens returning from assignments.'

'We will leave the same way you entered. Through the back caverns,' Tarek stated.

'Leave, sir?' Grim asked in disbelief. 'We can't leave yet!'

'Grim, I fought alongside the first two teams that fell right here in this lobby during the initial attack. We just lost the third team in the yellow mess, a team of paladins no less, fighting those two white cambion, and we still didn't kill them,' Tarek revealed. He was calm and firm, and Tiago couldn't help but admire him all the more. He was making a tough call—a decision with no right answer. 'We need to leave, regroup and retake the sanctuary later. If we can.'

'What about the other teams, sir?' Grim appealed.

'The remaining four teams were out on assignments,' he said. 'I've ordered the kathari to relay a message to them to get to the emergency sanctuary, which is where we are going.' With his last words, Tarek's voice carried a steel-like authority. Even Grim didn't seem to want to argue anymore. 'Well, I hope you've all got your harpy kickin' boots on,' Tiago remarked with a grin.

***

Aiden tried calming his nerves as Tarek led them through the centre corridor towards the back of the mansion and out into the cavern. He had done as Asha told him and stayed close to her in the previous battle and was thankful for it. They had entered the yellow mess and found Tarek holding off a horde of demons led by two cambion. They looked like the one from the casino, only their skin was pure white and they wouldn't die no matter what the paladins did. The paladin team that had been with them at the Salem Arena brought them time to escape, but paid with their lives. Aiden had come close to being struck down so many times by the inmai that fought alongside the cambion, so by now it was all he could do to keep his hands still. When they cut their way through the hallway and found the others, it was only a minor relief. He was glad they had made it, and the more wardens together the safer they would all be, but Aiden knew the white cambion wouldn't take long to catch up to them.

As they entered the cavern, Aiden almost ran into the back of Asha when the group halted. They had stopped and were looking around cautiously. Silence fell. For a moment it almost felt like they were home free. But the tension in the group told Aiden a different story.

Suddenly the silence shattered as a swarm of tiny demons came crawling out of the broken pipe and into the cavern. They rushed out in all directions like an army of angry ants, their claws digging into the walls as they climbed, their mouths chittering with delight. These weren't inmai. These creatures were a mismatched horde of grey-skinned demons, most of which only came up to waist height. The wardens went to work burning and slashing the demons as fast as they could.The battle went on for several minutes before a white cambion arrived. As it walked into the cavern, the other demons gave him a wide berth as he strode towards Tarek. Aiden did not recognise this one from the yellow mess. The other cambion looked much like the one they had killed, Eligos, except its wings and skin were white, like the white of fresh porcelain.

This cambion, however, had a strong and handsome face, despite the wickedness in his eyes. He wore spiked black steel gauntlets that matched the demonic looking fauds covering the outer part of his thighs, which were connected by a series of pointed metal shards that formed a belt. Under the fauds, flowing down on either side of ashen-black pants, was a blood-red piece of tattered fabric that circled around behind him, ending a few inches below the knee. To Aiden it looked like he was wearing the bottom half of a robe that had been shredded by some angry creature. The demon's chest was bare and had numerous black markings etched into it like demonic tattoos. They were reminiscent of the glyphs on the cursed blades that the wardens used. The tattoos didn't just appear on the cambion's chest either; they snaked around down his arms, around to his back, and even as high up as his neck.

The cambion continued its determined stroll through the sea of demons and was intercepted by two of the paladins that had been fighting beside Tarek. One launched a ball of fire which, without even a flinch from the cambion, dissipated harmlessly off his skin. The paladins moved in, attacking in unison. As they both swung their huge swords, the cambion raised a hand to grab one, while the other become embedded between the cambion's ribs.

Without even the smallest inflection of pain, the cambion yanked on the sword it had grabbed, tearing it away from the paladin's grasp. The demon then used it to impale its owner, pinning him to the floor while still standing. The paladin that had struck the cambion in the side struggled to free his blessed blade, but as it gave way, revealing a gouge in the demon, the wound had already half healed by the time the paladin regained his footing. He swung the sword again, aiming higher this time. The cambion leaned back just enough to dodge the blade. The paladin swung again, but this time the cambion blocked it with the back of its clawed hand. The paladin followed up with a fireball, which struck the demon in the face, causing his head to reel back with the force of the impact. Seemingly otherwise unaffected by the attack, the cambion then stepped in and grabbed the paladin by the neck, crushing it and throwing the body aside in one quick motion.

The cambion then set upon Tarek, who turned to face the demon as it walked unharmed across the cavern. Tarek readied his blade, an ornate flamberge with demonic glyphs on one side and angelic glyphs on the other. The blade itself had a golden tinge to it and seemed to glow.

As Tarek charged forward, the white demon summoned two swords of his own, which appeared in a flash of crimson sparks. Tarek swung his sword at the demon's stomach, slicing it as he stepped in and around the demon, striking again on the cambion's spine as he turned back around.

The wounds on the demon bled this time, but although it took a few moments longer, they closed up and healed, not even showing a scar. The cambion turned around to face Tarek again, his face showing the first touch of emotion so far—amusement. With a beat of its wings, the demon lunged forward, its feet leaving the ground and both swords above its head.

Tarek lifted his flamberge and placed his left hand against the flat of the blade to block the dual overhead attack. As his blade came into contact with the demon's, the force of the attack caused his left hand to slip off, and without the extra support, his own sword's blade was forced back on him, slicing into his collarbone. With his now-spare hand, Tarek launched a fireball at the demon with such force it sent the demon sprawling backwards. The point blank attack singed Tarek's face, but he pressed on while he could.

Tarek called upon the power of another rune, and green transparent needle-like crystals appeared around him as he walked towards the cambion. One after another, the shards were sent flying towards the demon and exploded as they broke on its skin.

The attacks themselves did nothing to hurt the demon, but the force of each small explosion kept it from being able to recuperate quickly enough from the previous attack to defend itself when the high paladin attacked again. Or at least that's what it seemed Tarek was hoping.

As Tarek lunged forward with his sword to impale the demon, the cambion closed its wings around itself, taking the force of the attack without as much as a scratch. Then the wings burst open, knocking Tarek hard to the ground. He lost his grip on his sword, and it slid away across the cavern floor just out of reach. He didn't have time to retrieve it, only to get to his feet again before the demon attacked with lightning speed. Now weaponless, Tarek called on the power of yet another rune and created a small force field in front of his hands.

The cambion pounded on the force field with his demonic blades, and white pulses of light rippled through the otherwise invisible barriers from the point of every impact. With every attack, Tarek seemed to feel it more and more. Once. Twice. Three times—before the whole field shimmered and broke into sparks. The fourth swing the cambion made met with steel, flesh, muscle and blood as it tore into the metal plating of Tarek's warden blacks and into his chest.

Even with a demonic blade now embedded into him, Tarek showed no sign of slowing. He stayed on his feet and summoned one more exploding green crystal. The demon dodged it with little effort, responding with a kick to Tarek's legs, which sent him down on one knee, struggling to breathe. The cambion smiled then grabbed Tarek by the throat and punched him half-a-dozen times in the stomach before letting go. Tarek fell back to his knees, and before anything else could happen, the demon grabbed Tarek's head in a single clawed hand and snapped his neck.

Tarek fell limply to the ground, and Aiden could hear Asha scream out his name. All he could see now was a sea of demons. His team were bloodied and tired, making more and more mistakes as exhaustion took over their bodies.

Next thing he knew, there was a sound like musical thunder as a horn called over the battle. Then there was no sound, only white light, then…darkness.

Chapter Fifteen
Two-day nap

Aiden's head ached, and his vision was nothing but a blur of grey that slowly came into focus as the details of the room he was in became clearer. He moved his head to the left, where he could see Sorterra lying unconscious in a bed. Aiden was shirtless, but almost covered in bandages. For the most part, whatever injuries he had sustained in the battle were healed, but as he tried to sit up, pain and stiffness told him where his injuries had been. He looked around and saw that he was in a large grey stone-brick room with simple pipe-framed beds in neat rows, about half of which had wardens in them in various states of invalidity. One warden was up and walking around, tending to the others. The warden turned towards Aiden when he let out a groan of pain as he sat up properly.

'Finally.' It was Tiago.

'I swear we've been through this,' Aiden said, looking around again. 'I didn't die again, did I?'

Tiago laughed. 'It seems not.'

'Where are we?' he asked.

'We're in the undercroft of the East Salem Church,' Tiago replied with a small smile. 'It's one of Salem's emergency sanctuaries. More a bunker really.'

'The last thing I remember was hearing someone scream and being overrun by demons.' Aiden stretched his arms and legs, wincing at the pull of fresh knitted skin. 'What happened?'

'Gabriel rocked up with his angel buddies and pulled our arses out of there.' He looked down at the ground with a grim expression. 'Most of us anyway.'

'Most of us?' Aiden asked. His first thought was of Kalli.

'Everyone from our team is fine. Kalli too, and Sorterra here is still hanging in there. William is over there but hasn't come to yet either.' Tiago gestured to each of them as he spoke. 'All in all we count twenty-four confirmed dead, including Tarek. Half our number. Gone just like that.' Tiago's face looked worn and tired.

'I still can't believe Tarek is actually dead.' Asha had raved about how skilled and strong he was. The way she spoke, anyone would think he was invincible. He was supposed to be their guide and their leader. 'Who's in charge now?'

'Gabriel led us here,' Tiago replied. 'He's gone now but left his second-in-command, Kára, in charge until we can restructure. Normally the high warden would step in until they could send a new high paladin from Sanctuary Prime, but Mason ran off, and the other chapters can't spare anyone, especially not someone experienced enough.' Tiago helped Aiden to his feet, and again pain niggled at him through various parts of his body.

'What now?' Aiden asked as he pulled a fresh black shirt over his head.

'While you've been taking a two-day nap, Kára has had us investigating,' Tiago said. Two days? Was he really out for that long?

'We've been trying to figure out a way to strike back and find a weakness to this new threat. These white demons are cambion, and cambion are created more often than not by a succubus'...' Tiago paused, and Aiden could have sworn he blushed a little before finishing. '...hands. Gabriel thinks these cambion are souped-up though. He reckons the only one who could do it is the queen succu-bitch herself: Lilith.'

'So we kill Lilith and that'll stop these white demons?' Aiden asked, knowing it wouldn't be that simple. Nothing had been since he woke up in Prime.

'No, but it'll stop her from making more at least, and we might be able to force information outta her that'll help get rid of them,' Tiago explained. 'Only problem is, she's not one for the sunshine on Earth. She's more for the lava-side scenery of hell, which is more than a little tricky to get to. So Amber and Grim are out questioning a known occultist group, while Asha and Kalli are trying to get help from Adley Black.'

'What should I do then?' Aiden queried, now fully clothed.

'Kára said she wanted to see you if you woke up,' Tiago said. 'I'll take you to her.'

Tiago led Aiden through the undercroft of the church. It was a series of grey open rooms made of brick, lit only by candles. The only decorations were the coffins in the wall cavities. Dimly lit tunnels and corridors linked each room, which were set up to accommodate the surviving wardens. Some had beds, while some had tables and chairs set up so they had somewhere comfortable to sit and eat. Wardens who were not too injured were eating, training or talking among themselves. Aiden and Tiago arrived at a small round room that could have been a prayer room at some point, but now the Order had converted it into an office for whichever warden commander needed it. At present, that was Kára.

Tiago didn't enter with Aiden, but gave him an encouraging shove inside as he turned to leave.

'You asked to see me?' Aiden asked, barely audible. It suddenly dawned on him that this was the first time he had spoken to an angel.

'Yes.' Kára extended her hand, which held a burned orange rune attached to a silver setting embedded onto a black band. 'Take this.'

'Um,' he whispered. 'A rune?'

'Yes, it is,' she stated. 'Normally there's a ceremony for this, but we don't have the time for convention. You are as of this moment a warden. Go see Tiago for instruction on how to use your rune.'

Aiden nodded and headed for the exit, but he felt a sudden surge of confidence. 'I need to know,' he said. 'Why haven't I regained my memories?'

'Why do you think you need to know?' Kára asked.

'Because someone's memories and experiences make them who they are,' Aiden intimated.

'Yet here you stand, a person all on your own without memories.' To Aiden she sounded like a school teacher giving a matter-of-fact lecture. 'You are a warden; whoever you used to be is of no consequence now.'

'How do you know that my memories don't contain something useful?' he pushed.

'How do you know that they do?' Kára retorted.

'I suppose I don't.' Aiden felt a little deflated at that. How stupid was he to even say something like that? As if his memories were important to anyone else but himself.

'And neither do I,' she replied, keeping the same tone of voice. 'What I do know is that Salem just lost half of its wardens *and* its commander, and we have seemingly unstoppable demons on the loose we know nothing about. I do not believe your memories would have the key to those problems.'

'But how can it be that I don't remember a single thing, yet everyone else knows at least bits of their past?' he pressed, determined.

'Like I said the day you woke, even angels make mistakes.' Her voice changed then. It was a subtle change, but to Aiden it almost sounded sympathetic. 'The process of collecting a soul is difficult. Souls are not physical things that can simply be placed in a box and carried away. We absorb the energy of the soul into ourselves, and by doing this some of our essence is transferred into it allowing the soul to exist within heaven, or in the case of wardens like you, it allows us to manifest whole new bodies, physically resembling your recently departed bodies, for your soul to be transferred back into when a new warden is needed.

'The initial process of taking the soul from the body is not perfect or instant, however, and if an angel is interrupted or rushes the process for any reason, further memory fracturing can occur."

'Or perhaps it was intentional,' Aiden blurted out, unable to contain his frustration. He instantly regretted it.

'I see Grim's distrust for angels is rubbing off on you.' This time the change in her tone was much more noticeable and clearly the start of irritation.

'Do you blame him?' he pushed on.

'I do, actually,' she said. The sheer bluntness of it was somewhat startling. 'I've worked alongside wardens for thousands of years, even before we founded the Order, and among those wardens there have been plenty who have had a very human-like ideal that angels are all-knowing and all-powerful. Prior to the Order, most of our heroes thought we were their ancient gods and were omniscient. We can travel to and from heaven quickly, allowing us to hop between different locations on the earth, but that doesn't mean we can be everywhere at once. If we could, where do you think that would leave wardens like you?'

He thought for a moment. 'We'd be pointless, I guess,' he deduced.

'Exactly. We formed the Order because we can't be everywhere at once, and must focus on where we are needed most. But, of course, humans are selfish, and even the ones who understand our limitations believe their plights are worthy of priority,' she said. The insult to humanity seemed to come with ease. 'We are few in number compared to the atrocities of this world, and fewer still are loyal to Gabriel.'

'What about God? God is supposed to be all-powerful, isn't he? Wh—'

'Enough questions,' she asserted with a definitive air of finality that crushed his confidence. 'Go find Tiago and start your training.'

Aiden decided that was a good place to quit while he was ahead. He left the room, making his way through the undercroft the same way he had come until he found Tiago again. He was still tending to the other wardens who had yet to regain consciousness in the infirmary.

Tiago's eyes lit up like an excited child when Aiden came back, but before Aiden could tell him what had happened with Kára, he urged Aiden to follow him to a room nearby. The room was much like the others—a grey brick room with a polished concrete floor. The only difference was that the wall was embedded with thick strips of steel. At the far end of the room someone had stacked a pile of grey brick squares.

'I believe congratulations are in order,' Tiago announced as they entered. 'Kára had me set this up after Asha convinced her you were ready for the rune.'

'Asha convinced the angel?' Aiden queried, looking at the rune dubiously. It was the same rune that Amber had taken from the demon in the casino.

'Kára was against it, but Asha insisted,' affirmed Tiago. 'She figured you were ready.'

'What about you?' Aiden asked. 'Do you think I'm ready?'

'I think you're as ready to face whatever is to come just as much as any of us.' Tiago let out a short, humourless laugh. 'Which is to say no.'

Aiden wrapped the black band around his wrist and attached it much like you would a watch. Although it had only one hole in which to push the metal arm into, it sat comfortably around his wrist. As he fastened it, Aiden could feel an electric-like tingling sensation pulse through his entire body.

'What do I do?' he asked as the odd pulsing eased until it was barely noticeable.

'Runes work kinda weird,' Tiago said. 'They kind of work like an extension of yourself, and every rune is different. Some are like limbs. Relatable and easy to imagine. Some are like learning to use a new set of gills. You've never had gills, have you?'

Aiden raised his eyebrow and gave him an amused smile. 'Not as far as I know,' he said.

'Exactly, so those are a little tricky. Teleportation, turnin' invisible, healin' and stuff like that are harder to teach yourself how to do,' he explained.

Tiago pulled out his pistol. 'Fortunately for me, my rune is simpler. My gun doesn't have normal ammo,' he stated. 'It fires aetheric ammo that I simply expect to come out when I pull the trigger. In doing so, I channel my rune's power through the gun and voila! Dead demons.'

'Simply expect?' Aiden asked knowing it wasn't simple at all.

'Yours is more like gills, unfortunately,' Tiago said, giving Aiden a hard, thoughtful look. 'I guess the fundamentals are the same: think it and it'll happen. But like, think really hard.'

'You guess?' Aiden asked, somewhat impertinent.

'Yeah, well, the not-so-high warden is the one who is supposed to oversee the rune training for the newbies, but since he ran off, you're stuck with my horrible teaching skills,' he said with a smile. 'Your rune summons aetheric blades, so just imagine it doing that.

Imagine that they are there and that you have control over them just as you would any part of your body.'

Aiden concentrated on the pulses of static-like energy he had felt earlier. When he'd first put the rune on and felt it, it had been like putting his hand in ice water—a shock at first. His senses had quickly adjusted themselves until the feeling had become like white noise that he grew accustomed to over time and subconsciously blocked out. It was still there just under the surface. He concentrated on the power of the rune that now ran through his body and willed the blades into existence.

As he did this, the power of the rune became clearer to his senses, like a blurred image becoming sharper. Yet as much as he concentrated, nothing happened.

'Keep trying,' Tiago said as Aiden's shoulders slumped in defeat. 'And for the love of God, aim for the targets.' He pointed to the square cement blocks on the other side of the room.

'Thought you didn't believe in God,' Aiden quipped.

'Funnily enough, I tend to get the sudden urge to find faith when I'm in the room with a guy who very well may accidentally impale me to the nearest wall at any given moment,' Tiago retorted with a snicker.

'Fair.' Aiden renewed his concentration. After half an hour of trying nothing happened, yet he continued.

He had felt helpless since he had woken up in Prime. This rune was more than just a weapon to him; it was a symbol of his ability to do better, to be a more integral part of the team. He wasn't going to give up.

Suddenly he felt it. The power of the rune, as if it were in the *hands* of his mind. He flexed this like any other muscle and felt the static energy rise to just under the surface of his skin. He tried once more to summon a blade and as he did, he felt the energy arc out just above him and materialise as a glowing, orange object: a sword.

The sword was almost transparent and about half as long as he was tall. Its grip was almost indistinguishable from the blade, separated by only a small guard. The blade itself was thin and ended in a needle-like point. Although it looked like a hologram, Aiden knew it could cut through steel.

'Impressive,' Tiago gasped. 'Whenever I've seen a newbie use one of these kinds of runes, they immediately lost control and sent the blade shooting off.'

As Tiago said that, Aiden noticed that the blade was indeed trying to launch forward. He was suddenly aware of the resistance he was holding back. He let go of it, and the blade shot forward like an arrow of flame smashing through the stack of bricks in an explosion of cement.

'Ha.' Tiago was laughing with genuine excitement. 'You're a natural, Rook. Just remember that runes need power, which they generate all on their own, but do so over time, so while you can draw more power from them, you risk running dry if you're not careful.'

Aiden nodded his understanding.

'Keep practising though.' Tiago headed for the exit to the room. 'But if it's all the same to you, I don't fancy being that wall, so I'll get out of your way.'

Chapter Sixteen
I need a favour

G rim and Amber had spent an hour searching a mansion in the northern suburbs of Salem for clues or information about the possibility of travelling to hell while still upright and breathing. Apparently 'still breathing' wasn't something these occultists could help them with, considering the state Grim and Amber had found them in. The occultists consorting with demons had caught up with them as it did more often than not, and one way or another, it cost them their lives.

'So, this occult group was worshipping laziness?' Grim handed Amber a note that detailed a member's frustration that they had not found Sloth.

'Only sin can wash away sin,' Amber read from the note out loud before scrunching it up. 'Yet another pack of occultists focused on making things stupidly easy for themselves and justifying it in ridiculous ways.'

They continued rifling through the mansion, but found nothing of use or interest. Just more occultist propaganda and instructions on summoning mephistos, which they promptly destroyed before they gave up and left the occultists' house.

'Once upon a time occultists were something to be feared,' Amber said as they walked down the street. 'The appearance of an occultist group meant more work for us while the occultists did serious damage consorting with demons for power. Nowadays there seem to be *more* occultists, yet they seem to pose *less* danger.'

'I blame the internet,' Grim grunted. 'Kids with twisted interests who are far too curious for their own good, playing with things they shouldn't, thinking it's all just a joke. But when they find out it's real, their first response is to make a deal for stupid crap.'

'Gone are the days of world domination attempts,' she said with a grin.

'Damn kids have no ambition.' He smiled back at her.

When they got to the car, Grim stopped just short of the driver's seat door.

'Can I ask you a favour?' he asked, suddenly quiet. 'You already saved my life so I have no right to ask more from you, but I need your help with something. I don't trust anyone else enough.'

Amber gave him a curious look, stopping at the opposite side of the bonnet of the car. 'Of course, Grim,' she said with a smile. 'Though I thought you were close with Asha?'

He scoffed a little louder than he meant to. 'I am, and I trust her more than anyone really, but the idea of her going against the rules is ludicrous.' He looked at her wearily. She looked back at him with patient interest.

'Do you remember Narki?' he asked. She nodded. 'On our way back to the sanctuary, I need to see him, but I need you to keep it between us.'

Her posture froze for a moment as her lips parted the slightest amount and closed again, and the sound of the fountain from the nearby lake suddenly seemed much louder. 'Why do you need to see him?' she asked. 'Does he know about the occult?'

'I wouldn't pretend to ever know what that guy is capable of knowing,' he said. 'But it's not about our task here, which is why I need you to keep it to yourself.'

He then proceeded to tell Amber the events that led up to his death. Everything the arbiter had forced him to tell, he now willingly told Amber as she stood in silence, listening to his story without a word.

'I'm so sorry,' she murmured as she walked back around the front of the car and placed a comforting hand on his shoulder.

'This may be the only chance I get,' he admitted. 'The Order is too preoccupied to be worried about what I'm doing, and with everything going on I want to find out what happened to my daughter before we all get ourselves killed.'

Amber's pause seemed to be much longer this time; during the silence, Grim envisioned her response going a variety of different ways. She could refuse and report him, which would end any further attempts, or he was about to gain his first shred of help in finding out what had happened to his daughter. Then again, maybe she'd turn around and cut is throat now for even considering doing something that might jeopardise his duties.

'Okay, Grim,' she said finally. 'I think you deserve that much for yourself, and I'd be honoured to help you. So long as it does not interfere with our primary purpose.'

Grim nodded and did his best to hold back a smile. 'Deal.'

'Twice in one week, Grim? I feel loved.' Narki was in his usual position when Grim and Amber walked into his store—lounging back behind the counter and watching them enter through half-closed lids. 'Oh, and you brought that pretty redhead along with you. Early Christmas present?'

Amber's only response was a cold glare.

'Trust me, I wouldn't be back here so soon unless it was necessary,' Grim said as they approached the counter. The surrounding room was the same as the last time they were there—half-built pieces of junk on poorly maintained shelves all around the room.

Narki reached upwards and stretched with a long yawn. 'Well, out with it then,' he said. 'How can I be of service to you and your friends today?'

'This is a personal request,' Grim began. 'I need information on a girl.'

'Can't you just use the internet like a normal stalker?' Narki complained. Grim couldn't tell if he was joking or not.

'Her name is Kiera Schatten,' Grim continued, choosing to ignore Narki's suggestion. 'If she's alive, she would be thirty-seven this year and possibly going under a different name. But I want to know what happened to her when she was ten.'

Narki looked at Grim, studying him with his baby-blue eyes. 'Who is she, Grim?'

'You don't need to know that,' Grim was stubborn, and didn't feel comfortable doing this as it was. 'Just find out anything you can about her.'

'The more info you give me, the more info you get,' Narki stated.

'She's my daughter,' Grim confessed after a few long moments.

'Okay, fine,' replied Narki. Grim pulled out his wallet, but Narki motioned for him to stop. 'I don't want your money this time, Grim,' he said. 'I need a favour.'

'I've known you to trade information for information,' Grim said. 'Or more often, money for information, but never favours.'

'Well, certain info I've purchased with my own info has given me info pertaining to something I need someone like you to do.' Narki gave them an impish smile.

'Someone like me?' Grim knew exactly what he was referring to, but never during his years of dealing with Narki had he ever outwardly admitted to knowing about the wardens, at least not in such a direct way.

'Let's just cut that little dance we do, hmm?' Narki said with a bored expression. 'I can't be bothered with it. I know you know that I know enough to know you're exactly the person I need.' He gave another playful smile.

'Go on.' Grim was now the one wearing the bored look across his face.

'Well, I also know you and your friends are looking for a way into certain place to deal with a certain troublesome being,' Narki divulged. 'That *being* has something I want.'

'I thought you were going to talk plainly?' Amber interjected.

'Sorry, force of habit,' Narki said with a lazy grin.

Narki passed Grim a piece of paper with a rough sketch on it. At first glance it looked like a dagger with a round handle. However, on closer inspection Grim could see that instead of a normal blade, it was screw-like with four blades twisting up into a point. There was some scribbling on the handle and on the blades, but Grim passed it off as unnecessary detail.

'What is it?' Grim asked Narki as he passed the sketch to Amber.

'You don't need to know what it is to get it, and you couldn't possibly afford to find out from me.' Narki said.

'How do you know Lilith has it?' Amber asked, passing the sketch back to Grim who folded it and slid it into a pocket.

'Again, that's info you can't afford.' Narki grinned. 'Just get it for me, and by the time you return, I'll have what you want.'

Grim looked at Amber, who looked back at him thinking the same thing. It was odd that Narki would suddenly ask for something so clearly demonic. The fact that they knew nothing about it, or what he planned to do with it, made it worse. On the other hand, Grim knew that once Narki set conditions on a transaction there would be no more negotiating.

'Deal,' Grim accepted.

After a quick handshake, Amber and Grim left the store for the cool night air and walked down the empty street.

'I'm not sure that was such a good idea.' Amber had stopped walking.

Grim turned to face her. 'It's the only way,' he explained. 'If anyone can find out what I need to know, it's him.'

'We don't know what that thing is,' she said. 'It could be dangerous in the hands of a civilian, especially one as questionable as him.'

'Once he's told us what I need, and if it turns out to be dangerous, we'll take it back from him.' Grim's eyes pleaded with Amber's.

'Okay,' Amber said with a resigned sigh. 'Just remember our agreement. So long as it doesn't interfere with our job.'

Grim nodded. 'Thank you.'

***

Asha knocked on the faded blue door, which swung open mere seconds later.

'Hello, wardens.' Adley's assistant, Katherine stood in the doorway wearing a professional smile and a blue pencil dress. 'Can I—'

'We're here to see Adley,' Asha said, asserting herself once inside.

'Sorry about her, we just need his help with something,' Kallista said with her best apologetic smile as she followed Asha inside.

Inside, Adley sat in the centre of the room at a large desk. He was so engrossed in whatever he was scribbling down that he didn't notice Asha until she was almost standing right over him.

'Ah,' he exclaimed, standing up. His face lit up with an overenthusiastic smile that, for some reason, annoyed Asha. 'So good to see you, Asha.'

'We need your help again, Adley,' she replied quickly. She didn't care for small talk or wasting time with pleasantries.

'Please,' Kallista added, returning Adley's smile.

'I am, as always, at your service, my dear,' he said.

'What do you know about getting into hell?' Asha asked in the same short tone.

'Without dying, I assume you mean?' Adley enquired. He gave her a quizzical look as if it were a trick question.

'Yes,' she replied. 'I know there are stories of it happening in ancient times. I need you to pry fact from fiction.'

'You're planning on going to hell? Whatever for?' Katherine interrupted.

'None of your business,' Asha barked. 'Adley?'

'The only way I know of, theoretically of course, to conjure up a two-way connection between hell and the earth is by creating an anchorage,' said Adley dubiously. 'But I doubt you'd wanna do that since that's like an open invitation to God knows what.'

'Adley, I didn't come down here to hear moronic ideas based on crap I already know.' Asha was already struggling to stay patient. Despite the tone she usually took with Adley, she knew he was knowledgeable and respected him for it, but that, more often than not, meant he took a while to sift through the parts that were of no use to her.

'Is there any other way, Adley?' Kalli asked.

'Hmm,' Adley ran a hand over his chin. 'Well, you mentioned stories from ancient times. If we can't create our own connection, perhaps we need to find a more permanent one.'

'You're talking about the hell gates. What do you know about them?' Asha had heard of them, but only from ancient mythologies and stories.

'Well, during the Second Aetheric War, the angels used the seven gates to seal hell shut after Lucifer's defeat,' he explained.

'That could work. Where are they?' Kalli asked.

'Well that's the thing,' he said with a shrug. 'They could be anywhere.'

'You're supposed to be an expert on this stuff,' Asha said harshly. 'Surely you have some idea where one could be found?'

'In all my studies I've never come across any evidence or rumour worth following up on. Even if I found one, I wouldn't know where to begin on how to open it,' he explained. Adley remained thoughtful, but Asha could see he was stretching himself.

'There must be a way?' Kalli said, more a statement of hope than a question.

'Well,' Katherine spoke up. 'Did you ever find the wielder of the Sword of Michael?'

'Oh yes!' Adley's dejected demeanour exploded into excitement and spoke so fast that Asha could only just keep up. 'During the Second Aetheric War, Michael used his sword to anchor legions of lesser angels inside hell when he invaded to kill Lucifer. Sort of the same way demons do on the earth, only in reverse.'

'So we need to find the Ghost of Salem?' prompted Kalli.

'What do you plan to do once you get to hell, exactly?' Adley asked with a tilt of his head.

'What does it matter?' Asha asked with a suspicious look.

'Well, hell's geometry doesn't work in the same three-dimensional way that the earth's does,' he said, still speaking a mile a second. 'Whatever it is you're looking for, you're far more likely to end up wandering in hell forever without a guide.'

'Are you offering to come with us?' Asha asked.

'Me?' Adley barked a short laugh. 'God no. For all my curiosity, that's where I draw the line, but I can give you something that will help you.'

'Hand it over then,' Asha demanded.

'No,' Adley said. At least she was pretty sure he said it. Asha had never heard him say 'no' to her before.

'Excuse me?' she asked, staring him down.

'Last time I asked for your help, you snubbed me,' he said, taking a half step backwards. 'This time I'll be offering something more important to me than just information, and I need your help.'

'That's not how this works, Adley,' Asha warned. She attempted to keep her patience despite Adley's unprecedented insolence.

'Normally I'd be happy to help, but I'm in danger here.' He looked terrified, but his sudden courage was unnerving. 'Besides, I know your chapter isn't exactly standing on solid ground right now. You can't afford to ignore me this time.'

'Fine, what do you want?' At this point Asha was more curious than she was angered by him.

'I made a deal,' he said plainly.

'Big surprise.' Asha rolled her eyes and shook her head.

'Not with a demon,' he blurted. 'I borrowed some money off some people one should not borrow money from. I need sanctuary.'

Asha was confused for a moment. It was so pedestrian for someone like Adley. An expert in demonology and author of several books on the subject. A man who chased demons for fun just to study them. Brought low by some thugs for money.

'First tell me how you plan to help us in return,' she said.

'Katherine will go with you,' he said quickly. Asha gave the woman a look of slight confusion. 'She…knows the way around.'

He wasn't that stupid. Surely not. 'Adley, are you saying what I think you're saying?' Asha asked.

'No!' He was defensive and frantic. 'Well, I mean yes… Katherine is my friend. She has served me loyally for years. But yes, she's…also a demon.'

'You've gone too far now, Adley,' Asha growled. 'Consorting with demons for research is one thing, but keeping one as a pet? No.'

The demon's eyes flashed with anger, and what Asha thought were press-on nails extended by an inch as she took a step forward.

'Try it, demon!' Asha shouted, her hand on her sword.

'Asha, we need them!' Kallista raised her voice above their aggressive displays. Katherine stepped back and her claws retracted, but neither took their eyes off the other. 'Besides, if we don't offer him safety, what kind of wardens are we? We'd be forsaking our primary duty.'

'No, I won't breach our sanctuary with a civilian who isn't being etched,' Asha said through gritted teeth. 'Let alone an occultist with a demon in tow!'

'Technically, we aren't breaking any rules because it's not really our sanctuary.' Kalli's voice was calm now, trying to even out the temperament of the room. 'Take them and let Kára decide.'

'Fine, but be it on your sanctimonious head if she kills them,' Asha snapped. She finally tore her icy gaze away from Katherine and back to Adley. 'Pack up your crap and then call me. I'll go speak with our current commander and smooth this over before I bring you in.'

'Thank you, Asha,' Adley said with a bowed head. He looked at Kallista. 'And you, ah...'

'Kallista, but you can call me Kalli.' She smiled.

Chapter Seventeen
Holy fire

Asha and Kallista arrived in the undercroft and were greeted excitedly by Tiago, who was standing in the main walkway next to the entrance to the infirmary.

'Kalli!' he exclaimed. 'William and your brother are awake, so you can go see them now.'

Kalli's face lit up with joy as she skipped into a run past Tiago and into the infirmary, stopping only once her brother's arms were firmly around her and they stood in a loving embrace, tears of relief in their eyes.

'How did you go with Mr Occultist?' Tiago asked.

Asha removed her gaze from the reunited siblings and looked at Tiago with tired eyes. 'We have an idea.'

Tiago looked at her with a raised eyebrow. 'Then why do you look like your dog just died?'

'Because we are no closer to killing Lilith than we were when we started.' Dejection riddled Asha's voice.

'Wanna explain that to me?' Tiago raised his eyebrow, continuing his look of a confused child.

'The only likely way we'll get into hell to kill the bitch is by getting the Sword of Michael,' she explained.

'Which is still being swung around by Casper,' Tiago said thoughtfully. 'I see the problem.'

'And we have no leads on the Ghost whatsoever.' continued Asha. 'To make it worse, the only way we'll find Lilith is by taking a demon in with us.'

'A friend of Adley's?' Tiago asked.

'Yeah,' she said, trying to get the displeasure out of her voice. 'Turns out his assistant is a demon.' The fact that he had been lying to Asha wasn't even what had made her mad. She expected that from an occultist. She was mostly angry at herself for not figuring it out after several years of working with him.

'Yeah, that's not *that* shocking when you think about.' He was nodding his head as if he were agreeing with something. 'I'd be more surprised if she was a normal woman who was both that loyal and good looking.'

'Since you're free enough to make jokes, you can come with me to pick up the pain in the arse,' she said. 'We have to go talk to Kára first.'

'Ah, right,' he said. 'Because of the whole demon thing. Don't want her turning the secretary into a sexy soup.'

Asha ignored his comment and elbowed passed him, but he brushed it off and followed her down the tunnel.

***

Aiden had been practising his rune ability for an hour and a half after Tiago left. By now the targets Tiago had set up were pretty much all destroyed as he became better and better at aiming the rune's aetheric blades. Once he had gotten used to feeling the rune's power, he could call upon it easily. Putting the blade where he wanted was a different story.

'You seem to be doing well,' Kalli said. Aiden had no idea how long she had been watching him.

'Thanks,' he replied. 'I was picking it up pretty fast once I summoned it for the first time, now it seems to be getting harder to summon.'

'Your rune is probably almost drained,' she informed. 'You'll get the hang of it and will be able to tell how much power it has after getting the feel for the power.'

'Oh,' he said, looking down at the rune.

'You should take a break; you don't want to overdo it, after all,' she said with a warm smile. 'Follow me. I want to show you something.'

Kalli led Aiden through the undercroft, past the infirmary and up a set of stairs, which swung around and up to a heavy wooden door.

'When Terra and I first became wardens, we used to come here whenever things got stressful,' she said as she pushed open the door. It opened with a fair amount of effort, groaning in complaint as it swung. 'Since the Order uses the tunnels below as a backup sanctuary, it stays abandoned. Has been for over a decade now.'

'It's beautiful.' Aiden walked over to stand in front of the altar, turning to take it all in. The inside of the church was smaller than Aiden would have expected, based on how sprawling the undercroft seemed to be.

It was simple yet elegant, with a silver altar sitting on a red rug that extended down the aisle between the wooden pews. All in all, it would have seated only about fifty people. Coloured light filtered in through the three stained glass saints that sat watching over the altar. Everything was in good condition despite the dereliction, yet it was all covered by a thin, even layer of dust, save for where the wardens had been coming in and out to access the warren underneath.

'It reminds me of the church Terra and I used to go to when we were kids,' Kalli said as she ran an affectionate hand over one of the pews. 'Almost a spitting image, actually.' She regarded Aiden, as if looking for answers to an unasked question on his face. 'You still haven't gotten back any of your memories, huh?'

'No, but I'm thinking I'll just to have to live with it.' He sighed.

For what seemed to be at least a minute neither of them spoke. They simply appreciated the serenity of the church.

'So have you thought more about things here? About our lives now?' she asked him.

'You mean about angels and demons and God?' He remembered the conversation she and Tiago had had in the mess hall a few days ago. 'Not really, but—' He paused, thinking of everything that he had been through in such a short time. 'It seems like we're alone here.'

'Would you like to know how Terra and I died?' she asked suddenly.

The abrupt nature of the question along with her hard-set expression took him aback for a moment, but after meeting her gaze, he nodded.

'It was a fire,' she revealed. 'In fact, we were the only two to be killed in the fire that burned down our church.'

'That's horrible,' he said. 'It's hearing those sorts of stories that make Tiago's and Grim's doubts seem more reasonable.'

'I don't see it that way,' she said with a slight smile. 'You didn't see the fire. It wasn't normal; it was a holy fire.' She stopped and looked around the church with a certain admiration. 'It seemed to spread with a will of its own as if all it wanted to do was take us. It was an all-consuming force, but despite that it didn't hurt. To this day, Terra and I have no clue how it could have started. Funnily enough, our pastor had a fear of fire. So no candles.'

It took Aiden a few long seconds before he realised what she was getting at. 'You think God chose you?'

'Isn't that how it works?'

'Well, yeah, but, I kinda thought of it as more of an afterthought when you died,' he said. 'Not some cosmic set of deliberate actions just to bring us here.'

'Everything God does is deliberate. All part of a plan.' Kalli flashed him a confident smile. 'Well, most of it. For everything else, there's us. I believe that's how most of us came to be here.'

'If we are soldiers of God, how come there are so many here who have different beliefs. Some outright believe God doesn't exist, and the angels don't seem to be interested in creating any sort of consensus.'

'If telling people what to believe worked, we wouldn't be necessary.' She gave a small laugh. 'Everyone would follow the same rules and there would be no evil in the world. But faith built on blind obedience is hollow.'

He remembered back to a few hours ago when Kára had said something of the sort. The wardens were necessary because nothing was perfect, but Kalli seemed to have the answers that Kára refused to tell him. What about God? Her answers, however, seemed to be more of a strong belief than any real explanation. 'What about the March?'

'What about them?' She gave him a suspicious look.

'They're angels; they serve God yet they kill innocents,' he said. 'In fact, I've heard some say they are the ones behind the increased demon activity. Like the white cambion.'

'I refuse to believe any angel who truly serves God would ally themselves with demons,' she said easily, as if she had been in this discussion a thousand times before. 'As bad as their actions are, I believe that they believe what they're doing is the right thing.'

'Maybe it's not directly?' he mused. 'Maybe they're just greasing the wheels. Y'know, riling up the demons and pointing them in the direction that best benefits their agenda.'

'I agree to a point,' she admitted. 'There is definitely something else going on, but what has best served me is to just trust in God's plan.'

'I dunno about God's plan, but I feel like I can trust in you at least.' He smiled at her, looking into the pools of honey that were her eyes.

'That's a fine start by my standards,' she said, returning the smile. 'Come on, I have a feeling we'll have more work to do soon.'

Chapter Eighteen
The spice of death

L ynus knew Adley Black. He was an author of several books on demonology, which he had written using knowledge obtained from demons themselves. He was an occultist as far as it concerned Lynus, no matter how well he conducted himself. Nonetheless, he wasn't as despicable as most who cavorted with aethereals.

Lynus and his brother had gone to see Adley when they had first arrived searching for information where they could find Hekate, who was the reason they had come to Salem. They knew she was one of the most powerful mephistos, and rather than shopping around for demons who could give them what they wanted, they went straight for the strongest one they could find. They were so desperate for revenge then, and now with his brother dead, the desperation they had felt seemed trivial compared to what drove him now. If an aethereal had his brother's soul, it meant his very essence was in danger. Lynus needed to free him from whoever had him so his brother could go wherever it was souls went after a person died. Making sure his brother had peace after death was the least Lynus could do after his foolish mistakes.

Adley had been helpful when Lynus had come seeking his help. He eagerly gave his advice for summoning Hekate, not because he had any desire for what Lynus wanted, but he just had a genuine desire to help someone in need. At least that's the feeling Lynus got from him. As such, he had a faint feeling of remorse for what he was about to do. But Adley was an occultist all the same, and Lynus knew better than most that there were consequences for dealing with demons.

Lynus walked down the alleyway that led to a small apartment at the back of a building. The building was an office complex, home to several small businesses and firms. Adley had taken up his residence inside one of these offices and had bought each of the surrounding offices as well, combining them into a large study for himself.

Lynus opened the door to Adley's office and stepped inside to see him rushing about collecting various pieces of paper and files. His assistant, Katherine, was doing the same.

'I'm sorry, but I can't help you today. I'm very busy as you can see.' Adley didn't slow his pace.

'Going somewhere?' Lynus asked.

'As a matter of fact, I am,' Adley said, still not looking up. 'So you must leave.'

'I'm sorry, Adley, but Hekate sent me.' Lynus' voice was even.

That made him stop and look up, recognition spreading across his face. When Lynus had first met Adley, he was known only by his name. Now, to most, he was the Ghost of Salem. Sadness mingled with the man's surprised expression. 'Don't tell me you made another deal with her, Ghost. Was it not bad enough the first time?'

'Don't lecture me. I'm here to collect for her because of a deal *you* made,' Lynus snapped.

'I took precautions,' he retorted. 'I didn't expect her to send someone like you after me. Even so, I wouldn't make the same mistake twice like you have.'

'I'm here to fix things, which means you have to settle your own debt.' Lynus' faint feelings of remorse had worsened, but

Lynus had already paid his price; now it was Adley's turn. 'I'm sorry, but it's my last chance.'

Adley shook his head, his own regret clear upon his face. 'If I had known what you were going to become when I helped you, or what would happen, I never would have helped. What happened to your brother is just as much my fault.' Adley's voice quivered. He lifted his head so he was looking Lynus straight in the eye. 'I'm sorry.'

'What do you think you're doing?' Lynus shouted. He projected his ghost form behind Adley, snatching and breaking a phone from his grasp.

'I truly am sorry, Ghost, but killing me for her will not fix anything, and you're a fool if you think it will!'

Lynus tightened his grip on the Sword of Michael. He and his…where was she? Katherine, Adley's assistant, was no longer rushing around with papers.

The assistant tackled him from behind with enough force to knock him to the ground. More force than a woman of her size should be able to achieve. When he rolled and sprung to his feet to face her, he could see why.

Her nails had become elongated, taking the form of claws, and her eyes had darkened to a near-black red. She snarled through sharpened teeth as she sprung for him again. She was far too quick for Lynus to move out of the way when she lunged through the air at him, crashing into him and forcing them both through the front door.

**

The undercroft where the wardens now took up temporary residence technically spread out of the bounds of the church's land and under various other buildings on the street. Since it was such a small church, nestled almost wall-to-wall between two much larger buildings on either side, the city made the exception so it could house a cheap way for families to store their dead. That was before cremation became mandatory within city limits and the faithful abandoned the church altogether, the dead left behind and forgotten. Soon after that, the Order had claimed it for themselves as an emergency sanctuary, but it had never been used as such until now.

The church walls were not quite touching its neighbours', and on each side ran weed-ridden paths that led to archways made of overgrown shrubbery on either side of a small patio area behind the church. The walls of the neighbouring buildings enclosed the patio, but tall shrubs bordered the sitting area. Within those shrubs were three round wooden tables and chairs.

Grim had come up for fresh air and to be alone. This was his favourite time of the night as much now as when he had been alive. It was about an hour before first light and the closest to sleeping the city ever got. He enjoyed sitting out alone and watching the stars as they faded with the coming light. He had been able to stare up at the night sky for a full five minutes before someone interrupted him. He enjoyed being alone, but he found himself not minding Amber's intrusion as she walked under one of the green archways and joined him at the table. Tiago though, who trailed along behind, he minded quite a bit more. He didn't dislike him, in fact he respected his skill with his weapon of choice, but he wasn't fond of him either. Maybe it was the innate distrust of cops Grim had adopted in his prior life, or maybe it was because he couldn't stand the way he turned everything into a damn joke.

'It's nice out here,' Amber said, looking up at the stars.

It was a cold night, but this was mostly because of the sea breeze that brought in the water's coolness. Enclosed within these walls, the breeze hardly reached them, so it was rather pleasant in their little corner of the city.

'Nah,' Tiago said. 'Too cold for my liking.'

'Feel free to go back downstairs then,' Grim grunted.

'Not feeling the love, Grimmy,' Tiago said with a grin. Grim rolled his eyes.

'You two worked together before, yes?' Amber asked, looking at Grim.

He nodded. 'When I first woke, Tiago was in a different team, but yeah. Our teams worked together occasionally for about sixteen years before he moved to Prime.'

'Why did you transfer to Prime?' Amber asked Tiago.

'Change of pace,' he said quickly. 'Spent ten years there but I missed this place too much. Not too sure I made the right decision, all things considered.' He laughed.

'Ten quiet years,' Grim added.

'It was not all bad.' Tiago chuckled as leaned back in his chair a little. 'There was the time you shot that gross pimple-demon-thing, and it exploded all over Asha.'

'I saved her life, and she still gave me the cold shoulder for a week,' Grim reminisced as they laughed.

'Does she have any other kind of shoulder?' Amber asked with the look of a wounded animal. 'It's been sparks between me and her ever since I got here.'

Grim offered her his best attempt at a comforting smile. 'She's all right once you learn how to handle her. She's just been under a bit of extra stress lately.' The truth was Grim could scarcely remember a time when Asha was anything but a hard-arse, but at one point she was just as frightened and confused as most of them were, before she got most of her memories back.

'What about *your* old team, Amber?' asked Tiago. 'Have not had the chance to ask about where you come from.'

Grim could see her think for a moment. 'Actually, they were all very similar to Asha,' she said. 'Very serious and by the book for the most part. You guys are all so different from each other yet you still work well as a team.'

'Well, y'know, variety is the spice of death,' Tiago quipped and Amber laughed, which made Grim chuckle despite himself.

'This place is much more like a family,' Amber said. She thought for a moment and then nodded to herself as if deciding something. 'I prefer it here.'

'Well, I for one am glad you're part of it.' Grim smiled at Amber who returned it as she placed her hand on his on top of the table. A sudden silence fell upon them.

'I'll take that as my cue to leave you two alone.' Tiago sat up with a cheesy smile plastered on his face as he left the patio.

There was a long silence following Tiago's departure, but Grim could not decide if it was an awkward silence or a comfortable one since they were now looking at the stars again, though Amber still had her hand on his.

'I've been a warden for twenty-seven years,' Grim said, meeting Amber's gaze once more. 'And I've never thought about someone as much as I do you.'

She smiled her way into another short silence. 'You know, I find myself drawn to you as well,' she said. 'I remember little of my life before, so this is kind of new to me, I guess.'

'My wife was the only person I ever remember feeling this way about,' Grim said, though a sudden tightness pierced his chest. His daughter was the only thing he had ever loved more than his wife, but Amber seemed to have a natural effect on Grim that pulled him towards her. Was it because she had saved him from that arbiter? Or was it something deeper within? 'You saved my life once already; I promise to you now I will make sure to return that favour as many times as I can. I won't let anything bad happen to you again.'

Grim was surprised when she smiled at him as though he had just told a joke. 'Favour?' she laughed, and Grim could feel his cheeks threaten to flush. He wasn't the greatest person with words when it came to this type of thing. 'There is no favour to return, but if your promise is for us to look after each other, then I too shall promise that.'

Grim's hand moved up Amber's arm as he leaned forward. Grim's heart quickened like it usually did when he was lining up a target in a fight. He leaned further in but Tiago's sudden re-emergence made them snap back into their chairs.

'The Ghost has been found!' Tiago shouted. 'We need to go. Now!'

Chapter Nineteen
Your last chance

G rim and Amber met up with Asha and Tiago in front of the church and sped their way through the streets of Salem until they arrived on Adley Black's street. Adley had messaged Asha, *'GHOST HERE HELP',* and by the time they arrived, a fight between Adley's assistant and a hooded man had spilled out onto the street. When the wardens' vehicle screeched to a stop, they jumped out of the car and drew their respective weapons, standing in a semicircle about a dozen metres in front of the Ghost.

For all the talk about this guy, for all the stories he inspired, he didn't look like much to Grim. He was of average height and build, and wore faded blue jeans and a dark hoody. To most other eyes, he just appeared to be a regular civilian, except for the sword in his hand, which was now pointed towards the group. It was a standard hand-and-a-half sword with a golden, ornate *S*-shaped guard. It had a silver blade with white filigree running through it that glowed with power.

Grim didn't admit it out loud, but he admired the man. Or at least the stories of him. Killing demons *and* angels without rules or restrictions. Doing what he knew was right because it was right, not because some aethereal pulled his strings and told him to dance.

'We've been looking for you, Ghost!' Asha shouted.

'You and half of both aethereal armies,' he slung back. 'Which one are you?'

'Neither,' she said. 'We are with the Order of Elysium, and we need your help. You can start by standing down from attacking our friend here.'

'The Order?' Ghost threw his head back in a short, fake laugh. 'My apologies then, I'll just stand down, and come quietly, then rejoin the ranks of you wannabe heroes, shall I?'

Grim was incredulous. The Ghost was a warden? He had heard stories of rogue wardens before but had never met one. His admiration of the man only deepened. He had done what Grim had fantasised about for over a decade. It wasn't all that surprising though—no normal human could do what the Ghost had done.

'We don't need *you*,' Asha growled. 'We just need the sword, so your choices are you help us or we kill you and get what we want, anyway.'

Grim could see the Ghost stare at them through cold, defiant eyes for a moment. 'I don't want to kill you, but I will if you try to stop me from what I need to do.'

'You can continue to do whatever you damn well please for all I care,' Asha shouted. 'Just give us the sword.'

'I *need* it!' he shouted back, enraged.

'Tiago, take Katherine and get Adley,' Asha ordered. 'Tell him to run.' He nodded and ran back into the apartment.

'The only place Adley is going is with me!' The Ghost charged forward, the Sword of Michael already arched back ready for a swing. Grim darted away, and the others took several steps back. He believed the stories of the Ghost, but knew the Ghost couldn't take them all on.

Grim saw blasts of ice fly from Asha's direction towards the Ghost, only to shatter into icy splinters as he sliced them from the air. While Asha engaged the Ghost from the front, Grim took the chance to attack with his hunting knife. He couldn't fight if they surrounded him. This would be over sooner than they had thought. Grim felt a slight pang of disappointment at how easy this would be. That feeling was short lived as what made the Ghost so special, and perhaps the real reason for his name, became abruptly clear. A smoky purple figure appeared from what seemed like inside the Ghost's body and lunged at Grim, blocking his attack with the full force of a solid being.

Grim stumbled back, though he kept his weapon within a firm grasp. Meanwhile, Amber had attacked with her axe alongside Asha, and it seemed to Grim that the Ghost could only hold one of those ghost-like things at once.

The three of them moved in quickly. While the Ghost dealt with Asha, Amber's next attack was deflected by a transparent force field that appeared from thin air. As Grim moved in, he was overcome with an intense heat as a ring of fire exploded from the Ghost, the force of which knocked all three of them back.

That made three. At least three runes on this guy. One was hard enough to master, and only paladins ever got a second. High Paladin Tarek was the only one Grim knew who had ever used more than that. The amount of willpower needed to use so many at once was a staggering concept for Grim to even think about. All that and the Sword of Michael, no wonder this guy had earned such a reputation so quickly.

The team got back to their feet and charged the Ghost once again. This time Asha rushed forward with a shield of ice forming around her forearm, while Grim melted into a near-invisible state as he approached. The Ghost met their charge and darted towards Amber. She swung her axe, and he blocked it with his angelic sword. As the two weapons collided, they let off a deep *clang* sound, which Grim could feel under his feet. Amber was lucky; Grim knew the Sword of Michael could shear through steel like any other sword through flesh.

The Ghost seemed taken aback but was still quick enough to flick the axe away and land a push-kick to Amber's abdomen. Amber stepped back and held her footing, but the Ghost launched a fireball at her, the force of which knocked her onto her back. Asha swung, aiming straight for the head. The Ghost ducked under and planted a fist into Asha's stomach. As she reeled back, he launched a fireball at her as well.

Grim didn't see if the second fireball had hit its target; instead, he went into a rage. He lost his concentration and his rune's power failed, rendering him visible again. As Grim charged, the Ghost's smoky purple avatar appeared again. This time it didn't just block but followed up with a few attacks of its own, slicing at Grim with its spectre-like blades, before disappearing again. When Grim turned back to face the Ghost, he saw a ball of fire flying through the air. He sidestepped to dodge the fire, but the Ghost was on him in seconds, now attacking him for real.

Grim sliced at the Ghost with his knife, but he leaned back, and the knife cut nothing but air. The Ghost countered, but rather than landing a blow with the sword, the Ghost planted an open palm on Grim's sternum and let loose a concussive blast, which knocked him back and out for several seconds. *Four runes?* When Grim's vision returned seconds later, Asha was down, but Amber was getting to her feet.

'I told you,' shouted the Ghost, his voice strained. 'I don't want to kill you, but I will if I have to. This is your last chance.'

Grim was about to shout back in rage when he felt something rumble through the ground that silenced him. Amber was on her feet now with her axe in hand. She looked calm as she burst into a run towards the Ghost, lunging at him with her axe overhead. The Ghost blocked her again, but as the weapons collided, with the same deep rumble of distant thunder, pure white wings burst from Amber's back. Her eyes had shifted from their cool blue to a glowing amethyst. Her axe, still pressed up against the Ghost's sword, transformed from boring steel to silver with golden edges and an ornate filigree of bronze.

Even through all the pain from his injuries, Grim felt his stomach go cold and sick through it all. Amber was an angel. A lying, deceiving angel, and he was a damn fool! The Ghost's surprise, which must have been just as severe as Grim's own, was all the distraction Amber needed to disarm him.

The Ghost jumped back as his weapon flew from his grasp and onto the bitumen. In a flash of light, the blade disappeared, and all that was left was the hilt. The Ghost attempted to continue defending himself using his invisible barriers, but Amber shattered them instantly, the force of which weakened the Ghost's legs. Amber kicked at one of his knees and he fell, Amber's axe on his throat.

'This is *your* last chance,' she said. 'We need your help. I'd prefer you gave it willingly.'

The Ghost, disarmed and defeated, stared up at the angel for a moment with the fire of defiance still in his eyes. Amber pushed on the axe just hard enough to draw blood, extinguishing that fire.

'My help?' he sneered. 'What in the hell would you need *my* help for?'

'You have been wielding Michael's sword for a while now. You've learned to use it well. For a human,' Amber said, and Grim's blood boiled as she said the word '*human*'.

'I've been keeping this sword out of angel hands for almost a year now,' he growled. 'I'm not about to just let you take it.'

'You're not in the position to *just* do anything. We could kill you and simply take it, but would prefer you alive,' the angel said. 'Besides, we are *not* the March.'

The Ghost of Salem shook his head defiantly. 'I don't care who you are; I need this sword, but more importantly, I need Adley,' he said.

'Why?'

'That's none of your concern, angel,' he spat. 'Let me take him, and I'll swing that sword in any direction you want.'

'Not going to happen,' Asha growled as she approached them. 'He is under our protection.'

'For now,' Amber said. Her wings, staying visible, folded back up, and her eyes faded back to their normal dark blue. 'But if the Ghost won't unless w—'

'No!' Asha shouted. 'I don't care if you're God's personal whore, I'm the loch warden here, not you, you lying bitch. Yours won't be the first angel arse I've kicked.'

'Enough!' Grim had walked over and helped the Ghost to his feet. At this point Tiago had reappeared with Katherine and Adley close behind. 'Asha is still in charge here. If she says Adley is under our protection, then he is under our damn protection.' Grim stared daggers at Amber. 'I'll help her stop you if I need to.' He turned back to the Ghost. 'You, on the other hand, will help us whether you like it or not. I'm sure we can help you without sacrificing Adley, but you help us first.'

'Doubt it,' the Ghost muttered. 'Fine. But if you can't figure out a way to help me, I'm doing it *my* way.'

'Grim...' Amber looked as heartbroken as Grim was furious, but he didn't care. She was an angel, which meant all those feelings she said she had were all lies. Some twisted agenda.

Tiago walked past and picked up the Sword of Michael's hilt, looking at it as if it were about to explode.

'Give it back to him, Tiago,' Asha ordered, still staring at Amber with icy eyes.

'If you say so,' Tiago said as he walked over, handing it back to the Ghost. 'Don't like that thing anyway.'

Asha removed her death stare from Amber and transferred it back to the Ghost. 'But I swear to whatever god there is—if you stab us in the back, we will put you down for good.'

Grim looked over to Katherine and Adley. 'You were told to run,' Grim growled.

'You seemed to have it all under control,' Adley stated as he and Katherine walked into the street.

'Besides,' Katherine said, 'with an angel with us, we can actually leave for hell right now.'

'The sooner the better, after all,' Adley added.

Grim looked at Amber with dead eyes. 'Is that true, Amber?' Grim scoffed. 'I mean, whatever your name is.'

'Ambriel,' she said, her eyes mocking sadness. 'Grim, I'm s—'

'We don't have time for that crap,' Asha interrupted. 'If there is a way we can leave and kill this Lilith bitch right now, we need to go right fucking now.'

Ambriel sighed. 'We angels cannot touch another angel's weapon without permission from its owner,' she said. 'But through another, such as the Ghost, we can channel our *grace* into the weapon, enabling the wielder to use more of the abilities of said weapon that they may not otherwise have been able to.'

'Wait, hold up,' the Ghost said. 'You need me to get you into hell? That's what you hunted me down for? You want me to literally go to hell?'

'And figuratively, as long as you're offering,' Tiago said.

Asha explained to the Ghost everything that had happened at the sanctuary and during the last two days that had followed. About the new breed of cambion and Gabriel's plan to kill Lilith.

'Fine,' the Ghost said. 'What do I need to do?'

'Well,' Katherine said. 'Theoretically, the angel woman here will use you to control the sword's ability to teleport us to and, hopefully, from hell, while I guide us in. Once there, we can grab the others the same as us demons do, only in reverse.'

'Sounds simple enough,' Tiago said. 'Terrifying, but simple.'

'Why can't you just use yours?' the Ghost asked Ambriel.

'My axe, although angelic, has nowhere near the power of Michael's sword, and quite simply does not have the ability,' Ambriel said. She walked over to the Ghost and placed a hand on his shoulder, and Katherine walked over to do the same.

'I hope you know what you're doing,' the Ghost said to both Katherine and Ambriel. They said nothing.

After a few seconds of silence, Grim could see Ambriel speak to the Ghost, but he could no longer hear them. Eventually there was a flash of blinding light and thunder rolling overhead. When Grim opened his eyes, the three were gone.

Suddenly, the street was dead silent as the team stood around eager to see what would happen next. Even Tiago was quiet, and if all of this was worth anything, it was that at the very least. As they waited, Grim's thoughts drifted back to Amber, and for the smallest moment his mind flashed with warm memories and feelings, but the plague that was reality tore that apart, infecting any kind thought or memory he had of her. When he had spent all that time watching over her when she had been wounded, he was caring for an angel. When he had confessed things to her that he never had to anyone before, he was telling his secrets to an angel. Every time he had risked his life for her in battle, he had done it for an angel. It made him feel sick, yet he couldn't help but fight back against those angry thoughts with the memories of when she had done the same for him.

There was another rumble of thunder and flash of light, this time completely blocking out his vision.

Chapter Twenty
The second circle

When the light had faded and Asha's eyes had adjusted, she looked around and briefly thought it hadn't worked. Asha had often thought about what hell would look like but never in a hundred years would she have guessed it looked anything like her world. The road that stretched out before her looked like any other city street with tall apartment buildings all around, complete with back alleys, fences, broken windows and cars parked on the side. It was as if they had arrived in a city suddenly abandoned and washed of all colour, save for varying shades of grey. Even the sky was pitch black as though they stood under a starless sky at midnight. Staring up into the blackness, an invisible weight seemed to push down on Asha, a feeling as though any hope and happiness she had, or would ever have, was draining from her.

'So this is it, is it?' Asha asked no one in particular.

'The first circle, to be precise,' Adley said. 'This is where the souls of the damned first arrive.'

As Adley said that, Asha spotted a grey figure in a window above, peering down at them. Her hand went for her sword, but Katherine urged for her to be still.

'Some souls never venture much further than this circle, instead becoming lost,' she said, and Asha noticed the figure wasn't looking down at them at all, but staring off at the bare wall across from it. 'Eventually the soul will either rot and become a casteless, or linger here until some hungry demon wanders over to consume it.'

'Lovely bunch, you lot,' Tiago said playfully.

'To think we are all the same is foolish,' Katherine scolded.

'Where do we go from here?' Asha asked.

'Lilith is in the second circle,' Katherine said. 'We will need to navigate our way through.'

'Can't we just, y'know, go inwards?' Tiago asked.

'Sort of,' Adley said. 'You're picturing hell to be a series of smaller and smaller circles until you get to the centre, yes?'

Tiago nodded. Asha agreed that's how she had pictured it, but then again never put much thought into its exact layout. Hell's geography didn't help her kill demons. At least not before now.

'That description is mostly correct. But as I explained before, hell's topography doesn't work in our three dimensions of space,' Adley said. 'Technically, you could walk inwards and still be wandering for weeks and not get any closer.'

'Only demons or experienced angels know how to navigate this place properly,' Katherine said. 'Follow me and stay close. I'm sure I don't need to tell you how dangerous even the first circle can be.'

'Let's not waste time then,' Ambriel said as she moved forward down the broken road a few steps behind Katherine.

For what seemed like an hour, the group trudged their way through the lifeless city without a word. Katherine's lead seemed aimless as she turned down random streets and alleyways, each one as empty as the last. The only sign of anything resembling life was more of the lost souls standing by the side of the road, huddled in a corner in an alley or lying down on the road, staring, unblinking, into the dark abyss that was the sky.

Grim walked next to Asha in a brooding silence that was all too familiar with him, but this time she shared his anger. Amber had rubbed Asha the wrong way ever since she had arrived. She always acted like she thought she was better than everyone else to the point where she seemed to ignore authority, and now it was clear why. She had lied to them for months, but Asha knew she wouldn't have done so without orders and a goal. There must have been an agenda as to why she had been pretending to be a warden for so long, and she wondered who knew about it. It made her sick to her stomach to think of the possibility that Delarin had known and kept it from her, orders or no.

All those times Amber had held back in a fight so she would appear to be a warden rather than an angel. She could have killed Eligos that night at the warehouse and Delarin would still be alive. Tarek would still be alive. It was her fault, and Asha would find out why and make her pay for it. But it would have to wait for now. Asha realised she was clenching her fist, so she relaxed her hand, trying to let her anger go—to lock it away for later when she needed it.

'So what happens if you go out too far?' Tiago asked Adley as they walked behind Asha and Grim. 'Do you fall off the edge of hell? Or is there a wall or something?'

Adley laughed. 'If you walk far enough out, you'll eventually just be walking back in, just on the opposite side.'

A silence followed that lasted several seconds. 'That,' Tiago paused again, 'is trippy.'

'Like I said,' Adley laughed again. 'Hell follows different rules.'

They continued for some time, though it was hard to tell how long exactly. Their perception of time was out of sync; Asha felt like it had been hours, while Adley was convinced they had only been travelling for half an hour. Katherine explained that the first circle was designed, for lack of a better word, to mentally dominate and confuse those within it. She assured them they weren't too far away from the second circle, and that the effects of the first circle would wear off.

Asha was finding it difficult to believe her. She was a demon after all, and their hopelessness had nothing to do with this place. They were in hell, by choice no less. They had lost the sanctuary to demons they couldn't fight, losing half of Salem's wardens trying. Everything was falling apart. Even their mission here was a last-ditch effort, and she'd no doubt see more of her people die for it, which was a thought that made her tempted to stay right where she was.

Asha deserved nothing more than to rot with the lost souls. She couldn't save anyone. Not Delarin. Not Tarek. She had lost two of the people she had most respected since becoming a warden, and now she couldn't even see when an angel had been planted in her midst. Her life as a warden was as washed out as the city that surrounded her. She looked up, and the buildings seemed to stretch further and further into the sky like talons ready to ensnare her mind. Someone grabbed her arm and pulled, snapping her away from her thoughts. She had stopped walking and hadn't even realised. She looked at Katherine, who then let go of her arm.

'This way,' Katherine said, leading them into a two-storey brick apartment building.

'You okay?' Grim had stopped beside her.

She nodded, still somewhat glass-eyed. 'I...'

'I'll walk with you,' he said, placing a gentle hand on her back and urging her forward. He didn't say it, but Asha knew him, and his show of compassion told her he had experienced something similar to her. He had the strength to push through it though. She didn't. Because she was weak. A leader who couldn't lead.

She caught herself, shaking her head to clear the thoughts from her mind before they took hold again. 'Thank you,' she said.

They walked side by side at the back of the group as they followed into the building, whose doors opened into a single hallway. The further they went, the more the walls deteriorated. The paint became cracked and peeled until there was no paint at all, and the brick was slowly replaced with jagged rock.

The tunnel opened up into the outside once more, and suddenly it were as if Asha could breathe again. Her thoughts of hopelessness were still fresh in her mind, but they were securely locked away again deep inside her where they belonged.

'Welcome to the second circle,' Katherine announced.

Like the first circle, this one was still somewhat reminiscent of a regular city, but here black vines with dark red thorns burst through the pavement, eager and hungry, ensnaring most of the buildings. A red blood-like substance dripped and oozed over most of the vines, some of it staining the bricks of the buildings they were attached to, making some parts of the buildings look like something out of a horror movie. The pitch black sky was replaced with one of blood red. Wispy black clouds rushed across the expanse and off into the void. The red of the sky was veined with black spider web-like cracks that throbbed and squirmed as if the sky itself was a living creature. A sudden feeling of unease settled in the bottom of Asha's stomach.

From the street, Asha could see sudden ends to the alleyways on their left, where a part of the 'city' had been swallowed up by what Asha could only imagine was a giant sink-hole. In the distance, she could see where the hole ended and more of the city continued off past the horizon.

'Between the second and third circles stands the Stygian Wall,' Katherine explained. 'It's a fortified barrier between where we are now and where true evil lies. No mortal has ever gone past that point.'

'Please tell me we won't be trying that today,' Tiago said, sounding like a child who didn't want to go shopping with his mother.'

'No. The Stygian Wall is dotted with fortresses that act as gateways through. During the Second Aetheric War, Lucifer manned these fortresses with his fallen lieutenants,' Katherine said.

'Traitors,' Ambriel muttered.

'Getting through was no easy task for The Divine March when they came,' Katherine continued. 'Since then the forts have been a point of interest for any and all ambitious demons who wish to lay claim to territories in the second circle. After Lucifer's defeat, Lilith managed to gain a lot of power, but within the last ten years she's managed to take full control of the entire circle.' Katherine pointed into the distance. Through the twisted mockery of regular city streets stood a dark monolith, rising into the deformed sky as if trying to escape the horrors below it. 'That's her nest. That's where we are going.'

'I didn't realise succubi were any good in a fight,' the Ghost muttered.

'They're not, and any other succubus would never have managed to hold so much power,' Katherine said. 'Lilith didn't become the queen of her kind by chance. Creating cambion isn't easy. Even when done with her level of skill, there is only a small chance of success, which is why you don't see cambion running around everywhere. But even for that small chance, other demons bend to her will. I don't know what accelerated her power a decade ago, but now that she's able to produce these white cambion, her power will only keep increasing unless we end her.'

'All the more reason for us being here then,' Asha said.

'Harpies!' Tiago shouted suddenly as he pointed towards the sky at a fast-approaching cloud of red.

Adley raised his voice over the commands Asha was giving out. 'No, don't,' he shouted. 'They aren't interested in us.'

This didn't seem to put the wardens at ease. 'Demons here are busy fighting one another for power,' Katherine explained. 'They don't care about us.'

'I thought you said Lilith has control over this place,' Asha remarked.

It was now Adley's turn to pitch in an explanation. 'Oh she definitely has, but demons are like animals. Uh, no offence, my dear,' Adley said excitedly, and Katherine smiled at him. 'While the rabble fight among themselves for their own little territories and armies, they'd join together and fight for her if she willed it.'

'That doesn't mean we should let our guard down,' Ambriel admonished as the harpies flew overhead and off into the distance. 'We sh—'

'Let's keep going.' Asha pushed passed Ambriel and walked next to Katherine as they led the group forward. She would not let this angel take charge of her team. They were her responsibility, and it was obvious to Asha that she couldn't count on Ambriel to come through for them, so why should she be fit to lead them?

As they walked through the twisted, broken streets towards Lilith's lair, Asha could hear Adley exclaiming his fascination with nearly everything they came by. A few times, Asha had to stop because his curiosity had sent him down an alleyway, and Katherine had to snap him out of his own world and get him to join the group again. Now that they had a reference point to where they were going, Katherine said they could simply walk straight towards the monolith, so Asha led the group towards it, keeping her eyes sharp for anything that moved towards them.

'What circle are you from, Katherine?' asked Tiago shamelessly. Asha didn't know if demons had any sort of social etiquette, but that didn't seem to be an appropriate question. Apparently Asha was correct in that assumption because the only response Katherine gave was a poisonous glare in Tiago's direction.

'Stop,' Asha commanded as she came to a sudden halt. She had seen something. Something watching them. She looked around and quickly studied each window in both of the buildings on either side of the group.

'There!' The Ghost ran into an apartment building to the right. Asha snapped her focus to the building just as a figure on the second storey fled from the window. She ran in after the Ghost, ordering the others to watch the streets for more.

She sprinted up behind the Ghost as he ran up a set of U-shaped stairs, almost running into the back of him at the corner when he suddenly jumped back to dodge a fireball that exploded off the wall. They continued up the stairs, and the demon continued running. Fortunately, the hallway was a dead end, and the demon stopped short of the window at the end and turned to face them. It looked like a fawn from a child's story book, but with sharp claws and blood-red eyes.

'What are you waiting for?' Asha shouted. 'Kill it!'

The Ghost did as ordered and took out the Sword of Michael with a flash of white light and attacked with an overhead swing. The demon held up his claws to grab the blade, but it glided through the flesh and bone of the demon's hand and into its skull.

Before the demon's body even hit the ground, a door in the hallway burst open, splinters and chunks of it exploding into the hallway, and another demon rushed past them, crashing through the window before either of them had time to react. Asha rushed the window and saw the demon unfurl bat-like wings and fly off into the distance towards Lilith's monolith.

'Great,' the Ghost grumbled. 'She'll know we're here now.'

Asha grunted in dissatisfied agreement, and they both quickly made their way back to join the others. 'We need to hurry,' she said as she returned to the group. 'Lilith will be expecting us now.'

'It's not too much farther,' Katherine encouraged.

An hour had passed before they arrived at the monolith. That demons had not attacked them was not a good sign. Lilith knew they were coming for her, and if she had not tried to stop them already, it likely meant she considered herself quite safe where she was.

There was no telling how many demons she had locked away with her. Asha regretted the decision to come here without more help. The monolith was easily at least a kilometre wide and sat in the middle of the city streets as if it had just been carelessly placed at random along the giant Stygian Wall. The walls, which seemed pure black from so far away, actually had a slight red tinge to them if you looked from the right angle, and didn't seem to have any sort of entrance.

'So what, we just waltz in like we're invited?' asked the Ghost.

'Is there even an entrance?' Tiago added.

'Of course.' Katherine walked out in front, leading them through a gap in the rubble that lined the front of the hellish building, and placed a hand on the monolith. A few moments later, a low hum of energy resonated from the wall, and a ten-metre-high section of it split evenly apart like a giant set of double doors, revealing a long hallway lined with braziers hanging from the roof on iron chains. 'This is one of many entrances to the monolith from this circle. Only a demon can open them.'

'And I guess all demons know exactly where to find these too,' Asha said flatly, her eyes throwing accusation. Adley said Katherine knew the way around, but who knew what sorts of things she had done, and for whom.

'Yes, I used to follow Lilith before my time with Adley,' Katherine replied, somewhat harshly. 'I lived in the second circle and it was pragmatic to f—'

'We don't want to know your life story, demon,' the Ghost interrupted.

Katherine simply shrugged, urging them inside.

'So, this is definitely a trap, right?' Tiago asked, already knowing the answer.

'If you ask me, this whole expedition is probably a trap,' Grim muttered darkly.

Katherine led the team through the inside of the monolith, where they were met with an unsettling lack of resistance. The sheer convenience of Katherine's help naturally made Asha sceptical of her, even if the fact she was a demon didn't already do that. The further they moved through the monolith unhindered, the more convinced Asha became that Katherine was purposely leading them into a trap. At this point though, she didn't care so long as it brought them face-to-face with Lilith.

The halls they moved down had pretty quickly become no wider than three people abreast and four metres high, all of which were made up from smooth black rock. Every now and again they would pass by a brazier alight with red flame, which would give some sections of the hallways a red glow. The maze-like design of the monolith's interior made Asha wonder what the building was supposed to be for. Was it designed to make intruders like themselves get lost within it?

Eventually the black hallway opened up into a large chamber with a highly decorative chair in the centre on a slightly raised platform. Down the length of the chamber were several columns, three on either side of the centre platform, dividing the room into thirds. To the left was a wall that was lined with handcuffs chained to it, and on the other side were several spa pools and lounging areas scattered with coloured pillows and rugs. It made Asha think of what she imagined a harem would look like.

'Looks like there's nobody home,' Tiago observed.

'I highly doubt they just up and left,' Adley replied.

Suddenly Asha heard the sound of pained moaning coming from somewhere nearby, and as she searched for its source, she noticed there was a doorway on the far side of the room.

'This way,' she instructed as she edged through a doorway into another, smaller chamber.

'Oh my god.' Tiago's voice mirrored the horror Asha felt as she looked around. Inside the smaller chamber were several cages all filled with people in various states of nakedness and consciousness. Those still clothed wore ripped and torn black clothes and coats. Asha's heart sank as she realised who they were: wardens. Asha didn't recognise any of them, but seeing them reminded her harshly of the reports of missing wardens from chapters all over the world. They looked dead, laying about their cages or propped up against the blood-stained iron bars. Asha didn't count, but she guessed there to be about twenty of them, which was only a fraction of the reported missing. Some of them groaned and sobbed.

'Quick,' Asha said. 'Get them out of there.'

Before they could get any of the cages open, Asha heard a voice come from the larger room.

'Oh, Kathdia!' The feminine voice seemed to dance through the hall.

'Adley, get those cages open,' Asha ordered. 'The rest of you with me.'

They went back into the main chamber, which was now far less empty. Standing in the centre of the room was a 'woman'. She was barely covered, wearing only a black semitransparent cloth that hid nothing of her naked form. She was flanked by four other human-like demons on either side, each completely naked. Their dark red irises were all that gave them away as non-human.

'Nice to see you, Kathdia,' purred the woman in a warm, almost genuine voice. 'And I thought you didn't have the gall to ever come back here.'

'You'll die today, Lilith,' Katherine hissed.

'Kill them,' Asha yelled to carry her order over Lilith's chortling. 'But leave Lilith alive.'

'As if you have a choice,' she called out with mocking laughter.

The opposing groups suddenly exploded into action. Lilith's minions were not built for combat, but still put up a surprising amount of resistance for things that were not even wearing clothes, and for each one they killed, more joined the fray.

Asha focused on Lilith, who had summoned a blade in each hand and was walking straight at her. Asha readied herself, encasing her left arm and fist in thick ice, which extended upwards and downwards, creating a makeshift shield that was reminiscent of a medieval 'heater' shield—flat at the top, narrowing down at the bottom to a dangerous spike.

Lilith did not attack alone, however, and Asha found herself beset on one side by another succubus and on the other by the male incubus. She turned to her left and swung a right-to-left slice across the demon's chest, which she paired with another, this time left-to-right. The demon stumbled back and hissed in pain. She followed through with the second swing, twisting to the right, and slashed the second demon's throat. The incubus didn't hiss or howl, only choked and fell to the ground.

By the time Asha had cut the throat of the incubus, Lilith was already within striking range of Asha. She blocked the first strike with her ice-shield and the second strike from Lilith's other sword with her own. As Asha's sword rebounded off Lilith's second blade, she kicked out for Lilith's stomach, forcing her back far enough so she had enough room to block an attack from the succubus to her left.

The demon's attack landed on the ice-shield, and Asha could hear the ice giving way. As the attack bounced off the shield, Asha swung for Lilith, who dodged it by stepping back once more, but darted forward with another attack using her demonic blade. Asha only just brought her shield back around to the front of her in time, blocking the attack. However, as the blade smashed into the shield, it cracked down the middle, and half of the shield fell to pieces.

Thinking quickly, Asha twisted to the left, embedding what was left of the ice-shield into the demon's head, snapping the shield off the ice around her arm. With the ice still encasing her fist, Asha twisted back to face Lilith and swung a left hook that connected with the succubus' head, shattering the ice and cutting Lilith's face. Lilith screamed in half fury, half pain. She slashed wildly at Asha. The strikes were unpredictable and sloppy, which made them easy to dodge. Asha blocked and dodged, which seemed to only make Lilith more furious. Eventually there was an opening, and Asha stepped in behind the limits of Lilith's effective range, stabbing her in the stomach with a shard of ice.

She screamed again, this time all parts pain, with maybe a bit of fear. Asha punched her again and pushed her hard onto the ground. As she fell, her blades clattered across the ground away from her. Asha looked around the chamber. Her team looked exhausted but alive, standing among the dead bodies of at least two dozen of Lilith's minions.

Looking down at Lilith now, despite all the power she had held only five minutes ago, she looked so small and fragile. Her fear was genuine, and any trace of her overconfident mocking had disappeared entirely.

'Order your cambion to stand down,' Asha demanded. She was firm and spoke as if giving an order to anyone else under her command.

'It's not that easy!' Lilith shouted, and she looked as though she may break down in tears. She got to her knees, looking up at Asha. 'Please, I can't.'

'Why not?' Asha kept her stoic tone.

'They are not under my control anymore,' she revealed. 'I made them for someone else.'

'Who?' Asha asked.

'I can't—' Lilith stammered.

Asha repeated her question and raised her sword again.

'An angel,' Lilith said. 'I can't—'

'Liar!' Ambriel seemingly came out of nowhere and struck Lilith, knocking her to the ground again.

'It's true!' Lilith pleaded, and she returned to sit back up.

Before Asha could ask her anymore questions, the sound of snapping lightning interrupted her. Asha looked to where the sound had come from, and a few metres behind where Lilith sat, a spark of red electricity arched from thin air, opening up into a ten-foot oval-shaped swirling mass of red liquid.

Emerging from the crimson portal were two figures standing side by side. They were humanoid, but it was not until they were all the way through that Asha knew what they were. They were white skinned, like porcelain, but had the black eyes of pitch. White cambion.

Asha took an instinctive step back and prepared herself for another fight, but the cambion were not alone. Another shape took form inside the blood-like swirling of the portal. This one was a woman. She was medium height with tidy brown hair tied up into a tight ponytail and hazel eyes to match. She was thin and feminine with beautiful yet hard features.

'Lust!' Asha heard Lilith cry out, now brave enough to scramble to her feet. The cambion did not attack, but instead took up a defensive stance on either side of Lilith, which made Asha and her team take another few reflexive steps back, and not just because of the cambion. If this woman was Lust, as in *the* Lust, and not just a lust demon, then the cambion were the least of their issues.

'I didn't think you'd make it in time,' Lilith said to Lust, walking over to her.

'Oh, Lilith,' Lust chided in the way you would if you were comforting a child. 'You should know by now that I am your biggest fan.' Lust smiled lovingly, brushing the back of her hand against Lilith's cheek.

'I know, and I am grateful you've come to help me.' Lilith stepped in as Lust pulled her into an embrace. 'I didn't think you would need me anymore, and that you'd let me die.'

'Shh,' Lust breathed as she materialised a demonic blade and ran it across Lilith's throat. Asha could hear the sound of the wound sizzling and Lilith choking as she fell to the ground. 'Unfortunately, you talk too much, my love.'

Lust turned to the group, a wicked smile upon her face. 'We won't be needing you anymore.'

Lust pointed at the Ghost. '*Mortika quod glaviras haber*,' she said to her guards before she turned away from them so casually that it infuriated Asha. Without another word, Lust disappeared back through the portal, and as she did, the cambion materialised swords of their own.

'Run!' Asha yelled as she called upon the power of her rune. She felt the familiar chill of it pulse through her body as she extended her arms and a miniature blizzard formed in front of them. When it cleared, the cambion were encased in ice. Asha felt her body go from icy-cold to unbearably warm, as if she had walked from a walk-in freezer into a sauna, and the sudden change in temperature made her feel as if her stomach were doing back flips.

'That will not hold them for long, and I've just used up all my rune's power,' she said, barely able to breathe due to nausea. Each breath made vomiting more and more likely.

A moment later, Adley came out of the other room with Katherine and six of the other wardens, who looked more dead than alive.

'Are we able to transport so many at once?' the Ghost asked Ambriel.

'In theory, yes, but doing it the way we are is risky,' Ambriel admitted. 'It should work, or it will kill you, or it'll kill all of us.'

'Oh good, so we get obliterated by the misuse of angelic power, or we get slaughtered by demons,' the Ghost said sarcastically.

'Isn't that how you've lived your life up until now, Mister I-Want-To-Take-On-Everybody?' Grim said dryly. 'It's not much of a choice, either we try and maybe die, or don't try and definitely die.'

Asha could see the Ghost about to say something in response to that, but the sound of the cracking ice took priority over the conversation. A moment later, the crack turned into an explosion of frozen shards, which left the upper bodies of the cambion free.

'Do it!' Grim yelled.

Ambriel leaped over to the Ghost, who held the sword up in preparation, with Katherine touching the Ghost's shoulder. Although they did not need her for guidance to get back, if she wasn't touching the Ghost when they teleported out, she'd be left behind. The sword wasn't exactly meant for transporting demons.

There was another sound of cracking ice as one of the cambion completely freed himself of his icy prison. Asha readied her sword, knowing it would not do much, but she had to slow the demon down at least and give Ambriel and the Ghost more time.

Before the demon crashed into Asha, who had moved into its path, there was a sudden flash of movement as someone barrelled into the cambion, knocking it to the ground. It was Katherine.

'Go!' she yelled at them as she got back to her feet. She turned back to face the cambion, who had also returned to its feet. Asha saw Katherine summon dual blades as the second cambion freed itself from the ice. It was too late to stop her as the familiar clap of thunder came, taking them home.

Chapter Twenty-One
Enlighten me

Asha's team helped the surviving wardens back to their hideaway and set them up with beds in the infirmary where Kára was waiting for them. She instructed Asha to come and see her when they were done and for Tiago to set the Ghost up with a room, or rather Lynus, as was his name. Kára then left with the lying bitch, Amber, in tow.

Once she was sure the surviving wardens were comfortable and well looked after, Asha followed her instructions and made her way to Kára's office. As she approached the door, she could hear voices behind it. The words she heard sounded familiar, yet vague, as if she could understand the language, just not the words. She knocked on the door, and the talking ceased immediately. Kára invited her inside.

Inside the room, Kára stood behind her desk, but several feet away from her stood another angel. She had long hair that reached the small of her back, and to say it was dark wouldn't do it justice. It wasn't just black; it was void of colour, like the light died before it could even reach it. She had a pretty face that featured the light orange eyes of a seraph, a first-sphere angel equal to Gabriel within their ranks, but where his eyes were like a raging sun, hers were more akin to that of a smouldering, dying fire. As Asha joined them at Kára's desk, it were as if this black-haired angel was looking at her through the ash-pit of a recently smothered forge.

'I have called the other lochs in as well,' Kára said. 'Please wait for them.'

There was about a minute of painstakingly awkward silence while she waited, but before long each of the other three loch wardens entered the room. First to arrive was Jason, who was an arrogant piece of demon crap as far as it concerned Asha, and if she hated anyone more than she had High Warden Mason, it'd be him by little margin. She figured he took top spot now since Mason was likely dead.

Jason was a wannabe paladin with no skill to suit; instead, he wielded his team like his own personal weapon to complete assignments, which he usually did at their expense. In the last three years, he had had a complete turnover of wardens due to fatalities in the field because of his poor leadership. He had a high success rate on assignments, higher than any other team in fact, but if the chapter had been working under normal conditions, Asha doubted he would have kept his position for as long as he had. Maybe all that was the reason she hated him, but it could just as well have been that he thought he was better than everyone else and seemed to have a constant smug expression stuck on his face.

Second was Ophelia. She was a small mousy woman who didn't say much, and she was the exact opposite of Jason, which wasn't a good thing. Her team failed most assignments they were sent on whenever demons were present, so most of the time nowadays, Tarek had sent them on clean-up duties. She was capable, as was her team, but she was far too careful. Though the positive of that was, in stark contrast to Jason's team, she had not lost a single warden in three years. She seemed to look up to Asha too, which made her feel a little uncomfortable. She'd smile at her when she entered a room like a small child seeing her mother, and always wanted to talk to her. Asha avoided her any chance she could.

The third and last to arrive was Sorterra. He had made a full recovery after the events at the sanctuary, physically at least. He had lost a member of his team during the initial attack, and then another during the ambush in the cavern as they tried to leave. Jessica had died shoving Kallista from the path of an inmai's spear, which made him feel like he had failed to protect them both. To make it worse, he had been sweet on her for years but had said nothing. He showed none of the pain from this now, but Asha could relate to Terra the most out of all three. He embodied what she wanted to be and was the closest thing to a role model she had since Delarin had been killed. He was no-nonsense and did whatever it took to do the job without taking unnecessary risks, but rarely hesitated when it was required. Regrettably, like her, he had also experienced losing his own loch and a few lances along the way.

The angel that was unknown to Asha stepped forward. 'Thank you for gathering here,' she began.

'With all due respect, who are you?' Asha asked.

'I've been called a great many things over many centuries,' she replied with a confident smile. 'Yama, Ferryman, Mara, and I believe your western culture calls me the *Grim Reaper*.' The angel spoke with a clear inflection of pride. 'But my brothers and sisters call me Azrael. I am a seraph—archangel and leader of The Ankor Legion.'

The Ankor Legion was another sect of angels like The Divine March and The Valkyr Guard. Their job was taking the souls of the dead—that is, the souls that the valkyr didn't claim for wardenship. She was *the* angel of death. This didn't bode well.

'She has come to deliver a message,' Kára stated. 'Salem was not the only sanctuary attacked. In fact almost half of the sanctuaries across the globe have been assaulted by demons led by the white cambion, and half of those were destroyed, leaving only a handful of survivors from each at best.'

'Sanctuary Prime was among them,' Azrael added. She said it so simply, like it was a fun fact you give someone in passing. 'We know not the condition of all sanctuaries presently; however, some have reported that demons have taken up residence in at least six other sanctuaries and are now relentlessly defending them from counter attacks. We have lost even more lives, warden and angel, in these failed attempts to re-secure.'

'And Prime?' Asha asked.

'They repelled their attackers, but they killed many of the council,' Azrael said. 'Including the arch paladin.'

'Asard is dead?' Terra cried out.

'He is,' Azrael confirmed. 'His death is the only reason I risk interfering by bringing this news as a favour to Gabriel.'

'The Order is in disarray, and we are vulnerable,' Kára said. 'Gabriel is doing what he can to keep things together until they choose a new arch paladin, but for now each chapter is on their own. But there is some good news.'

'I was informed that during the attack on your Order's headquarters it was found that neither blessed nor cursed blades could hurt these white cambion, as you already know,' Azrael said. 'But I *have* heard reports of angelic weapons having harmed them. None of the legions are about to start handing them out, but it is something.'

A few moments passed as the news and ramifications sank in. They were without their own high paladin, and now the Order's leader was dead along with half his potential successors. They were without a proper sanctuary here and had just lost half of their own numbers. Azrael was right though—knowing they could kill the white cambion after all was at least a small light of hope.

'What do we do now?' Ophelia asked. It was the only realistic question that was no doubt on everyone's mind. They seemed all but completely defeated.

'We keep going,' Kára said. 'Nothing has changed. Your duty remains the same. On that note—Asha.' She looked at her. 'I wish to offer you praise on your team's success within second circle. Tell us how it went. Is Lilith dead?'

'She is,' Asha confirmed, somewhat shocked Kára had given her praise instead scolding her for rushing off without more help.

'So the cambion are dead?' Jason asked. He was about as dumb as he was arrogant. Whatever he did in his previous life to be considered worthy of wardenship was beyond Asha.

'They aren't a hive-mind, you moron,' Sorterra grunted. Asha had only held back because of the presence of the archangel, but the somewhat aggressive display didn't seem to faze her.

Kára spoke before Jason could reply. 'Did you discover anything else about the demons?'

'No.' Asha shook her head somewhat ashamed of how little their mission actually achieved. 'But there is more to this than the white cambion. We went to kill Lilith, and now she's dead and unable to create more, but it looks like whoever was using her was already finished with her. We were not the ones who ended up killing her, and we ran before we could investigate.'

'Who was it that put an end to her, Asha?' Azrael asked.

'Lust,' Asha said.

'Your team was chased out by a lust demon?' Jason laughed hard. 'Maybe the problem here is that the right teams are not doing the right assignments.'

'Shut up, Jason!' To Asha's surprise, it was Ophelia who had yelled. It must have been a shock to Jason as well, since he did as he was told, albeit for being at a loss for words rather than compliance.

'It wasn't a lust demon,' Asha said. 'It was Lust herself.'

The room went quiet, and the angels looked at each other as if they were speaking telepathically.

'What does this mean?' Sorterra broke the silence, but his question fell unanswered for several long moments as the angels pondered it over.

Azrael finally spoke. 'I do not know,' she replied, looking back to Kára. 'I will have to tell the others and try to ascertain what this means. For now, do what it takes to continue your duty here in Salem and keep what's left of the team safe.'

'Yes, sister,' Kára replied.

Azrael nodded to Kára and stood up straight, her arms crossed over her chest. She emitted a light from her entire body. Suddenly there was a flash, and when it cleared, the angel was gone.

'I want all teams to spend the day resting,' Kára directed as she turned her attention to the group of loch wardens. 'As soon as night falls, I'll have assignments for you that I will brief you on throughout the afternoon. You may leave.'

With that, the teams turned on their heels and left. As Asha approached the door, Kára called her name.

'Before you retire for the day,' she said. 'Send the Ghost to me.'

Asha nodded in acceptance of her instruction, which she fulfilled quickly to make it to her room as soon as she could. She and sleep were not friends, but today she had a feeling they'd bury the hatchet and get along just fine.

***

The sun had begun its ascent into the clear sky as Grim sat among the cold concrete of the walls that rose around the church garden. Apparently all wardens had been told to rest, and in his experience the only time wardens were actually instructed to sleep was when the higher-ups knew bad things were about to happen. Grim had no interest in sleep, despite not having done so for two days, which even for a warden was pushing it.

Everything was going to hell, and no matter what they did to stem the tide of shit falling around them, it just carried on like a tidal wave through a small town undeterred by their efforts to stop it. But Grim knew this was always the way it was; he knew he was letting it get to him more now than usual because of what was going on in his own life, a life that wardens were discouraged to have in the first place. But that would not stop him. Screw Amber and her lies; he wasn't going to give up on finding his daughter. He wouldn't let this shit-storm swallow him up before he knew what had become of her. But his only hope had been that demonic artefact that Narki wanted, and Grim hadn't had the chance to even look for it in Lilith's nest, let alone bring it back. He had to think of a way to convince Narki to help regardless.

He sat there for quite some time, watching the last few stars disappear as the sun's light swallowed them up, by which point he almost felt relaxed enough to sleep, but then *she* walked in under the hedge archway and approached with care.

'You aethereals are not very good at being where you are wanted,' Grim said without looking at her.

'Grim, please,' she pleaded. Her eyes almost looked sincere. 'I'm sorry.'

'Don't give me your fake sentiment,' he snapped. He wanted nothing more than to just yell and scream obscenities at her, but he held back. 'I know you things don't feel. I opened up to you like I've never done with anyone before as a warden, and everything you said in return was a lie.'

'Angels feel, Grim.' She looked sullen, but it didn't bother him. 'Everything I told you was the truth. Why do you think I'm here?'

'You tell me,' he said firmly. 'I take it you're here to grovel, hoping you can trick me again.'

'What point would that serve?'

'Who am I to know the agendas of your kind? Why do you think I distrust you things so much?'

'I am not a thing, Grim.' This time there was a flare of offence mixed with her fake desperation. 'We angels are not that much different from you wardens.'

'Enlighten me then, because you sure as hell don't act like it,' he said.

'Second- and third-sphere angels were once human. Our souls were reforged from human souls who made it to heaven,' she said. 'We remember nothing, nor will I ever remember my human life, but we know what it's like to be human. We may not feel emotions the same way humans do, but we still feel them in our own way. Our physical form is different, but our soul is the same as yours.'

Grim wanted that to be true. At the back of his mind there was something scratching at his resolve. Something that wanted to believe her. Something that desperately wanted to just embrace her. He knew what that something was too. It was nothing more than the affection she had seeded within him with her lies.

'So far all you've shown me is your human-like ability to deceive,' he said.

'I am here to apologise, yes. But I also want to show you that you can trust me.' She moved in front of him and locked eyes with him. Her eyes spoke to him of a gentle defiance. It reminded him of the looks his wife used to give him when he was being stubborn and she was trying to convince him of something for his own good.

'Ask me anything, and I will answer it as best I can,' she said.

It was an interesting offer. What would stop her from lying about anything he asked her? How would this prove anything? Regardless, he took her up on it.

'What kind of angel are you?' he asked. 'You took down the Ghost pretty easy, so I figure you're up there.'

'I'm second sphere, a temperance angel of The Virtuous Guard,' she said. The look on her face showed that she knew further explanation was necessary. 'Sort of like the equivalent of a wrath demon, except we guide humans away from wrath, rather than towards. I was only able to pin the Ghost because he had already spent a lot of his rune energy, and he wasn't expecting me to well...show myself.'

If what she said was true, and that she was a virtue angel, it would explain why she expressed human emotion better than most other angels.

'Your eyes. They're wrong now. Too light,' he stated. Before she had revealed herself, her eyes were like sapphires, now they were a perfect sky blue.

'Oh,' she said, and just like that the blue of her eyes darkened. 'Since we work as guardians and guides to lost humans, angels of virtue can disguise themselves as human,' she said. 'We're also more resilient to the negative effects of indulging in human emotion. The more reason you should believe me when I tell you I meant everything I said last night.'

'Why are you here? Why the deception?' he asked. Despite himself, he was starting to crack. The scratching was breaking through.

'I can't tell you that,' she said.

'So much for full disclosure.'

'I can't tell you because I don't know,' she said quickly. 'Gabriel asked my legion's seraph, Raphael, to borrow one of his angels. They chose me. They ordered me to join a team in Salem to help protect the chapter. I was told to stay disguised for as long as I could. I was never told why, and it is not in our nature to question our betters.'

'Maybe if you did, you'd be able to make me believe you,' Grim said, doing his best not to indulge his urge to scream at her. 'You angels, all you care about are your own agendas and plots. You're as bad as demons; you don't care about us.'

'That's not true!' she railed.

'Prove it.' He had slunk back into fiery stubbornness.

Amber exhaled a sigh of resignation as she reached into her coat and pulled out what Grim thought was a dagger. It had a bone-white handle with engravings on it that looked like demonic glyphs. The blood-red blade was three-in-one, which twisted up into a screw-like point. When he realised what it was, the fires of his stubbornness were extinguished. It was the artefact Narki had wanted in exchange for information about his daughter Kiera.

'I grabbed it as we were leaving,' she said as she placed it in front of him. 'I still want to help you. I want you to have it either way, but I will join you if you'll still have me. If this doesn't prove that you can trust me, I have nothing else to give.'

There was a full minute of silence as Grim stared at the artefact, thinking of ways that giving this to him would work in Amber's favour. It was a demonic artefact, which she should by all rights destroy or hand in. For her to not only *not* do that but be willing to forsake her duty as both a warden and an angel by letting this thing go was beyond anything Grim would have expected from her. She was choosing to gain his forgiveness rather than reward from her superiors, not to mention risking punishment.

'Okay,' he relented. 'But only because I care more about finding Kiera than I do about being able to trust you.'

'I suppose that will have to do for now,' she said.

'Meet me in here in three hours,' he said. 'Oh, and I'm still calling you Amber.'

'I wouldn't want it any other way,' she smiled.

***

With their sanctuary destroyed, demons on the loose and the world coming to a swift end, Tiago could think of nothing more than his bed. After he had shown Lynus to his room, Tiago made his way to his own, though there was one thing he needed to do before calling it a night.

Tiago didn't know the exact difference in the time progression between hell and the earth, but he figured Aiden must have been training for at least most of the night. He liked that about him because it reminded him of his days as a police officer. He had met many new recruits who were scared, clumsy and a little unsure of themselves. Then there were recruits who were far too confident and far too brazen for their own good, who ended up making more work for him. As a warden, Tiago considered Aiden the former of the two, but he liked him for more than that. He was scared a lot, but they all were at some point when starting this life, and Tiago had seen multiple occasions where Aiden had shown courage despite being scared out of his head. He was clumsy at times, but always did his best to do better at everything each time he did it. He was unsure of himself, but he always seemed to seek answers, and Tiago had always told his recruits, in his past life and in this one, that he'd much prefer to answer a stupid question than to fix a problem caused by a stupid mistake.

Tiago walked into the room where Aiden was training, being watched by the holier than thou Kallista. 'He has the eyes of God watching over him, I see.'

'The eyes of the Lord are in every place,' she recited with a smirk. 'Keeping watch on the evil and the good.'

Aiden turned away from the targets. 'You're back!' he exclaimed, looking far too happy for someone at five in the morning. 'What happened?'

'Did you find the Ghost?' Kallista asked. 'What took so long?'

'I am. We did. Went to hell.' His flippant response was met with blank stares. 'We found him, yes, but he didn't want to come quietly so he kicked all of our arses until Amber turned into a freakin' angel and kicked *his* ass instead. Then he agreed to help us, so with his help we rushed off to hell, kicked Lilith's arse, got our arses kicked and ran away, so now we're here with some rescued wardens and stories to tell. The end.

'Sorry we didn't take you guys along with us; we were kind of in a hurry and didn't have time to pick up extra passengers along the way.'

'It's fine,' Kallista said. 'I've spent both my lives in such a specific way to avoid ending up there.'

'Wait,' Aiden said with a look of bewilderment on his face. 'Amber is an angel?'

'Kinda obvious looking back on it, I guess,' Tiago said.

'So the Ghost is helping us now?' Kallista asked dubiously.

'Apparently, he has some deal with a demon he wants to fulfil,' Tiago explained. 'So we agreed to help him with that in exchange for him helping us into hell. How we're gonna do that is a matter of debate between Amber and Asha though.'

'I couldn't imagine it thrilled Asha to find out Amber was an angel this whole time,' Aiden chuckled.

'Let's just say it wouldn't surprise me if they killed each other before the day is out,' Tiago said with a half-hearted laugh. He didn't take the revelation as badly as Asha or Grim, but he had no personal reason to. This sort of thing had never happened before that Tiago knew of, but it didn't surprise him. These were strange times, and with a possible traitor within their ranks, perhaps an angel in the mix wasn't such a terrible thing. Who knew really? Either way, Tiago would not let it get to him.

'You said you ran away,' Kallista said. 'Does that mean Lilith is still alive?'

Tiago shook his head. 'No, she's like super dead,' he said. 'But it was Lust who showed up out of nowhere and killed her.'

Kallista's reaction was about what Tiago expected. She went very pale very quickly. Aiden's was also what he expected, though very different.

'So is Lust a demon?' he asked, still looking confused.

'She's a Sin,' Tiago said.

'Okay,' Aiden nodded slowly. 'So are Sins demons?'

Tiago barked an amused laugh. 'Yes and no.'

'Well, that's helpful,' he said, his eyes narrowing.

Kallista rolled her eyes at Tiago and explained further. 'There are sin demons whose power embody the seven deadly sins,' she said. 'They have the power to bring out the vices that exist in even the deepest parts of ourselves. But Tiago is talking about the Sin, Lust, itself.'

'What's the difference?' Aiden asked.

'A demon of sin can manipulate all those naughty feelings people keep locked away based on the sin they represent, and are a pain in the arse because they cause havoc wherever they go,' Tiago explained. 'They are usually easy to deal with though.'

'An actual Sin itself can create those vices whether they exist or not, and manipulate them with a much higher intensity.' Kallista divulged, still pale, and Tiago could tell she hated speaking of them.

'They are also immortal and aren't demons technically,' Tiago said. 'They're called primordials and are much worse than demons.'

'Luckily for us, they can't get out of hell and can't be summoned to the earth in any form,' Kallista explained. 'They have to escape hell itself, body and soul. That's why they have sin demons to do their bidding.'

'They're content feeding off of the sin their demons spread,' Tiago said. 'The fact that one is scheming about in our business is not good.'

'How do you kill one?' Aiden asked.

Tiago burst out with a genuine belly laugh. He wasn't laughing at the ridiculous thought of them being able to kill a Sin, but the fact that Aiden's first thought was how to kill it. He really was coming into his own as a warden. It almost made Tiago feel like a proud father, or older brother.

'Primordials are probably older than God,' Tiago joked after he finished wiping the tears of laughter from his eyes. 'You can't.'

Aiden looked resigned, but Tiago could see his mind working over the implications of such a thing. Probably, like most, he was thinking of the worst-possible scenario that came along with this information.

'So, yes,' Tiago said. 'We escaped with some rescued wardens we found and got away mostly unscathed. Now we have been ordered to rest up for the day, and in my experience that means we will have one hell of a night tonight, so get some rest.'

With that, Tiago left them to probably smooch goodnight or something so he could go do some smooching of his own—with his pillow.

Chapter Twenty-Two
Eleanor

Oh, good morning,' Narki said in surprise as he shoved a page of scrawlings under the table into a drawer.

The pair of them said nothing as Grim produced the artefact Narki had requested in exchange for his information. It was not until Narki grabbed it with eager hands that Grim spoke. 'We literally went through hell to get this,' he said without a hint of humour in his voice. 'The information you give me now had better be worth it. Otherwise, we'll take it back from you.'

Narki gave them a sly smile bereft of any hint of the trepidation that Grim had tried to instil in him. 'I've always believed that an item is only worth as much as someone is willing to pay for it,' he sniggered. 'It is similar with information. It is only worth as much as someone is desperate to have it, and I know you are very desperate, but don't you worry because the price is exactly as it should be.'

'Are you going to tell me or not?' Grim interrupted.

'Historical cases like this, especially with all the other complications involved, are not exactly my forte,' he said. 'I couldn't find much in such a small amount of time. However, I found you a solid starting point.'

Grim and Amber stood in silence waiting for him to continue. A *starting point* was a little less than Grim was hoping for, but it was much better than he had ever gotten before. Besides, if Narki screwed them around and the lead ended up nowhere, Grim was prepared to let Amber do whatever it took to take the artefact back.

'After your ah...*departure,* your daughter was badly injured,' he revealed. 'They took her to Saint Juliana Hospital where she was cared for, but with no parents to take her, she was sent to an orphanage.'

'So she lives?' Amber asked.

'I don't know if she does now or not,' he replied. 'But she survived after the last time you saw her, Grim.'

Grim felt relief swell in his chest to the point where he felt as if he would burst. Yet a lump grew in his throat as he thought of all the terrible implications of her survival. Her last parent dead, killed in front of her no less. Forced to live horribly scarred and raised by strangers. He dreaded to think what sort of long-term effects it had had on her mentally, and how that in turn controlled her life.

'Which orphanage?' Grim asked. He could feel Amber's gaze on him, but he didn't look at her. Looking at her face while struggling to keep his emotional wall intact would send the wall crashing down.

'Jerome Hope Orphanage,' Narki said. 'Do you know where that is?'

Grim shook his head. 'No, but just because I can't find my daughter, it doesn't mean I can't look up an address.'

'Well, the thing is, it's no longer listed,' Narki said apologetically. 'Which works well for you because it's been abandoned, bought by some rich folk who are going to tear it down.'

'How is that good for us, exactly?' Amber demanded.

'Because all their records are still there,' Narki replied. 'I'm sure you'll be able to find something on Kiera.' He then passed Grim a piece of paper with a printout of a map on it.

'Thank you, Narki,' Grim said.

'Well, holy crap,' Narki laughed. 'Hearing you thank me for a change would have almost been worth the information alone.'

The paint on the sign above the archway into the front yard of the orphanage that read 'Jerome's Hope' in thick red letters was chipped and sun damaged. It had been clearly in disrepair well before they had closed down. The Victorian-style two-storey house that been the orphanage peeked over the tall hedges that served as the front fence to the property.

Inside the archway was a wrought iron gate that stood defiant again their desire for entry, but it was not about to deter them. Amber walked up to the gate, grasped the padlock and pulled downwards, breaking the lock with ease.

'That's a neat trick,' Grim said with a smirk.

'What kind of angel would I be if I let human locks get in my way,' she chuckled as she opened the gate. She didn't notice Grim's face turn sour at the reminder she was an angel. It's not like he had forgotten; he just didn't enjoy hearing it. Especially so casually from her.

Not that it would have mattered, but the front door to the building itself was left unlocked. It opened with little noise as it swung inwards. They walked into the house and stood within a wide but otherwise small foyer with nothing in it except a simple green line running down its length, a few cheap paintings hanging from the red floral wallpaper and an empty desk in the middle against the wall opposite the front door.

On their left was a closed wooden door while on the right-hand side of the room was a doorway opening up into a parlour, which they walked into. The room was a little more decorated than the foyer, with a much larger, more ornate rug dominating most of the floor space. There was a red leather two-seater lounge sitting opposite two single-seater couches of the same design, with a coffee table between them still holding an open book and several mugs.

'It's like they just got up and left,' Amber said, looking around at the almost-immaculate condition of the room.

'Whoever purchased it must have been in a hurry to get them out,' Grim said.

'Hmm,' she mused. 'Which makes little sense considering they've left it abandoned.'

'Let's be thankful for that,' he said. 'Where do you think they'd keep records of the orphans that came through?'

'In this day and age, I'd assume they would record everything digitally, overseen by whichever organisation runs this place,' Amber speculated. 'But if they kept physical records, I'm not sure. I noticed this building had a particularly large loft, so perhaps we should look there?'

Grim nodded in agreement, and they made their way through the house. It was a lot bigger than it looked from the outside and reminded Grim of pretty much every Order sanctuary he'd ever been in. From the parlour, they walked down a hallway with the same red floral wallpaper as the foyer had, which then led them to the back half of the house where they came across a staircase.

Grim watched Amber as she climbed the stairs in front of him. She walked with such grace, making hardly a sound while she glided upwards, her hand caressing the wooden railings as the stairs spiralled up to the second floor. The part of him that wanted to hate Amber for what she had done lost a lot of its conviction despite his anger, and because of that, his admiration for her had pushed it back down inside him. But he was too stubborn to let it die completely. Despite this, he could feel its warm disdain, fuelled by a sense of betrayal, becoming cooled by her presence. He thought he needed to keep it as a reminder, but he was beginning to realise that the thing he needed to remember instead was that she was here now despite herself, and the act of her desire for redemption in his eyes was all he needed to let his anger slowly die. Maybe there was no betrayal. After all, this war made them all do things they didn't want to do.

From the second floor they made their way up a smaller set of stairs that led to the loft. This door creaked a welcome to the pair as they pushed it open into the third level of the house. It was about what Grim had pictured: a giant room under a pitched roof with dark grey floorboards and the occasional support beam. It was without any kind of furniture except for dozens of file cabinets set up along the sides of the room all the way to the back of the loft where a single window let in the only source of light.

'Looks like you were right,' Grim said, looking over all the cabinets.

She nodded with a smile as she lifted an arm and extended her palm. Her hand glowed and several orbs of light formed and floated up to the peak of the roof, illuminating the room.

'So is that like your angel ability or something?' Grim asked.

She laughed a short, gentle laugh, like that of a mother to a child struggling to understand something. 'Not exactly,' she said. 'We don't have abilities of our own, like you wardens do with runes; we share more of the same abilities. Certain angels just excel in different disciplines.'

'And what type of ability are you good at?' he asked.

'Illusions,' she said with a facial expression that told Grim she was not unaware of how that may have sounded. 'It's how I led the team to find you when the arbiter had captured you. I could track you by using your blood, as all angels would have been able to, but I couldn't admit to that, so I used an illusion that your team would remember as a locater crystal.'

'So such a thing doesn't exist?' Grim probed.

She shook her head. 'No, but I had to help them find you and going alone with no explanation would have put suspicion on me.'

'Fair enough.' He nodded his understanding. 'Where should we start?'

Grim and Amber began their search through the cabinets. To say they were poorly organised would have been far too kind. Despite this, and after an hour of searching, Grim opened a file that contained a picture of Kiera.

The sight of her photo almost invoked tears, but he held them back as he read the file, giving Amber a summary of its contents as he did.

'She came here after the hospital, just as Narki told us,' he said. 'She was admitted with lacerations to her face, and after minor surgery, they sent her here. The state refused to press charges against the men who did it.' Grim cursed and clenched his fists until his knuckles were white. 'Fucking cowards were too afraid to go up against the mob, not even for a little girl. I swear I'll kill them all myself!'

'Grim.' Amber's soothing voice cut through his anger. 'Let us focus on finding out where she has ended up.'

She was right. It was after all what he had always wanted. Not only to find out if she had survived, but to find out what kind of life he had forced her to have. It broke his heart each time he thought of all the bad things she must have gone through. He needed closure.

'You're right,' he consented, taking a deep breath. He read through the rest of the document and found something else. A new lead. 'She was adopted a year later, the address is listed here.'

'That's great news, Grim,' Amber said with a bright, genuine smile. 'I am—'

She was cut off by a sudden cacophony of shattering glass and exploding tiles as parts of the roof and the window imploded. When Grim was able to regain his senses, he saw what had just invited itself into the room.

Two white cambion now stood at the opposite end of the loft and wasted no time in charging at them. Grim lifted his rifle and fired as many rounds as he could until he needed to reload. The power of the rounds kept one cambion back, but did nothing to harm it. Grim called upon the power of his rune and faded into the shadows as he reloaded.

Amber raced forward, her wings appearing as she materialised her angelic axe and swung. To Grim's surprise, Amber's and especially the cambion's, Amber's attack made contact, biting into the cambion's arm and drawing dark red blood. The demon hissed in pain and anger as it counter-attacked with a punch to Amber's stomach, forcing her to take a step back. The cambion's wound stopped bleeding, but it didn't close up. A thrill of hope rose up through Grim—they could be killed.

Grim had reloaded and fired at the cambion who was now walking in his direction. He fired the first two rounds at his target, but saw that the other cambion attacking Amber had summoned his own blade and was about to land an attack on her. He fired at the cambion, disrupting his attack enough that Amber could get in first with a solid strike to the demon's ribs. Doing this put Grim in danger as the break in the shots on his target allowed the other cambion to close a significant gap between them.

The cambion bearing down on Grim summoned a demonic blade and brought it down from overhead. Grim blocked the strike with his rifle, but it knocked him to the ground. The cambion suddenly howled in pain and spun around, a large gash in its back spilling out blood onto Grim. Amber engaged the demon from the front as Grim got to his feet. The other cambion was coming in behind Amber, and Grim suddenly felt panicked. He moved towards the cambion that was currently fighting with Amber and fired directly into the demon's wound on its back just as it was about to close up. The demon screamed in agony and fell to its knees, and Amber relieved it of its head before turning towards the other cambion just in time to prevent what would have been a lethal strike. Instead, the demon's blade tore into her left shoulder. She yelled in pain but it didn't stop her from attacking in return.

She took flight over the cambion's head, landing on the other side before swinging her axe. The demon blocked the swing, but the axe dissipated like smoke. It was an illusion. Grim looked above the demon and saw that Amber had never landed at all. She came rushing down, but the cambion was too quick and used its own wings to dart away just in time. Grim half-ran towards Amber to help, but before he could do anything, two more cambion came crashing through the roof, landing beside the other.

The cambion stalked towards them with a quiet confidence. Grim knew that even with Amber, they were screwed. 'We need to run,' Grim said. 'A week ago, I'd love to have to died taking these arseholes out, but I'm too close to finding Kiera.'

Before Amber could respond, there were more sounds of destruction behind them as something else burst through the roof, something that made even the cambions stop, look at one another and promptly fly away like scared insects. Grim and Amber turned around to see Gabriel, the sight of which sent an immense wave of relief through him.

'What are you doing here?' His voice was that of a father that had just found his kids somewhere they shouldn't be. Grim knew they were in trouble, but this kind of trouble was much more preferable.

'I am sorry, sir,' Amber said. 'We had something we needed to look into.'

'Whatever it is, it is not Order business,' Gabriel chided. 'You two have been poking around in things you do not understand, with people you do not know and for reasons you should not.'

'I'm sorry,' Amber repeated.

'Markus,' he said looking at Grim. 'I understand your pain, but you know well enough that personal business is to forsake the duties given to you by the Order.'

'I needed to know, sir,' he said. 'I'm sorry as well, but not as sorry as I would be if I were to die before knowing.'

Gabriel looked at the two of them thoughtfully. 'Clearly sending you to Salem was a poor choice, Ambriel' he said. 'I did not realise…'

'Realise what, sir?' Amber asked.

'It does not matter now,' he said. 'The artefact will be collected and given to me.'

Grim's attention was diverted away from Gabriel as the cambion returned. Three of them entered the room, blocking the exit. Somehow with Gabriel at their side, the sight of the cambion did not have the same impact of fear on him as they did before. Nonetheless, Amber and Grim got ready for a fight.

'Sir, we figure—' Grim's words were cut short as he looked down at the source of the sudden pain through his body. A spear jutted out from the left side of his chest. Gabriel's voice whispered into his ear.

'I do not need your kind any longer,' he said as Grim fell to his knees and then onto his back. He could hear Amber screaming out his name, and he looked at her with wide eyes as she rushed over to him, tears already streaming down her face. He looked at her as if seeing her for the first time. It made sense now. 'Eleanor,' he breathed as the light faded from his world.

**

'Why!' Amber screamed as she charged at Gabriel, who swatted her aside as though she were nothing more than a human.

'I did not know your connection to this human would continue to be so strong after your soul was reforged. Nonetheless, you've done your part, and the sword is exactly where it needs to be,' Gabriel said, displaying a genuine albeit shallow regret. 'It is unfortunate it ended this way.'

Amber didn't understand what he was saying, but it didn't matter. Her tears streaked her face and wet the hollows of her eyes. She felt the anger inside of her explode into all parts of her body and take root. The wetness of her eyes became hot, and she screamed at the ceiling in pain. Her hands burned where her tears had splashed against them. She looked down and saw the splotches smoke and burn her skin black. She charged at Gabriel again, who swung his spear with almost no effort. This time she ducked and swung her axe, but he dodged the attack, taking to the air.

'Kill her,' he ordered his cambion, before escaping through one of the many holes now in the orphanage's roof.

The three cambion attacked her simultaneously, but even when they landed an attack, her anger swallowed the pain, allowing her to attack again and again and again. Despite her wounds, she killed two cambion before the last one attempted to run.

It took flight, and she swung her axe as hard as she could, letting it fly through the air, connecting with the cambion, severing a wing and causing the demon to plummet into the floor. She rushed over to the demon, took her axe back and took the cambion's head off with it.

Amber rushed over to Grim, but it was too late. He was gone. The anger that had taken hold inside her flared into a white-hot fury that surged in every part of her. She stood up as agony shot through her wings like lightning. She screamed a cacophony of pain and sadness as her feathers began to slowly fall from her wings. Another flash of pain struck her, and her feathers shot from her with such speed they embedded themselves into the walls and floorboards before turning black and blowing away into dust.

The pain ceased and her fury settled as the last feather fell from her. Her wings were now only a silhouette of shadow, a dark mockery of the brilliance they were. The rage that settled inside her calmed like the ocean after a storm in the night. It churned inside her but did not crash and break. It sat restlessly within its new home, coursing through her body and darkening her mind. It whispered to her, promising safety if she let it drag her under. Promises that it would be all right. Nothing could hurt her. Her anger was her shield, her armour and her sword now. It would keep her safe from the emotions that had destroyed her. Fallen, she was an angel of temperance no longer.

Temperance had become wrath, and wrath would become vengeance.

Chapter Twenty-Three
Last thing you remember

Aiden spent several minutes walking up and down the main corridor of the undercroft, looking for members of his team until he realised he was the first one awake. It was only about three in the afternoon, but Aiden guessed after the mission in hell and everything else that had been going on lately, they'd taken advantage of their orders to rest. Aiden on the other hand had missed most of the excitement centred on the Ghost and Lilith, so he'd been sleeping for about as long as his body would let him. Now he was full of energy and with no one else in sight, he headed back into the training room.

He had spent hours training, most of the previous night in fact, while the others were gone, with no one for company except Kallista for the last few hours he'd been in there. Aiden enjoyed listening to her views on the world they now lived in as they were almost polar opposite to most other wardens'. She had faith that most things happened because God willed it and believed that God had something planned. She thought every bad thing that was happening was either a part of it, or what God was planning to stop. Much of what she tried to explain to him he didn't understand, and he wasn't sure what to believe even when he did. What he did understand though was that she believed it completely. Her faith was enough to reassure him a little, even if he didn't agree with or understand everything she said. It was inspiring considering how negative everyone else seemed to be all the time. Not that he blamed them.

He had seen the wardens that Asha and the others had brought back. They looked like zombies. It made Aiden shudder to think what things hell had subjected them to, and for how long. The things he had seen in just the last few weeks were almost enough to make him despair about everything. He couldn't imagine what it was like for the other wardens like Asha and Grim, who must have seen and done horrible things over the years they had been fighting.

Aiden concentrated on his rune, and two orange translucent blades took shape above him. The previous night it had taken him an hour to summon a single blade with great deal of effort and several hours of practice after that to do so in under five seconds. Before Tiago had come in earlier that morning, he had just got the hang of summoning two at once.

Kallista had been giving him lessons about runes as he had practised. She explained that in theory, Aiden should be able to summon as many blades as he wanted given his rune had enough energy. Tiago had explained a lot of it to him already; however, she did it in a much more precise and technical way. She had explained that the more runic energy he used, the longer it would take to recharge. She was unsure how it recharged and said it was beyond her ability to understand since the runes themselves were angelic artefacts, so it may as well be magic from a storybook for all it mattered.

Kallista had also explained the bigger, sharper or generally the more impressive the blades—or the more he summoned—the more it drained the rune, so using it effectively was key when in battle. Aiden noticed a correlation between how hard he concentrated and how much runic energy he was using, so the more he practised the better he got at using less energy for more impressive things, such as using two blades. Now that he could summon them quicker, the less energy he needed to do so. When he had pointed this out, Kallista had cautioned that no matter how good he got at using a rune, the rune still had its own limitations.

He had become so used to her talking to him as he practised that being in the room alone now in silence was an odd feeling. Though the silence did not last long.

'You're keen.' It was Asha standing in the room's archway. She looked like she had just walked out of a job interview. She was dressed in her blacks already and had brushed her wavy dark hair, pinning it up at the sides to keep it from her face.

'Yeah, I uh…couldn't sleep much more.' Aiden looked up at his blades and made them dissolve into thin air, something that had taken a surprising amount of practise to do.

'Yeah,' she said, walking in. 'Decent sleep in this life is like an estranged family member. You love it, and when you get the chance to spend time with it, you should take it, but once it's gone, you don't know when you'll see it again.'

Aiden was still unsure how to speak to Asha. She was very authoritative, yet didn't like being called by her title. She was the team leader but didn't seem to like answering questions. Because of this, a somewhat awkward silence followed for a few moments.

'You seem to be going well with your rune,' she said suddenly.

'Well, I wanted to prove you right,' he replied.

'What do you mean?' she asked.

'Tiago told me you convinced Kára that I was ready for it,' Aiden said.

'Hmm,' she grunted. 'Well, I need everyone on my team to be at full strength.'

He knew he should have just said *thank you* and left it at that. As much as he had tried to hide it, she must have noticed his deflation.

291

'Look,' she began. 'You're not bad as far as new wardens go, but you need to understand that this life we live is unforgiving; it will not only punish you for mistakes you make but it will punish everyone around you as well. It's my job to make sure you don't get anyone else killed.'

Aiden nodded, feeling a little dejected. 'I understand.'

'It's also my job to make sure no one else's mistakes, my own included, get you hurt either.' Her voice softened a little. 'Now, have you eaten?'

Aiden shook his head. 'Came straight here.'

She looked at him in his grey hooded jumper and black tracksuit pants. 'Yes...I can see that.'

Asha and Aiden walked out of the training room and down the corridor towards the exit of the undercroft. They didn't have a mess hall here like at the sanctuary as the logistics of getting the food and equipment down there would have been a nightmare. Instead they were told to go into the city and buy food, but not to do so as a large group. It was not until thinking about food that Aiden realised how hungry he was.

As they were making their way through the undercroft, a warden walked out in front of them, almost knocking Aiden over.

'Lynus,' Asha growled. 'Watch where you're going!'

Aiden recognised the name: It was the Ghost of Salem. He had been looking forward to meeting this guy, but as Lynus turned and looked at them, he looked horrified, as though Aiden were a demon.

'Aiden?' the Ghost breathed. 'How?'

As Aiden looked at the Ghost's face, a pain shot through his head. He felt as though a demon had grabbed his entire head and was squeezing. His vision blurred, and his hearing became fuzzy. He was barely aware of what was going on around him, but the Ghost was frantic, and Asha seemed no better. All he could hear was someone shouting about someone being alive.

The blurriness worsened, and he vaguely knew that he was no longer upright. There was another bolt of pain through his head as he blacked out.

***

'Dad needs rest, Lynus,' Aiden said, placing a hand on his brother's shoulder.

'I'm not letting that bitch tell us when we can see our own father,' Lynus retorted as he turned away from the bedroom door. His face softened as he met with Aiden's narrowed eyes. 'We moved back here to help look after him, right?'

'Yeah,' Aiden said. 'But Meredith said he's resting.'

'She always says that,' he said with a roll of his eyes. 'Just because he married that crone, doesn't mean we have to listen to her. We're here to look after him, so that's what we'll do.'

Lynus was older than Aiden by two years, which meant even now at the age of twenty-three, he still had the tendency to take charge. Aiden usually found it easier to just follow his lead, especially since he agreed most of the time anyway.

'Fine,' Aiden conceded. 'But if Meredith finds us in here again without her, I'll be making sure she knows whose idea it was.' Not that it mattered; along with taking charge, Lynus also usually took as much of the blame as he could when things didn't work out.

They walked into the bedroom as quietly as they could. The room was dark, and much like the other rooms in their house, it was larger than it needed to be and filled with classy antique-looking furniture. A small bedside lamp was the only illumination, the light of which did not reach the walls, making the room look as if it were floating in a void.

The room was also a lot warmer than the rest of the house, so Aiden took his jacket off, placing it on a nearby chair before the two brothers tended to their father. No one seemed to know what was wrong with him. They had admitted him to hospital with shortness of breath, cramps, nausea and lethargy, yet none of the tests they did could pinpoint what it was, despite the many theories they had come up with.

After a few days of being in the hospital, he went into a coma. Meredith had power of attorney by that point, despite only being married to him for a few weeks, so she insisted he be transferred home since they had the money to buy the necessary equipment to care for him. Lynus and Aiden had agreed since they knew their father hated hospitals, which was a feeling they shared.

The brothers wiped the beads of sweat from his brow, changed his blankets and ever so carefully gave him a fresh pillow. All the while, their father lay unmoving; only the subtle rise and fall of his chest gave any indication he was even still alive. Once they were done, they left the room as carefully as they had entered it, but just before Aiden closed the door behind him he remembered something.

'Crap,' he whispered. 'I forgot my jacket.'

Lynus kept walking down the hallway as Aiden walked back into the room, but it was no longer just his father in there. A woman in a green cocktail dress leaned over the man in the bed. It was Meredith. At first Aiden thought she was kissing him, but their lips were not touching; instead, a green mist moved from his father's mouth and into Meredith's.

Aiden must have made a noise because she abruptly stood upright and turned to face him.

'How many times must I tell you little shits not to come in here!'

'What the hell are—'

Her face contorted into rage and she lunged at him, knocking him to the floor. To his horror, her eyes had become blood-red, and her fingernails had become black talons that tore into him as he struggled to kick her off.

Suddenly he was free as Lynus tackled Meredith. Aiden got to his feet and saw Meredith clawing at Lynus' forearms while he tried to defend himself. Aiden grabbed a small golden statuette of a woman from a nearby table and swung it at the Meredith's head. She stumbled away.

Her screams of pain became screams of rage as Aiden swung again. This time Meredith caught Aiden's arm and twisted. He yelled in agony as the bone broke, and Meredith knocked him down with a slice of her nails to his stomach. He couldn't move enough to get back to his feet and could feel the warmth of his blood pooling under him. Lynus was screaming out his name, but all Aiden could see was the ceiling, and even that was becoming a blur.

The ceiling faded to grey, yet his vision became clear. The ceiling melded into stone, and he was naked. He got up to the sound of someone calling his and Lynus' names. He sat up on the bed he was on and twisted so that his feet were flat on the floor. Across from him was Lynus, who was looking as confused as he felt.

The room was stone-walled and bare, except for a pair of fluorescent tube lights on the ceiling. He was inside, yet there was a prominent draft that chilled his skin.

'Aiden and Lynus.' A large man dressed in black clothing placed a duffel bag beside them. 'I understand you are confused, but we will explain everything soon. Please get dressed and follow me.'

They did as the man told them and followed him down several corridors until they came to a set of double doors.

'Through here you will find all the answers you need,' the man said.

They pushed the doors and stepped into a large room filled with people who looked just as scared and confused as Lynus and Aiden were.

They dawdled through the crowd of people and as they did, Aiden noticed that a lot of them were wearing long black coats. As they approached a raised platform at the far side of the room, they turned around to find that the large crowd of people, as well as the room itself, had become considerably smaller, and they too were now wearing the warden blacks...

...Aiden turned away from the crowd and back around to face their high paladin and the angel that presided over their initiation. The high paladin stepped down and handed each of them a necklace with a rune attached to it.

'You are now officially wardens,' said the high paladin. 'Your rune training will start tomorrow in between missions at your loch's discretion.'

After their time at Prime, and now almost a month as lances, Lynus and Aiden had finally received their runes and had become full-fledged wardens.

Aiden turned to Lynus, and they shared a smile. Lynus opened his mouth to speak when the room they were in changed again...

…Now they were in the sanctuary's cafeteria and Aiden was sitting opposite his brother.

'Now that we have our runes, I say we go hunt down that thing that killed us and Dad,' Lynus said in a hushed tone.

'We don't know that he's dead for sure, Lynus,' Aiden replied with hope, even though he knew there was none. They had since learned what had killed him: a demon that slowly killed its victims by feeding off their life force. Normally they'd do it quickly over the course of a week, but the more patient ones savoured their meals over months, like their father's killer had. They had since concluded the only reason Meredith had not killed them sooner was because it had planned on feeding off them next.

'Besides,' Aiden said. 'We're not allowed to go off on our own.'

'This has always been the plan since we figured out what we have become, Aiden,' Lynus asserted. 'Revenge.'

'Yeah, I know,' Aiden responded.

'So what's stopping us?'

'Just because we have runes now, doesn't mean we can kill it.' Aiden tried to reason with his brother.

'No, but I've been doing some research.' Lynus placed a mostly black book on the table. It had the title A Pocket Guide to Demonology by Adley Black on the cover. 'I overheard those angels that were in here the other day talking about how a demon named Hekate was in a city called Salem. She's a powerful deal-making demon. And the author of this book…he lives in Salem too.'

'So we go to Salem, find this Adley guy and then what?' Aiden asked.

'He can tell us where to find Hekate, and she can help us get revenge,' Lynus concluded. Aiden could see the determination in his brother's eyes. He had already made up his mind, and although Aiden did not like the idea of breaking the rules, he too wanted revenge, and he knew Lynus would just go on his own either way.

'Okay, fine,' Aiden conceded. 'When do we go?'

'First thing in the morning,' his brother said with a grin.

With that settled they got up from the table and headed for the exit. As Lynus stepped through the canteen door, it shut abruptly behind him, and the door was suddenly a faded blue wooden door…

…The light of the canteen faded, and the room itself disappeared and was now an alleyway. Aiden waited patiently by the door. They had travelled to Salem and, after a full day of searching and asking questions, they had found where Adley held residence. Lynus had gone in by himself, saying that if the Order had come looking for them, they'd be asking about two people, not one. Aiden tried telling him they'd figure it out, but he insisted they needed to do anything that made it even a little harder for someone to track them down.

Eventually Lynus came back outside with good news. Adley was able to direct them to Hekate, who could apparently be summoned by throwing a key into a lake and saying some fancy words. Aiden and Lynus spent several hours finding a park with a lake with which to perform the ritual, but as Lynus said the words and Hekate rose from the lake…

…The lake became a rooftop, and the image of Hekate morphed into one of two angels who seemed to be arguing by the ledge while Lynus and Aiden hid behind an air-conditioning unit.

'What do we do with the thing Hekate gave us?' Aiden whispered to his brother.

'For now, we wait,' Lynus replied. 'This rune is powerful. Apparently it's used by some special legion of angels to incapacitate other angels, but it's only good for one use, so we have to wait for Gabriel to leave.'

Aiden peered around the corner to look at the two angels. 'Which one is the one with the sword?'

'The one of the left,' he said. 'Michael.'

Aiden watched the angels and waited. For a moment Gabriel looked over in their direction, and for a second Aiden was sure they had been found out. However, Gabriel turned back to arguing with Michael for a few more moments before saying something that seemed final before flying away off into the darkness of the night.

'Now!' Aiden shouted.

Lynus threw the rune. Michael snatched it out of the air and laughed.
'What is this, some kind of assassination at—'

The rune burst into a wave of blue electricity that engulfed Michael, forcing him to drop to one knee. Lynus took the opportunity to snatch the sword from his grasp.

'No!' Michael shouted. 'How did you get—' his words were drowned out by his pain.

'Come on!' shouted Lynus. 'This thing doesn't last for long.'

Lynus and Aiden ran towards the rooftop's ledge and jumped to a lower ledge below, but before Aiden landed…

***

Aiden shot upright. Sweat drenched his hair and dripped down his forehead. Looking around, he soon realised he was now awake and back in the infirmary. Tiago and Kallista stood over him wearing concerned faces. He looked to his left, and Lynus stood there watching him with an anxious smile. When Aiden saw Lynus' face, he recognised him as he was: his brother. Everything from the dream seemed to click into place, the visions settling into his mind where they belonged among his memories. There were still empty spaces where memories remained lost, and some details were hazy, but it was enough for him to feel more like himself again.

He rushed to his feet and wrapped his arms around his brother in a tight and long embrace. 'I remember,' Aiden said as he took a step out of the hug. 'Mostly everything. Father, Meredith, getting the sword and most importantly, you.' Aiden looked to Tiago. 'I remember waking up too.'

'Your memories as a warden shouldn't be affected by the process, Rook,' he said. 'Of course you remember waking up to this handsome face.'

Aiden shook his head. 'No, I remember waking up in Prime once before.'

'How?' Tiago asked. 'This doesn't make sense. Wardens can't be brought back a second time.'

'Perhaps it wasn't an angel's doing?' Kallista offered.

Tiago looked at her with dull eyes. 'Don't even start with me.'

Kallista shrugged. 'Guess we better ask Kára then.'

'That's exactly what I intend to do.' Asha was standing in the doorway to the infirmary, and she looked far from pleased. Aiden having been supposedly brought back a second time raised a lot of questions and a lot more implications. Something was not right.

'Kalli, we better go make sure she doesn't get herself killed by pissing off our angelic leader,' Tiago remarked.

'Good idea. These guys probably want some time to talk anyway.' Kallista gave Aiden a smile and left the room with Tiago.

Aiden looked back at Lynus. He looked tired and worn— far worse off than when he had seen him last.

'What's the last thing you remember?' Lynus asked.

'I remember incapacitating Michael and taking the sword,' Aiden said. 'But nothing past that point. What happened to us after?'

Lynus' expression went sour as he recalled the events that led to them being separated. He sat down on a bed and gestured for Aiden to sit down opposite him.

'We found the thing that killed Dad, then we spent the months afterwards killing as many demons as we could find. When the March angels started coming after us for the sword, we killed them too,' he said, his expression worsening as he went on. As Lynus spoke, pieces of Aiden's memory came back to him as flashes of fights with demons and angels. 'It didn't take long for the damn March to wise up and throw their best at us though. There was no ramp-up to it either. Suddenly we went from killing third-sphere angels to being ambushed by much stronger angels who captured you and tried ransoming you for the sword.'

At the back of Aiden's mind, somewhere buried deep in his memories, he knew what had happened next, and the pained look of regret on his brother's face made it all too obvious he was right.

'For Hekate's help, we promised her one of our dying souls, but in my eagerness to complete the deal I didn't even consider that you would die before me. When the angels captured you, we upheld our agreement,' Lynus said.

'We knew it would end this way,' Aiden added slowly as if repeating something that had just become clear in his mind. He had said that. Those were his last words before losing his memories again. 'We knew we'd be taken out eventually, and we promised that we would never give up the sword until we were both dead.'

'By the time I realised the angels planned to follow through with their threat, they killed you right in front of me.' Lynus' jaw clenched and he looked away, but Aiden could see his eyes brimming with tears. 'I'm sorry.'

Aiden placed a hand on Lynus' shoulder. This was as best a gesture to comfort him as he could think of. 'It's okay, Lynus,' he reassured. 'I don't know what happened after the angels took me, but I woke up at Prime again with none of my memories, so obviously Hekate didn't get to me.'

'I know, but who did?' Lynus asked, after having wiped his tears away.

Aiden shrugged. 'I have no idea what happened, I guess The Valkyr Guard got to me again.'

'I didn't think that was possible,' Lynus mused.

'Me neither,' Aiden agreed. Then Lynus said something that surprised him.

'Let's get out of here.'

Chapter Twenty-Four
Combat ready

Asha burst into Kára's office, the wooden door almost bouncing back off of the wall. 'What the hell is going on here!' she hollered, before realising she had done so.

Kára rose from behind her desk, extended her wings and stared Asha down. 'I don't know what you are angry about and until you calm down, I do not care,' she barked. 'You will remember your place!' When she spoke the last word, as if for emphasis, her wings shuddered and a gust of wind forced Asha to take a step back.

Before anything else could be said, Kallista and Tiago crept into the room, a touch of panic on each of their faces as if they half expected Asha to be dead. A hard stare from Kára was enough to make Kallista turn around instantly. It wasn't until Asha also turned around and had an if-looks-could-kill competition with Kára, using Tiago as their battleground, that he followed Kallista out of the room.

'You've been lying to us,' Asha shrilled, looking back at Kára with fire in her eyes, though her tone was a little more level. 'Aiden got his memories back.'

Asha half expected Kára to react with at least a bit of fear, as one does when they've been called out on a lie. Yet her face portrayed no emotion, so either the revelation did not come as a shock to her or she expected them to find out.

301

'What did he remember that has you so riled up?' Kára asked as she sat back down. The question seemed innocent enough, but if she didn't know what Asha was referring to it made her wonder what other things Kára was hiding from them.

'He remembers dying and waking up as a warden. Twice,' Asha alleged, not breaking eye contact with Kára.

'Impossible,' she said with a slightly furrowed brow.

'Impossible he remembers, or impossible that could happen?' Asha asked accusingly. 'I believe him, because guess what, he's the Ghost's brother, who remembers the same things.'

There was a long silence as Kára seemed to become lost in thought, no doubt trying to think of a way to cover it up. If wardens could have been brought back to life repeatedly, it would solve a lot of problems, and Asha personally would not have lost so many people. Why would they lie about it?

'Asha,' Kára said finally. 'Trust me when I tell you that we cannot bring the soul of a warden back a second time; it truly is impossible. We've tried many times, but it never worked out.

'When we take the soul and turn them into a warden, we imbue it with a part of ourselves: our essence. It is only a drop in a proverbial ocean, but it is enough to give you the strengths you have,' she explained, and her expression darkened slightly as she continued. 'To raise a warden a second time, we would need to use more essence, which has always gone very badly.'

'In what way?' Asha felt sick to her stomach.

'I assume you have fought with a husk before?' Kára asked, to which Asha nodded in response. 'Husks are first-sphere angels that have fallen, given too deeply into human emotions, depleting their grace without returning to heaven in time to renew themselves. Husks are what's left of the bodies. Wardens rising a second time almost instantly become something of the sort. Something, however, far more grotesque and dangerous than any husk you've ever faced.'

'Then how is it possible that Aiden has memories of waking on two separate occasions?' Asha asked, trying to push the images of husks from her mind. Normal ones were creepy and disgusting, but picturing what Kára was describing was bad enough to give even her nightmares.

'I regret to say that I do not know, Asha,' she conceded.

'How could you not know?' Asha asked, keeping herself from raising her voice again. 'You are the erelim of The Valkyr Guard. Don't you oversee all of that stuff?'

'That I am sitting here before you should indicate that I cannot possibly be there to oversee everything.' Kára stared at her with eyes that threatened anger. 'Can you account for every member of your four-person team? No. I have a legion under my guidance. I cannot possibly be responsible for all of their actions. Besides, I may be the guard's erelim, but there are still those with higher authority that will use that power if they see fit.'

'What are we going to do about Aiden then?' Asha asked.

'He is still a warden, is he not? He still has control over himself? We do nothing except our jobs,' she said. 'I will look into this mess with the utmost intrigue. For now, we have work to do.'

Asha clenched her jaw and let out an internal sigh. 'What do you need me to do?'

'I want you and Lynus to go back to the sanctuary and do reconnaissance,' she requested. 'I don't know what the demons are doing there, and it doesn't matter because whatever their intentions are, there is no way it won't be worth putting an end to. But to get in there to evict them, we need to scout the entry points and plan an attack.'

'Yes, ma'am,' Asha said with a nod. Kára was right. It would be dangerous to try to take back the sanctuary. Many others had failed at other sanctuaries around the world. But if the demons wanted the sanctuary, the wardens needed to want it more. 'Why me though? Why not send Grim with Lynus? He's better suited for this kind of mission.'

'Because I do not trust Lynus yet, but I trust that you can keep him in check,' she explained. 'Besides, Grim has not been in the undercroft since early this morning. He has been out all day, and I am unable to contact him.'

'Last time he went missing, a damn arbiter had kidnapped him. We should be looking for him.' Asha normally didn't worry about Grim. It wasn't unlike him to go off to brood somewhere, but after last time, and everything that had happened lately, she was admittedly a lot more worried than usual.

'We have other teams to do that,' Kára said. 'Don't worry about him; you just focus on the assignment I have given you. However you choose to do it is up to you. Now go.'

Asha thought better than to lose her temper again, although she dearly wanted to. Grim was her team member, and although he pissed her off on a regular basis, he was her longest and most trusted friend. If anyone would find him quickly, it would be her. She knew the assignment Kára had given her was important, but she had every intention of helping to look for Grim afterwards if he didn't show up by then.

Asha turned to walk out when Kára spoke again.

'And Asha, if you ever come to me with such anger again, misplaced or otherwise, I will not hesitate to show you what the storm of true anger looks like.'

Asha found Lynus with Aiden in the bunkhouse room. The large room held a dozen simple beds for the wardens to sleep on. They were several decades old by the looks of them, but they served their purpose. Aiden sat on his bunk and watched his brother as he wrapped the hilt of the Sword of Michael in black clothes and concealed his various runes.

'What the hell are you doing?' Asha was less than pleased. Lynus was collecting his runes and attaching them to different concealed spots on his clothing.

'Uh, leaving,' Lynus replied sullenly.

'What do you mean you're leaving?' she demanded with a scowl. 'You can't just go.'

'I helped you people, and whether you meant to, you helped me,' he said as a matter of fact. 'Now Aiden and I are leaving.'

'Funny how keen you are to adhere to a deal so strictly yet how ready you are to leave the Order again,' she sneered. 'How did that work out the first time you two left your sanctuary?'

'Look around you, Asha,' he said, gesturing to the space around them. 'This is not our war to fight. I will not play soldier under these angels. If I'm going to fight aethereals, I'm going to do it my way.'

'Y'know, I used to believe that as well, that this isn't our war to fight. But I've learned that in truth we are the only ones who *can* fight this war,' she said seriously. 'All this fighting is over *our* home, and they have given us the opportunity to represent humanity in it all. It doesn't matter what the angel's intentions are, or whether we are their tools or weapons or whatever else.

'The point is that under these black coats, without our runes or our supernatural resilience, we are just humans protecting humans, and doing so under the angels' guidance helps us do that the best way we can.'

'Look how that has turned out so far,' he spat, his voice rising. 'Aiden and I are family, and the only family we have left. He is the only one I'm interested in protecting.'

'You're just being selfish,' she said with a slight roll of her eyes.

'Selfish?' he asked incredulously. 'We helplessly watched our father slowly drift towards death because of a demon. We had to watch each other die, and then because of angels, I had to watch my brother die a second time. Call it what you want, but we're done here.'

'Boo-fucking-hoo,' she snarled. 'Every single person here has a story at least as sad as yours, and none of us are crying over it. I have seen my own share of death, including my loch warden's, who I served under for almost twenty-five years along with many other members over that time.'

'And you want us to endure the same just so we can help you fight for the angels?' Lynus asked. 'Who's being selfish now?'

'You hold the Sword of Michael and whether any of us like it, if we have any chance to succeed, we need you,' she said. It was true, but it made her a little angry to have to admit it to him, and for what she was about to say next. 'Believe it or not, you've built up quite a reputation within the Order. People have heard of you cutting down whole groups of demons by yourself. I have no idea what truth there is in the myth, but regardless, you're seen as a hero to some.'

'I'm not a hero, and I'm not invincible just because I have this sword. I've done things that the Order would not approve of.' He looked down, his expression a reflection of what he must have been remembering.

'I've done things I'm not proud of in this life or the one before,' Asha said, her tone suddenly soft. 'My father was horrible to me, yet I spent my life trying to please him. My biggest regret in either life is that I died after betraying my own family to put something right that he did wrong.' Some wardens had a strange compulsion to tell people their stories about how they died, and some even wore them as badges of honour, whether they deserved to be seen that way or not.

Asha on the other hand was always secretive of her life before, and even out of the people she spoke of it to, none of them knew all the details. It wasn't so much that she wanted to hide her past, more that she was trying to forget it. 'But like I said, after everything else, we are only human. There is only so much we can put on ourselves.'

Aiden interrupted before Lynus could perpetuate the argument even further. 'Lynus,' he said firmly, with pleading eyes. 'Asha's right. We can't make the same mistakes again.'

'You think she's right?' he roared. 'You of all people think what we did was a mistake? We did what we had to do to avenge our father, and that's exactly what we did!'

Aiden nodded. 'It wasn't a mistake to have gone after the demon, but what if we hadn't? What if we had failed and died again before we could? That demon would still be out there hurting innocent people just like us. Chances are it would be stopped by another warden eventually, and I want to be that warden for all the other demons who need to be put down just as much as she did. I want to fight for those who couldn't achieve what we did. The mistake we made was leaving the Order to do it.'

'You've seen for yourself exactly how the Order achieves things,' Lynus snapped. 'They tie one hand behind their back because they don't want to take risks and instead dally about with things that are unimportant. If we had stayed in the Order, we would never have killed that demon-bitch.'

'Maybe not,' Aiden agreed. 'But things are changing now, and the Order will need unity if it's going to survive whatever happens next. You're my family, brother, but so are the people I've fought with now. I've woken up twice, and no one seems to know how or why. Maybe God wants us to stay.'

'Since when do you believe in that stuff?' Lynus huffed. Asha could tell Lynus had changed his mind before he even said it. Lynus rubbed his face with his hands and groaned, which was followed by a deep silence. 'Fine,' he relented. 'We'll stay, but only if you promise me something.' Asha nodded for him to continue. 'If there ever comes a time when keeping me alive will put Aiden in danger, I want you to choose him over me, sword or no sword.'

Aiden went to protest, but Lynus silenced him with a raise of his palm.

'I can promise I'll do my best,' Asha said. Although she knew that there were some that would put the possession of that sword above all other things. She could only speak for herself, but she wasn't going to point that out.

'I guess that will do,' Lynus replied. 'What did you come in here for anyway?'

'Get combat ready,' she announced. 'You and I have an assignment.'

Chapter Twenty-Five
Grim

Asha and Lynus pushed the door that led from the church to its undercroft until it groaned and gave way. They had just returned from a four-hour surveillance of the Salem Sanctuary, though they looked like they had just returned from battle. Their footsteps seemed to echo off the narrow walls as they made their way down the steps into the lower levels. Looking down the main corridor, Asha could see several wardens stare at her as she and Lynus came into view. Their gazes were so pointed and so wrapped in a heavy silence that it slowed Asha's gait. Just as she was about to ask one of her onlookers what it was that had them so spooked, Tiago came out of one of the side corridors and stood in front of her.

Tiago was always pale, but what little colour he usually had was nowhere to be seen at that moment.

'Asha…' his voice broke. 'Something has happened.'

It felt as though an icy finger had slithered down Asha's back, sending a chill to her stomach. 'What? What happened?'

'Kára sent out a group of wardens to look for Grim and Amber,' he said softly.

'Don't tell me we lost another team,' she thundered, her heart feeling heavy.

'It's not…' Tiago's voice broke, and he shuffled his feet, his face going from pale to a light red as he blinked repeatedly.

The anxiety that was growing rapidly in Asha's heart let loose a spark of anger, and Asha shoved Tiago. 'Tell me!'

'It's Grim,' he said, losing his battle against tears as several escaped his eyes. 'He's dead, Asha.'

The heaviness, the anxiety, the cold feeling and the anger all faded away from Asha's entire body in an instant, leaving her with nothing but a hollow, empty feeling that swallowed up everything like a black hole in her heart. Her mind refused to process what Tiago had just said; the words were just repeating in her mind like a loop in a nightmare, losing their meaning a little more with every iteration.

'They found him at the Jerome Hope Orphanage,' Tiago said, wiping at the few tears that had gotten away from him. 'They believe a group of white cambion ambushed them.'

Asha said nothing, still stunned with disbelief. The emptiness in her had grown into utter helplessness. For all wardens could do, for all the power they had…she was helpless. Unable to do a single thing to undo this.

'What about the angel woman?' Lynus asked.

'Amber wasn't there when they arrived,' Tiago said. 'But they found some of her feathers, though th—'

'No!' Asha's helplessness exploded into rage. The wardens in the main corridor watching it unfold ducked away when Asha's fists clenched and turned glacial blue as ice formed around them. She pushed passed Tiago and stormed into the nearest room, which was luckily empty. She allowed her rage to overcome her as she let loose bolts of ice and destruction upon the room. The ice shattered and the bricks and mortar exploded with every impact. The air around Asha became so cold it was physically noticeable with clouds of fog forming. Several minutes went by that saw the room utterly destroyed, and the areas untouched by her fury were iced over. It was not until she had drained her rune that she stopped, by which time she walked over to the nearest wall and instead slammed her fists into it, screaming in rage through her tears. It was at that point that Lynus came in and restrained her to prevent her hurting herself more than she already had; her knuckles were covered in her blood.

Lynus and Tiago pulled her away from the wall, and she crumpled down to her knees. 'Haven't we lost enough?' she whimpered to no one in particular. With Delarin gone, and now Grim, she was the last of her original team alive, not to mention losing Tarek. Just then Kára entered the room.

'I need to see everyone in the main chamber,' she commanded, paying no mind to the destruction of the room. 'As soon as you can,' she added before leaving again.

Tiago and Lynus looked at one another. 'I could have sworn there was a bit is sympathy in her voice just now,' said Tiago with a forced grin.

It was another several minutes before Tiago and Lynus could get Asha to leave the room. She sat there, staring at the floor while they spoke to her, trying to coerce her to get up again, but she was only vaguely aware they were even there. In times like these, most people said it felt like hell, but she had been there, so she knew that it was exactly like that. She felt as though she were in the first circle again, crushed with hopelessness and wanting nothing more than to fade away into the crushing void that was now burning in her chest.

Eventually they got her to her feet, mostly by gentle force. As Tiago guided her through the hallways of the undercroft, her surroundings slowly started to exist within her world again. By the time they got to the main chamber, the entire Salem chapter was already congregated inside, or at least what was left of it. When Asha walked into the room, her mind was still unfocused and for a moment all she could do was stare aimlessly.

The main chamber was the largest of the undercroft's many rooms, and from what Asha could tell, it was more or less in the centre of the maze of corridors that made up the undercroft. Above them, the ceiling was made up of lines of shallow vaulted squares, the descent of each corner narrowed down to form pillars. Just in front of the middle of the far back wall was a small altar, and behind that was a set of shelving cut into the stone of the wall. Behind this altar stood Kára and much to Asha's surprise, Gabriel.

'Asha.' Gabriel had seen them come in and called out her name. All twenty-something wardens that were still alive turned to look at them. 'Could I have you and your team at the front please?'

Asha, Lynus and Tiago moved to do as they were asked; however, when Aiden was the only other one to emerge from the crowd, it threatened to knock the wind from her again.

'You have been told about Grim's death, yes?' Kára asked like the blunt side of a hammer to the stomach.

Asha nodded. She didn't even feel the threat of tears as her focus remained numb, but she wiped away a tear that ran down her cheek at the mention of his name. She looked up at Gabriel as he spoke.

'There are two reasons I have gathered everyone here,' he began. 'The first is that I want to take this opportunity to reassure everyone that even though things seem so dark it feels as if we may never see the light again, it is crucial we continue to fight. I must say to you all that I could not be happier with how, through everything, every single one of you has fought with the tenacity and the conviction of the first wardens.'

Asha could see the wave of pride and inspiration pass through the crowd as everyone stood that little bit taller, and their faces lifted slightly. Even Asha herself felt a small swell in her chest kick back against the darkness engulfing it.

'But while all of you have done your part, and each has been vital to our survival this far, there is one I would be remiss not to adulate,' Gabriel continued. Asha tried to see if he was looking at anyone in particular, but he addressed the crowd with an even gaze. 'The title of loch warden was thrust upon her after hers was killed. She was unprepared for the role yet fought on. She has led her team bravely, and together they dealt a massive blow to a new demon drug ring, found the Sword of Michael and with it ventured into hell itself to stop the source of white cambion.' Now he looked directly at her, gesturing with a hand and all. 'Asha, congratulations. I am personally promoting you to the rank of paladin.'

Becoming a paladin was never something Asha really aspired to, and even now as it was given to her she didn't feel as excited about it as she perhaps would be any other day before this one. It seemed empty and meaningless to her as she stepped automatically towards Gabriel when he gestured for her to. He held out an open palm, revealing a dark grey rune.

'This is a barrier rune,' Gabriel said. 'It was Tarek's. He'd be proud of you, and I know he'd want you to have it.'

An enthusiastic applause rumbled through the crowd as she picked up the rune, but she felt no pride. Everything Gabriel has just congratulated her and her team for was all luck. It was a collection of coincidences and being in the right place at the right time that had led them through it all. Sure, their skills as wardens definitely played a major role, but no more than any other team would have been able to manage. The fact it was them and not another team was sheer dumb luck.

She thought back to when they had fought Eligos. In his dying words, he had called them puppets. Like most things demons hissed and taunted when they were feeling overconfident or angry, Asha had passed it off as just that. But hearing her team's achievements listed out like that made it all seem more than a coincidence. In a world so chaotic, how could things line up so well in their favour? She took her thoughts with her and joined her team again, listening to Gabriel as he continued.

'Secondly, we wanted to tell you all that we can kill these white cambion. During the attack on Prime, angelic blades were seen to harm them, and the wardens found several white cambion dead where Grim was found. Luckily we have a powerful one in our midst thanks to Asha and her team, and will use it to take back your home.'

Another loud murmur moved through the crowd. Asha was glad to know that Grim did not go quietly at least. At the idea that they could kill these demons, Asha could feel the emptiness inside her twist and turn into thoughts of revenge. If these things could be killed, that's what she planned to do to every single one of them.

'If we are going to assault the sanctuary, we will need help, sir,' Asha said, the fire returning to her voice. 'Even with the Sword of Michael.'

'I know getting this sanctuary back is important,' Gabriel agreed solemnly. 'But unfortunately with everything else going on at all the other chapters, my angels are spread too thin.'

'Azrael was here before,' Asha said more as a question. 'Can't her angels help us?'

'The Ankor Legion is constantly busy ferrying the souls of the dead. They seldom have the time to fight demons alongside us,' he explained. 'Which, truth be told, is only one of many reasons they remain neutral in our conflicts, save for when Azrael deems something important enough and can intervene without damaging her claim to neutrality.'

If only humans were given that option, Asha thought.

'Ophelia, Sorterra, Jason and Asha,' Kára called the other lochs from the crowd. 'Your teams are the least decimated, so together you will spearhead this assault, with me there to guide you. We will consolidate the other wardens into teams of their own and to support us once we clear a way in.'

A series of verbal acknowledgements told Kára that each of them understood. 'Asha, I want you and Lynus to meet with the other lochs to give details on what you found out during your scouting assignment. That way, we can work on specifics for the attack.'

'Yes, ma'am,' Asha said with a nod.

Kára now addressed the whole room again. 'The rest of you begin some warm-up training and be ready for what is coming, whatever that may be.'

'I must leave now and tend to other chapters,' Gabriel advised. 'But I wish you all the best of luck.'

The crowd of wardens dwindled as each of them set out with renewed vigour and the fire of revenge in their eyes, but Asha remained with her own rekindled flame: that of answers. With Gabriel about to leave, now was the time she had to ask him about the thoughts that swirled in her mind.

'Sir,' she said.

Gabriel had been talking to Kára as she approached. He turned away from the other angel and stepped out from behind the stone altar. 'Yes, Asha?'

'How did he die?' Asha asked.

'He and Ambriel went off together for who knows what reason, and white cambion ambushed them,' Kára explained.

'What about Amber?' she asked. 'What happened to her?'

'She has fallen,' Kára said. 'It is likely that Grim's death was enough emotional distress to push her over the edge. As it was, she was dangerously close to that line, but despite my warnings, she refused to listen.'

'We believe she had become attached to Grim,' Gabriel said gently. 'She must have had her reasons for delving so deeply into her emotions.'

'Nothing can be done about that now,' Kára interrupted.

'Sir, with due respect to Kára, would it be okay if I spoke to you privately?' Asha asked, not daring to look at Kára. She knew Kára wouldn't approve of leaving considering how she was so protective of Gabriel. Asha supposed she had been no different with Delarin.

As predicted, Kára moved to speak, but Gabriel lifted a finger before she could get a word out. 'It's fine, Kára. Tend to the wardens, see that they are ready,' Gabriel ordered. Kára did as she was instructed, but not before giving Asha an almost unnoticeable glare. 'Now, what is it, child?'

'I was curious about Amber,' she said. 'Why did you put her in my team?'

'Are you asking why I placed an angel in the chapter, or why into your team specifically?'

'Both, I guess.'

Gabriel smiled. 'She is a new angel, relatively speaking anyway,' he explained. 'And your chapter was dwindling somewhat more than most others. I thought your city could use her help. As for why your team, that was for Tarek to decide.'

Asha felt a pang of discomfort in her stomach as he said that. Tarek had known, which meant Delarin must have known too. How could he not? Delarin would always give in when Amber suggested something be done a certain way. That hurt a little.

'So it was just by chance then?' she probed.

Gabriel nodded. 'Something that worked well in your favour.'

'Despite the obvious, there seems to be a lot of that happening,' she said.

'I'm not sure I understand, Asha,' Gabriel said with a furrowed brow.

'We found the Ghost, Lynus, just as we needed him the most, and we were able to get in and out of hell fairly easily,' she explained. 'Lynus was found by us, who just so happened to have the brother he had been looking for, who didn't have any memory of having already been a warden, which on its own presents a new set of questions.

'I don't know, sir, it just seems like we are being moved around like game pieces. Like everything is being orchestrated by something we are not seeing.'

'It is,' Gabriel said pointedly. 'When my father abandoned us, many of the angels lost faith in him. I still believe everything that is happening is all a part of his plan.'

'Abandoned?' Asha asked, confused.

Gabriel seemed genuinely taken aback for a moment. 'I simply mean that is how some other angels see his disappearance.'

'Like Michael?'

Gabriel nodded solemnly. 'Yes. He believes the sins of humans grew too wild, and it caused our father to punish us by leaving. It's why Michael fights so ruthlessly to eradicate sin, whether it be demons or within humans themselves. He thinks doing so will bring our father back.' Gabriel looked away in thought, as if looking at something in the distance. 'Other angels would prefer Michael simply destroy the entire world and start fresh with the angels enforcing their will on humans, rather than relying on humans to figure out what is right by themselves. Other angels in the March, of course.'

Asha realised how off topic they had become, with none of her questions having been answered with anything that led her to any sense of closure. None of it seemed right to her, and she wasn't sure what to make of the *God's plan* explanation. Even the angels seemed to lack consensus on God's intentions.

'Before you commit to this counterattack, know that I am not ordering it,' Gabriel said softly after a brief silence.

'What other option is there?' Asha asked, taken aback. Anything other than taking back their home did not seem agreeable.

'Leave the demons be for now, and let come what may,' he said. 'Take your wardens elsewhere and rebuild the chapter. Garner your strength and then deal with the infestation.'

'My wardens?' Asha felt her heart sink.

Gabriel smiled a sweet smile, but his eyes were serious. 'Yes, Asha,' he said. 'You are now the highest-ranking survivor of this chapter. If you choose to take your wardens elsewhere, the appropriate protocols will take place later, but for now whether you fight or rebuild is a decision only you can make.'

A dozen outcomes forced their way into Asha's mind all at once, only a few of them positive, and each one in her hands. She missed Delarin more in that moment than ever; he would know exactly what to do, and he'd have made the decision in an instant. Seconds ticked by as she considered each choice, but she kept coming back to one truth. The attack on the sanctuary was not random, so they needed to stop whatever the demons were doing *now*, not later. She had always taught those under her not to hesitate but to strike before the enemy could gain the advantage, and this should be no different.

'We attack,' she said.

Gabriel nodded deeply. 'Very well,' he said. 'Go see to your wardens; they will need you.'

Asha watched as each of the other lochs left the room, leaving her with just her thoughts in the now-empty chamber. The chamber was small and basic, most likely a storage room many years ago. Now it was a briefing room of sorts, and Asha had just finished devising a plan with Kára and the other team leaders, the details of which swirled around in her mind.

The teams were split up into two groups. The first group would assault the front of the sanctuary through the main cavern to draw out the bulk of the horde within and hold them for as long as possible. Group two was to go in through the back entrance and find out why the demons wanted the sanctuary so badly, or better yet to find and kill the white cambions that no doubt anchored the other demons infesting their home. Kára would lead the first team, consisting of Ophelia's and Jason's teams, along with the survivors they had brought back from the second circle. Asha and Sorterra would lead the second group alongside Lynus, who was the only one capable of killing a white cambion with Michael's sword.

Asha's thoughts were interrupted when she noticed a figure standing in the room's archway. It was Adley. She had not seen him since they had returned from hell, nor had anyone else for that matter. She felt a little guilty that she had not checked up on him, especially after the death of Katherine.

'I want to come,' he said sternly.

'You're not a warden; they'll slaughter you,' she replied evenly.

'I know that to you, my loss doesn't hold up to yours,' he said, walking closer. 'But I want revenge. I cannot swing a sword or use a rune like you people can, but I want revenge for Katherine anyway I can.'

'What we are going into is worse than what we faced in hell, Adley,' she admonished. Normally by now she would have lost her temper at him and told him to get lost, but she didn't have it in her.

'I can help.'

'How?'

'You're up against demons that can only be harmed by angelic weapons, yes?' he asked, and Asha nodded. 'Well, as it happens…I have one.'

'Since when did you start messing with angelic things?' she asked with a furrowed brow. 'I thought demons kept you in enough trouble.'

'Opportunity, is all,' he answered. 'I had set up a meeting with a demon.' He put his hands up in front of him as Asha went to speak. 'For academic reasons, I assure you. Just some questions.

Anyway, a group of angels attacked the demon, killing it. Before the angels moved on, however, they were counter-attacked by more demons. One angel went down, and while the fight continued, I grabbed the sword and ran off.

'Now, I'm no good at swinging a sword, but I'm sure you could make use of it. There is only one problem.'

'Of course there is,' Asha sighed. 'What is it?'

'Well, angel weapons get their power in a similar way that runes are given theirs,' he explained. 'They're imbued with a small amount of grace. The difference between runes and weapons, however, is that an angel links themselves to their own weapon, which gives it its power and prevents other angels from using it without permission.

'Humans on the other hand can wield them, except when the angel dies, the grace within the weapon dies with them. So at the moment the blade is powerless.'

'So why keep it?' she asked.

'Well, let's say you have a rune that can hold an angel's grace. It'd hold raw angelic power like a rune, but without the necessity of the angel linking themselves to it. So essentially you'd have a sort of *grace-in-a-bottle,*' he explained in his usual excited way.

'I've never heard of such a thing,' Asha said with a tinge of impatience.

'That broken rune you brought me was one such rune. It would have allowed whoever possessed it to temporarily wield the weapon of a dead angel,' he explained.

'I take it you found a rune that could do what you're describing,' she said.

'Do you remember when I asked you for a favour, and you declined by saying that you letting me live was my reward?'

'What I said was that I would ignore your fraternising with demons in return for the information you gave me,' she corrected.

'Yes. Well, regardless, the favour I was going to ask was to have you take a rune from me and have it charged by an angel,' he said. 'I sought it out especially for the sword. Once charged by an angel, it can imbue the sword with grace.'

'Why not just use it on any weapon?' Asha asked.

'Only works on angelic weapons,' he explained.

'Why?'

He gave a casual shrug. 'No idea. Like you said, demonology is my thing, not angels.'

'Where is it then?' she demanded.

'The rune is with me,' he replied as he put his hand in his jacket pocket, taking out a pearl white rune. The rune was so white that Asha could barely make out the etching of a symbol inside. 'The sword is in my office.'

'Having a second angelic weapon would be useful, and if I had one, then we could send Lynus to the front where he'd be more useful,' she mused more to herself than to Adley. 'Thank you, Adley, but I still don't see how coming with us will help.'

'You have no idea why the demons took over the sanctuary. I might be of help in determining the reason,' he said hopefully. 'No one knows how demons think better than me.'

'If the sword and rune work, then yes,' she said. 'Now let's go. We don't have much time.'

***

Aiden felt a tinge of disappointment when he saw that the church above the undercroft was empty. He had hoped he'd be able to see Kallista there seeking refuge from the drama below. They were only a few hours away from beginning their attack on the sanctuary. He should have been down below with the others training, checking his gear or helping where he could, but his thoughts were too much of a distraction. Ever since his memories had come flooding back, so many things had been going on, and he didn't have any time to talk to anyone about anything, leaving him alone to process the plate of spaghetti that was his mind.

Lynus had said they should leave and fight demons on their terms rather than dying at the orders of angels. Aiden saw freedom in that, but there was no sense in repeating the same mistake. Nonetheless, he was prepared to follow his brother anywhere, but was relieved when Asha had convinced him to stay. His team had become important to him over the last few weeks, and he felt a level of attachment to them he had not felt for another person other than Lynus since their father had died. Asha was rough with a harsh tongue, but she cared, and Aiden had seen her softer side more than once, if only briefly. Tiago was someone he especially wouldn't want to leave behind. He had guided Aiden when he'd felt like a lost little boy with no idea what was going on. Now at least he remembered his training from the first time he'd woken up and didn't feel so helpless.

Then there was Kallista. She had given him a calming sense of hope whenever she was around. Nothing seemed to be able to get through her strong faith that everything would be okay. However, the more memories that came back to him, the more parts of himself clashed within his mind, struggling against the reassurance of Kalli's comfort and the reality of what they'd been through.

He sat down on one of the pews and stared up at the stained-glass windows. There was a creak to his left as someone pushed the heavy wooden door and emerged from below.

'There you are.' It was Lynus. He was wearing warden blacks, something Aiden had not seen him wear for what seemed like a very long time.

'Asha give you a new uniform?' Aiden scoffed.

'They're giving out paladin coats to all teams going in first,' Lynus said as he sat down next to Aiden.

'Thought you were with us?'

Lynus shrugged. 'Apparently Asha has an angelic sword now too, so they want me with the first group instead.'

'What's the difference?' Aiden asked, tugging at Lynus' coat. 'Looks the same to me.'

'They're lined with some sort of poly-armour or some crap,' Lynus shrugged. Aiden reached out and felt his brother's coat. It felt soft but thick like their normal coats, which offered mild protection from glancing blows, but it was also a lot more rigid with hard pieces in it that bent under pressure before returning to their original form.

'Still not gonna help us from a cambion attack,' Aiden muttered.

'True enough, we'll still have to rely on ourselves,' Lynus agreed. 'Speaking of, how has your training been coming along now you've regained your memories?' he asked. 'From what I've heard it seems that not all your muscle memory was lost at least. What luck to end up with your old rune.'

Aiden looked down to his wrist where his rune sat within a black band. He now remembered it from before. This was the rune they had given him when he first became a warden. Whatever had caused him to lose his memories the second time also saw him lose his rune. Somewhere along the way, it came to be in the possession of a demon, the same demon they had killed at the casino. It explained why he had picked up its use with relative ease.

Aiden shrugged. 'Not bad,' he said. 'Was getting used to it before my memories came back anyway. Now I just can't wait to use it on a demon's face.'

'Good to hear,' Lynus said with a wide smile.

'Been meaning to ask, what exactly have you been doing all this time we've been separated?' Aiden probed.

'What you and I promised,' Lynus said. 'Been killing as many demons as I could before one of them got me instead.'

'How did you get so many runes?' Aiden asked. Lynus wore a purple one around his neck and a red one in a band similar to his on the wrist, but Tiago had told Aiden that he had used at least four during their battle with him.

'Well, I always had my fire one, but the purple rune was one I grabbed from a collector demon, as was my barrier rune. I took my concussive rune from an occultist I killed,' he said, and the look on his face as he said the last bit told Aiden he was expecting him to react the way he was about to.

'You killed a civilian?' Aiden cried, his eyes going wide with shock.

'I killed an *occultist*,' he corrected.

'Doesn't matter, Lynus!' Aiden raised his voice. 'What would Dad say?'

'Do you think Dad made sure we trained in swordsmanship for fun?' Lynus asked.

'Well…I never really thought of why,' Aiden said.

'I loved Dad just as much as you, but we both know he was into something he shouldn't have been.'

It was true. Aiden's memories were still incomplete, but Aiden could remember bits and pieces of being home-schooled, and their father insisting on strange subjects. Aiden could not bring any to mind, but he had vague memories of Lynus complaining about having to study those subjects and how none of the other kids had to learn them.

'It doesn't matter,' Aiden said.

Lynus looked down at his feet. 'Salem is an odious pit of sin. I've killed plenty of occultists who have been actively trying to make it worse, and I've killed civilians who have tried to hurt others.' He looked up at Aiden. 'I've done many things I'm not proud of, Aiden, but I don't regret them. This city needs saving from more than demons. We need to cut out the beacons of filth that bring them here.'

Aiden didn't know what to say, so they sat in silence for a few moments before either of them spoke again.

'We should go get ready for the fight,' Lynus said, breaking the silence. Aiden nodded and together they went back down into the undercroft.

Chapter Twenty-Six
Ready to die

N ightfall to demons was like light to moths. It was easier for demons to move around in shadow and feed their desires, or even out in the open when all those around them didn't care to know any better. The inebriated people looking for vice and the deviants of the night were all playthings to demons. Wardens had long since adapted to this behaviour, carrying out most of their assignments at night, thwarting the machinations for demonic indulgences and power grabbing.

It was easier for wardens to use the shadows of nightfall against the demons who hid within. This morning was different, however, as there was no time to wait for nightfall. The Order would not allow the demons who had taken their sanctuary to infect it for even a single day longer, no matter what they were doing within. Not while they lived.

The seasons were changing. The sun had just crested over the horizon to the east and would soon spread its warmth over the city, but winter wasn't ready to let go just yet and brought with it a bitter wind that sliced through the temperate autumn air. The extra lining of armour within the warden blacks shielded Lynus from not only a demon's talon, but the cold bite of the wind even as high up as he was where the wind howled the hardest.

Lynus stood at the safety railing of a four-storey building that overlooked the street closest to the beach and the sanctuary entrances. To his left was the ocean, choppy and wild as it battled the wind. To the right were the streets, void of all life as they usually were this early in the morning. In front of him, only two streets away, was the alleyway that led to the rear entrance of the sanctuary.

'When do we go?' asked a female voice behind him. Lynus turned to see Ophelia, a loch warden of one of the two teams Lynus was supposed to be accompanying.

'We go once Kára has arrived,' Lynus said. 'Is your team ready?'

Ophelia nodded. Lynus found her to be an odd warden, especially for a loch. She was short, with long light brown curls and matching eyes. She was timid in the way she spoke, walked, and as Lynus had heard, in the way she conducted her team.

'I mean are they ready to die?' Lynus asked, keeping pointed eye contact. Ophelia's already large eyes widened a little, and her mouth opened to say something but no words came out. 'A soldier who isn't ready to die is a soldier who is not willing to fight as hard and for as long as they need to.'

'I don't thi—' Ophelia started to speak but the other team's loch walked up and interrupted.

'You don't think anyone should ever die and we should all live on rainbows and eat candy all day long,' Jason sneered. He then looked at Lynus. 'My team is ready and willing.'

Jason was the same height as Lynus and had shaved his blonde hair with a number one clip. He was lean but with broad shoulders and muscles that bulged under the sleeves of his warden blacks. 'You think you're better?' Lynus asked with an arched eyebrow. 'It's not better to be so willing to send wardens to their deaths just to kill a few demons. You think the demons care if they lose even ten to one of us? On paper you lead your team to success, but your price is too high. If we are ever going to one-up these arseholes, you need to learn to use your head.'

'How dare you talk to me like that!' Jason snarled, storming up to Lynus. He halted as Lynus drew the Sword of Michael and held the tip inches from Jason's neck.

'You want to know what else bothers me about you in particular?' Lynus continued. 'I've been told you've had more successful missions than anyone, but at the cost of numerous fatalities. Yet here you are alive and well. That tells me quite a bit about the kind of warden you are, and I find it severely wanting for the merit of your accolades.'

Jason backed off, and Lynus lowered the blade. Lynus looked at the both of them with a look of appraisal. 'You,' he said, pointing to Ophelia, 'need to find the strength to really fight these demons. Death will always be a part of what we do and it will always suck, but if we don't give all we can to fight them, then there goes humanity.' Ophelia nodded, but Lynus was not convinced.

'And you,' he continued with a look towards Jason, 'need to learn to lead from the front. You mock Ophelia but at least she's right beside her wardens. If you were willing to die just as much as those under you, maybe they wouldn't need to.

'I honestly have no fucking idea why The Valkyr Guard chose either of you, but I really hope you can both show me the reason today by being a little bit more of each other.'

Jason and Ophelia both stood beside each other, their eyes to the ground. 'Now go get your teams ready. I mean really ready.' Lynus commanded. They both turned and walked to the other side of the roof where their teams waited with the teamless wardens, the ones saved from hell, among the survivors of otherwise decimated teams with no loch.

When Lynus turned back to the railing, Asha stepped up to stand beside him. 'I don't know why they seem to care what I have to say,' Lynus said. He didn't mean to lecture them like he had.

What right did he have? It had just come out of him when he saw how pathetic they both were. They embodied the reason he wanted to stay away from the Order.

'They know your reputation,' she said. 'They're both scared and in awe of you, and they aren't the only ones among the wardens in Salem either.'

'My reputation?' he scoffed. 'What me and my brother did was stupid and dangerous, and after I thought I lost him…' Lynus paused, looking across the streets and at the city skyline beyond. 'All I wanted to do was go down swinging. But I scraped by on luck most of the time. I'm no hero.'

'Trust me, you'll never hear me say you are. Heroes don't exist,' she stated flatly. 'Not as people anyway. Before I died, I looked up to heroes all my life from what I remember. The heroes I worshipped betrayed me, and I disappointed those who saw me as theirs.' She joined him, lost in thought looking over at the city. 'It took my own death for me to learn that heroes aren't people; they're just ideas that inspire people to do stupid and dangerous things.' She turned to look at him. 'But sometimes stupid and dangerous is what needs to be done.'

'More often than not for us it seems,' he sighed as he turned away from the city and back to Asha. 'Y'know speaking of reputation, you're not as much of a bitch as yours implies.'

'And you whinge more than yours does,' she grunted.

'I thought you said they had sentries guarding the entrances,' Kára said as she approached them. 'Where are they?' During their reconnaissance assignment they had watched the streets from the same rooftop and had seen that they were being patrolled by demons.

'Isn't it obvious?' Lynus asked. 'They know we're coming, just like they always do. So my guess is they're ready to ambush us. Because isn't that exactly what they've been doing for months now?'

Lynus' impertinence didn't seem to bother the angel. 'It makes little difference,' she said.

'If anything, it might make it easier for us to not have to fight them on the streets,' Lynus said. Kára nodded in agreement.

'Asha, join your team below and make sure they're ready to go,' Asha nodded and made her way into the streets where her team had assembled in a nearby side alley.

Kára led Lynus and the others onto the beach, which, besides the wind, was eerily quiet. They made their way across the sand with the other wardens close behind. All up, they had mustered twenty-four wardens between the two groups. Six wardens had gone with Asha and Sorterra, while they had the remaining eighteen, not including himself. Ten were from Ophelia's and Jason's teams, while the other eight were comprised of the surviving wardens that weren't present during the initial attack and had made it back to the church. Along with them there were also the three out of six that had survived the escape from hell—three hadn't made it through the night after they returned.

The gate to the sanctuary was lying nearby the entrance, bent and broken in the sand. They never meant it to be strong enough to keep demons away, only curious civilians. A hundred years ago, demons would not even think to attack a sanctuary even if they had stumbled upon one. Lynus wondered why the Order didn't think to reinforce their security measures with demon attacks in mind when things started to go downhill. With Kára leading, Lynus walked into the entrance to the cavern with the others close behind.

After an immediate right turn in the cramped tunnel, it curved around to the left and opened up into the cavern. Lynus had never seen the Salem Sanctuary before, but Asha had told him about it. It had fallen from the city above many years ago, but looking at it now on the other side of the vast open cavern, it looked like some eccentric millionaire had simply built a mansion inside a cave. It was in perfect condition after years of renovation and restoration despite the demons that played host to it now.

As Lynus took his first full step inside the cave, there was a blur of motion followed by a loud thud as a humanoid demon landed in front of him. It swiped its clawed hand at him. Lynus couldn't bring his sword up in time, but the attack was deflected all the same by his purple ghost form as it darted from him, parrying the demon's attack and then just as suddenly disappearing. He had not even thought about it. It had been a pure knee-jerk reaction; he was glad for it and took full advantage by thrusting the Sword of Michael at the creature's stomach. The demon screamed as the sword sizzled its flesh and muscle. Lynus pulled the sword back out and with another quick movement severed the demon's head. It was an inmai demon, a dark brown monstrosity with small white horns dotting its body and two large horns protruding from its head that curved backwards almost all the way to its neck. It wasn't alone either and more dropped from the ceiling along with a host of imps.

Lynus charged forward as the demons rained from the cavern ceiling, and the others followed his lead. He sprinted past one demon on his left, slicing its abdomen as he went. Another landed in front of him, and he tackled it to the ground, piercing its throat before it could land an attack with its razor-like claws. When Lynus returned to his feet, they beset him on all sides.

Lynus let launch a fireball at an imp as it lunged at him, turning to face another inmai before the fireball struck, confident the flames would incinerate the smaller demon. Lynus launched another weakened ball of fire at the inmai; the ball exploded on the creature's skin with just enough force to set it off balance, enabling an easy strike to the heart with his sword, killing it quickly so he could face his next target with as much speed as possible.

He continued like this for a while, killing one demon after the next as they got close to him, and when there were too many to block at once, his purple ghost form would appear long enough to block, counterattack and then vanish. When he became so engulfed that even his ghost was not enough, he drew power from his concussion rune and sent out a blast of pure force, causing any demon within five feet of him to be flung away like ragdolls.

With the crowd of demons in his immediate vicinity temporarily cleared, he could see colourful flashes of power from the runes of the other wardens as they cleared the area around the entrance. Lynus leaped into motion as he fought his way back through the thinning crowd of demons and re-joined the other teams. Kára was at the front of the group, cleaving demons with so much ease she looked bored. To Lynus' disappointment, but not to his surprise, Ophelia's team sat back behind the others in relative safety as some of them used long-range rune powers to kill demons, while Jason's team was ahead of the group killing demons easily, yet they were scattered and vulnerable.

'God dammit,' Lynus muttered as he re-joined the group and began slaughtering demons, once again doing his best to cover Jason's team, all the while shouting at them to stay together.

Suddenly Kára rushed past Lynus, and her wings erupted from her back, stretching outwards to reveal their white radiance, which, even in the cavern, reflected light as if directly in the sun. She held aloft a long halberd that looked like something between a spear and an axe. The shaft was capped off with a tear-shaped blade, and on either side of that were long bearded axe-blades that mimicked the curves of an angel's wings. The halberd was alive with energy, and sparks of electricity and lightning arched out as she plunged into a large group of inmai, cleaving left-to-right, right-to-left, cutting them down like an archaic farmer to his crops. Soon after, the battle was over. It was if Kára's boredom reached its peak and she had simply decided to end it.

Lynus surveyed the cavern floor as he caught his breath. At least a hundred imps and lesser inmai littered the area, and it turned

Lynus' stomach to think what was anchoring them all here. How many cambion were here waiting for them?

'It is not over yet, Ghost,' Kára said.

'I'm guessing that little ambush was a test,' Lynus answered, looking over at her. Her brilliant wings were still outstretched and her bladed stave still in hand—she was a force to be reckoned with. 'Luckily no one died, but that just means they'll be attacking us with a lot more force as soon as they rally.'

'Asha needs to hurry and find what is anchoring them,' Kára replied.

'Obviously,' he fired back. 'But we are all going to be slaughtered if the lochs don't pull their heads out of their respective arses and fight.' He raised his voice over the commotion of the crowd of wardens. Kára gave the slightest of regards in their direction before an almighty crash stole their attention back towards to front of the sanctuary.

The large double doors had been blown apart from the inside as more demons emerged. This time it was not imps that spewed forth, nor was it either variety of inmai. Three white cambion strode out from the sanctuary. The cambion that stood in the middle was larger than the others, and black tattoos marked his white skin.

If the cambion were not bad enough, the shadows above them began to move, dislodging small rocks and debris that fell to the cavern floor, shattering into pebbles. Lynus looked up, but all he could see were shadows—moving shadows that did not stay up there for long.

As the cambion came to a stop fifty metres away, the shadows from the ceiling dropped into the light. They moved so fast that all Lynus could see was a blur as they landed in front of the cambion, sending an explosion of dust and dirt in all directions. Lynus strained his eyes, ignoring the sting of dirt as he tried to see what they were, but all he could see was a swirling cloud of dust that suddenly began to clear with a rush of wind.

'Hellbats,' Kára said casually. Between them and the cambion stood half-a-dozen huge deformed-looking bats. Standing straight up, Lynus estimated they'd be at least ten feet tall, not including the massive curled horns on their head or their elongated ears. They were nothing but solid muscle under black fur that covered most of their torso, with extra around their necks. Unlike a regular bat whose arms were more a part of their wings, the hellbats' wings were a leathery membrane attached to spines under their human-like arms. Their muscular legs had thorns dotted all over them, all the way down to their talons. Lynus had never seen a hellbat before, but he had heard stories about them during his training at Sanctuary Prime. They were ferocious, tenacious and hard to pin down. *Like harpies on steroids*, he had once heard someone say, and it seemed accurate. Besides all of that, they were totally subservient to their masters and more protective than any breed of dog.

One of the bats let out a screech that was like a knife to the ears. Before Lynus' knew it, they were galloping on all fours towards them. Lynus looked back; the others were ready, and with Kára at his side, they went to work.

***

Aiden remembered that Lynus and Asha had told everyone during the briefing that the back entrance was just as guarded as the front, yet they encountered no resistance as they entered in through the back, which could only mean one of two things. Either they were walking into a trap or the plan was working.

'Wait,' Asha ordered from the front of the group. They were all spread out behind her, their eyes probing the cave for any movement. 'We need to wait a moment and make sure Kára and Lynus have drawn away as many demons as possible.'

'Where to once the fun begins?' Tiago asked. He stood next to Aiden, his handgun already drawn.

Asha looked to Adley. 'We have to assume they are planning to open an anchorage,' she said. 'How exactly would they go about doing that?'

'I uh… I'm not sure,' Adley stuttered.

'I thought this guy knew everything there was to know about demons, Asha,' Terra grumbled.

'Don't be absurd, of course I don't,' Adley spat back. 'I know the general idea for the ritual, but not the specifics. There are many variants to the process. I've never been able to find out any consistent data on the subject, much to my frustration.'

'So where do we need to start looking?' Asha asked. To Aiden, it looked like she was ready to hit Adley.

'If one has already been created, then we need to look for a room large enough to hold the anchorage portal and the demons that will be coming out of it,' Adley explained.

'What about the mess halls?' Aiden offered. 'They're the biggest rooms in here, aren't they?'

'That would be a good place to start,' Asha said.

'Agreed,' Sorterra affirmed. 'There are two mess halls. Should we split up?'

'No,' Asha replied immediately. 'We stay together and take our chances doing one at a time.' Asha led them into the mansion from the greenhouse and through the hallways, which were bereft of demons. The only noise they could hear was the distant sounds of battle from the caverns where Lynus and Kára were keeping the horde busy. They searched the blue mess hall first and found it just as empty as the hallways and seemingly untouched by demons altogether. Their way to the yellow mess hall was slow as Asha became extra careful when the sounds from the cavern quietened.

Aiden couldn't help but worry about his brother. Had they killed all the demons or was the opposite true? If Lynus and the others had beaten the demons back, there was only one place they would retreat to, and Aiden and his group still had not run into any. Aiden tried to focus on the mission as they crept through the building, but the worst-case scenario kept forcing its way back into his mind. When several loud thumps shook the ground under them, and the sounds of battle once again started, Aiden was actually relieved.

They made it to the yellow mess hall, but as Aiden watched Asha enter, he saw Terra almost run into the back of her as she stopped dead in her tracks. Aiden was the last of the seven to enter the room and see what had shocked her: the room was gone. It had been excavated, and only the ceiling remained. Even some adjoining rooms had been destroyed as the demons had expanded the new cavern.

Where the floor had been, there was now a rocky descent that transformed the room into a giant amphitheatre-looking cavern. Where the ground evened back out, there was a large ring of reddish rock at least ten metres in diameter.

'What the hell are they doing?' Asha asked out loud and to no one in particular.

'Looks like they're carving something out of the rock,' Terra observed. 'But what?'

Aiden crouched down by the ring. It wasn't rock at all. It was made up of bricks that looked to Aiden more like smooth, red limestone. Each one of the bricks had a glyph on it that Aiden had never seen before. The most interesting part of the ring, however, was the inside. The stone there was darker and waves rippled across its surface. It looked like an unsettled ocean had been captured within stone.

'I don't think they carved this,' Aiden said, running his finger along the bottom of one of the bricks. The rock of the ground looked very different to the rock of the circle. 'It looks more like they are excavating something, not carving it.'

'You're right,' Asha said crouching down beside him. 'These are demonic glyphs too, but I've never seen these kinds before. Adley?'

Adley was already scrambling for a book that he had secured within a leather pouch on his waist. He flicked through the pages with a look of frantic horror on his face. He was muttering something, but Aiden couldn't hear what it was. Suddenly he stopped, and the look of horror turned into plain fear as he handed the book to Asha.

'No,' she breathed. 'Sitting under us this whole time?'

'A hellgate.' The voice came from behind them, at the top of the stairs. Aiden and the others spun around to see Gabriel standing by the doorway.

'Sir, what are you doing here?' Asha stammered.

'You lot are proving to be far too smart for your own good. I should have known you wouldn't just attempt a brute force attack at the front,' he ranted.

'I don't understand,' Asha breathed.

Gabriel laughed. 'Yes you do, child,' he said. 'You've already began piecing it together, but your denial, fuelled by blind obedience, has prevented you from seeing the truth.'

'It's you...' Asha's voiced cracked, and she looked like she had just lost another team member, and in that moment it clicked in Aiden's mind. Everything they had gone through: the abductions, the spy, the unseen guidance that led them to unlikely victories again and again. It was all him.

'There were those among you who were closer to the truth than others, and too soon than I would have liked. People who had to be dealt with before they ruined several millennia of planning.' Gabriel smiled again, a smile more sinister than any demon Aiden had seen. 'People like Grim and his pet angel.'

The next moment, Asha shouted in rage as she charged at Gabriel so fast that Aiden's eyes could barely catch up to her before an unseen hand tossed aside her. She landed hard against the rock wall and then fell flat. Tiago and Terra rushed to her. Rage filled her eyes, but they were wet with tears as she struggled to her feet. 'I'll kill you!' Asha shouted as she tried to rush him again, held back by Terra and Tiago. Even in her weakened state both men struggled to hold her back.

'You say that a lot, child,' Gabriel muttered. 'But the only ones you get killed are your friends. Here, let me help you.'

Aiden was too focused on Gabriel to notice the two white cambion that had entered the room until they had moved into position on either side of the angel. With a low, mocking laugh, Gabriel turned and exited back into the hallway.

Aiden watched as Adley slunk to the back of the room, wisely getting out of the way of the fight to come as the others prepared their weapons. Asha's voice came over their communication units, trying to warn the others, but there was no response. Tiago had his weapon drawn the moment Gabriel had walked in, Terra had his kukris and Asha had her sword. Though she was now drawing a second, which she held in her left hand. It was an angelic blade— a simple arming sword that gave off a dull white glow. She and Adley had retrieved it from his office, and Kára had agreed to imbue some sort of rune that charged it with angelic energy. Aiden looked at her with awe. She stood with fury in her eyes and a blade in each hand. One was iced over and the other had a glow that made it look like it would burst into flames any second. At that moment, he was not sure who he'd rather fight: the cambion or her.

'Get ready,' Kalli said from behind. This would be Aiden's first fight since regaining his memories, so he hoped all the important stuff was still there in his mind. But more than that, he hoped that Asha's new sword would actually help them. The tattooed cambion that had killed Tarek had done so with relative ease, and these ones would be no pushovers either, so their survival now rested on Asha, or a miracle.

William was the first to break into a charge. He was fearless, and his beast-like roar was the first time Aiden had ever heard any sound come out of him. He was the oldest warden Aiden had seen besides Tarek and Mason, and easily the biggest. The man was a giant, and his sword was large enough to stand as high as some fully grown men, yet in his hands it looked no bigger than Aiden's did in his. As William charged, Aiden noticed a red tinge cover his body.

William and Asha raced to the cambions, but one of them leaped from the high ground, the air around its right hand crackling with red electricity as it summoned a demonic blade just in time for it to land mere feet away from William. It swung. William countered in turn with his own sword at the same moment. To Aiden's surprise, he managed to not only connect and match the demon's strength, but force the demon to take several steps back.

Kallista capitalised on the demon's failed attack and let loose an arrow of lightning that crackled overhead. Aiden had seen Kallista's lightning arrows before when they had saved him from an angel at the Salem Arena, and then the next day from a harpy, but he had never seen her use the bow itself. It was a modern blue recurve bow, and when she pulled back the string, as though there were an arrow nocked, a burst of electricity arched out from the string, forming an arrow-shaped bolt of lightning. She let the string go, and the arrow flew in the demon's direction along a perfect trajectory, hitting it square in the chest with a loud crack. Sorterra was quick to join in, but Aiden's attention was drawn to the second cambion that focused on him and his team.

Several imps joined the battle as Asha charged at the cambion. Aiden slashed at the imps, keeping them off Asha as she fought, while Tiago fired his pistol at the tiny demons as they fell from the ceiling and lunged at them from the walls. Aiden had just decapitated an imp with as much ease as he had ever killed anything since he woke up the second time. A thrill of confidence shot through him. He turned to Asha just as she had swung both her swords that the demon blocked, locking blades for a moment before pushing her away. She was relentless and attacked again.

As Asha and the demon struggled, Tiago moved quickly and fired a few rounds from his pistol once he was in a better position. The bullets, even though powered by his rune, did little more than irritate the cambion. Though after a dozen rounds to the demon's head, it was enough to make it flinch, opening it up for Asha to land an attack. Her regular sword slashed the demon's abdomen, a strike that would have gutted a human. The wound barely had enough time to ooze blood before it healed up, and for the cambion to attack Asha again. Aiden took this as his chance to join the fight with the cambion and broke into a sprint. Avoiding the demon's blades, he ran past the creature and took up a position behind.

Aiden charged at the demon from behind, summoning his blazing orange aetheric blades above him and launching them at the demon as he did. Aiden's ghost-like blades exploded into shards as they struck the cambion. Some of the shrapnel tore into the demon's wing, but just like the wound to its stomach, the tears healed up before Aiden even reached the cambion. As Aiden got within striking distance, the cambion quickly broke off its attack on Asha and spun to strike out against Aiden, who only just blocked the attack. The force knocked Aiden to the side; he stumbled but managed to keep his footing. Meanwhile Asha took the demon's distraction as an opportunity to swing the angelic blade.

The cambion turned back to face Asha, but not fast enough as Asha's angelic blade made contact, cutting into its left side. For the first time, Aiden heard the demon cry out in pain, but with a single beat of its wings it was airborne, hovering several metres above the ground. Aiden saw its thick dark red blood ooze from the gash in its side and run down its white skin. A few seconds later, the wound closed up, but it did so much slower than before. A flare of hope and relief lit up in Aiden's chest.

Tiago was still firing at imps from his bottomless clip, keeping them away from Asha and Aiden. The cambion turned towards Tiago and lunged, kicking up dust and rock as it landed in front of him. In a flash of movement, one of the demon's swords disappeared in a red electric flash, and then he had Tiago in the air, held up by his throat.

The demon sneered at Tiago as he struggled, lining up his demonic sword to impale him. Aiden summoned and launched as many blades as he could, as quickly as he could. The blades impacted with as much force as Aiden could muster, which was enough to stagger the cambion long enough for Asha to close in and stab it through the stomach with the angelic sword. The demon howled in pain and dropped Tiago. Aiden could hear the hissing of hot blood as Asha pulled the sword free.

'Shoot the goddamn hole!' she screamed. Tiago scrambled to pick up his weapon. He turned, lying on his back, and fired his pistols as fast as he could. With each round that struck the wound made by the sword, the healing process halted as demon blood spurted with every bullet that tore apart the wound. The cambion roared in tenacious defiance, once again beating its wings, only this time instead of taking flight, it knocked Asha aside. Aiden jumped back to avoid the wing and launched more blades towards the cambion. The summoned swords struck the wound and exploded, letting loose shards of ghost-like glass that embedded itself inside the demon. Asha recuperated and struck another blow to the demon with the angelic blade, then another as the demon stumbled. She struck out once more as the demon fell to a knee, this time severing the cambion's head from its body. Asha kicked its decapitated torso over and buried the sword into its chest for good measure.

Aiden looked over to where the others were fighting the second cambion and saw William swing his massive sword down onto the demon. The demon caught the sword with its bare hand and swung at the warden's side. Aiden acted quickly enough to send an aetheric blade at the cambion, striking the demon's hand and preventing the attack. The cambion snarled and pushed against William's sword, causing his knees to buckle. Kallista let loose another lightning arrow, and it struck the demon in the face, causing the demon's head to reel back. The cambion roared in frustration, pushed William's sword away, grabbed him by the clothes on his chest and tossed him aside. The warden, despite his considerable size, was thrown twenty feet through the air, landing hard mere metres away from Aiden. Aiden rushed to help him up, but the giant warden was already on his feet with his sword in hand by the time Aiden and the others got to him.

Asha didn't stop by William like Tiago and Aiden did. Instead she continued running at the cambion as it approached Kalli and Terra for an attack. She approached from behind and planted her angelic blade through the demon's calf, shattering its shin as it erupted from the other side. Asha pulled out the sword when the demon fell to the ground. It moved quickly, but as it got to its knees trying to rise, Asha attacked again relentlessly, opening a gash across the demon's chest.

'Attack the wound!' she yelled.

In response, Terra launched himself at the demon, plunging his kukris into the demon's chest through the wound, and rode the demon back to the ground. After it was down, Terra pulled the kukris apart, carving a bloody chasm into the cambion's chest that sparked white lightning from the power of his rune. As Terra kneeled on the demon's stomach, slashing and stabbing wildly with electrified blades, Asha finished the cambion off with another successful decapitation.

Tiago and Aiden tended to William, who was groaning in pain, his hands on his side, covered in blood.

'Let me see,' Tiago said to William, who removed his hands from his side, showing a wound that would have sent most normal people into shock.

'Doesn't look like it hit anything important,' Tiago observed, assessing the wound. 'You're lucky. We'll get you to the medic station down the hall.' Asha sounded an agreement as she and the others came over to them. Asha herself had several lines of cuts on the left side of her face that were still bleeding.

'Let's hope we don't run into any more of those arseholes,' Terra snarled.

'Alright, Adley?' Tiago asked as Adley made his way over from the far side of the room.

'Those things are abominations,' he stuttered.

'This coming from a guy who makes friends with demons,' Tiago quipped.

'I'd sooner go to a demon's dinner party before willingly seeing one of those up close again,' Adley commented. 'They'll be one page of my compendium gladly left blank.'

'Enough talking,' Terra interrupted as he helped William to his feet. It was a strange thing to see as William was at least a foot taller. 'We need to get to the medical bay.'

Gabriel knew they were here now, and William was losing enough blood to kill a normal human as it was, so they made their way to the medical bay with speed rather than subtlety. Luckily each wing had its own medical bay, so the nearest one was a short walk away, although with William's wounds slowing them down, they took several minutes to get there.

The medical bay was, to Aiden's relief, free of any demonic presence. It had five beds on the left-hand side and a large bench that ran along the room's right side, featuring a sink and cabinets full of medical supplies.

'Kalli find some med foam,' Terra ordered. Kallista opened one cabinet and searched around, knocking boxes of pills out as she did. She huffed, closed the cabinet and opened the next one, soon thereafter producing a large needleless syringe filled with a grey substance.

She delivered the syringe to her brother, who tore off a plastic seal from the tip. He then placed the tip a few centimetres away from William's wound and pushed in the syringe's plunger, squirting a thick grey liquid that coated the inside of the wound and began to expand. William hissed in pain as the foam did its work, sealing the wound and stopping the bleeding. Once the foam had finished, Kallista secured a bandage over it and around William's waist.

'Good as new, eh?' Tiago grinned.

Chapter Twenty-Seven
Nephitus

I t was not long after the hellbats had started the next attack that the inmai appeared again. There were not as many as there was during the first attack, but the demonic bats made up for that at least twice over. The battle around Lynus was a cacophony of screams, yelling, demonic roaring and explosions of fire, ice, electricity and the slicing of flesh. They had started strong, able to form some semblance of a defensive line and push the demons back steadily, but as Kára left them to engage all three of the white cambion, the line soon broke and they became overwhelmed. Many wardens were dead already, with Ophelia and Jason's teams only just holding out. The only solace at this point was that all but one of the hellbats were dead, which was now gliding through the air towards Lynus to avenge the three he had killed himself.

Its wing was torn, so its flight was uneven and it landed with a stumble, allowing Lynus to dart to the side. He swung the Sword of Michael at the beast's neck. The demon bat folded in its torn wing to defend itself, but the sword sliced through the membrane with ease, widening the wound to where there was no way the hellbat could fly again. After a few failed attempts at swiping at Lynus with its talons, it threw its entire self at him, pinning him to the ground. Its talons sank into Lynus' shoulders making it almost impossible to move his arm and attack. Instead he focused on the power of his runes and let out a concussive shockwave, which pushed the demon bat off of him, its talons tearing out of him with bits of flesh. He could have sent the bat head over talons to the other side of the cavern, but he limited the output just enough to get the beast off him. Even with so many, it would be easy to get overzealous and drain his runes, and as it was, with most of them still at full power, it was exhausting and time consuming forcing his mind to focus on the different runes.

The hellbat got back to its feet and awkwardly leaped into the air towards Lynus again, though this time the creature stopped in mid-air as if hitting an invisible wall, crashing to the ground in a heap. It was then that Lynus noticed the line of bright light trailing across the ground just in front of where the hellbat now lay, struggling to get back up again. The air along the three-metre-long line, and several metres above it, looked as if it shimmered ever so slightly, like the shadow of heat off bitumen on a hot day, only golden.

Lynus looked around, trying to find the source of the wall of light, and saw Ophelia several metres off to his left, holding out her hands towards the bat. When she dropped her hands, the wall of light fell. Lynus turned back to the bat, ready to attack, but the demon didn't charge towards him. Instead it had figured Ophelia for an easier target, which she may well have been, but she was quick enough to summon another wall of light in front of herself, which the hellbat crashed into once again. Tenacious? Yes. Smart? No. Having had its full weight go from a gallop to a sudden stop left it stunned long enough for Lynus to sprint over to it and, putting the full momentum of his run into a swing, he brought down the Sword of Michael onto the hellbat, slicing through its mane of fur and through its neck. This severed its hideous head from its body, which thrashed about in the rapidly growing pool of dark ichor that was forming underneath it.

The hellbats were all down, and Kára had killed two out of the three white cambion, their leader being the only one to remain. Just as Lynus was about to refocus on his next target, the sound of an explosion rumbled through the cavern. Lynus looked around and saw Kára, who slammed down the butt of her halberd, which sent out an explosion of sparks that spread out over the demons. It looked like a powerline transformer exploding in slow motion into a million tiny suns, each then cracked and shot out bolts of lightning that arched and snapped through the air from one demon to the next. When the lightning stopped, the remaining demons fell, spasming on the ground, which left only the tattooed cambion left alive. He grinned like a child who was about to have dessert.

Lynus looked over at the wardens, or what was left of them. Three of Jason's team were dead, though Lynus knew that even if Jason had taken what he had told him to heart, he wouldn't have been that much better off. Besides, he had seen Jason fighting demons just as much as anyone. Ophelia on the other hand had saved Lynus from a few new scars at the very least, but she had two dead in her team. Lynus knew he should feel some sorrow for her, but he also knew that right now there was no point in mourning the dead while they still had work to do. As cruel as he knew it was to think, their deaths would help her in the end. All up, they had gone from nineteen wardens to seven in the space of about half an hour. This wasn't great any way Lynus thought about it, made worse by the fact that two more white cambion stepped out of the mansion and stood on either side of their leader.

For a moment, the tattooed cambion stared at them before speaking. 'Hand over the sword, and we will kill you quickly.' Its voice sounded like multiple people speaking at once, each trying to be heard over the other.

Lynus knew that even with their angelic essence it wasn't enough to shield the white cambion from the fact they were mostly demons, and holding the Sword of Michael would cause them to combust into an unholy funeral pyre. He toyed with the idea of handing it over and watching the show, but there was something off about this cambion. Its eyes held more intelligence than any other demon he had seen before.

'The only time you will ever lay your fetid hands upon the Sword of Michael is when it is removing them from your abominable body, demon,' Kára hissed.

The two smaller cambion didn't take kindly to her insults and showed their displeasure by erupting into a sprint towards them. Before they got more than halfway though, there was a sudden flash of light that illuminated the entire cave. It lingered for a few moments and then receded quickly, and when it did, Lynus could see a large white object protruding from the chest of the cambion. Lynus stared in shock and realised it wasn't a single object, but a collection of feathers. The cambion didn't scream or yell, it simply froze in horror before there was another quick motion and something severed its head from its body as another feathered object sliced through its neck. As it fell, Lynus could see Gabriel, who wound his arm back, summoning a bolt of solid light, which he then hurled at the other cambion that had charged at them. The cambion turned to face Gabriel just before the golden spear pierced his chest, impaling it at a forty-five degree angle into the rock, pinning the demon in place. The cambion tried to remove the spear frantically, but failed to do so before Gabriel flicked one of his wings out, once again severing a head from its body.

'I gave explicit orders for the cambion not to attack until I was ready,' Gabriel intoned as he pulled out his golden spear from the demon's body, which then fell into a heap alongside its head.

The tattooed cambion, who had taken several sharp steps away from Gabriel when he had appeared, now stepped forward towards him, taking a kneeling position by his feet. 'My apologies, master,' it rumbled. 'These cambion are like rabid dogs at times.'

Lynus always knew there was something off with the Order, but he never imagined this. Had all their problems been because of Gabriel? Lynus didn't consider himself a warden, not really, not like the others at least, but even this revelation hit a nerve that sparked a rage in him.

'You fucking traitor!' he roared.

'A creator is not a traitor to its creation for using it as he intended,' Gabriel's said, his voice calm and even as his four wings folded back up behind him. 'A creator becomes a traitor to its creation when he forsakes its purpose for the benefit of another. My brothers and sisters, the seraphim, were created to protect God and all of creation from the darkness. A darkness that many humans have willingly embraced, and yet God did not destroy them as he should have. No, he tasked me to protect them from themselves! He turned me and my legion into an army of caretakers for mortals intent on destroying themselves by inviting the darkness in with their sin and savagery. *That* was a betrayal!' Gabriel's temper seemed to flare for a moment, but he made no move to attack, though Lynus prepared for one at any moment. The anger Gabriel showed passed like a receding tide. 'Kára, my most loyal angel, help me free this world of its filth. I do not want to hurt you.'

Lynus looked over at Kára. He could never have imagined her, of all angels, showing the expressions she did now. First it was utter disbelief then it looked like she might burst in to tears. Then rage. 'No!' she screamed. 'How could you do this? You've betrayed the valkyr. You've betrayed the entire Order, and the guard!'

'I betrayed nothing,' Gabriel replied. The golden spear he held in his hands disappeared in a small flash of light. 'The Order was a tool I created for *this* purpose. They were *meant to keep* the March busy. They were *meant* to keep the demons at bay, making them easier for me to control. They were *meant* to make my new demon soldiers possible. Most importantly, they were *meant* to bring me Michael's blade. How is using them for what they were meant to do a betrayal?'

'What use do you have with the Sword of Michael? You can't use it,' she hissed.

'No, but he can.' Gabriel gestured to the tattooed cambion who was now standing behind him. The cambion stretched its wings out with a sly grin.

'A cambion, even with the essence of an angel, is still a demon,' Kára scolded. 'The blade will smite your foul mutt before he has time to swing it!'

Gabriel responded to her anger with a short humourless laugh. 'Nephitus is not simply a cambion,' he said. 'Nephitus is my own creation. He's so much more than a mere cambion, even more than the white cambion Lilith created for me. He is the culmination of many failed experiments finally perfected. Just the right mix of the three so he can use the blade to its full potential, rivalling even Michael himself.'

Lynus' grip on the sword tightened until his knuckles were white. 'That thing won't be loyal to you like I was!' Kára yelled. 'How naïve do you have to be to think it won't cut *you* down as soon as it has the chance?'

'It knows true loyalty. You were loyal, yes, but like all lesser angels, your kind is still imperfect, tainted by the mortal soul within you,' Gabriel said. He looked over at the tattooed cambion. 'Nephitus knows no anger, no jealousy, no agenda and no ambition for anything save for pleasing me. It is imprinted into his very soul to be loyal to me.'

'You don't have loyalty, you have a puppet!' Kára spat. 'A slave whose eyes reflect what is within your own soul—nothing.'

Gabriel grinned. 'The entire world is my puppet, Kára, and it has been for longer than your own soul has existed—it just doesn't know it yet. But it will when I burn it all down and create the perfection that my father refused to.' In another flash of light, Gabriel once again held his golden spear, and was now looking directly at Lynus. 'I'll ask you only once, hand over the blade.'

'Better angels than you have tried taking it from me,' Lynus said in defiance.

'Oh, I doubt that,' Gabriel sneered as he brought down the butt of his spear, sending out a concussive blast throughout the entire cave, accompanied by a flash of golden light. The blast blew Lynus and the rest of the wardens off their feet, and only Kára held her ground against it. When Lynus got back to his feet, Gabriel had stretched out both pairs of his magnificent white wings, and he and Kára were exchanging blows several feet above the ground. The cavern was not high enough for a full aerial battle, but they each took full advantage of their ability to use all the space they had available to them, darting up and down dodging and returning attacks with their pole-arms, their fists and even their wings.

Gabriel's attacks landed more often than Kára's, producing small flashes of aureate light as they did, but Kára gave almost as good as she got, sending sparks of lightning out with each strike. It was clear Kára was outmatched though, and she wouldn't last long.

Lynus' attention then fell to Nephitus who was walking casually towards him, a demonic blade in each hand. He could feel the presence of the other wardens take up positions next to him, and it gave him a twinge of pride. If Jason and Ophelia could stand beside him against this, perhaps there was a chance for them yet. They'd have to survive this though. He was ready to die, and he had been for a long time now, but he wasn't going to just let these bastards get what they wanted without bleeding for it.

'Lynus!' It was Aiden, rushing in the cavern with Asha and the rest of their team. Lynus felt a rush of relief to see them mostly unharmed.

Nephitus turned to face the newcomers. A pair of inmai demons, the larger, meaner kind, followed closely behind. Aiden and the rest turned to attack their pursuers. All except Asha who was already charging at Nephitus like a crazed demon herself, a sword in each hand just like the cambion. She swung the angelic blade first, but the cambion dematerialised one of his swords, leaving a hand free to catch it. The blade did nothing. Not a scratch. Nephitus flexed his arms and squeezed, shattering the blade in an eruption of light as the angelic power exploded outwards. The force of the power knocked Asha back, but she kept her footing and rushed in again. She was insane.

Lynus rushed forward to help her, as did the others behind him, but not before Asha was engaged again. She swung her sword, and the cambion swatted the blade from her hands with a quick swipe of his own and retaliated faster than Lynus could track by grabbing her by the throat and lifting her into the air.

'I will enjoy cutting your strings,' Nephitus hissed.

The cambion's sharp nails dug into Asha's neck, and her blood dripped down the demon's arm. He pulled back his other arm, blade in hand and thrust the demonic sword. Lynus swung the Sword of Michael, and it sank into the flesh of the cambion's abdomen, but Asha's shriek of pain told Lynus he was too late. He made the mistake of looking at Asha before pulling his sword back. Asha screamed as the demon removed his blade from her. It did not impale her as the demon had intended—Lynus' attack had thrown Nephitus off his mark. It did, however, still make contact, stabbing deep into the side of her stomach.

Nephitus pulled the blade out and threw Asha to the side. He then took advantage of Lynus' distraction to backhand him across the face. Lynus' ghost form attempted to take the blow, but was, for the first time in a long time, too slow, and the demon's talon-like nails tore bloody gashes into his face. Lynus stumbled back, and his grip on the Sword of Michael released. Nephitus grabbed the sword and pulled it out of himself, the wound healing up almost instantly. The blade glowed, and Nephitus grinned wickedly. Before anyone could react, he slammed the sword blade first into the ground, sending out a visible shockwave of golden light, much like that which Gabriel had used at the beginning of his fight with Kára.

Lynus could hear shattering all around the cavern, like a hundred tiny glasses breaking as he and the others hit the ground. A powerful feeling of fear swept over Lynus as he realised what the sound of broken glass was: runes shattering. He looked down and was relieved to see his purple rune was still secure in its place on his wrist. He checked his other runes and found that the blast had destroyed all the others.

Nephitus obtaining the Sword of Michael drew Gabriel's attention; he was still airborne fighting Kára. When he saw that Nephitus had the sword, he attacked Kára with the blade of his spear once more, a strike that landed hard against her face. The impact of the attack caused her to fall like a shooting star, slamming into the ground near Lynus and causing a small crater where she lay unmoving, blood spattered on her wings. Nephitus turned away from the wardens and walked over to Gabriel, who now had his feet on the ground. Nephitus planted the sword into the ground once more. Lynus winced, expecting another shockwave, but instead Nephitus kneeled at Gabriel's feet.

Lynus struggled, but he got back to his feet, his legs shaking slightly from pain and exhaustion. Despite this, he rushed over to Asha where Aiden and the others were helping her get up. She could barely walk on her own, so Aiden put her arm over his shoulder, propping her up.

'We need to get out of here,' Lynus asserted.

'No...' Asha managed to say. She spat blood.

'Gabriel alone is worth running from,' Lynus said. 'Now they have the sword, and I don't know about anyone else, but that last blast destroyed most of my runes. We have nothing to fight with!'

'We'll come back when we know how to fight them,' Aiden reasoned.

'Don't be stupid!' Jason barked. 'We get out of here and we never come back. There's no fighting that!' He pointed at Gabriel who was now standing two dozen feet away.

'He's right,' Gabriel said. 'The key is in my hands, and I will open the door. No matter how far you run, no matter what weapons you obtain, none of you will even live to see the fires of The Shattered One.'

There was a flash of motion to Lynus' left, and a bolt of lightning crashed into Nephitus. It was Kára's halberd. The blade did not pierce the demon's skin, but it was enough to send the demon stumbling into the dirt. Kára was screaming an order at them. 'Go!' Then, like a bolt of fury herself, she tackled Gabriel, and they both glided along the ground, tangled against one another as they disappeared, crashing through one of the front-facing walls of the sanctuary.

The wardens did as they were told, despite Asha's groans of protest. Nephitus was too preoccupied running after his master to be bothered giving chase, so the group of wardens made it out into open air through the cavern's main entrance unhindered; the only thing that followed was the commotion of Kára's sacrifice as she held off Gabriel and his pet.

Lynus moved to help Aiden with Asha, and together they all made their way up to the beach, ignoring the stares of people on the streets as they moved as quickly as their broken limbs would carry them. Most of them were still bleeding badly, while some like William and Asha could barely move on their own. They had patched William up, and he could push through his pain, but Asha was another story. The wound had likely punctured her stomach, and even for a warden that wasn't good. Lynus himself had a gaping hole in his arm, and several deep lacerations in his shoulder and face, but those had at least stopped bleeding.

Finally they made it to their car garage. Tiago punched in the code for the roller doors on a nearby console, and with a loud whirring of machinery, the doors lifted. They separated into the two black vans that waited for them inside. Sorterra jumped into the driver's seat with Kallista in the passenger seat. Lynus got in the back with Aiden, Tiago, William and Asha. Sorterra took off the moment everyone was in, and the others carefully placed Asha on the floor of the van. The other group of wardens followed closely behind in the other van as they took the fastest route possible out of the city.

'Get some med foam,' Tiago barked, pointing to a red duffel bag that was strapped to the back door. Lynus complied, unzipping the bag and finding the large syringe filled with a grey liquid. 'Terra, keep the car as steady as you can. I'm going to try to close the puncture in her stomach. Ghost, be ready to pump that into her wound as soon as I say. Aiden, find something for her to bite down on.' Tiago looked at Asha. 'This is going to hurt like a bitch.'

Chapter Twenty-Eight
Only human

A slight bump in the road sent a bolt of pain through Asha's stomach as she half lay, half slouched on the van's back seat. She looked down to see the gash in her blacks, still damp with her blood. The med foam held though, and the internal injuries had already closed up thanks to Tiago's work. She tried to sit up straight, but as she did, a hundred cuts and bruises reminded her of their presence. They'd be gone soon though. She checked on her runes, both of which were still intact.

Everyone in the van looked exhausted and sat in silence. Even Lynus had his head back with his eyes shut. Asha looked out of the van's back window as they travelled down a highway, the skyscrapers of Salem still just visible on the horizon in a haze of blue. She guessed they were at least an hour out of town at the highest part of the northern hills. It was hard to wrap her head around how much had happened in such a short time. She looked up at the midday sun and felt an overwhelming sense of dread.

Light had always been a metaphor for hope. The light at the end of the tunnel. The light of the dawn. Yet as she reflected on everything, she couldn't help but wonder if the light that now covered the city was the last time it ever would. Would Salem survive the night to come?

'How did you do that anyway?' Asha heard Aiden ask.

'Do what?' Tiago replied.

'You basically performed surgery in the back of a van with little more than a needle and thread,' Aiden said, dumbfounded.

Tiago barked a short laugh. 'When I was a cop, they trained me in emergency first aid,' he explained. 'When I was at Sanctuary Prime, I had a lot of time on my hands so I expanded on that skill with the warden medics.'

'Still. It was pretty amazing,' Aiden marvelled.

'Yeah, maybe, but if Asha were a normal human, she woulda died no question,' Tiago stated. 'It's a little easier to do that sort of thing on us.'

Asha continued to stare out of the window, her thoughts getting further and further away from the casual conversations starting within the van. She couldn't help but feel responsible. She had known going into the sanctuary was a suicide mission. Gabriel hadn't ordered it and she should have waited to come up with a better plan after getting more information on what they were walking into. Gabriel had tricked them, but she had let her blind obedience prevent her from figuring it out, and her wardens had paid the price. But he had fooled everyone for who knows how long, so how could she have known? She couldn't help but feel she still should have. Now more warden blood was on her hands. It was her fault.

'Asha.' Terra's voice broke through her thoughts, and it was clear it wasn't the first time he had said her name.

'What?' she grunted, her gaze still fixed on the steadily disappearing city.

'Getting out of the city is a good start and all, but what are we going to do now?' Terra asked, his attention swapping between the road and looking at her through the rear vision mirror.

She turned her head and saw that everyone was looking at her, waiting for her to reply. 'I don't know,' she admitted after a few moments. 'Keep driving until Salem is well behind us.'

'That's it?' Lynus asked, opening his eyes and looking at her dubiously.

'I'm happy with any plan that gets us well away from cambions, especially white ones,' Aiden piped up.

'There are things worse than cambion, kid,' Terra stated. 'Even white ones.'

'Maybe,' Aiden acknowledged. 'But Gabriel has an army of them.'

'At least we know we *can* kill them,' Kalli said from the passenger seat.'

'Yeah, with angelic swords,' Lynus grumbled. 'And in case you missed it, we're fresh out of those. Then there's Nephitus...

'Exactly,' Asha said. 'So for now we just...keep driving.'

They drove for several hours until they were forced to stop at a petrol station and fill up. Luckily the Order credit cards still worked, at least for now. Asha took the opportunity during their break to check up on the other van. Ophelia and Jason were riding with what was left of their teams, and Adley was at the wheel. To Asha's surprise, Adley didn't have much to say, and Ophelia and Jason had not killed each other yet. When the vans were full of fuel, they continued driving for at least another three hours. The cramped van didn't do much to lift anyone's spirits.

The sun sank below the horizon as they drove, though apart from the occasional farm or roadhouse, there wasn't much to see in the light besides patches of forest anyway. Even they were getting smaller and fewer between, giving way to dry scrubland. As Asha watched fence posts and trees go by and the light fade, she once again wondered what would become of the city in their absence. They were not the only wardens in the city. There were still kathari, but Asha had no idea what their status was, or if they even knew what was happening.

Asha's thoughts were abruptly interrupted by the sudden crash of thunder and an explosion of lightning falling from a cloudless sky in front of them. Everyone lurched towards the front of the van as Terra slammed on the brakes, almost causing the other van behind to collide into the back of them.

Fearing the worst, Asha nearly kicked the van's back doors off as she exited the vehicle ready to fight whatever aethereal Gabriel had sent after them, but halfway between the van and the aethereal she saw who it was and stopped dead, as did the others behind her.

In the middle of the road, rising from a kneeled position was an angel holding a polearm in her bloodied right hand. Blood spattered her wings, and wounds that were only just healing riddled her body. She slowly managed to stand upright.

'Kára?' Asha asked cautiously.

Kára walked towards them. 'Is everyone okay?'

'More or less,' Tiago said.

'Good,' Kára replied, her gaze scanning over them.

'Are you okay?' Asha asked. 'How did you escape?'

'I'm fine,' she replied. 'But I have little time. Asha I need you to lead these wardens. I—'

'Me?' Asha interrupted. 'But I—'

'I can't pick up these pieces on my own, Asha,' Kára beseeched. 'I need to return to heaven. This experience has been…draining. I fear I will fall if I do not return soon.'

'Is it safe there?' Tiago asked.

'I believe we may be the only ones who know of Gabriel's betrayal. He wouldn't reveal himself just to attack me in heaven,' Kára said. 'The Divine Authority's laws will prevent Gabriel attacking without sanction. Besides, he won't want the others to question why he is attacking in the first place.'

'Heaven politics. Nice,' Lynus' muttered.

'What do we do now?' Asha asked.

'Gabriel mentioned a door, and something called *The Shattered One*. I will use my time in heaven to find out what he was referring to,' Kára said. Her voice seemed different. She spoke with more emotion than Asha had ever heard from an angel, besides Amber at least. 'While I search for answers in heaven, you search for them here.'

'Where should we start?' Asha asked. 'The city isn't safe for us.'

'We could start with outlying towns around Salem,' Terra suggested. 'There is an emergency sanctuary about fifty kilometres east of here.'

'Won't it be monitored?' Kallista asked. 'Surely they'll think to look there.'

'It's better than wandering around aimlessly,' Terra countered.

'Okay,' Asha said. She turned back to speak to Kára, but the angel was gone. 'Guess we're on our own now. We should get going.'

'Before we go, Asha,' Kallista said sheepishly. 'Maybe we should say goodbye?'

'What do you mean?' Asha asked.

'I mean we've lost a lot of wardens. Wardens we have not had time to give the proper rites to,' she said, looking like she was holding back tears.

'Let's go find something to burn then. Who has some dust?' Terra asked the group.

'I do,' Ophelia said, offering up a large silver flask.

Most of the wardens spread out into the dark to find wood, while Adley moved the two vans from the middle of the road. After about half an hour there was a pile of what was mostly branches, which was large enough to last a full night of camping. If only that's all it were for.

'My fire rune was destroyed,' Lynus said. 'Anyone else got a lighter or something?'

Jason scoffed. 'Don't look at me. Mine was screwed by you letting Nephitus get the sword.'

'Enough,' Terra growled as Lynus' hand balled into a fist. 'Kalli, your rune wasn't destroyed was it?'

'Luckily.' She pulled out her bow and let loose a bolt of lightning. In mere seconds, the wood was engulfed in flames, and they had their pyre.

The group stood side by side, forming a crescent line a few feet away from the now-raging fire. One by one they stepped forward, throwing a handful of dust into the flames. Terra was first. He stood for a moment with his eyes closed. 'Gerard,' he said as he opened his fist and dropped in the dust. The powder enlivened the fire and for a moment the flames grew twice their height before shrinking back once more.

Kallista went next. With tears running down each cheek, she approached the fire and dropped in her dust. 'Jessica,' she said. Using the dust was symbolic. Under normal circumstances, they used it on the body of the warden within a fire to represent that, unlike the first time they died, they were truly finished with their body. It was also practical as burying the body of an already-dead person proved to be a logistical nightmare.

Next was Tiago. He walked up to the pyre, a firm expression on his face as he dropped his handful of dust into the fire. 'Tarek,' he said. It hurt Asha to realise that through all that had happened since the sanctuary was first attacked, they had not had the time to honour his death. He deserved better.

Ophelia stepped forward as soon as Tiago had taken his place back in the line. She was sobbing, her face wet with tears. When she fed the fire with her dust, Asha could not understand the names she spoke through her sobs.

When Jason didn't budge from the line to drop in any dust, Asha stepped forward. She looked into fire and her eyes danced solemnly with the flames. She brought up her hand but hesitated. All the years came down to this. It was always going to for one of them eventually, but she would never have been prepared for how hard it was. As soon as she let go, that would be it. The last act of his life was for her to honour his death. 'Markus,' she whispered as she let go of the dust.

The group was quiet for a long time as they stared into the fire, reflecting on all that had happened. One by one they each broke off, and even when they had split into groups and chatted away, Asha remained looking into the fire as if waiting for it to swallow her up and punish her for her failings.

Asha spotted someone at the corner of her eye stand next to her. 'You don't have to stick around if you don't want to,' Asha said, not looking away from the pyre. 'My screw ups have already made you lose almost everything.'

'Almost everything,' Lynus replied. 'Not Aiden though. He's more important than the sword.'

'I'm glad for that,' she said, nodding at Aiden as he joined them. 'But this isn't even close to being over, and I'm not sure that we'll get through it.'

'I'm staying,' Lynus said firmly.

'Why?' she snapped, finally looking at him. 'You didn't care before.'

'Before I had the sword,' Lynus said.

'Oh, I see,' Asha grunted. 'Now that you don't feel invincible, you want to be part of a group?'

'I think I've made it clear I don't care if I die,' he said. 'When Aiden and I left our sanctuary, we knew how it would end. With our deaths. But I promised I would die with the Sword of Michael in my hand and dead aethereals at my feet.

'Since I no longer have that sword, I need to stay alive at least until I get it back,' he continued. 'And the chances of me doing that on my own are well...non-existent. Don't get me wrong. My feelings about the Order haven't changed.'

'I don't think your chances are that much improved by being under my leadership,' she said, looking back into the fire. 'Just like before I died and became a warden, my inability to see past my obedience led me into a fight I couldn't win. I knew something was wrong, but I was too naïve to even entertain the possibility it was Gabriel all along.'

'He's been fooling people far stronger and far smarter than any three of us combined for who knows how long, Asha,' Aiden consoled. 'There's nothing you could have done.'

'We could have planned the counterattack better,' she said. 'More wardens died than necessary and for what? We lost everything.' She hated how she felt. She hated how weak she sounded. Most of all she hated that she couldn't see anything within herself to fix it. 'The Order is gone. We're just remnants of a lost cause now.'

'Bullshit,' Aiden spat, surprising both Asha and his brother. 'Gabriel may have led the Order of Elysium, but that doesn't mean he *is* the Order. The Order is every single warden dead or dying that upholds its virtues.'

'What virtues?' Asha asked with a scowl. 'Everything they based the Order on was to trick us into helping Gabriel's twisted plot.'

'Someone I know once said that it doesn't matter what the angels' intentions are,' he said. Those were her words yet her guilt made them taste bitter after everything that had just happened. 'We fight to protect humanity, and it's important we keep doing that, especially now that it's clear who the real enemy is.'

'Nothing is clear at all,' she sighed. 'We know nothing. There is so much going on that we can't even begin to understand.'

'We just take it one day at a time. We survive,' he said. 'It's like you said, 'We're only human.'

Epilogue

The glare of the full moon reflected brightly off of the water streaming from a large alabaster fountain, the centrepiece of an already beautiful garden. The radiant flowers and the lush bushes and trees were a much less stunning sight than the front of the residence they decorated, however. It was a veritable mansion, complete with clean cream bricks, decorative white pillars by the front door and large windows from which you could no doubt see the dozens of dead bodies strewn across the lawn.

Some bodies looked like private security with stab wounds and guns by their side, while others looked like regular civilians with gunshot wounds and knives lying by their sides. A hooded angel walked among them with white wings extended, holding a simple wooden stave in his right hand and a thick whip curled up on his hip. He stopped by a corpse, and the tip of his stave glowed before a light arched up slightly, curving into a descent to the body. As the light touched the security guard's body, the colour of the angel's wings went from pure white to murky grey then to a black that would almost not be visible if not for the moonlight.

As the light receded back into the stave, the angel's wings steadily became white once more, and he moved again, this time to one of the regular-looking people. Once again, the light arched out from the tip of the stave and into the body, and just like before, the angel's wings became black for a moment before returning to white as the light disappeared.

The angel stopped by a woman's corpse. She stood out from the other bodies, so to speak, as someone had shot her, but she didn't share the back-alley attire of the other civilians. In fact, she looked as though she may have lived in the house. The angel placed his stave down once more, ready to do what he had done half-a-dozen times already tonight when a woman's voice stopped him.

'This one is mine,' said another angel, appearing beside him.

The first angel looked inquisitively at the one who had interrupted him from his work. 'I didn't think your kind were still around.'

'It is true that most of The Valkyr Guard believe that Kára betrayed Gabriel and led the Order against him, but I believe the opposite is true,' she said. 'And while there is still light in the darkness, I will fight for it. *My* kind is not going anywhere without a fight.'

'Commendable,' the first angel said. 'I don't know if I'd have the same resolve as you if Azrael suddenly turned on The Ankor Legion.'

'And who would collect the dead then?' asked the female angel. 'We cannot take them all on as wardens. Though we might not need the wardens if angels such as you and your kind helped us fight the darkness.'

'We are, as we always have been and always will be, neutral in this war, Brynhiel,' he said. 'Besides, there is clearly contention on who represents that darkness, especially now.'

'What Gabriel has done does not change anything,' she said. 'Anyone who would see father's world destroyed is the enemy, no matter what their intentions may be.'

'You put it so simply, but in all my memory there has only ever been one thing that has been as black and white as that.' He gestured with his free hand to the garden and to all the dead that lay around them. 'Life and death. That is, unless one of you shows up.' There was a short silence as the legion angel looked around again, then down at the body he was about to take the soul from. 'What is so special about this one? What do you plan to do with her?'

'All of those that we choose to become wardens are special in their own way, and this one is no different,' said the female angel. 'Like all of them, she will help to keep the light in the darkness alive.'

Acknowledgements

I want to give special thanks to the people who made this book possible. To have even finished this book is a great personal achievement to me—one that I am immensely proud of. More than that, however, I am proud of the people who helped me achieve it and that I get to call them my friends and family.

First, thank you to my parents, Aaron and Darrelle, who always fanned the flames of my creativity when I was a kid. Without your support and encouragement to immerse myself in the things I enjoyed when I was growing up, I never would have fallen in love with reading.

Thank you to my childhood friend, and still my friend now of seventeen years, Charlotte. If not for you and our shared loved of fantasy, I don't think I would have found my spark for writing. You were always, and still continue to be, a literary inspiration to me far more than any of my favourite authors.

Thank you to my aunties Rachael and Teri. Thank you for being so keen to be my among my test readers, and thank you for letting me talk your ear off with questions. Thank you for, like my parents, always encouraging my creativity and sharing your own love of fantasy, which helped to inspire me into the genre at an early age.

Thank you to Chris, my best friend and fellow book nerd. Thank you for always having a book suggestion for me and introducing me to pretty much all of my favourite authors' books.

Thank you for being a test reader and taking to the task with such an air of importance and interest.

Thank you to my gorgeous wife, Lisa. It's not a coincidence that it took me the four years before we got together to get half the draft finished, and then have it finished, edited and all, within two years after. Your never-ending encouragement, unwavering support and the fact that you are always so excited to talk about the lore of the book were the reasons I accomplished what I set out to.

Thank you to my editor, Juliette from The Erudite Pen. You helped to elevate my book and the content within by pushing me to answers questions I didn't think of, or was too content to simply not address. The book is now the best it can be in large part to your amazing work.

Finally, thank you to Ian from Book Reality. The unfamiliar and daunting process of getting my book ready for the digital shelves was a serious point of anxiety for me. However, your constant professionalism and willingness to go above and beyond for me has kept me feeling grounded and confident throughout.

About the Author

Dean Buswell was born in Perth, Western Australia. He grew up in the southern suburbs of Rockingham where he cultivated a small but close group of friends to share his love for gaming, reading, and eventually writing. For as long he could remember, Dean has always loved the idea of writing a book, often writing fan fictions that never got past five chapters, or original ideas that never got past one.

Eventually one stuck, and what was originally a half-formed concept he came up with for him and his friends to play around with, evolved into an ongoing project that would go on to see the light of day as his first book, *The Order of Elyisum*.

He has a strong respect for loyalty among his close friends and family, which are the two most important things to him. During his free time, when he should be writing, he enjoys playing video games with his wife and best friend or binge watching through a never-ending Netflix list.